REALMSLAYER
LEGEND OF THE DOOMSEEKER

Other great stories from Warhammer Age of Sigmar

REALMSLAYER
LEGEND OF THE DOOMSEEKER

DAVID GUYMER

BLACK LIBRARY

A BLACK LIBRARY PUBLICATION

First published in 2023.
This edition published in Great Britain in 2024 by
Black Library, Games Workshop Ltd., Willow Road,
Nottingham, NG7 2WS, UK.

Represented by: Games Workshop Limited – Irish branch,
Unit 3, Lower Liffey Street, Dublin 1,
D01 K199, Ireland.

10 9 8 7 6 5 4 3 2 1

Produced by Games Workshop in Nottingham.
Cover illustration by Anna Lakisova.

ISBN 13: 978-1-80407-638-5

See Black Library on the internet at

blacklibrary.com

Find out more about Games Workshop
and the worlds of Warhammer at

games-workshop.com

Printed and bound in the UK.

The Mortal Realms have been despoiled. Ravaged by the followers of the Chaos Gods, they stand on the brink of utter destruction.

The fortress-cities of Sigmar are islands of light in a sea of darkness. Constantly besieged, their walls are assailed by maniacal hordes and monstrous beasts. The bones of good men are littered thick outside the gates. These bulwarks of Order are embattled within as well as without, for the lure of Chaos beguiles the citizens with promises of power.

Still the champions of Order fight on. At the break of dawn, the Crusader's Bell rings and a new expedition departs. Storm-forged knights march shoulder to shoulder with resolute militia, stoic duardin and slender aelves. Bedecked in the splendour of war, the Dawnbringer Crusades venture out to found civilisations anew. These grim pioneers take with them the fires of hope. Yet they go forth into a hellish wasteland.

Out in the wilds, hardy colonists restore order to a crumbling world. Haunted eyes scan the horizon for tyrannical reavers as they build upon the bones of ancient empires, eking out a meagre existence from cursed soil and ice-cold seas. By their valour, the fate of the Mortal Realms will be decided.

The ravening terrors that prey upon these settlers take a thousand forms. Cannibal barbarians and deranged murderers crawl from hidden lairs. Martial hosts clad in black steel march from skull-strewn castles. The savage hordes of Destruction batter the frontier towns until no stone stands atop another. In the dead of night come howling throngs of the undead, hungry to feast upon the living.

Against such foes, courage is the truest defence and the most effective weapon. It is something that Sigmar's chosen do not lack. But they are not always strong enough to prevail, and even in victory, each new battle saps their souls a little more.

This is the time of turmoil. This is the era of war.

This is the Age of Sigmar.

Your Celestial Highnesses,

I arrived in Anvilor through the Stormfire Gate as we discussed and a few days earlier than hoped, posing as a water-seller from Kurnotheal in Ghyran. There are apparently fortunes to be made delivering water to this arid hell, though I do not personally understand the appeal. I go where your Celestial Highnesses direct, as always, but be assured that I feel especially motivated to make my stay in the Great Parch a brief one.

Under my merchant guise, I attached myself to a trade caravan bound across the Pyroc Plains for Vostargi Mont. It had been my intention to follow it all the way to the Salamander's Spine, but after the third Bloodreaver attack in as many days, each one greater than the last, it became clear that the attention the caravan drew outweighed any supposed protection that it could offer. After abandoning it, I saw the smoke rising from the road as I made my first day's ascent into the Salamander's Spine. I cannot say for certain that it was the caravan. Smoke is not exactly an uncommon sighting on the plains of Aridian.

All that I have been able to observe since my entrance into Fyreslayer lands would appear to justify my mission here. Your portents spoke of a great power that will emerge from the stronghold of the Unbak and, despite the war to the south, the Fyreslayers have abandoned their outer holdings almost completely and locked their magma-vault tight. Some great work is afoot. What is more, I sense that I am not alone in my interest. More than once I have felt eyes on me, and have almost disturbed other watch-ers as I investigated the mountain's hidden ways. I have come to the conclusion that if I am to enter Karag Unbak then I must do it today.

I leave this missive here, in the hope that any Swift-hawk agent passing nearby will notice the seal and deliver it.

I will contact you again soon, with this new power safely in my possession.

Your most loyal and faithful votary,
Maleneth Witchblade

PART ONE

The Face of the Doomseeker

ONE

'*Khazuk!*' Broddur roared, hefting the icon of Grimnir Doom-seeker aloft. In the shifting, golden choler of the lava sea it seemed to frown, as though condemning whoever was fool enough to breach the inner wards of the Unbak lodge to a fiery end. Broddur sucked in his belly and marched. Today, he would make his master proud.

Two hundred Fyreslayers of the Forn Fyrd, a sixth of the might of the Grand Fyrd, marched five abreast. The Salamander's Spine was the oldest and hottest volcanic chain in the known lands of Aqshy. It was here that their god had fallen in titanic battle, and here that the first and largest of the Fyreslayer lodges had been founded. Karag Unbak had never been the greatest of those early lodges, but where they had fallen to abandonment and disrepair, the Unbak had endured through the long ages. The magma-vault was hewn from a basaltic isle in a volcanic sea known as the Caldur, deep under the ancient mountain. The Caldur Bridge extended across that seething ocean, jutting from one rocky atoll to the next, linking the disparate outer holdings of the Unbak to the main lodge before disappearing into the same haze of heat and cinders. Most were long abandoned: once cities in their own right, now little more than hunting lodges and ranger posts. Lava lapped sluggishly at their fortifications. The sky, such as could be seen beyond the shield of the volcano, was burnt and angry.

Many were the warbands abroad in the Salamander's Spine Mountains of late, and few of those could resist the chance to test their mettle against that of the Unbak lodge before heading on to their war in Hammerhal Aqsha.

Riding over the bridge at the marching column's head in a war-throne of pitted basalt, Forn beat his fists on his chest and roared. 'Unbak! Broken, but unbowed!'

'Unbowed!' Broddur returned, with a thrust of his glowering icon.

'*Khazuk!*' the fyrd rumbled, as though the stone beneath them might split.

The runeson, Forn, was a champion in Grimnir's mould. Not a warrior but a *fighter*. His chest was a barrel of muscle. His neck was so thick that it would take two duardin together to wrap their hands around it. His hands were like a runesmiter's hammers, so heavy were they with golden runes. They simmered with a barely controlled power as the low-slung gait of the magmadroth he rode swayed him back and forth. The great reptile's name was Yellow-scale. Forn had stolen her as an egg and slain her mother. Her temperamental fury was a perfect match for his own.

The smouldering rock face that was her jaw split open for a roar that shook the entire bridge and left a thunderous ringing in Brod-dur's ears. When his hearing returned, he heard Forn laughing.

'I know that the lodge elders think me foolish and Aruk-Grimnir thinks me harmless.' Forn turned in his high seat so that he was looking back on the golden-helmed and high-crested heads of the fyrd, raising his voice in a boisterous shout to address them all. 'So what then does that say about the kinbands he's given me to lead?'

The fyrd answered with affectionate cheers. Forn was the youngest of Aruk-Grimnir's six sons and widely held as the most likely to burn too hot, too young, before ever threatening to succeed his father. While the lodge elders tutted and shook their heads at his recklessness, the kinbands loved him for it.

'My father and brothers stand now with the Zharrgrim Hearthguard. Runemaster Krag Blackhammer nears completion of his life's great work and whatever the foe waiting for us, the magmavaults are to be defended at all costs.' Yellowscale delivered another punishing bellow, spraying the exuberant front ranks with cinders. 'It is a sign from Grimnir's own mouth! While they all play at being Grungni, the Forn Fyrd will make war!'

'*Khazuk!*'

Broddur felt a tingle run down his spine as he looked up at his friend. 'Your father'd be proud, runeson.'

'Hark at you,' Forn mumbled, leaning over the arms of his throne so only Broddur could hear. '*Runeson*. Was a fyrd of ten-score and twelve all I needed for you to start showing me the respect I was due? Call me Forn, Broddur, lest I start calling you battlesmith.'

'We'll make them both proud.'

Forn's fierce expression cracked for a moment. It was only ever for a moment. 'I've only five brothers to surpass after all. We can at least be gold-mad enough to try.'

He drew a long spear from the stone quiver carved into the side of his throne and thrust it into the air with a roar. His warriors duly cheered.

'Do you remember when we were flamelings, Broddur? When we would steal hammer moulds from Skorun's forge and play berzerker in Az Skorn?'

Broddur smiled to consider the rare innocence of the memory.

The realms were harsher and hotter than they had seemed then. 'The Firebrand had me working his forge for six months with no rest to pay back what those moulds were worth.'

'And now you're a battlesmith yourself. His equal.'

Broddur scoffed. 'I wouldn't go that far.'

He looked up to the face at the top of his icon pole, regardless. It had been fashioned from ur-gold and fyresteel, finished with a beard of magmadroth-hide straps studded with rubies and yellow citrine. The eyes were grave and deep, little more than hollows in the metal. The expression was grim, as it should be grim. There were a hundred aspects of Grimnir. Few were the non-duardin who could tell them apart, but to a Fyreslayer they were as distinct as one form of gold was to another. Even amongst the Fyreslayers, however, only a lodge's battlesmiths had earned the right to forge their likeness and tell their stories.

'Grimnir the Doomseeker,' said Forn, following his gaze. His voice was grave now, as was right. When considering the Shattered God, drunken despondency or earth-shattering fury were the only states that were acceptable. 'He was always your favourite when we played.' The runeson grumbled under his breath, but was unable to hold off the small smile that Broddur could see threatening. 'You always made me be Vulcatrix.'

'Someone had to be Vulcatrix.'

'And me a runeson, too.'

Broddur sighed as he shook off their reverie and returned to the moment. 'Something in this face always spoke to me.'

'Well, it's yours now. So show the Firebrand you're handier with more than just a hammer and tongs.'

With a nod, Broddur raised the icon high. The jewelled straps flapped in the heat rising off the Caldur beneath them. His free hand fell to his belt, feeling out the marks in the story beads that he had himself cut from cubes of solid gold.

'The earth did tremble!' he roared, projecting his voice, as his master would, to address the marching fyrd entire. 'The sky wept fire. Seven times did the axes of Grimnir carve the molten scales of Vulcatrix and seven times was he savaged by the ur-Salamander in turn. As Grimnir fought so his beard and crest did burst aflame, but hotter still burned the killing rage in his heart. And when Grimnir stood at last bestride the broken body of his foe, the earth did respond with a fury that turned mountains into plains and plains into oceans. But Vulcatrix, in her great spite, would suffer no god his victory.'

'*Dreng tromm.*'

'The ur-Salamander did turn her fire upon herself. Even in her death throes her breath was hotter even than that of the Great Drake Dracothion, the grandfather of all dragons, and with that last breath did she destroy herself and Grimnir with her.'

'*Dreng tromm!*'

'The peak of our ancestors did crumble and the High Star of Azyr showed its white face upon their halls. Much was the ur-gold that fell upon them and many were the magmadroths that hatched in the fires below. Karag Unbak did they rename it. The Broken Volcano. We are the children of Grimnir. We fight as Grimnir fought. His strength is now our strength.' He yelled louder, his voice finding a strength that countless hours of practice in front of reflective plates in his private forge had not prepared him for. 'We are the Unbak lodge. Broken, but unbowed.'

'Unbowed!' Forn bellowed.

'Khazuk!'

'*Khazuk!*'

'*Khazukan kazakit-ha!*'

'Maybe we'll make both our masters proud after all,' said Forn, as the cheers simmered down.

The Fyreslayers halted before the yellow-glowing, semi-molten gates of Az Skorn, at the end of the Caldur Bridge's initial span. The isle was so named because, when viewed from the sundered caldera high above, its outline resembled that of an axe. When he was younger, Broddur had asked the Firebrand if it had been Grimnir's axe. His tutor had laughed and told him no: Grimnir's axe would be bigger. Ordinarily, the cluster of castles would be home to a kinband of scouts, a small trading post, and any number of truant flamelings depending on the time of day. Its gold walls wobbled with the heat. They were currently silent.

'Weapons ready and hold,' Forn barked, beating Yellowscale with the stick end of his javelin to get her to stop with the rest of the fyrd. 'Hearthguard to me.'

The elite warriors of the lodge wore elaborate golden helms and tough magmadroth-scale kilts. They formed up around Yellowscale and presented a thicket of smouldering pikes.

'See that?' Forn jabbed his spear into the magmic haze.

Broddur squinted. 'I see nothing.'

'That's because I spend my days hunting magmadroth while you spend yours squinting at klinkerhun and letting the Brew Matron's pies come to you.'

Broddur gave his round belly a paternal pat. 'She says I'm a proud figure of a duardin.'

'You're the proud figure of at least three duardin, and she'd have to say it since she made most of it.'

'Wait up,' said Broddur, silencing the Hearthguard's chuckles and staring forwards.

The outline of something solid had appeared within the wandering haze. It appeared to be approaching from the gates.

'Blood and gold!' Forn snapped. 'Show them fyresteel!' There was a hiss, as of heated steel being drawn from an anvil, as the fyrd readied their weapons.

The squat, powerful-looking shape plodded out of the heat.

Broddur lowered his icon. He felt more than a little foolish. 'It's... it's a duardin.'

Forn swore, practically throwing his javelin back into its quiver. 'One chance to win honour and gold while my brothers are elsewhere. One! Do I ask too much?'

'It must be a trader from one of the outer holdings,' Broddur murmured.

'I don't care if he's Grimnir's favourite brewer. What's he doing on the Caldur now?'

Broddur shrugged.

'One measly duardin?' Forn grumbled. 'The whole fyrd mustered over *one duardin*. My brothers are going to love hearing about this. Bloody Blackhammer. Damn him, and his Master Rune. I'm going to take it while it's still white from the anvil and shove it right up his *grimaz*.' He clambered down from his war-throne as he scowled and complained, gave Yellowscale a kick in the ankle to indicate that she should stay, and then stomped off in the direction of the approaching duardin.

Broddur shared a look with the karl of the runeson's Hearthguard. With Forn in this mood, he would as soon toss an unfortunate duardin merchant head first into the Caldur and then push on to the Great Ash Road as stop and ask questions. Together, they hefted up their heavy poles and hastened after him.

The figure that came stumbling out of the heat was indeed a duardin, but he was like no Fyreslayer Broddur had ever seen. His beard was a fiery orange, but it was not the living spirit of Grimnir that made it smoulder as it did Broddur's and Forn's. It was dyed. Brown hair was showing through at the roots. His hair, similarly, had been drawn into a flattened, slightly singed crest that was reminiscent of the Unbak style but without the war-helm that would usually hold it in its shape. And the duardin was big. Bigger even than Forn and thicker with muscle.

'Grimwrath,' Broddur muttered fearfully.

'Rubbish,' said Forn. 'There's not a single rune on him.'

That, Broddur decided, was the most unsettling thing.

Primitive-looking tattoos traversed the duardin's flesh. His fore-arms were clapped in bracers of scuffed and blackened gold, steel chains that may once have been attached to weapons dragging their broken ends along the ground. Yet his body bore none of the ur-gold that lent a Fyreslayer the vigour and strength of his fallen god.

'He looks meaner even than your father, Forn.'

Broddur could hear the clenching of the runeson's fists over the rumbling of the Caldur. The rune embedded in his swelling bicep began to smoulder.

'Some homeless *scruff* from one of the Dispossessed clans dressed up as a Fyreslayer. I have all the luck.' He gesticulated angrily towards the seemingly senseless duardin. 'Well? What've you to say for yourself, you witless *wanaz?*'

The duardin swayed on the spot as he turned to frown at the runeson and his Hearthguard. His eyes slowly uncrossed. Gobbets of lava hissed where they clung to his body.

'Grimnir's blood,' Broddur muttered under his breath. 'It's as though he just climbed out of the volcano.'

'Got drunk and fell in, more likely.'

The strange duardin glowered at the Fyreslayers as though something about their existence enraged him. 'Daemon fire dwarfs and wingless runt dragons,' he growled in a voice as cracked and sore as burnt skin. 'Where in the far reaches of the Chaos Realm have I landed this time?'

'The middle of a painful embarrassment is where this is.' Forn closed the remaining distance between them and rammed his face into the other duardin's. The smell of burnt hair made it to Broddur's nostrils as their crests tangled. 'Are you so block-headed you don't realise Karag Unbak is at–'

Whatever question the runeson had intended to ask ended with a howl of pain as the confused intruder bit down on Forn's nose. Cartilage crunched under his brown teeth, blood and snot spraying his scruffy beard as Forn issued a strangled roar. The other duardin shoved him off, spitting blood and skin back into the runeson's face. His licked his lips as they split into a brutal, humourless grin.

'Tastes like dwarf. A decent effort, daemon.'

'I'm sixth son of Aruk-Grimnir,' Forn shrieked, clutching at his mutilated nose with one hand, his rising fury causing the runes embedded in his body to ignite one by one. 'I'll kill you, you–'

The duardin punched Forn in the face.

The runeson staggered, blinked as though fighting to wake himself from some terrible dream, and then hit the ground in a clatter of fyresteel armour and magmadroth scale. Broddur looked down in shock at his unconscious friend. Say what you like about Forn Aruksson, but no one had ever denied his ability to take a blow to the head.

He felt his gaze drawn to the face at the top of his icon.

The duardin picked a scrap of skin from between his teeth and flicked it onto Forn's body. 'A blight and a ruin on the Dark Gods. Fight if you're going to fight, or simper about your accursed blood-lines if you'd rather. But bear in mind that Gotrek Gurnisson will be doing the former.'

The duardin, apparently calling himself Gotrek, stumbled towards the rest of the Hearthguard like a punch-drunk pugilist.

'Don't make me choose between you now,' he growled. 'What kind of wimpish daemon breed are you?'

'Defend the runeson!' yelled Forn's karl as the Hearthguard belatedly levelled their magmapikes. 'Hearthguard! Bring him down.'

Blasts of molten rock slammed into Gotrek's chest. He staggered through the impacts like a dazed beast, only to curse as he found one of his legs dragging him, the cooling magma hardening into rock and encrusting the foot to the ground.

'Is that all you've got?' Gotrek bellowed. 'Rocks?'

The Hearthguard loosed another volley of magma from their pikes, and charged. Two veteran warriors threw themselves at the duardin, one at each shoulder, meaning to tackle Gotrek to the ground, but succeeded only in wrenching his foot up off the floor. Gotrek merely staggered and reset and cracked their skulls together. They dropped like two rolls of hide. The rest piled in, Gotrek and the four remaining Hearthguard yelling wordlessly as they grappled with one another.

'How did he… get so… strong… without runes?' Broddur heard one of the Hearthguard gasp.

With an infuriated roar, one of the struggling Hearthguard held underarm in a headlock, Gotrek barged his way through the scrum. 'You look like dwarfs, but you fight like girly elves.'

Again, Broddur found his attention summoned by the face of the Doomseeker atop his icon pole.

Gotrek Gurnisson cackled, even as a punch from one of the Hearthguard sent a tooth flying from his mouth. A second was clubbing at his head, a third pulling on his beard. The warrior being crushed in his headlock was slamming his elbow furiously into Gotrek's stomach. He was still raging, still cursing, as the rest of the Forn Fyrd, all two hundred strong, roared past Broddur to join in the fight.

TWO

The water bubbled energetically as Maleneth plunged her hands into the bucket. The reek it gave off was sulphurous. Whether the bucket had been left for her out of genuine compassion or for her gaolers' amusement, Maleneth was unsure. She intended to make a point of asking just as soon as she was free. She withdrew her hands, sloshing water over the sides. It evaporated before it hit the floor. Dabbing her hands with a strip of silk torn from her purple cloak, she hissed where it touched the burns. *By the Bloody-Handed, it hurt.* That would teach her to forget whose gaol she was occupying and touch the bars.

'I know, mistress,' she murmured softly. 'I know.' Her singed fingers went to the locket she wore about her neck. It was made of silver, rather than the gold that everyone knew the Fyreslayers coveted, which was the only reason they had let her keep it. It held a single droplet of blood in a crystal vial. 'You instructed me better than that. That is why your blood is around my neck now and mine is not filling your cauldron to buy you one more year of beauty.'

The sound of a stout duardin key turning in a lock caused her ears to prick. She looked up from her burns as a band of Fyre-slayers in characteristically boisterous mood, and almost certainly drunk, burst into the Hall of Censure. They tramped down the long corridor towards her.

There were no other cells. The Fyreslayers did not typically take prisoners in her experience. Not unless they were confident that their captive could be sold back for gold. She wondered if that was what Aruk-Grimnir had in mind for her. If it was, then the runefather of the Unbak was in line for a disappointment.

'Kindling-bearded goblin sniffer!' the Fyreslayers' new captive snarled as he was herded towards her cell by a small forest of magmapikes. 'Try that again when my hands are free. Or better yet, just try it again right now and see what happens.'

The duardin was impressively muscular, tattooed like the kind of hill-tribe barbarian who were said to hit one another over the head with rocks in Azyr's Eternal Winterlands, though his threats struck Maleneth as somewhat ludicrous while both his hands and one foot were encased in solid rock. Nevertheless, the Fyreslayers seemed to take them seriously. One of the Fyreslayer Hearthguard pushed him towards Maleneth's cell with an uncompromising prod.

'Can you believe he's still fighting, Broddur?'

'Just get him in,' said a large, severely frazzled-looking Fyreslayer carrying the face of his god on a golden stick. Maleneth recog-nised him as one of Forn Aruksson's little friends. Broddur, that was right. Since her capture, he had cast her the occasional apolo-getic look through the bars. At least, she had assumed them to be apologetic. With Fyreslayers, it was difficult to tell. 'Forn'll decide what to do with him when he comes around.'

'Oh woe of woes,' Maleneth called from the back of her cell, clasping her hands around the talisman at her neck as though offering a prayer to poor, sad Forn, ruining it only with the sneer on her lips. 'Please tell me that nothing terrible has befallen dear Forn.'

Broddur scowled. 'We've had enough lip from you, Darkling.'

'I would hate to hear that he had fallen from the war-throne of his magmadroth, or maybe had a rune beaten somewhere painful and embarrassing.'

'Enough.'

'You do know that there is only so much stamina and strength that even your magic gold can confer.' Maleneth chuckled nastily as Broddur's face flushed. Duardin were such painful prudes, and the Fyreslayers were no exception.

The master of the Hall of Censure, a scowling drunk in his ember years named Lokar, opened up the door. The captive was shoved inside. Lokar slammed the door shut just as quickly and locked it behind him.

The duardin tottered around as the heavily armed Fyreslayers outside withdrew from the bars with amusing haste.

'I demand a cell without an elf in it.'

'No offence taken,' Maleneth murmured.

'An eternity of battle in the Realm of Chaos is one thing, but this is cruel and unusual.'

Only Broddur remained with his burly fists around the bars. He stared at his belligerent prisoner as though searching for a familiar face in one beaten out of shape by too many centuries of being a combative oaf.

'Gotrek? Is that your name?'

The duardin scowled. 'For what that's worth.'

'Who are you?'

'The Ice Queen of Kislev, who are you?'

Broddur looked perplexed.

Maleneth burst out laughing at his expression. She could not help it. 'The fabled eloquence of the Fyreslayer battlesmiths. The tales told in Azyr are but pale reflections of the genuine article.'

'What would a Darkling aelf know about it?' Broddur snapped. 'You don't even honour your ancestors with a family name.'

'Aye,' Gotrek added, throwing her a sideways look. 'Butt out of it.'

'Do I need to remind you which side of the bars you're on? I didn't ask to share my living quarters with some Dispossessed hog.'

Gotrek dismissed her with a snort.

'The sacred role of a battlesmith is not to amuse, aelf,' said Broddur, sucking in his ample paunch and adopting a ridiculously proud air. 'We are the keepers of the living history of the lodge. We record and remember its battles, its debts, its grudges, and we heed the lessons of Grimnir.'

Up until the mention of *Grimnir*, Gotrek had seemed almost interested.

'Grimnir?' He scowled, clenching his fists so tightly that Maleneth feared the rock encasing them was going to split. 'I met him once.'

To Maleneth's surprise, the battlesmith reacted with neither scorn nor ridicule, either of which would have been correct. He pressed in closer, eyes eager for something other than gold. She wondered what else could excite a Fyreslayer battlesmith. A grudge? A story? What else had been mentioned in his little speech before? Surely, he could not expect to prise anything of value from some disgruntled Dispossessed who believed he had met Grimnir.

'And?'

'He killed me. Then he lied to me. If I ever see him again, I'll spit in his eye.'

Maleneth collapsed into hysteria. This really was becoming too much. Here were two supposedly adult duardin idly discussing the dead Slayer God as though he was a great uncle that popped by every so often and still owed one of them half a comet for a hundred-year-old unpaid tavern bill.

'*Enough!*' Broddur smacked the bars with his fist. The flesh at the back of his hand sizzled, but it did not seem to trouble him.

'Aye. You sound like something being strangled by a cat.'

'I believe that the correct form of that expression is–'

'Could it be…?' Broddur interrupted her, ignoring both of his prisoners as he drew back from the bars. 'The legend has always been that he would return when enough of his remains had been gathered. I've never heard of as much ur-gold being assembled in one place as Runemaster Blackhammer gathered for his Master Rune. Could he have accidentally…?'

The young battlesmith was almost incandescent with excitement as he backed away.

'I need to speak of this to the Firebrand. And to Aruk-Grimnir.' He bowed to Gotrek, which Maleneth would have found more amusing were she not imprisoned in the same cell. 'Forgive me, but I must go.'

With that, the battlesmith turned on his heel and departed in haste. The Hearthguard seemed relieved to be leaving with him. Lokar gave Maleneth an ale-stained grin in which the occasional glint of gold shone like the foolishness of hope, then ambled back to his pathetic excuse of a life at the end of the hall.

'So,' she said, turning to Gotrek with poisonous brightness. 'What did you do?'

Gotrek's stony glare hardened.

'Easier to walk on water than bandy honest words with an elf, and I daresay more pleasurable to boot.'

'Forgive me for being curious. But I have had no one else to talk with and you're clearly no friend of the Fyreslayers.'

'The what?'

Maleneth could not be sure that Gotrek was not being deliberately dense. Every beggared aelf-child in the Witch's Quarter of Azyrheim knew of the mercenary duardin and their lust, bordering on obsession, for gold. But then, with his crude tattoos, matted crest, clinking nose chain, and fiercely animal stench, Gotrek did more closely resemble some backward Darkoath chief than he did any of the Dispossessed who would occasionally wander into Executioner's Row and 'disappear'.

'How can *you* not know what a Fyreslayer is?'

'Because I care not for illusions and lies.'

'Just where did you come from?'

'The Realm of Chaos, of course.'

'A little advice from someone with experience of telling lies. If you don't want to tell me, then at least come up with something less ridiculous than that.'

'Dwarfs don't lie. Not even to elves who wouldn't know the truth if you gave it to them in a box.'

'No one trapped in the Realm of Chaos just walks out of it.'

'Trapped?' Gotrek looked genuinely insulted. Maleneth had no idea why. 'Whoever said I was trapped? I went there by choice.'

Maleneth adjusted her posture against the wall and sighed. 'Fine, I'll play along. Why would *anyone* do that?'

'Maybe it's because I thought there'd be no elves there to pester me with questions.'

Gotrek sat down heavily, as though suddenly weary. He brought the massive lump of rock encasing his right hand to his eyes and then, with a grunt, smashed it down onto the similarly massive lump encasing his left. As Maleneth watched he fell into a rhythm, huge muscles rippling across his chest and shoulders, raising one huge weight, controlling it, and then smashing it down into the other. It was like watching a Kharadron steam engine that had been switched on and left to run. She had the feeling that she may have terribly misjudged the duardin's strength.

'Let us say, just for the moment, that you entered the Realm of Chaos by choice. Why then leave?'

'Let me tell you something, elf. For years I've battled the daemons of Chaos. Most likely a great many years, for that was the doom that was promised to me. But the gods are fickle. Eternity means less to them than it means to a dwarf. They got bored of me, I think, and turned away, and so I went looking for them. They like to play games sometimes, the Dark Gods.' He paused to glare at her. 'And I have less patience for that than I do for fighting their dregs, so don't sit there and pretend like I've *left*.'

'You think me a daemon, sent to bewitch you?'

'You flatter yourself, girl.'

The rock around the duardin's left hand finally split. He grunted in satisfaction as rubble crumbled away from his wrist. He wriggled his fingers and then made a fist. Veins popped from the tattooed flesh as his bicep bulged.

Maleneth shuffled warily to the other side of the cell. Even unarmed, she was more than capable of fending for herself. A woman alone in Aqshy did not get very far if she was not. But there were some fates that it was better not to tempt.

Gotrek mopped sweat from his unwashed brow and proceeded to smash the remaining rock-manacle against the bars of the cell. Maleneth peered through the faint hazing of heat towards the end of the hall. She knew that Lokar did not take his responsibilities as gaoler terrifically seriously, but this was absurd. Gotrek sounded like he was trying to punch through the bars. She wondered if he was even still inside the hall. She cursed Gotrek and his mindless din. If the master of the hall had left his post and stepped outside without her noticing then she would personally see to it that the fool never made a sound again.

'It's hotter than the time that the manling and I were thrown into a pit in Ind,' Gotrek complained. 'I wonder if that storysmith would bring me a beer.'

'Battlesmith,' Maleneth corrected him, distracted.

'What?'

'It's a battlesmith, not a storysmith.'

'When I ask for the opinion of an elf then the End Times really will have come.'

'I thought we were figments of the Chaos Realms anyway.'

'A beer conjured by the Dark Gods to taunt me is still a beer.'

Ignoring the duardin and his bleating for the moment, she leant as near to the bars as she could without burning herself again and peered out. There was definitely no one out there.

'Lokar?' she called, in what she imagined a Fyreslayer might consider a non-murderous way. There was no answer.

'What is it?' said Gotrek. 'What's going on?'

'The signal for us to get out of here.'

Gotrek made a grand show of crossing both arms over his barrel chest. One was still firmly encased in rock. 'No. Tell your god I tire of playing his games. Or her games. Whichever seems more insulting.'

Maleneth rolled her eyes as she moved to examine the lock. It was typical duardin craftsmanship, too solid to force, but far subtler and more complicated than immediately met the eye. Still, it was nothing that she had not dealt with a thousand times as a child with a taste for other people's lives and property, as a daughter of Azyrheim's Khailebron Temple, and in her training as a Shadowblade of Khaine. She picked up a flat shard of crystal that Gotrek had shattered from the rock around his wrist and turned it appraisingly in her hands.

'Fine then,' she said. 'You can enjoy watching my escape.'

THREE

Broddur stared out over the Unbak Khaz, the great hall of the Unbak lodge, open-mouthed. Skaven warriors in tattered robes and rusty chainmail were scuttling across the walkways in huge packs, their shrill voices drowned out by the periodic blasting of the forge temples and the churn of magma flowing through ducts. Skaven infiltrators in fluttering black cloaks chittered excitedly as they abseiled down from the magma-ducts, knives held between their yellowed teeth.

Where had they come from? And how in Grimnir's name had they got so deep into the lodge without triggering any of the outer wards?

Looking around the hall, he soon found his answer. A tracked drilling machine lay in the rubble of a forgehome. The giant drill bit glowed a sickly green as its whirring slowed, spraying out bolts of purplish lightning. It looked as though it was about to explode, but instead a hatch opened in its side and skaven Stormvermin in a kind of heavy half-plate and carrying halberds flooded out. Far more than a vehicle of its size should have been able to hold.

Broddur drew a fyresteel hand-axe and started towards the infernal machine. He still had four of Forn's Hearthguard with him and he was sure he could go out in a suitable blaze of glory.

It was Lokar, the old gaoler, who held him back. 'It's Black-hammer's Master Rune they're after. Get yourself to the Zharrgrim and defend the forgeflame.'

'What about you?'

'I'm going to defend my hall!'

The whizzing shriek of powered tools sounded from the space before them. Broddur saw nothing but an unsteadiness in the air that could have been readily explained away by the heat, but some instinct made him throw himself out of the way just as a skaven tunneller tore through a rip in the air where he had just been. Its long, rat-like head was enclosed by a goggled mask, ears poking out the sides, tail hidden under a lengthy coat. Another ratman skulked behind the first. They carried what looked like a handheld version of the larger drilling machine engine between them.

'Die-die!' the ratman chittered through the thick leather mask, and stabbed its grinder tool at a Hearthguard who had not been as quick on his toes as Broddur.

The Fyreslayer howled as his flesh and bone disintegrated just as readily as the air through which the skaven had just emerged. The tunneller squealed delightedly as its efforts resulted in a bloody hole big enough for a swarm of skaven warriors to spill through. They looked horrified by whatever they had been through to get here. They were wide-eyed and foaming at the mouth, and unusually happy to throw themselves at a kinband of veteran Hearthguard if it meant getting *away* from whatever nightmarish under-realm they had just come from.

What the skaven lacked in courage they more than made up for in frenzied energy and sheer weight of numbers. The first was on

Broddur before his axe was ready for it. The second, third, fourth, fifth, sixth and seventh were not a tail-length behind it.

The first ratman had a rusty spear in one bandage-wrapped paw, but had been driven to such desperate heights of fear that it ran straight into Broddur's axe as he tried to swing it. The weight of its pack-mates drove its squirming body onto him. The ratty stink made Broddur gag. It scrabbled at him in a death frenzy, blunting its claws on his rune-toughened skin. Broddur finally managed to get in a swing and brained one with the cheek of his axe, bludgeoned another with the butt. Even at the risk of being swarmed, he couldn't use the actual blade. The skaven were too numerous and too fast. All it would take was for him to spend a second pulling his axe out of some ratman's mangy corpse for him to become its companions' next meal.

'You tire, I think,' something squeaked. 'Beard-thing too fat for war. Yes.'

A clanrat hacked at him with a notched scimitar. Broddur struck another chip into its blunt edge with his parry, but the fighter had already slunk back into the horde and his return blow merely hacked the arm off a squealing spear-rat. Broddur followed after the tittering clanrat with a roar, splintering another skaven's ribcage and feeling the scrape of a flesh wound down his side as he shouldered the frothing vermin aside. The scimitar-wielding skaven reappeared, scuttling around to come at him from a different side. This time, Broddur got a decent look. It wore a scuffed mail coat and a kettle helm and carried a wooden shield with the tripartite sigil of its verminous deity scratched into the boards. A leader.

'Big-fat. Yes. Yes. Slow.' The skaven licked its pointed teeth and lunged. 'Die-die now.'

It was nimble, but Broddur was five times its weight. It staggered away from the meeting of their blades with jangling paws, squealing as Broddur caught the ratman by the goatee-like tuft of fur sprouting from under its muzzle and tossed it over the nearest magma-duct.

The heat haze above the monolithic stone channel turned briefly pink.

The fiery dissolution of their leader seemed to be enough for the remaining skaven. They scampered over the corpses and rubble they had left behind them in their first mad charge, biting and clawing at one another in their determination to get away.

Broddur held his sides ruefully and watched them flee.

'By Grimnir, they're quick when they're going the other way.'

Lokar bent to pick up his slingshield and wrenched his axe from a clanrat's scrawny chest. The grinder tool continued to rev fitfully, in spite, or perhaps because, of the Hearthguard's bare foot crushing the wielder's trigger finger. With the exception of the one warrior gone back to the flame in the initial ambush, the three remaining Hearthguard had emerged with no more than scratches.

'To the magma-vault!' Lokar yelled at them. 'Get on with you, go!'

Broddur could already see several Fyreslayers running in that direction, and turned to join them when something even more important than the sanctity of the Zharrgrim struck him.

Gotrek.

There was something about Forn's prisoner that he could not yet explain. He claimed to have met Grimnir – *Grimnir!* – and though Broddur knew he should dismiss his claims as nonsense, he could not. Perhaps it was the workaday way in which he spoke of meetings with gods and battles with daemons that made his outlandish tales seem believable. And had he not seen Gotrek down Forn with a single blow, and then proceed from there to fight his way through half the runeson's Hearthguard? Whatever he was, Broddur could not leave him in the Halls of Censure for the skaven until he knew.

'Do as he says,' he ordered the remaining Hearthguard, even as he started running in the opposite direction.

The clash and squeak of battle became muted as the heavy gilt-inlaid doors of the Hall of Censure closed behind Broddur.

'Stand back, Gotrek. I'm going to smash the l–'

He halted mid-stride as he noticed that something was amiss. Feeling like a fool, he pushed open the already-partway-open door of Gotrek's cell. It swung in on well-oiled hinges.

'It wasn't me, if that's what you're thinking,' Gotrek said with a scowl. He was sitting sullenly in the middle of the floor, surrounded by the rubble of his stone cuffs. Broddur could not be astonished by that feat of strength just then. He looked quickly around the rest of the cell.

'Where's the Darkling, Maleneth?'

'About somewhere doing *elf* things, no doubt.'

Broddur stepped back from the wide-open door. 'What are *you* still doing here?'

Gotrek gave a deep, rumbling sigh. 'As I already explained to the elf, I want no part in these games. One of you is at war with the other one again, aren't they? And whatever god you serve hopes I've taken enough knocks to the head to play along and join their side.' He rapped his knuckles on the side of his head to demonstrate. 'Well, dwarfen skulls are thick. So begone, before I demonstrate on your forehead just *how* thick.'

'There's no time to argue. We need to join the Grand Fyrd in the magma-vault before this hall is overrun by skaven.'

'Did you say skaven?' Gotrek took a long, aggressive sniff. 'I knew I recognised that smell. Even that seems fouler than I remember it.'

Broddur tossed his hand-axe into Gotrek's cell. The big duardin caught it by the haft in one gigantically muscled fist.

'Well here's a handy thing. A daemon surrendering his weapon to a daemonslayer.'

'I've my icon, and seeing what you did to Forn with just your fists, I think you'll make better use of an axe than I.'

Gotrek grumbled under his breath, but stood up. 'All right, I'll go with you, if it means you'll stop yammering about it. But only because it's been centuries since I last killed a skaven. And a change is as good as a rest.'

'We'll find Skorun Firebrand and Krag Blackhammer in the magma-vaults. They'll know what you are.'

Gotrek muttered something that sounded disparaging, but nevertheless hurried after Broddur as he pounded back to the fight.

Broddur and Gotrek emerged from the Hall of Censure to find skaven warriors everywhere. They scampered in and out of scurry-holes, darted under the monolithic stone feet of the magma-ducts, peeped over gold-veined parapets to take aim with bizarre long-barrelled firearms. The Unbak Khaz would ordinarily have been a bustling hub of industry and trade, but a swathe of it had since collapsed around the skaven tunnelling machine. Those Fyre-slayers not already fighting were yelling in frustration at the skaven snipers. A *crack* rang out over the din, seconds before the wall next to Broddur's head exploded under a sniper's bullet, causing him to duck his head and curse.

The skaven's scattergun approach was starting to organise into two main prongs. The first, centred around the tunnelling machine that was still disgorging armoured warriors, effectively owned half of the Unbak Khaz, but only because those Fyreslayers not already locked in combat or dead were ignoring it in favour of the second. It was the larger and seemingly better organised of the two hosts, comprising dense ranks of warriors, mutant warbeasts, and several rattling war-machines of indecipherable function. It was pushing hard on the great, rune-inscribed doors of the magma-vault. That was where Gotrek needed to be too, and where Broddur was determined to get him.

'Skaven,' Gotrek spat. 'I'd like to say I missed killing them, but I don't.'

'Khazuk!' Broddur yelled, raising his icon aloft so that the face of the Doomseeker might rally his kin from afar, and breaking into a run. '*Unbaki* to me! Khazuk!'

A skaven straggler in ill-matching half-plate hissed at him in alarm. Being so far to the rear of the main skaven attack, it was either an important leader, unusually cunning, or simply a coward. Broddur brained it over the head with his icon. Another, this one swaddled in black rags, pounced from behind the tumbled storefront awning of the smithy it had clearly been looting, only to jerk back and fall over with a Vulkite slingshield buried in its collarbone. More Fyreslayers emerged from their dwellings as Broddur huffed by. Two at first, then five. Then fifteen. Then twenty. A drop of fire in an ocean of fur, but the least and youngest amongst them was worth ten skulking clanrats, and twenty when in defence of the ur-gold in his magma-vault.

'As the fathers of the Unbak did best Ignimbris, first and greatest of the children of Vulcatrix, and drove him back beneath the Caldur, so too will we drive this menace from our halls this day!' Broddur yelled as the warriors rallied about him.

'*Khazuk!*'

'You're handy with a speech, I'll grant you that,' Gotrek grunted, giving every indication of struggling to keep up.

With a wild bellow, a Fyreslayer berzerker hurled himself from a four-tier foundry roof. The warrior burned bright as ur-gold runes poured fire into his veins, landing amidst the clanrats milling around below like an explosive charge.

'*Dawi zharr* sorcery,' Gotrek muttered darkly as bits of rat rained over them and the maddened berzerker set about the broken survivors with an axe in each hand.

Broddur recognised the syllables that Gotrek was using, but had no idea what the words meant. He wanted to ask, but there was no time. He held his icon aloft to rally the disparate kinbands before any more could be tempted to break off and attack the skaven alone. 'To the magma-vaults and to Aruk-Grimnir. Cut through them!'

'Not that it's any business of mine, but what's that one over there up to?'

Gotrek was pointing to one of the nearer magma-ducts. Teams of skavenslaves were hacking away at one of the basaltic support columns, their skeletal, patch-furred bodies almost bald from repeated strokes of the overseer's lash. Their attempted vandalism was being overseen by a chittering warlock engineer in an armoured coat and heavy brass gauntlets. A loose-fitting helmet bugged its eyes with a plethora of coloured lenses, and it wielded a wire-pronged glaive that sputtered out a halo of dirty electricity.

'They mean to bring down the magma-duct,' Broddur gasped. 'To flood the chamber and capture the Zharrgrim before it can be reinforced by the kinbands on the other side of the Unbak Khaz.'

'I thought you lot were made of fire, or lava, or something similarly unnatural.'

'I could put my hand into a forgefire, true. Or hold a hot rune in my hand and not burn. Can you not?'

Gotrek brandished his borrowed axe threateningly. 'I'll happily show you what this Slayer can do.'

Broddur stared at him. For a moment, he forgot all about the skaven and the battle for the lodge. This Slayer, Gotrek had called himself. *The* Slayer.

'What are you gawping at?'

Broddur returned from his reverie. 'Well, a flood of lava will stop a Fyreslayer as surely as anyone else. Kill them all!' he yelled, for the benefit of those nearby. 'Khazuk! Blood and gold!'

He remained behind, urging the Fyreslayers on as they sprinted past him, waving their axes and hammers in the air. Partly, this was from a desire to ensure that no skaven trickery saw the duct brought down while his attention was elsewhere, but mostly it was because he was quite thoroughly out of breath. Axe-work? Yes. Singing the stories? Yes. Both at the same time? The Firebrand had always made it look so easy...

Nevertheless, he watched with pride as the Fyreslayers hurled themselves into the squealing vermin, their axes making mince-meat of the hapless slaves.

It was the perfect position to watch them all die.

'There-there!' the warlock engineer squealed, its voice ampli-fied and weirdly distorted by its helmet. 'Throw them there. No. *There*. Big-beard and beard with stick.' It stabbed a gauntleted claw to where Gotrek and Broddur were standing, and a volley of dirty glass spheres shattered in the midst of the melee. A pall of filthy green smoke rose to envelop skaven and Fyreslayer alike. The warlock engineer pulled the fur from its head in frustration. 'No-no!' it screamed, gesticulating furiously towards Gotrek and Broddur. *'There!'*

The Fyreslayer kinbands swung their axes about wildly, blinded by tears that turned to acid in their eyes, their mouths welling up with froth. Broddur saw one warrior sway like a drunkard in an attempt to fight his way clear of the poison cloud, tripping over the asphyxiated corpse of a skavenslave. His mouth gaped open in a last effort to draw breath, all his rune-given strength in Aqshy made worthless by the insidious nature of the skaven gas.

'For the forges of the first fathers!' Broddur croaked. Even the tiny amounts of poison gas he had inhaled made his voice unrecognisable. 'We are Fyreslayers and our axes thirst for blood and gold! We are Grimnir's children. We fight as he fought, to bloody triumph or bloody oblivion, and to celebrate them both the same. Khazuk!'

He turned to check on Gotrek, but the Slayer was no longer beside him.

In the confusion of the gas attack and the hand-to-hand fighting, he had disappeared.

'Gotrek! Gotrek, where are you?'

The warlock engineer was still crouching on the stone lip of the magma-duct overlooking the combat and was surrounded, Broddur saw now, by a gaggle of rubber-masked globadiers. It aimed its wire-pronged glaive at Broddur, squealing in glee as electricity tormented the air around the sorcerous apparatus.

Then the engineer exploded. Broddur's first assumption was that the warlock's weapon had misfired, as skaven technology was often wont to do, but then he noticed the fresh lava fountaining over the lip of the magma-duct and realised that a third party had been involved.

The ground quaked and the remaining skavenslaves and their masters broke in terror.

Broddur turned as a huge magmadroth with fiery yellow scales stomped through the rubble of the Unbak Khaz. The giant reptile delivered a deafening bellow and then proceeded to spew magma over the fleeing skavenslaves. It was this, Broddur realised, that had slain the warlock. Gas grenades shattered ineffectually against the magmadroth's yellow hide, their corrosive contents dissipating harmlessly in the fierce heat emanating from it. High up in the war-throne lashed to the beast's back, Forn wafted his hand through the thinning cloud as though someone had just broken wind. Not that the runeson could have smelled a thing through the mess of his nose.

'Did you miss me, Broddur?' Forn yelled over the carnage. 'Admit it, you missed me.'

Yellowscale turned her head towards the skaven globadiers that were pestering her from the rooftop and blinked slowly. A pinprick of yellow-white heat ignited deep in the well of her gullet and the ratmen shrieked as the ensuing stream of lumpen magma incinerated them, along with most of the structure that they had been cowering in.

Broddur could only grieve for the handiwork of his kin.

Forn gave a fierce laugh as he reined the magmadroth in. 'I've been a fool, Broddur! After the debacle on the Caldur Bridge, I actually thought this was going to be a bad day. Let the Unbak Chronicle remember the day that Forn Aruksson led his fyrd to the defence of the magmahold. Remember it, Broddur. Or better yet, write it down!'

Ignoring him, Broddur beat his hand through the thinning cloud of green gas, searching desperately over the staring, open-mouthed corpses of skaven and Fyreslayer alike.

'Where's the Slayer?'

'Who?'

'Gotrek Gurnisson! The duardin from Az Skorn.'

'Why're you looking for him here?'

'Because I released him from the Hall of Censure.'

'Hah!' Forn barked. 'Good for you!'

A Fyreslayer's rage burned hot, but as the examples of Grimnir and Vulcatrix had taught them, the hottest flame burned the shortest. Not for them the slow, eternal burn of Dracothion. They did not cleave to their grudges as other duardin did. Had Gotrek been there with them now then Forn would probably have laughed about the fight at Az Skorn and bought the Slayer an ale to celebrate it with him.

'No duardin should die in a cage.'

'He was right here with me. Where would he go?'

'He'll be fighting somewhere, and doing all right. We've our own blood to honour and gold to claim.'

'No! No, we've got to–'

'We're not flamelings now, Broddur. I'm a runeson, and you're my battlesmith. We go on to the magma-vaults! For blood and gold!' Forn stood tall on the seat of his war-throne and yelled. *'Khazuk-Haaaaaa!'* as Yellowscale threatened to deafen them all with a trumpet of her own.

The surviving kinbands rallied around the enormous magma-droth and Broddur reluctantly acknowledged that Forn was right. If Gotrek was who Broddur was starting to believe that he was, then he did not need Broddur, or the Unbaki, to look out for him.

He was more concerned about what the Unbaki were going to do today without Gotrek.

FOUR

The magma-vault was quiet. The roar and thunder of the battle between the idiots of the Unbak lodge and the skaven was muted by the thick basalt walls, subdued by the consonant hum of the runic wards that glowered menacingly from every surface. Maleneth moved carefully, more wary of the defences she could not see than the dozen or so that she could. The duardin were cunning artificers, and the Fyreslayers clove to those same traditions, in their own boorishly violent way. In her experience, jealous peoples tended to devise the most fiendishly deadly wards. There was no shame in acknowledging, to herself at least, that there were artisans like Krag Blackhammer whose skills surpassed even the Hags of Azyr.

Why, even Sigmar had been forced to concede to the Chaos Gods, had he not?

Silently, she padded towards the rune-inscribed anvil in the centre of the vault. Her feet were shod in black Spiderfang silk, more material torn from her shirt. It was sleeveless now, her whipcord arms pale and perspiring. The magma-vault was an oven. No hint of a breeze moved the air that deep under the volcano. Tools lay in drums at the anvil's feet. A sense of wary animus hung about them, as though their proximity to the anvil's power had infused them with a limited sentience, awareness enough to be aggrieved by her intrusion. Graven effigies of the Slayer God, Grimnir – twenty-foot-high likenesses carved into the columns against the walls – burned her back with their gazes.

The Unbak lodge was one of the oldest in the Salamander's Spine, that volcanic range that was itself rumoured to be the birthplace of the Fyreslayer lodges. Its magma-vault was a honeycomb of hidden chambers. Each was a trove of treasures, secured by its own cunning wards and defences, the secrets of which had been lost even to the descendants of the runemasters who had first cast them. But Maleneth Witchblade was no petty thief, to grab the first trinket to catch her eye. She was a daughter of the Khailebron, a disciple of the Bloody-Handed God, a student of the Shadow-blades. For all their ancient wealth, the Unbaki had only one treasure that interested her, and it was here.

Why else would she have worked so hard to ensure that that blundering clod, Forn, had been able to capture her and bring her into the mountain? The magma-vault was a veritable fortress, after all, and much easier to enter from within.

She stepped up to the anvil and gasped as she looked down into the golden radiance shining from its face. It was what she had been sent here to steal. Blackhammer's Master Rune was a thing of beguiling simplicity and deep power; a thing of beauty, even to her jaded heart. Its golden symmetry burned into her retinas like the fiery outline of an eclipsing sun. She reached for it, only to immediately pull her hand back as she felt its heat against her already burned fingers. The Master Rune boiled and churned like the core of the World-that-Was.

'I am not going to be carrying that out of here by hand,' she murmured, tapping the locket above her heart as if for luck or guidance.

It was not often that the spirit of her former mistress replied, but when she did it was generally worth listening to. Not at all like the first decade or two after her confinement there, when her threats and curses had run through Maleneth's thoughts almost constantly, day and night.

Maleneth smiled to herself. She missed those little talks.

Stepping back from the anvil, blinking her eyes to restore her vision after the brilliance of the rune, she crouched by the tool stand. Carefully, as silently as she could, not that she expected to be overheard over the battle raging without, she removed the tools one by one and lifted the now empty drum. She needed both arms just to raise it, but it should be able to bear the heat of the Master Rune. It would be inelegant, but it would suffice her to carry the rune out of the mountain.

A pair of iron-capped boots scuffed the floor behind her.

She whirled towards the unexpected intrusion, a pair of long fyresteel knives singing as they slid from her belt. The Zharrgrim Hearthguard from whom she had 'borrowed' them had considered them little more than eating utensils. But then, as he had since learned, one type of meat could be cut just as readily as another.

She hissed in annoyance as she saw who it was who had followed her. She should not have been surprised. Neither skaven nor Fyreslayers wore shoes.

'I thought that you weren't interested, Gotrek.'

The duardin in the threshold shrugged his massive shoulders. He appeared to have found a weapon of his own somewhere in the maze of vaults: an axe, and this one no culinary tool. A caged flame, a genuine ember of the Unbak's sacred forgeflame, burned between two gleaming wedges of rune-engraved fyresteel.

'I've absolutely no idea what's going on out there, it's true. But if there's one thing in life more certain than the trickery of the Dark Gods, then it's the treachery of elves.' Gotrek spun the massive greataxe one-handed, flames roiling from the molten brazier at its core.

'That is no ordinary axe. Where did you get it?'

'I found it. That storysmith gave me one, but I like this one better. It's bigger, for one, and it reminds me somewhat of the one I used to have.'

'And they call *me* a thief.'

'I call you a dirty elf. What *they* call either of us is neither here nor there.'

'You know, you remind me of my former mistress. Every year when the dark moon, Dharroth, waxed full and showed the Mallus its darksome face, the Hag would rouse herself for the revels of Death Night, convinced that she was a young woman and that it was a thousand years ago, looking for long-dead foes and replaying long-lost games.'

'I take it she came to no happy end.'

Maleneth smiled distantly, playing idly with her blood-drop pendant. Oh, it had been happy. For Maleneth.

'Maybe you really have just stepped out of a tablet from the Age of Myth and been spat from the Unbak crater. Or maybe you really were consigned to the Realm of Chaos and robbed there of your wits. I do not care. All my masters demand of me is the Master Rune. They will not care if one addled duardin walks away unscathed, but stand between me and the door as you do now and it will be the Bloody-Handed God who will receive you next.'

'If I had a penny for every time someone promised me that, I'd be High King of the Everpeak by now.' Gotrek ran his thumb down the blade of his axe until a bead of blood welled up between his calloused skin and the metal. He stuck his thumb in his mouth and sucked it dry. 'Instead, I'm in this hellhole. My axe thirsts, elf, and I would lead her to drink.'

Seeing that her gifts of persuasion were going to waste on this fool, Maleneth launched herself at Gotrek with a hiss, intending to overwhelm the flat-footed pig with her speed.

Her two long knives butterflied across his muscular torso, but Gotrek was as preternaturally good with an axe as someone with his contempt for the entirety of the Mortal Realms would have to be, allowing deft flicks and feints to prick his skin while killing blows were batted aside. He was bleeding in several places even so when Maleneth jinked back, knives fluttering about her to distract the duardin's eye as she put distance back between them.

He glared at her, ignoring the sharp edges completely.

She licked the duardin's blood where it had fallen on the back of her hand.

'It tastes aged. Like a fine bitterberry wine.'

'You don't know the half of it!'

The duardin swung his flaming greataxe with a roar. She willowed to one side, allowing the monstrous rune-weapon to boil across her. Gotrek grunted in annoyance as she ducked and weaved around his efforts, turning his phenomenal strength to redirecting the greataxe mid-stroke and slashing it across her waist. She bent at the knees, back parallel to the ground as both the axe and its ensuing fireball rolled across her.

'Don't toy with me, elf. I get enough of that from the gods.'

Letting the haft of his axe run out to its fullest length, Gotrek threw a blistering haymaker across Maleneth's shins. She pushed up off her feet and into a handstand, launching herself into a backward flip that landed her neatly on top of Krag Blackhammer's anvil.

'Tell your unholy master that Gotrek Gurnisson hasn't forgotten his oaths. I'm coming for them all, and I want my axe back.'

Tossing the flaming axe over to his left hand, which seemed no less muscular and powerful than the right, Gotrek sent it rippling overhead towards her. With his strength and the greataxe's obvious runic enchantments, the blow would have carved her from hip to shoulder had she remained where she was to receive it. She leapt lightly from the anvil, putting its solid, rune-encrusted mass between herself and the mad duardin.

'Idiot! With a weapon like that you might actually damage the Master Rune.'

'Wouldn't that be a shame.'

Gotrek circled around the anvil, holding his axe menacingly in both hands. Maleneth mirrored his steps, keeping the anvil between them.

'Do you know how difficult it was to get captured by that meat-headed imbecile, Forn, in the first place, just to get this close to the Master Rune? If I had known that the skaven were so close behind me then I would not have put myself to such trouble. I would have just snuck in and killed everyone who got in my path, the way my beloved mistress taught m–'

With a sudden explosion of violence, Gotrek slammed his shoulder into the side of the anvil and roared. Maleneth started to laugh as the effort bulged the duardin's shoulders and popped veins across his body. It would have taken a Stardrake to move that anvil. No, two Stardrakes!

No sooner had it reached her mouth however than the anvil, impossibly, was teetering on two of its four feet and leaning perilously towards her.

'Lord of Murder!'

She leapt clear just as the anvil crashed over, pulverising the tile she had been standing on. The empty tool drum and all of its assorted tools clattered across the floor with an almighty din while the Master Rune itself thumped to the ground with a solidity and mass far in excess of its size. Something under the tile it landed on went *click* and Maleneth gave voice to a second curse.

'Sweet Hag of Azyr!'

The many faces of Grimnir engraved into the walls, ceiling and floor opened their mouths and sprayed beams of magical fire, forcing Maleneth into a wild dance to evade them all. Wall panels gave way to reveal articulated clockwork arms with spears attached. They stabbed with a mechanical frenzy; Maleneth wove her mad dance with sudden limbos and cartwheeling turns until she was no longer certain which way was up and which down. She jinked, weaved, spun, skipping towards the one small square of unmolested ground, which was where Blackhammer's anvil had stood before Gotrek had thrown it. Somersaulting over a jabbing spear-thrust and rolling through a sheet of flame, she landed in a crouch beside the ten-times-accursed Master Rune.

'Got y–'

The flat of the duardin's axe struck her square across the jaw. Sparks from the captive forgeflame exploded over her as the floor spun and raced up to have her.

'I hate it when they jump about,' that hateful, faraway voice said over her as she slipped into unconsciousness. 'Like goats in bloody spring.'

FIVE

Broddur stood in amazement as Gotrek Gurnisson emerged from the magma-vault and dumped the Darkling, Maleneth, on the ground. He lowered his axe. Threescore rune-hardened veterans of Krag Blackhammer's Zharrgrim Hearthguard and the handful of Vulkite warriors of the Forn Fyrd not intimately involved in putting the remaining skaven to flight watched the Slayer with expressions of belligerent awe.

'Shatter me,' Broddur muttered.

'She wasn't that tough.'

'Not the aelf, Gotrek. The axe.'

The Slayer cocked his head to regard the flaming greataxe he was carrying propped against one shoulder. 'Not a bad axe.'

'Not a bad axe?' sputtered Forn.

'Aye, not a bad axe. My old one was better.'

'It's Zangrom-Thaz!'

Faced with Gotrek's blank, slightly dangerous expression, Broddur hastened to explain. 'It's the fyrestorm greataxe of the Unbaki.

Only the mightiest of Grimwrath Berzerkers can wield it, those Fyreslayers who've proven themselves strong enough to take on Grimnir's fire without being driven insane by it or killed.'

'Look.' Forn spread his arms to display the ur-gold runes that had been hammered into his torso. 'I've seven runes in my body. Broddur there has three, but he's younger than me and not son to Aruk-Grimnir. A legendary Grimwrath, like Braegrom the Blessed...' He turned to Broddur for help. Forn never had read as much as he ought.

'Twenty or more,' Broddur supplied helpfully.

'And you don't have any! Could the axe have lost some of its potency, Broddur?'

'There are many fyrestorm greataxes in the Salamander's Spine, but Zangrom-Thaz is one of few to contain a shard of Grimnir's axe.'

Gotrek laughed suddenly at that, and Broddur blinked, unused to any Fyreslayer taking the Unbak Chronicle as a subject of ridicule. 'I don't think so, storysmith. Whoever sold you that bedtime tale should be run out of the hold with his beard shaved.'

'Excuse me?'

'Grimnir gave his axe to me. It's *my* axe.'

Forn's kinband and the Zharrgrim Hearthguard muttered to one another in disbelief. Broddur's own mouth worked silently as he thought through the implications of even that much he already knew to be true.

'A Doomseeker strong enough to wield Zangrom-Thaz, but without the borrowed strength of Grimnir?'

'You're a strange and pitiable people,' Gotrek went on, scowling at them all. 'As I'd expect from the Chaos Gods' attempt at conjuring a dwarf.' He prodded the unconscious Darkling with the iron-capped toe of his boot. She moaned softly as she came around. 'Wakey, wakey, elfling.'

'Gods curse you all,' Maleneth muttered, without leaving the foetal ball she had curled herself into on the floor. 'I have seen Flesh-eater Courts with more grounded delusions than these.' She spat on the ground, almost catching Broddur's bare toes. 'As far as I can see, you all deserve one another.'

A loud *bang* went off in Broddur's ear before he could reply, an explosion of smoke and ash striking him in the face. Too late, he threw up his hands to shield it, his eyes stinging as a string of secondary pops and bangs rippled through the smoky cloud.

Another huge, smoke-muffled explosion knocked through a slab of the magma-vault wall. It blasted outwards, as though blown from within, stonework and sculpture crumbling as the resultant blast wave rolled out over the coughing Fyreslayers. Broddur strained his ears, convinced that he could hear the chittering of rats over the ringing.

'To arms!' Forn was yelling tinnily, somewhere in the murk. 'To arms!'

Skaven! Broddur tried to yell, only to end up hacking his lungs up into his mouth. *They're inside the vault.* 'Forn Fyrd,' he managed to croak. 'Khazuk!'

He heard Fyreslayers charging about in the smoke. A wail of grief and fury arose from within the walls of the magma-vault.

'Congratulations, Gotrek Gurnisson,' said Maleneth. 'You have allowed the skaven to get away with Blackhammer's Master Rune.'

Gotrek kicked the aelf in the stomach. 'Congratulations on allowing my boot to fall into your belly.'

Yellowscale was a beacon of red heat in the middle of the smoke-cloud, rumbling like an erupting volcano in a crown of ash. Leaving the Slayer and his captive aelf for the time being, Broddur stumbled towards her. He was not alone in doing so. A dozen or more Fyreslayers bustled around the runeson and his magmadroth in agitation.

'Which way did the ratmen flee?'

'Scatter,' Forn bellowed. 'Someone will find them.' He struck his javelin across Yellowscale's rump, urging her to claw fat sparks out of the ground and roar. 'They shan't be allowed to escape.'

'Shouldn't we find Aruk-Grimnir and your brothers?'

'There's no time,' Forn replied, more aggressively than Broddur had expected. Of course, the theft of the Master Rune while his elder brothers had been cloistered away in the heart of the Zharrgrim was his shame to avenge. 'They must be deep inside the magma-vault if they've not roused themselves already. After the skaven, battlesmith. If they make off with the rune then I'll never be runefather.'

Fyreslayers broke off in all directions at the runeson's bellowed order. Broddur found himself running again, and in a direction seemingly chosen for him at random by the scattering kinband. He rowed at the air with his hands as the smoke began to thin, clearing away enough of it to see that he had essentially run back the way he had earlier come. The magma-ducts gurgled to his left. The Hall of Censure was directly ahead. He pulled up, wheezing, at the sight of a Fyreslayer corpse. Bodies were plentiful enough between here and the Hall of Censure, but this was different. It was one of the Zharrgrim Hearthguard, a throwing star giving off an eerie green glow embedded in the bridge of his nose.

This was the way they had run.

'A thousand curses of vengeance upon the skaven race,' he said, leaning down to draw the dead warrior's eyelids open so that he might see his enemies on his way to the Stone Sleep. 'Go to the fires, my kin. You walk in Grimnir's footsteps now.'

He flinched, looking up suddenly, as a filthy, emerald-tinged explosion consumed one of the gold-plated support columns of the magma-duct. It was either terrifically bad timing on the part of the warlock engineer that Yellowscale had slain earlier or astonishingly good. The stone channel began to lean onto the blown column, cinders blowing over the injured side as the whole structure began to creak.

Leaving the fallen Hearthguard to the fire, Broddur ran ahead of the listing magma-duct. His legs pumped. His paunch shook. His cheeks blew until they were as red as tongs from the forge. He could just about see the skaven ahead. Black-clad assassins. Nothing but a wriggle of tail as they disappeared through the outer rune-gates for the Caldur. They were just too damned fast.

The magma-duct gave a tumultuous groan. Broddur could not help but glance back over his shoulder as the great channel finally surrendered to gravity, shrugging off its remaining uprights and crashing to the ground, slopping the stone floor of the Unbak Khaz with hot lava.

'*Bugrit!*' Broddur wheezed, as he strained to make his legs move faster. 'Bugrit, Bugrit, Bugrit.'

More molten rock splurged from the broken channel like blood from a severed artery. Faster than any duardin could run.

'Hang in there, Broddur!'

Broddur turned to see Yellowscale thundering through the spreading lake of magma. Forn stood tall in the war-throne, sprayed by sparks like the figurehead of a lava ship at sail. He lowered his javelin and Broddur grabbed it with both hands as the magmadroth stampeded past, yanking him from his feet just as the lava flow oozed over the flagstone where he had been standing. Forn roared with elation, and with the effort of pulling up Broddur's bulk. Broddur did his part by wedging his toes into Yellowscale's craggy sides and pushing. They collapsed together on the stone platform of the war-throne.

'You… fat… *duraz*,' Forn gasped when he could breathe again. 'Where's the Slayer?'

'Always the blasted Slayer. He was with the Darkling on the steps of the Zharrgrim when I saw him last.'

Broddur took a grip on the war-throne's rocking back and peered after the fleeing skaven. 'They're taking the Caldur.'

'Escaping the old-fashioned way, are they? Good!' Forn beat the magmadroth with his javelin for more speed. 'They're quick, these vermin, but Yellowscale's no sluggard herself when she's angry.'

The furious magmadroth and the two white-knuckled Fyreslayers on her back exploded through the awesome rune-gates of the Unbak Khaz and onto the Caldur Bridge. The skaven assassins were fleeing the Zharrgrim atoll by the bridge, barely visible through swirling clouds of cinder ash and fire. One of them turned to look over its shoulder, crouched low and rolled something back along the bridge. It was a brass orb.

'Watch ou–'

The device went off with an unspectacular *pop* and a fizzle of poisonous-looking gases, but the main strength of the charge seemed to have been directed downwards. Hairline cracks split the obsidian paving slabs. Chain detonations pummelled the Caldur Sea, summoning geysers that sprayed molten fire hundreds of feet into the air. Pyroclastic rain clattered across the bridge, thumping harmlessly off Yellowscale's thick hide. Broddur held his arms protectively over his head as the magmadroth thundered through the boiling hail. Forn laughed.

'Is that it? Is that all you have?'

'Children of Grimnir!' Broddur yelled in terror as the bridge began to shudder.

'Raised to fire!'

A deep tremor disturbed the surface of the lava sea, like the footsteps of a mega-gargant in a body of water. The bridge's paving slabs shivered in their mortar.

'Forn? What is–'

A great reptile easily three times the bulk of Yellowscale rose from the magma, its scaled body glowing with an infernal heat.

Its head was like an armoured war-forge, leaking fire and malice with every breath as it hauled itself up onto the bridge behind the Fyreslayers.

'*Urkar*,' Broddur swore. 'Ignimbris, the godbeast, first of the children of Vulcatrix. It can't be.'

The skaven, further along the bridge from the monster, shrieked in terror.

'I don't think this was part of their plan,' Forn yelled.

The godbeast, Ignimbris, drew a deep breath. Its head shook like the roof of a volcano. White heat blasted through the cracks in its neck and jaw.

'Get down!'

Forn threw himself into Broddur, sending them both over the side of the war-throne as Ignimbris sprayed the bridge with molten rock and boiling gases. Yellowscale bellowed in pain as her armour bore the brunt of the onslaught. She collapsed to the bridge with a heavy thump and a plaintive roar.

'Yellowscale!' Forn cried, dropping to the beast's side and cradling her enormous head in his hands.

Through the smoke and cinders, Broddur saw the bomb-rolling assassin itself catch fire in the magma torrent. It flapped about in a panic before its fellow skaven arrived to beat out the flames. That done, they then stabbed the singed ratman in the chest, bent down to collect the heavy thing it had dropped, and scurried away as quickly as their verminous cowardice could blur their limbs. In spite of everything, Broddur felt sickened by their fratricidal treachery.

'No, no, no. *No!*' Forn wailed, desperately trying to rub life back into Yellowscale's craggy brow. 'You don't die, girl. I raised you from an egg, and you don't get to die until I say so.'

'They still have the Master Rune.'

Forn looked up, a fiery shimmer in his eyes. 'To the flame with the rune.'

'We have to go after them.'

'To what end? It's Ignimbris, the first of the magmadroths. It'll destroy the entire Zharrgrim atoll.'

'Then we stop it, and then we go after the skaven.'

The Forn that Broddur knew would have leapt at the chance to earn glory with such a fight, and within sight of a friendly battlesmith, no less. He had felled Yellowscale's mother with the very javelin in his hand, but to Broddur's dismay that hand was now shaking.

'This is no scavenging Chaos warband,' Forn hissed. 'No wild magmadroth to be hunted for sport. It's a godbeast.'

'Now this is more like it. Get ye down here, dragon, that my axe might reach you.'

Broddur and Forn shared a horrified look.

The battlesmith alone found the nerve to stand on tiptoes and look back over Yellowscale's cooling flank. The Slayer stood alone in the middle of the Caldur Bridge. Embers swirled around him, the forgefire of his greataxe giving out a blustering flame of its own. Sweat soaked him, his muscles shining in the fevered heat. Ignimbris lowered its head towards him, diamond-hard scales hissing and splintering as they cooled and shrank. A blast of cinder-hot breath ruffled the Slayer's crest and beard and jangled the gold chain that pierced his nose. Gotrek clutched his axe and glared up.

'Skjalander was bigger!'

Ignimbris gave a titanic roar that brought rock tumbling from the distant roof and lava seething from the surface of the sea, as though hearing the challenge in the Slayer's words and seeking to match them.

'I've fought Chaos dragons and liche kings. I've fought greater daemons and the gods themselves. I bled Be'lakor, the prince who would be king, and I crossed axes with Grimnir himself and walked away.'

Ignimbris hauled its chest up onto the bridge and roared in Gotrek's face. The Slayer stared the godbeast down.

'I swore an oath to die in battle, but outlived a world. Come try me, beast. Maybe you'll have better luck than every monster I've ever slain before you. Maybe we both will.'

Broddur could hardly make himself breathe. Godbeast and Slayer glared at one another for what felt like an age of the world until, with a rumble of submission, Ignimbris, firstborn of Vulcatrix, left the Caldur Bridge and slipped back under the lava sea.

'I don't believe it.'

'What's happening, Broddur? I daren't look.'

'It's backing down.'

'Impossible!'

Further back along the bridge, alone, the Slayer slumped his shoulders and lowered his axe. He had just vanquished a godbeast without having to so much as swing his axe.

And he looked oddly disappointed about it.

SIX

It was night by the time the Fyreslayers dared the wrath of Ignimbris and approached the Slayer. The sky had turned from a burnt umber to a brooding red. The few stars capable of shining brighter than the lava sea twinkled above the flames like rubies. Sigendil, the High Star of Azyr, Broddur noted, with some appreciation of what that portent meant, shone amongst them. They had found the Slayer still sitting there, staring over the Caldur Sea towards the great fissure that Vulcatrix's death throes were said to have left in the volcano's wall. The stars could just be seen there.

'This is no trick, is it? No dream. No jest of the Dark Gods.'

'This... is Karag Unbak,' said Broddur. 'The Salamander's Spine. Aqshy. One of the eight Mortal Realms. If it's an illusion then it's a great one and surely claims us all.'

'That beast, it knew me. Or it thought it did.'

The Slayer looked over his shoulder. In addition to Broddur and Forn, a score of Zharrgrim Hearthguard under the command of Krag Blackhammer himself stood watching. The runemaster's forge-worn flesh was the black of slate, bedecked in tokens and runes. He stood with the aid of a staff, naked before the fire but for a belt of heavy golden keys. His temper, on finding the skaven long gone before he and Aruk-Grimnir had even emerged from the vault, had been volcanic. A worthier and more volatile duardin did not exist in the Mortal Realms.

The Slayer acted as though he could not care any less.

He tossed a stone into the lava where the godbeast had disappeared. It sizzled, turned red, and melted into the sea.

'My world is gone. The manl–'

He stopped himself there, like an old warrior instinctively pulling on a muscle he forgot was sore. Some stories, Broddur knew, hurt more with each telling. That was their power.

'The people I went to my doom to save, they're all gone too. They've been gone for thousands of years. I told you Grimnir was a liar.'

'Did you really see Grimnir?'

Gotrek tapped the top of his cheeks with two fingers. 'With these very eyes. He even gave one of these eyes to me, as though restoring half my sight would earn him my forgiveness.'

'What was he like?'

The Slayer snorted, but did not answer. Broddur could not help but be disappointed.

'Where *do* you come from, Doomseeker?'

'It hardly matters now, does it?'

Krag Blackhammer's staff rapped on the bridge's stone. Broddur bowed his head respectfully and fell silent as the honourable runelord approached.

'Indeed,' said Krag. His voice was a fiery rasp, worn by age and heat, the word uttered like an anvil dropped upon the ground. Firm. Final. Quite possibly a challenge. 'It does not. Only retrieving my Master Rune from the skaven matters now.'

'Sod your rune,' said Gotrek.

Broddur gasped.

'What?' said Krag, too astonished by the insolence to take proper offence.

'Did someone hammer some gold between your ears? I don't care about your sodding rune.'

'You've taken Zangrom-Thaz and it hasn't killed you. It's clear that you've been sent here for a reason.'

Gotrek sighed miserably. It was difficult to remember that this was the same duardin who had charged happily into the jaws of a godbeast. 'Aye. Probably. Ask the elf girl I left by your vault. She seemed to know something, and had more interest in it than I.'

'There was no aelf outside the magma-vault.'

Broddur and Forn coughed and silently interrogated their feet.

'We might've... er... left her unguarded. A bit,' said Forn.

'I take none of it back, even if you do happen to be real,' said Gotrek. 'You're a strange and pitiable excuse for real dwarfs.'

Krag bristled. 'You've been accepted by Zangrom-Thaz, the greataxe of the Unbaki Grimwrath, and you've bested the godbeast Ignimbris – but who in the fires of Aqshy do you think you are, to speak to a runelord and his lodge with such disrespect?'

'Maybe if you wore more than a bit of jewellery and a beard, I'd–'

Broddur struck the haft of his icon on the ground, wincing only slightly when Krag, Gotrek, Forn, and all the Hearthguard turned their attention on him. 'He is Grimnir,' he breathed. 'Made whole and returned to us.'

Most of the gathered Hearthguard scoffed, muttering amongst themselves at the battlesmith's foolishness and throwing accusations of *zaki* in his general direction. A few though, those who had seen the duardin emerge from the fires of the karag or heard the stories from those who had, who saw now that same duardin wielding Zangrom-Thaz having bested Ignimbris, were less certain.

'I know the face of the Doomseeker has always called to you, Broddur,' said Forn, unexpectedly reasonable. 'But this sounds like madness.'

'Do you deny that he'll return one day as promised? When enough ur-gold has been gathered and the Great Four arise again to await his challenge?'

Forn looked suitably abashed. A few of the muttering Hearth-guard looked at Gotrek anew. The Slayer just sulked, as though the Fyreslayers were talking amongst themselves and none of it concerned him.

'Age, skill, wealth, I used to respect those things, called a king a king. I don't even know what makes a king any m–'

The Slayer stopped himself short as thunder pealed far away through the crack in the mountainside. He looked up, and Broddur followed his gaze to where lightning bracketed the karag's broken wall. He could see why it had drawn the duardin's attention.

'I must have been longer without a proper drink than I'd real-ised,' said Gotrek, rubbing his eyes and then looking again. 'I thought I saw a man in that lightning.'

'Much has changed in the world, Slayer. The might that Grimnir's brother, Grungni, forged out of the Winds Celestial in repayment of his debt to Sigmar brings a tingle to my beard even from a thou-sand leagues away.'

'Grungni, you say? Sigmar?'

'You know them too?'

'Hush, beardling, and tell me what it is I'm looking at.'

'It's been two centuries since Sigmar retook the Gates of Azyr, but Chaos isn't so easily beaten. In all the lands below the Sala-mander's Spine, where the first lodges stand, their hordes march. Sigmar dispatches his Stormcast Eternals to contest them, but that storm there...' Broddur paused, as though lands of consequence had names that rightly took time to say. The Fyreslayers obligingly fell silent. 'That'll be the free city of Hammerhal Aqsha.'

'That's where Chaos in the Great Parch will be broken in the end,' said Forn.

Broddur caught the flicker of something like interest, or perhaps just recognition, in Gotrek's world-weary gaze.

'Tell me of these *Stormcast Eternals*.'

Broddur looked to Krag for support. The runelord could surely answer the question better than he, but the Blackhammer's frown suggested he was not currently minded to.

'I know little. Only that they are said to be the greatest heroes of humanity, souls stolen from across the Mortal Realms and from the annals of history to be remade into Sigmar's warriors.'

The Slayer scratched his beard thoughtfully, the claws of whatever depression had been encroaching on him visibly receding from his face. He stood up, bending to retrieve his greataxe.

'Heroes of men you say? I knew one of those. Once. Perhaps there is something for me to do here after all. Maybe I *was* returned for a reason, as you say. I would see one of these Stormcast Eternals for myself, if nothing else.'

He turned to Broddur and the battlesmith's heart pounded for joy. He had the distinct impression that the Slayer had not genuinely looked at him until that moment.

'Who here knows the way to Hammerhal?'

PART TWO

Unremembered

SEVEN

'Left face, left face! Come about and form ranks!'

The long column of Edassan swordsmen clattered to a halt. Jordain peered fearfully into the charcoal-black trees that flanked the Great Ash Road, but it was no good. The regiment's torches could not penetrate the forest's gloom. Lifeless trees ground and scraped in the smoky, acrid breeze. There was nothing in this forest that was not long dead, but Jordain shivered at the feel of it all the same.

At Manezomo Osayande's order the Freeguild had marched through the night, hoping to make Twinfire Keep before dawn: better a torchlit march, the manezomo had reasoned, than to make camp within the Charwood.

With Iyase Loba screaming for order, Jordain drew his long-hilted sword from its scabbard and turned to face left. The rest of his unit, swordsmen in red-and-black livery and golden chain mail, followed suit. Further along the column, Jordain expected to find the same manoeuvre being simultaneously performed by five thousand Edassan infantrymen, but he could not see any of it.

In spite of the sudden halt, the dark, and the desperate yelling, it had not yet fully dawned on him that he might be in danger. He was the crown prince of Edassa. These things did not happen. It was almost as though he was still in the university, half-asleep and late again for his classes, listening from his dormitory window to the drillmasters on the Red Sand. An ambush in the dead of night and a forest melee simply did not live up to the tales of heroism he had devoured as a boy at court.

'Ready!'

Jordain thought he could hear something now. The bird-like calls of things that were most definitely not birds. The rustle of trees that bore no life and felt no wind. He felt a rumble through the loose-packed surface of the Great Ash Road. It put him in mind of charging cavalry, but there was still nothing to be seen. His mouth felt dry. He shuffled his feet in the dust, as though preparing himself to flee, but he knew there was nowhere for him to run to with Edassa's swordsmen ranked up all around him. He told himself that it would be the man-ezomo's outriders, but something about the rhythm and gait put him in mind of a flock of flightless birds. Cavalry with two long-taloned feet instead of four.

Sigmar, he thought, *I'm really about to fight.* He was horribly reminded of the countless hours he had spent daydreaming through Memihir Akpani's *History of the Realmgate Wars,* ruing the misfortune of being born too late for those glorious battles.

Jordain took his sword in a two-handed grip. His hands were so sweaty he was genuinely worried he might drop it. He didn't want to think how that might look to the men and women under his supposed command. He had been made ezomo of the First Edassan Lions for three reasons. Firstly, he was the only son of Queen Karine. Secondly, the manezomo was his cousin. And thirdly, he was the thrice-great grandson of the legendary Kyukain

Hammer-Friend. None of these reasons seemed to him to be particularly good ones just then.

He glanced to Iyase Loba for reassurance.

The woman emerged from the darkness, inspecting her front rank with a critical eye and an occasional approving nod. Loba was shorter than most of the men in her company and as wrinkled as the desert sand. She was a faint gleam of sword steel and gold mail in the dark. There was a rumour that she had fought in the last battles of the Realmgate Wars, though Jordain was almost certain that she could not be that old.

'The Arcanites of the Seeing Legion are little more than barbarians,' Loba yelled hoarsely as she limped down the line. 'Old men gifted strength and long life by their twisted master. Not like us. Our skill is earned through sweat and toil and faith in Sigmar. The cost of our strength is not to our souls, but freely given to the Red Sand. Look to the woman on your left. The man to your right. Stand together. Lions of Edassa!'

The First Edassan Lions roared like the patron animal-deity of their city as the iyase slotted into the front rank alongside Jordain. None of the veteran swordsmen seemed particularly astonished by his deference to the iyase and were certainly not in any way troubled by it. Jordain could not even be offended. He felt the candour in Loba's gaze as she looked him up and down, taking in the lamellar plates of rich Edassan leather, the red woollen cloak emblazoned with the Flamescar Lion, and the steel crown of a regimental ezomo.

'My eyes must be failing me, my years catching up to me at last. It looks as though your hands are shaking.'

Jordain flashed a nervous smile. He had hoped that, in the dark, she would not notice. 'Just eager, iyase,' he lied.

'No final suggestions?'

'I'm not so great a prince that I don't know when it's time to keep my mouth shut.'

'So, we did finally teach you something.'

'When you say final–'

With a flurry of piercing, inhuman shrieks, the enemy that Jordain had still been hoping would turn out not to be there came surging from the treeline. Their white faces shone as they entered the circle of light cast by the Edassan torches. With their beaked helms and long, blue-feathered cloaks they looked like a flock of riotous, glittering birds descending from the dead branches of the forest. Here then was the Great Enemy that Jordain had yearned to fight since he had been old enough to read Alio, Koundja and Kyukain Hammer-Friend. He felt proud that his courage passed its first test and that his first encounter with the forces of Chaos had not ended with him fleeing in terror.

'Charge!' Loba yelled.

'Edassa!'

Jordain collided with a pillar of muscle. The warrior was unarm-oured but for a bird-like helmet and a single golden shoulder plate bearing the lidless blue-eye emblem of the Seeing Legion. Even so, Jordain practically bounced off the burly Arcanite. The barbarian followed up with a wild swing that Jordain only just managed to duck. Instinct took over.

The Arcanite cultist shoved Jordain back to clear room for his larger sword and delivered an overhead swing. His heavy scimitar smashed across Jordain's hurriedly raised sword, screeching down to become ensnared by the lion claws of its hilt. Jordain smoothly sidestepped, as he had been taught in swordsmanship classes on the Red Sand, and kicked the barbarian in the backside as he stumbled across him. The Arcanite fell straight onto Loba's sword.

Jordain grinned savagely. 'The Flamescar Plateau is *Sigmar's* land. Death to the Hosts Duplicitous, and death to the Eye That's Seen!'

A moment ago he had been terrified. Now he felt more alive than he ever had before. Sigmar, was he alive! He saw now how those who had lived through the great wars of the past had been able to write so graphically about their experiences.

'Nicely done, ezomo,' Loba panted, drawing her sword from the slain cultist. 'The peacock that would strut about in cloak and crown for the ladies at his mother's court has some steel in his blade after all.'

Jordain laughed. In the middle of all that mayhem it seemed the only right thing to do. 'We are like the heroes from the Realmgate Wars, iyase.'

'Steady, prince.'

'God-King!' Jordain roared, looking around the melee for more foes. 'God-King!'

'Behind you!'

He swung around as a bald-headed warrior with a long, curved sword in one hand and a round shield bearing the Eye lunged towards him. The warrior's cheeks had been drawn up and stitched into a smile of perpetually enlightened rapture. He had no eyelids.

'Your enlightenment will be brief and final, Edassan,' he said in a surprisingly cultured drawl, as though he was another university tutor nitpicking Jordain's Azyrite grammar as opposed to a barbarian hacking at his chest with a sword.

Jordain leant out of the way. The Arcanite's sword tangled in his cloak. The black Flamescar Lion stitched into the cloth wrapped around the cultist's weapon and flapped madly as though mauling his arm.

'Your soul belongs to the losing side. You will never reach the great gates of Hammerhal Aqsha!'

Jordain threw his elbow at the Arcanite's face. There was no room left between them for either of them to use their swords. The cultist took the blow with a grunt and retaliated with a bash to the wrist with the rim of his shield. Jordain cried out as the wind flew out of him and he lost his grip on his sword.

It landed flat in the churned, bloody ash of the road.

'Ezomo!' Loba cried, shouldering the Arcanite to the ground. The barbarian vanished under a scrum of legs.

A sword-point erupted from Iyase Loba's neck.

'L… Loba!'

Jordain watched, stricken, as the veteran iyase gurgled her last breath around a serrated sword. It was not the hero's end that the legends had prepared him for.

'No, no, no. That's not how it's meant to be. That's not how heroes die in the old stories.'

'What was it you were told about the manner of your enlightenment, young prince?' The barbarian wrenched his sword from Loba's throat and, in the motion, swung his shield at Jordain.

In trying to step back from the blow, Jordain tripped over an arm, landing heavily on the Ash Road. By some piece of luck, he managed to land close to where his sword had fallen. He snatched it up off the ground and stabbed back, furiously raking the Arcanite's unarmoured shins.

'God-King!' Jordain gasped, his heart exploding with terror and elation as Loba's killer dropped to his knees with a cry. Some warrior he never saw seized the opportunity to hack off the barbarian's head.

As the headless corpse collapsed, it burst into giddy pink and blue flames. By the time it hit the ground, the blaze was already spent. Before Jordain's eyes, the muscle-bound cultist that he had fought withered to an old man in homespun robes. Madness, Jordain thought. *Madness.* He wanted to be sick. He had read about the so-called 'Kairic Test of Nine' in which men and women who had devoted themselves to books and learning could, in selling their souls to the Changer of the Ways, transform themselves into hardened warriors, but he had not believed that it was possible.

If anything, much like his tales of war, they had failed to fully convey the horror.

Loba's body lay in the ash of the road where it had fallen. Her back was arched as though her last moments had been spent in pain. Her mouth was wide, a bloody hole opening her up like a discarded fish that the hook had not come out of cleanly.

He felt ill.

He crawled away from the melee as fast as he could. Insofar as he was still thinking at all, he thought that if he could just get clear of the road and into the Charwood then the Arcanites might miss him in the slaughter.

And slaughter was the word for it. The Seeing Legion had caught the Edassans entirely unprepared. It was not a battle any more. It was carnage. Bodies littered the road between him and the forest. Some had faces he recognised. Isoke. Nourbese. Geywe. Soldiers he had trained with and supposedly commanded. Now he lay with them. He supposed that was fair. The taste of sick filled his mouth.

His shaking hands found the iron-rimmed wheel of an Edassan war-wagon. It had been parked on the opposite side of the road from the Arcanite ambush and appeared to have been abandoned. He used the large wheel to pull himself upright and promptly threw up over it. Feeling slightly better for it, he got himself back onto his feet, wiped his mouth on the hem of his cloak, and brought his sword up to guard.

'Sigmar preserve us.'

Everywhere he turned, the Freeguild of Edassa were being overrun.

Skyborne embers and the earth's fiery glow, a kind of permanent Aqshyan false dawn, illuminated the dozen or so Edassan standards fleeing east along the Great Ash Road. Marauders mounted on monstrous blue-feathered war-birds howled the foul name 'Tzeentch' as they mercilessly rode them down.

'How?' he murmured, dazed. 'How did this happen? Where are the manezomo's outriders?'

He looked west. A few hundred swordsmen and handgunners were continuing to fight there. It was obvious that they would not hold out for much longer.

A sudden, crushing sense of disappointment swept away his panic. Was this really how he was going to die? He had had dreams. Ambitions. He had wanted to see the Lion of Edassa fly over the walls of Hammerhal Aqsha, to fight in a war that mattered like Kyukain Hammer-Friend. His ancestor had led the Azyrite Free-guilds alongside the First-Forged Host of the Stormcast Eternals, the Hammers of Sigmar, and had liberated half of the Ashlands, founding the free city of Edassa as his crowning achievement. A twenty-foot-high sandstone statue to him stood over Heroes' Gate. A week of holy days commemorated his victories. Perhaps it had been a childish fantasy, but Jordain had wanted that.

A trio of Arcanites advanced unhurried towards him, savouring his imminent enlightenment with regard to his mortality. They no longer felt any need to rush things. There were hardly any of Jordain's regiment still fighting. Jordain slumped into a ready stance, the great wagon-wheel at his back. A kind of resolve settled over him. More than being afraid, he was embarrassed at himself.

'See me, Sigmar,' he prayed, 'as you once saw my great-great-great grandfather–'

'Die!' the first of the Arcanites shrieked, taking the final few yards in a spring and forcing Jordain to rush the conclusion to his prayer.

'–and stole him from the battlefield at the point of death!'

With a quick sidestep and a powerful cross-stroke, Jordain beat the sickle-curved blade of that first warrior aside. 'Dancing scorpion,' he muttered under his breath as he stepped back, light on his toes, every form and movement that Loba had drilled into him on the Red Sand suddenly written for him in memory and blood. 'Aqxen leaning.' He caught a serrated shortsword on his blade and turned it, sending the Arcanite sprawling. 'Lion's paw.' The move left him perilously off balance himself, and he was duly shunted onto his back by the third warrior's shield. He should have known better than to try and fight three of them at once.

He closed his eyes. He was ready.

He heard a *thunk* and flinched as something very heavy and sharp hit something that was, up until that moment, very alive. Jordain blinked as blood splattered across his eyes. The Arcanite that had knocked him over with his shield burst unexpectedly into flame while his two compatriots twisted around to face some new threat.

'*Khazuk! Khazuk!*'

'See that, storysmith? I appreciate the way they burn themselves up for me when they die.'

Jordain looked up at the sky, wondering if this was the miracle from Sigmar that he had been praying for. He thrust up from the ground with his sword, impaling the Arcanite with the sickle-blade through the base of the spine. The last warrior standing spun back towards him, wide-eyed, and drove his shortsword towards Jordain's throat. Jordain seized the Arcanite's wrist. He strained with the effort of holding the cultist's sword-point above his neck. It inched lower, lower, the Arcanite's unholy strength slowly beginning to tell.

'I will carry your soul with me to the Labyrinth, Edassan.'

And then suddenly, the downward pressure on the sword-point released.

A thundering axe-blow struck the warrior's skull in half, a breath of flame cooking it through before his own wyldfires could claim it, wafting the stench over Jordain. He gagged, grateful that he had already been sick, covering his mouth with his hand as a terrifically muscular duardin with a bloody crest of orange hair struggled to shake the charred corpse off his axe.

'Naught but gristle and bones,' the duardin complained as he finally got his enormous weapon free.

Jordain stared up at him, struck dumb by the overwhelming experience of not being dead.

'On your feet, then…' The duardin looked at him for a moment. '*Manling*. There's killing work yet to be done.'

EIGHT

The sky was turning orange, a monstrous fireball rising from beneath the eastern horizon to engulf the lands behind them. Jordain was not sure how it could possibly be dawn already. He wondered if he could have fallen asleep without realising it. He blinked at the skeletal black trees encroaching onto the sides of the Great Ash Road, tinted bloody by the dawn and the things they had seen.

Ten metal gibbets were spaced along the roadside. A skeleton hung by a chain from each. They were all deformed in some way. Some had horns, a tail, an arm sprouting from the chest, a third socket in a permanently grinning skull. By some sorcery the dry bones continued to burn, albeit fitfully, their shadows flickering and convulsing in undying agony across the ashen black road. Ten more hung from the gibbets opposite.

Jordain pulled on the reins, drawing the rumbling war-wagon to an exhausted stop. The horses snorted and stamped ill-temperedly on the ash. Clad in metal helmets and draped in lion-skin caparisons, they were feeling the heat. As creatures of Aqshy, they did not take their discomfort with equanimity. Jordain wished he had some water to offer them. He would not have minded some himself.

'What fresh devilry is this?' Gotrek grunted. He was sitting in the seat beside Jordain, staring at the twenty burning gibbets. He did not seem the least bit tired.

'They are mileposes. We are twenty miles from the keep.'

'I'm referring to the things hanging from the poles, manling. Are they human?'

'Not unless you've seen humans with horns, wings or tails.'

'I'll not trouble your sleep with the things I've seen, manling. They've clearly been dead some time. How is it they still burn?'

'This is Aqshy, the Realm of Fire. Beyond that...'

He trailed off, but Gotrek seemed satisfied with the answer.

'Wait with the wagon, manling.'

'Uh-huh,' Jordain mumbled sleepily as the duardin got clumsily down from a platform intended for a human twice his height and half his weight.

'I'm going to take a look and stretch my legs.'

Jordain nodded tiredly, struggling to keep his eyelids up. The duardin stumped on a way into the grim shade of the Charwood, his large battle axe flicking like a torch as he carried it past the mileposes' eerie sphere of illumination. The farther he got from the wagon, the less discreet the pushing and shoving from the back became.

'You're standing on my foot.'

'You touched my leg.'

'You'll be going over the side in a minute if you don't keep to your bit of the bench.'

Jordain sighed. The war-wagon's rearcastle was packed with nine fractious Fyreslayers and their gear. They were shorter than a man, but stupefyingly muscular. Each took easily twice a human man's space in a compartment designed for six. The duardin wore little beyond torques, bracers, key chains and elaborate headdresses, but all of it was bulky and all of it looked to be made of solid gold. There was wealth enough there to buy a man a kingdom. If Jordain had not already been the heir to a kingdom, then he might have been tempted. It would probably be easier to take Edassa than it would be to take the Fyreslayers' gold, though, if the destruction of the Arcanites was any guide to their bellicosity.

'What are you looking at?' said the one called Broddur.

He was a leader and a spokesperson of sorts, whose role seemed to be interpreting Gotrek's gruff utterances into his own flinty tongue for the benefit of the others. This he would invariably do at unlikely length, leaving his compatriots tugging on their beards and looking wistfully into the forest at the profundity of what they had just heard. Whenever his patience wore low, which seemed to be often, the rough ends of his beard and hair would kindle. Jordain wished he knew what he could possibly have done to offend the Fyreslayer so.

'I was just wondering if you are all right in there?'

'Golden.'

'If I've offended you somehow, I hope you'd tell me.'

Broddur grumbled, but looked away, as though embarrassed by something. 'It smells like cat in here.'

'I suspect that it's... uh... the Flamescar Lion pelts that the horses are wearing. It's the sacred beast of Edassa.'

'Give me hot stone and sulphur and I'll be better pleased.'

'Or room to swing an axe in,' grumbled one of his kin.

'And a battle like that last one to do it,' said another, to much back-slapping and cursing and seesawing between mirth and violence that Jordain did not pretend to understand. He felt as though he was riding in a powder keg.

He felt his own thoughts return to the battle. His memories were confused and fearful. Everything else was a blur of blood and fire.

'You mean the ambush. Sigmar, it was a slaughter. They're all dead except for me. Some prince I turned out to be. Some hero of legend.'

There was a creak as Broddur leant forward from the rearcastle battlements. 'Do you know the tale of these woods? When Vulca-trix breathed the first fires into Aqshy, the forest was scoured by an inferno so hot that the trees were turned instantly to ash. Ten thousand years have they stood thus. No hero has stood as long, nor even their legend.'

The infighting from the rearcastle quieted down. At first, Jordain thought it was the story, as the Fyreslayers seemed to have almost as much respect for a good tale as they did for gold and violence, provided the tale was about gold or violence, but then he realised that Gotrek was stomping back towards the wagon. He muttered to himself all the while, climbing awkwardly back into the fore-castle. The sudden amity from the rearcastle was striking.

'I always thought the only good tree was a dead tree. I've changed my mind.'

'If the Flamescar Plateau is not to your liking, then know that Aqshy is a vast realm,' said Broddur. 'There are the continents of Aridian, Vitrolia and Capilaria, to explore. Each has its own character. I've even heard it said too that the fire of this world diminishes as you venture nearer the centre of the realm. Green things grow from the earth and the sky is blue.' He scoffed. 'If you can imagine such a thing.'

'Sounds wonderful.'

Jordain could not tell if Gotrek was being sarcastic or not.

'And don't forget there are seven other Mortal Realms beyond Aqshy's edge to explore, Lord Grimnir.'

'I prefer the Realm of Chaos. At least that's still as it always was. It makes sense in its own foul way.'

Jordain picked up the reins and leant in towards Gotrek. 'Why does he keep calling you Grimnir?' he whispered.

With considerably less tact, Gotrek growled loudly back. 'Because his kind are short-bearded nugget foragers with kindling for brains.' The Fyreslayers in the rearcastle grumbled but, most uncharacteristically, did not argue. 'Hand me the reins, manling. Twenty miles is a long way yet and you look half-dead already.'

Jordain was half minded to protest, but when it came to it, he didn't have the strength.

'Do as the Doomseeker says,' said Broddur. 'Duardin need little rest.'

'Aye,' said Gotrek, gripping the reins so tightly that Jordain could hear the leather creaking under strain, glaring belligerently at the horses' caparisoned backs. 'How hard can it be to drive this thing anyway?'

The fortress was uniformly black, built using the dark coal that could be hacked from the dead trees of the Charwood, and loomed imposingly over the road. Its high walls sprawled between the two rivers that converged on the site and pinched the Great Ash Road to a naturally defensible point between them. The river to the right was a slow-moving sludge of oozing lava. The body to the left was a wide flow of water, bubbling forever at the very brink of evaporation. The Charwood had been hewn well back from the fortress, which reassured Jordain enormously. Gotrek had allowed him to sleep on past the final milepole, but he was still feeling edgy from lack of sleep.

'So, this is Hammerhal then, is it?'

'Gods no. Hammerhal is the mightiest city in the Mortal Realms. It is home to a million men, duardin and aelves, and is defended by entire Stormhosts. Its walls are a thousand feet high and surrounded by a moat of fire. This is Twinfire Keep. It guards the Great Ash Road across the Flamescar Plateau and is maintained equally between Hammerhal Aqsha and Edassa.'

Gotrek gave the castle an appraising look. 'Shoddy work. Who builds a castle out of coal?'

Feeling his national pride stung, Jordain pointed to the great statue that stood bestride the gatehouse. 'He did.'

The statue's black armour had been so highly polished that against the glare of the lava fields it looked almost golden. A flared halo ringed the warrior's closed helm. His great warhammer was thrust high towards the Celestial Realm.

'Friend of yours?'

Broddur leant in from the back and cleared his throat. 'That, I believe, would be Vandus Hammerhand. He led the first battles in what the Azyrites insist on calling the Realmgate Wars. As if the Unbak lodge never lifted an axe over the centuries that *they* spent locked away in their precious realm.'

'If they hadn't, then all the Mortal Realms would now be overrun by Chaos,' Jordain patiently explained.

The Fyreslayer snorted. 'So they like to tell us.'

Gotrek frowned up at the effigy. Jordain wished he knew what he was thinking about, but there was something thoroughly inhuman about the duardin. There was a distance between them that could not be bridged. Jordain could not explain why, but he felt a closer kinship with Broddur and his Fyreslayers than he did with Gotrek.

A lonely horn sounded from the walls of the keep. Jordain pulled on the reins and the weary horses stamped and clattered to a halt. The heavy war-wagon trundled to a stop. Jordain squinted, spotting what looked to be five men on the battlements above the gates.

'Who approaches?' one of them yelled down.

Jordain cupped his mouth with his hands and shouted back up. 'I am Ezomo Jordain of the Edassan Freeguild. These duardin are friends who would come unbidden to the aid of men of Sigmar on the Great Ash Road.'

'Just like men of Sigmar,' he heard Gotrek grumbling. 'Needing aid on their own road.'

'Edassan Freeguild, you say?' the watchman replied. 'The Edassan Freeguild has already passed these gates. Not three hours ago.'

Jordain felt his mouth fall open while he considered this. Was it possible that the massacre of his cousin's army had not been as total as it had looked at the time? It was true that it had been dark, and the fighting in the centre had been especially chaotic. Perhaps the forward elements of the column had managed to fight their way clear and had remained far enough ahead of Gotrek and the Fyreslayers to go unnoticed. It was also true that he had seen many of his countrymen fleeing into the Charwood. He had attempted the same himself. With Twinfire Keep only half a day ahead and a road to follow, it made sense that they would try to make their way here rather than home to Edassa.

'We were ambushed by the Seeing Legion of the Hosts Duplicitous. About half a day's hard marching back down the Great Road. But I saw a few hundred escape.'

'Mayhap a little less,' Gotrek muttered.

'They said nothing of an ambush,' the watchman called down. 'And it was five thousand men, not a few hundred, that passed through these gates.'

'But that's impossible! It was five thousand men that set out from Edassa in the first place.'

'And what's more, there was an Ezomo Jordain of the Edassan Freeguild that greeted me then.'

Jordain simply gawped. His mind had become a blank. He had the horrible crawling sensation that he had, in actual fact, died on the Great Ash Road, and that he was now wandering the Ashlands as a spirit watching others living his life for him. It did not make sense. How could there be another Jordain? And where could he, whoever *he* was, have mustered another five thousand Edassan soldiers?

'Twinfire Keep is a thousand leagues from Hammerhal, but the enemy is never far from here.' The skin of Jordain's forehead prickled in the punishing heat as the watchmen spoke on, suddenly highly aware of the crossbows and ballistae being cranked his way. 'The Seeing Legion, the Thrice-Poxed, the skaven of Clan Boil, they have all been seen abroad in the Charwood. And you should know that even the twisted wiles of the Hosts Duplicitous will not catch us off our guard.'

'Wait. You are making a–'

'Osayande even warned us there might be agents of the Seeing Legion on his trail, seeking to slip through our gates and reach Hammerhal with one of the Freeguild regiments.'

'*They're* the infiltrators! I am Crown Prince of Edassa and I will not be dismissed as some vagabond or brigand.'

Even from the top of his wall, the guard looked amused. 'Five thousand infiltrators? Or a dozen? Which would you think more likely were you up here and I down there?'

With a growl, Gotrek drew his axe to his scarred chest. He breathed over the flame held between the two great blades, causing it to billow. 'Just say the word, manling,' he muttered. 'One lick of this axe and that gate will go up like a kegfire on the Feast of Grungni.'

'Wait,' said Jordain, holding his hand placatingly towards Gotrek and then turning to the crossbows above the gate. 'Wait! You said that Manezomo Osayande led them. Describe him to me. Was he black-skinned like me? And did he wear a cloak like this, red with a black lion, and a crown like mine, silver, but with a golden edge?'

'He did,' the watchman answered, uncertain where this was going.

Jordain slumped back into the driver's bench. He had no strength left in his knees. That was why the column had received no warning of the ambush. Osayande had let them through. Worse, it seemed he had replenished his losses from the ranks of the Seeing Legion and was leading them on to Hammerhal under the Lion of Edassa. The combination of exhaustion and shame almost blacked him out. Suddenly, he no longer cared if the watch captain gave the order to shoot them all or not. His permission for Gotrek to have at the gate was on the tip of his tongue.

'I don't understand. How does a man like Osayande turn against the God-King? How does any man?'

'You know him well then, this...' Gotrek scrunched his face up. 'Osa-yard-ee?'

'He's the commander of my mother's armies. The fiercest lion in Edassa, they say. Popular with the men and women who fight in her armies. And my eldest cousin.'

'Family, eh. Some things never change.'

'I will have his head for this and see it fed to the lions. The same goes for every man of Edassa that follows him.'

Gotrek slapped Jordain on the back, almost throwing him over the side of the wagon. 'Good for you, manling. There's naught worthier than vengeance upon a kinslayer and an oathbreaker.' The Slayer's mood took a sudden turn as his gaze appeared to go inwards. 'We were going to Hammerhal anyway. Might as well get our arm in on your cousin before the killing really starts.'

'You'd do that for me?'

'You'd do that for *him*?' said Broddur.

Touched, though he could not say why, Jordain turned back to the wall. 'I beg of you, please let us pass. Can you not see that the survival of Hammerhal itself may depend on it? Look at me! Is it not obvious to you that I'm a man of Edassa?'

'I wouldn't know,' the watchman replied. 'I've never been to Edassa.'

'Someone here must have. My mother's gold pays for half of this place!'

'Easy, manling,' said Gotrek. 'No one likes an over-entitled princeling.'

'*Dorki wannaz.*'

Grumbling in his fiery tongue, Broddur clambered up onto one of the rearcastle benches and stood. He pulled in his enormous belly and planted his strange icon on the parapet. Mounted on a high pole it bore a face that Jordain presumed to be the Fyreslayers' god, Grimnir. Carved from a forge-bright steel alloy and a wealth of gemstones and gold, it glared at the keep with angry eyes and an open mouth, as if cursing its very existence.

'You know, Gotrek, it does look a little bit like y–'

'I am Broddur, battlesmith of the Karag Unbak Fyreslayer lodge, and we'll prove our good faith to you and your cause.' Broddur fished about in a pouch attached to his belt and withdrew a golden bead about the size of his thumb.

'Throwing away good gold...' one of the others grumbled as the battlesmith held it up.

'We are soldiers of Sigmar,' the guard called down. 'You think you can buy us with your gold?'

There was a sharp intake of breath from the Fyreslayers.

'Buy you?' Broddur's jowls trembled with anger. 'What mannishness is this? This is a piece of my god that I hold in my hand. You think I offer it lightly?'

The wall fell silent for a moment, presumably while the watch captain and his subordinates argued over what to do. Jordain saw them put their heads together and confer.

'Might as well just roll it down the mountain for all the good it'll do,' one of the Fyreslayers complained.

'They'll slam the gate in your face as soon as it's left your palm,' said another.

'Well then,' said Gotrek pointedly. 'We'll know where we all stand on breaking the door down.' He leered at Jordain. To his surprise, the duardin winked. 'Won't we?'

The watchman drew Jordain's attention back to the wall with a polite cough.

'Keep your gold, Fyreslayer. It's too rich for us. The offer is proof enough that you are who you claim to be. You may enter, and have lodge and board within the keep for the night.'

Horns sounded from the keep beyond the wall. Jordain heard the clank of gears and chains, and the gates before them ground slowly outwards.

'We thank you for the offer, but don't have the time. We need to keep going lest we fall any further behind my cousin.'

'Those are the terms,' said the watchman firmly. 'Warden Karame is Edassan by birth. She rides beyond Hammerhal Gate, hunting the Tzaangors of the Eternal Conflagration, but is due back tomorrow. I'd still have her vouch for you before you walk another foot along the Great Ash Road.'

Gotrek ran his thumb along the blade of his axe. The fire blistered his flesh, but if anything he seemed to enjoy it. 'Just say the word, manling.'

Jordain let out a breath and shook his head. 'No. I'll not fight true men of Sigmar.' Shouting up to the top of the wall, he added, 'I look forward to meeting her in the morning!'

He snapped the reins and the war-wagon started rolling through the open gates. From over his shoulder, he saw Broddur sitting back down, pocketing the shining ingot.

'Thank you for the offer of your gold, battlesmith.'

'I didn't do it for you,' Broddur said, scowling, and Jordain had the impression that he had once again done something to anger the Fyreslayer. 'Now we'd best find another way out of this keep. Just in case this Warden Karame is unconvinced by us in the morning.'

NINE

Broddur's beer sat untouched. It was barely even boiling and lacked the mouth-wateringly sulphurous aroma of the Unbak brews he was used to. Watching the ever-present Twinfire soldiers from the corner of his eye, he rolled the golden bead between forefinger and thumb. Gotrek sat on the other side of the sticky black table, noisily demolishing a trencher of ham and eggs. Jordain was seated beside him with his head on the table, snoring lightly. Broddur looked at him sourly. He wished he knew what this thoroughly unspectacular human could possibly have done to so endear himself to the Doomseeker.

The other Fyreslayers were scattered about the crowded common room, boisterously belting out a well-known Unbaki drinking song about a brew matron and her missing gold coin.

'Valdarinn wanrag ek brynit?'

'Guz! Naraz! Valdarinn wanrag ek brynit?'

'Guz ong!'

'Guz tvo!'

'*Guz dwe!*'

'*Nai brynit bin or kup. Anguz valdarinn! Ut anskrat ekbrynti.*'

'*Guz fut!*'

'*Guz sak!*'

'*Guz siz!*'

'*Guz set!*'

'*Guz odro!*'

'*Nai brynit bin or kup. Anguz valdarinn! Ut anskrat ekbrynti.*'

And so on...

The various servants, wagoners, off-duty soldiers and home-steaders that filled the crowded alehouse did their best to ignore them, but eight Vulkite Berzerkers of a mind to drink and feast were hard to ignore at the best of times. The place had been full even before Gotrek had arrived and 'found' an empty table. He supposed that was what humans did when Chaos marched across the Mortal Realms. They ran to the nearest walls rather than fight the enemy and take their gold. Broddur watched his hard-drinking kin ruefully. Of the thousands that carried the fire of the karag in their belly, these eight alone had seen the truth of the Slayer's divinity.

Gotrek belched loudly, wiping yolk from his chin on his forearm. 'What's that you're mumbling about, storysmith?'

'Nothing.'

'These eggs are rotten,' Gotrek complained, apropos of nothing. 'And the ham tastes like... What was that runt dragon you lot rode as though you were a bunch of mountain elves?'

'I assume you mean the magmadroth?'

'Aye. Magmadroth. It tastes like ham that's been pissed on by a magmadroth. What end of the lizard did you say it was cut from?'

'Actually it's hagidd, which is a type of burrowing bir–'

Gotrek drained his flagon before unleashing another voluble belch. 'And the beer's too hot. It tastes as though these eggs were poached in it.' He sighed. 'A world without Bugman's is not one I care to live long in.'

Broddur felt his teeth grinding as he listened to Gotrek's diatribe. Every day was the same. The sun was too big. It moved wrongly. Could Broddur shut up now: his accent reminded him of a Kraka Drak jester. Despite what he had told Jordain about a duardin's endurance, he was far, far beyond the limits of his with the Doom-seeker's carping.

God or no god.

Biting his lip, he returned his attention to the gold bead between his fingers. Examining the scratches he had already made into one square face, he frowned thoughtfully, drew a small chisel from the collection of writing tools hanging from his belt, and began to scratch at the adjacent face.

'What are you doing there, storysmith?'

The Slayer sounded peeved at having his latest tantrum go unacknowledged. Broddur felt unexpectedly pleased with himself.

'This is how the Unbaki battlesmiths record our histories. In gold. On beads like this one to be read by touch. See.' Broddur passed the gold to Gotrek, who rubbed his greasy, callused thumb over the nascent rune. 'Skorun Firebrand gave me twenty of these gold beads as a parting gift.'

'What does this first bit say?'

'It is the first chapter of my travels with Gri–' Broddur coughed nervously. He and his kinband had learned that the Slayer could be kept more-or-less agreeable so long as they refrained from calling him by that name. 'With Gotrek,' he finished.

'So, you're some kind of a *rememberer* then?'

Broddur felt some of his old belly fire flicker, and he grinned across the table at the Slayer. Finally, he had been able to show Gotrek something that he seemed to understand and appreciate. 'I suppose you could call it that.'

Gotrek scowled at his platter. It was as if a darkness had crept up and wrapped its arms around him, jealous of the attention he had been paying to Broddur. He picked up his knife and fork and attacked the food he professed to hate. 'I've no more need of a rememberer.'

Broddur looked up as the cheerful hubbub faded, and noticed that a man had just walked in. At least, Broddur assumed it was still a man. He had seen hexwraiths with more flesh covering their bones. His amethyst-coloured robes were tatty and covered with soot. His black hair was mildewed and greying. Even the Fyreslayers faltered at *Guz dwe* as he surveyed the room like a carrion snake wary of magmadroths. He shuffled towards the bar.

'A glass of your Skull Isles arrack.'

'Of course, master.'

'Leave the bottle.'

'Whatever you say.'

Broddur watched as the man retreated to a corner table that remained suspiciously free, as though it had been held for him, just in case he should make an appearance. The noise gradually resumed as he sat down. The Fyreslayers decided that all eight of them should have a drink and start again from *Guz ong*.

'I didn't think even humans could get that scrawny.'

'His name's Uthan Barrowwalker,' said Gotrek around a mouthful of ham and eggs.

'How do you know that?'

The Slayer jerked a thumb to the thin plank of charred wood that separated the common room from the kitchens. 'The barkeep told me. Said he's just the man we need if we mean to sneak out of here before dawn and that we'd recognise him as soon as he arrived. You think I've just been sitting here enjoying my eggs?'

'Why would I be thinking that?'

'Some of us are capable of eating and being useful at the same time.'

'Why's everyone so nervous? I think they're more scared of him than they are of us.'

'I'm told he's a wizard, or is the dress too subtle for you?'

'He's covered in soot.'

'Aye. According to the barkeep, he's something of a hermit with all sorts of secret little ways in and out of this castle. Oh, and he's mad, so there's that.'

'Do you know how many times in the recorded history of my lodge that a kinband has been aided by a wizard they met in a tavern? Never. No times.'

'Are you going to finish that beer, storysmith?'

Broddur looked down. 'It's barely even bubbl–'

Gotrek reached across and took it before Broddur could finish. He downed it in one gulp. 'I've never trusted a dwarf who can't finish his beer.' He slammed the empty flagon back on the table. 'Let's go over there.'

'Why would he even want to help us? He doesn't know us, and Sigmar's war isn't ours. Not until he pays enough to make it ours.'

'He'll help.'

'Should we wake the princeling?'

'I know how to talk to wizards, storysmith.'

With a sigh, Broddur picked up his icon and followed Gotrek to the wizard's table.

'Oi, wizard!'

Uthan Barrowwalker startled like some kind of wild bird as Gotrek stomped towards him. He gripped the edges of his table with skeletally thin fingers, motes of purplish energy flaring within the deep sockets of his eyes.

'Who?' he asked in sibilant panic. 'What? How? Where?'

'Easy, wizard,' said Gotrek. 'I seek a favour off you is all.'

Uthan relaxed, although just a little. To Broddur, it still looked as though he might take wing at any moment. His fingers tapped skittishly on the table, and Broddur noticed the way tiny spirits crawled out of the charcoal to wind about his knuckles like ghostly rings. 'A favour, you say? Duardin ask no favours. Especially not of men. Our lives are too short.' He chuckled as though he found the idea amusing, but could understand why others might fail to see why. 'Generally. What to do when the human dies unrepaid? What then, duardin? *What then?*' The wizard's fingers tapped furiously on the tabletop.

Gotrek eyed the petty conjurations seeping through the tabletop with open disgust. He tightened his grip on his greataxe. 'Liche. The barkeep said nothing to me of necromancy. Dismiss your minnow spirits, and I'll make your end as painless as an axe with a volcano bound to its steel will allow me.'

Broddur placed a restraining hand on the Slayer's arm. 'Wait!'

'Unhand me or be the next to feel my axe.'

'You aren't in the Realms of Chaos any more, or wherever it was you say you were before that. You can't just kill anyone that stokes your fires the wrong way.'

'And that includes necromancers now as well as dark elves and fire dwarfs, does it?'

'Sigmar once led a broad pantheon of gods that included both Grimnir and the Lord of Undeath. We were all allies throughout the Age of Myth.'

Gotrek reluctantly lowered his axe, though he continued to glare suspiciously at Uthan. 'Were?'

'A lengthy story,' said Uthan.

'You see,' said Broddur, 'Nagash betrayed Sigmar at the–'

'I don't care!' Gotrek bellowed, making the wizard flinch in his seat. 'I've no interest in what's going on now. What makes you think I'd care any more about what happened back then? Be silent, storysmith, and by Grungni's hairy arse stay that way until you're spoken to.'

Broddur sullenly clamped his lips shut and folded his arms over his chest.

'I believe I heard something about a… favour?' said Uthan.

'Don't you try my patience either.'

'I think he's offering to help.'

'I know. I don't like it, it's unnatural. And what did I *just* tell you, storysmith? What part of being silent is challenging you? Stop your mouth from running before I stop it with my fist.'

Taking a deep breath to calm his temper, the Doomseeker set his axe across the table. The Unbak forgefire caged between the two runeblades lapped hungrily at the charcoal. The wizard stared at the caged flame while Gotrek scraped back a chair and sat in it.

Broddur remained standing. He was too awed by his glimpse of the Slayer's divine rage to sit.

'There's an army moving along this ash road of yours. A friend of mine wants to catch up to it and murder the kinslayer who leads it.'

Broddur stiffened at the Slayer's description of Jordain as a 'friend'. He glanced back towards the slumbering human prince with a frown.

'And you wish for me to draw the life of this one from the hereafter?' said Uthan. 'It would be my pleasure to–'

'No, liche, no. Where would be the honour in that? How could we say vengeance was rightly served on the say-so of your unclean sorceries? No.'

'Then it seems your need for a necromancer is at an end. I hope you were pleased with my work. Good evening.'

'I'm told you like to roam the Charwood at night, that you know how to get in and out without seeking the permission of the guards.'

With his eyes locked on Gotrek's axe, the necromancer shook his head. 'Take you outside?' The necromancer gave a strangled little laugh. 'No, no, no. *No*. I couldn't do that. I can't. The last time I ventured into the Charwood I was almost killed. A Khainite assassin! I barely escaped with my life.'

Gotrek and Broddur exchanged a knowing look. The necromancer appeared too distracted, drumming his fingers on the tabletop and muttering to the spirits floating around him, to notice.

'A dark elf was it?' said Gotrek.

'A Darkling Shadowblade, yes. The most feared of the God-King's assassins. They say that once given a mark, a Shadowblade can track the doomed man's soul to anywhere in the Cosmos Arcane they might try to hide.'

'A slip of a girl?'

'You know her?'

Gotrek grunted. 'Our paths have crossed.'

With a snap of his fingers, Uthan banished his carelessly summoned spirits into the aether from which they had arisen. He sat back, steepling his fingers under his chin and regarded the Slayer. A last spirit, more defiant than the others, hissed angrily before it too slithered back into the cracks in the table.

'Then it would seem that we are all on the same boat down the Stygxx. My condolences to you both.'

'She tried to steal an item of great power from the Unbak lodge,' said Broddur. 'If she's nearby then she's either on the trail of the skaven that took it or bound herself for the war in Hammerhal. Or both. No disrespect, but what's the interest of a killer like her in a... Well, in you?'

'Interest, interest.' The wizard looked at his pale fingers and tittered. 'I am an interesting man. But as for the Khainite's attentions? I did not ask. Better to cower amongst the living, however cloying and wretched, than be ushered into Shyish for the final time.'

'That's the Realm of Death,' Broddur muttered out of the corner of his mouth.

'I know what it is!'

'But maybe...' Uthan looked around nervously, then leant forward, inviting Gotrek and Broddur to do the same. 'The Burning Gate,' he said.

'The Burning Gate?' said Broddur.

'What are you, an echo? Let the man finish.'

'It is a realmgate.'

'Uh-huh.'

'It's a–'

'Not now, storysmith!'

'It is little known and less often used. If I take you, then maybe you will help me. I know the ancient rites to open the portal. A dead man told me. I can even guide you thereafter through the lands of Shyish.'

'And what are you after in trade?' said Gotrek. 'Gold?'

'*My* gold, you mean,' said Broddur.

'Can you eat it? Can you tame a spirit with it? No,' said Uthan. 'Keep your gold. All I want in return for this favour is for you to see me safely to Hammerhal.'

'What makes you think we're going to Hammerhal?' said Gotrek.

Uthan gave a jerking shrug. 'Everyone's going to Hammerhal. Living and dead. But even a Khainite assassin will have trouble getting into that mighty city while an army of Chaos stands on its threshold. From there I can slip through the Stormrift Gate, be lost in the forests of Ghyran before she even knows I left this keep.'

Gotrek glanced at Broddur, looking for guidance without wanting to *look* as though he was looking for guidance. To be so angry and so proud about everything he had lost, but to have so little understanding of the world he had since found... It was almost enough to make Broddur feel sympathy for him.

'We bring nine Vulkite Berzerkers of the Unbak lodge and the Doomseeker,' said Broddur. He nodded towards Gotrek. 'He's bested the aelf once already. I think we can guarantee your safety on the road to Hammerhal.'

Uthan grinned toothily. 'Then I am ready to leave when you are.'

Gotrek turned to Broddur and grunted. '*Now* you can wake up the princeling.'

TEN

Nothing living moved through the Charwood. Fossilised trees creaked like gigantic skeletons in blackened armour. The air was ash. The wind was dead. Even the light was stultifying. It leaked through the wizened canopy to striate the knee-deep ground ash with shadows. There was not even an insect buzzing. To walk through it was surely to skirt Shyish's boundaries without ever having to venture near to the Burning Gate.

'The Charwood,' Broddur was muttering reverently from somewhere up ahead. He and his brethren were the occasional gleam of gold within the tangle of scorched boles and branches. 'I never thought I'd live long enough to walk under the canopy that Vulcatrix burned.'

'I'm not sure we need to go any further at all,' Jordain murmured. 'We're practically in the Realm of Death already.'

'Something ails you, manling?' Gotrek asked.

Jordain was not sure how to answer. Of them all, the mad necromancer included, Gotrek alone seemed impervious to the forest's oppressive mood.

'Can't you feel it?'

'Feel what?'

'We walk through a forest that was scorched bare by a godbeast before the Age of Myth even began. There's probably at least one Chaos warband between us and the realmgate, and a Khainite assassin is apparently hunting our guide.'

The Slayer chuckled grimly and stroked his axe. 'At last. Someone who knows how to look on the bright side.'

Jordain had the horrible feeling that the duardin was not joking. Indeed, far from perturbed by the menacing air, Gotrek had been in positively buoyant mood since taking their leave of Twinfire Keep. To Jordain's horror, the Slayer broke into a tuneless whistle.

'Shhhh!' Uthan Barrowwalker hissed back at them. 'We are far from alone in this wood. Not all that is quiet is peacefully dead.'

Jordain looked at the crooked bowers with newly fearful eyes. 'I knew it,' he murmured.

'Here, mutants,' Gotrek called into the wood in a sing-song growl. 'Here, daemons. Here, beasty beasty beastmen.' He chuckled darkly. 'This Slayer has an axe for you.' Jordain cringed, convinced that he saw one tangle of shadow scrape across another. 'I've walked through the Drakwald and the Dead Wood of Mordheim and come away. I fought blood-drinking vampires and giant lizards in the jungles of the Southlands, giants in the forests of Albia, and things I'll not name even here in the Hinterlands of Khuresh. I fear nothing from this wood.'

'Please, Gotrek. If we don't make it to the Burning Gate in one piece, then Osayande will face no punishment for his betrayal. Edassa will be shamed for generations.'

Gotrek grumbled under his breath, but to Jordain's surprise relented. 'You're right, manling. We'll just have to kill whatever lurks in this wood on our way back.'

'Shhhh!' Uthan hissed again.

'I'll be silenced by no liche!' Gotrek bellowed, evidently forgetting his promise to be quiet.

'I haven't thanked you, Gotrek,' said Jordain quietly. 'For getting me even this far. If not for you then the Seeing Legion would have left no survivors. They would be marching on Hammerhal in friendly colours with no one to carry the warning.'

Gotrek shrugged and muttered, perfectly comfortable in a god-blasted forest haunted by Sigmar knew what but apparently ill at ease with words of gratitude. 'The storysmith and his lot would've handled it well enough, I'm sure.'

'Would they even have been on the road if they weren't following you?'

'Nine bad pennies is what that lot are.'

Jordain turned briefly from the bleak wood to consider the Slayer. He had known duardin in Edassa. They were common enough in the merchant's bazaars and the university campus, and even at court on occasion. Loba had once goaded him into challenging a Kharadron sky-captain to a duel on the Red Sand, which he regretted to this day. At least the Kharadron had been gracious about it. Gotrek was different. He moved through the realms like a rich man through a crowded bazaar, apart from it even as it clamoured for something from him. Jordain could see a sadness behind his eyes that went deeper than he could fathom, as though the Slayer had lived too long, seen too much, and could not simply go on as before.

'Why Hammerhal?' he asked, after a time.

'What?'

'You were already heading to Hammerhal before you found me. I was curious why.'

The Slayer brooded on the question for so long that Jordain had given up on an answer and returned his attention to the Charwood by the time he spoke.

'I mean to find someone there.'

'But you're uncertain whether you will or not?'

Gotrek grunted, unwilling to be drawn further. 'I came back for a reason. The storysmith and his brain-addled kin are right about that much.'

'Back?'

One of Broddur's Fyreslayers, Jordain noticed, had fallen back from the rest of the group and was wandering close by in a surreptitious bid to listen in. Gotrek did not appear to notice. Either that or he did not care.

'There was a time when nothing mattered more to me than having my story remembered. To cut short a tale I've no wish to tell, I was offered the mightiest doom of any Slayer. Naturally, I accepted it. To stand forever against the daemons of Chaos, so that Grimnir might rejoin the world. *This* world, as it turns out. It appealed to my pride, manling. But no one remembered. No one. In time, even Chaos forgot. Grimnir tricked me. And because of that, all my oaths are now ash and there is no one still alive as remembers.'

'Sigmar remembers.'

'Does he now? I wonder.'

Jordain heard the snap of a twig and looked sharply to where the eavesdropping Fyreslayer had been standing. There was no one there.

'What is it, manling?' said Gotrek, lifting his axe and letting its light stab in between the trees. 'Did you see something?'

Jordain looked a moment longer, then shook his head.

Perhaps the Fyreslayer had heard that particular story before and gone ahead to rejoin Broddur and the others. Even so, had it been Jordain then he was sure he would have wanted to hear it told again. It would have been like meeting Kyukain Hammer-Friend in the flesh, asking him what it had been like to fight alongside Vandus.

He turned back to Gotrek.

'What was the world before I–'

The branch immediately above his head creaked and snapped and a bloodied lump dropped to the ground at his feet with a plume of ash. Jordain started back. Before him lay the vanished Fyreslayer, face down, his runes glowing with a faltering brightness. Something had practically torn him in half.

There was a moment of gobsmacked silence in which Jordain wondered what could possibly inflict such brutal damage on a Fyreslayer, and then the Charwood came to life around them.

Spindly, crooked shapes bounded out of the wood, howling like banshees. They were feminine in aspect, but a long way from human. Their bodies were armoured with charred bark and calcified lichens, barbed and horned with splintered amber and limbs that cracked as they ran.

'Even the blasted trees can't be trusted to keep still!' Gotrek yelled.

'They're not trees, Gotrek. They're Sylvaneth!'

'Back!' Broddur was roaring from the far end of the line. 'Back, for the Doomseeker!'

'*Khazuk!*'

The eight remaining Fyreslayers burst out of the darkness in explosions of golden light. Ordinarily, Jordain would have marvelled at it, but he was forced to focus on the tree-revenant rushing his way. Its gait was shambolic, stumbling into the cracked trunks of ancient trees and spilling itself over others, but it covered the distance at an appalling speed.

'Where is Uthan?'

'Cowering in the woods with his skirts over his eyes, most likely,' said Gotrek, brandishing his axe at the frantically closing Sylvaneth. 'Come on then, tree-kin, it's firewood for you!'

'Here they come!'

Gotrek laughed.

With a harrowing shriek, the tree spirit lashed at Jordain with a long, tapering set of claws. He blocked with his sword, but the branch tips whipped around the blade to scratch his leather sleeve. Jordain cried out in alarm, backing away as quickly as the deep ash underfoot let him move, angling his blade across him as a swipe came in from the other claw. This time he felt thorns rake his face from jaw to eye.

'Unburned,' the Sylvaneth rasped, its voice like a cold wind through dead wood.

Jordain thrust his sword through the creature's heart. It did not try to get out of the way. He was not even certain whether or not the Sylvaneth had a heart. The lion-hilted blade split the bark of its woody chest and became stuck.

The revenant's neck cracked and popped as it raised its dully glowing eyes towards him and bared the blackened stumps of its teeth.

'Unburned this one.'

'What the...?' Jordain struggled to pull his blade out of the Sylvaneth's scorched bark. 'How do you kill them?'

'*Unburned.*'

Ignoring the sword in its chest, the Sylvaneth swiped for Jordain's head. He struggled to fend it off with just his arms and the pair of them tumbled together. Jordain took a deep breath before his face hit the ash carpet of the Charwood floor. Woody talons found their way around his neck and squeezed. He found the handle of his sword but could not pull it out of the Sylvaneth's chest. Instead, he used it as a handhold while he tore the skin of his knuckles repeatedly with punches to its hard wooden chest. His own chest burned, desperate for a lungful of air. The Sylvaneth, he realised, did not need to breathe.

'Oh no you don't!' someone yelled.

There was a sensation of heat followed by a muffled crunch. The hands around Jordain's neck slipped away, cutting his skin with thorns even in that, and then Jordain felt a muscular arm hauling him out of the ash by the collar of his cloak. Jordain gasped, disturbing the ash that he had managed to swallow, and then fell against the side of a tree in a fit of coughing.

'Thank you again, Gotrek,' he croaked.

The fight appeared to be over. Scores of the tree spirits lay in splintered heaps, torn apart by Fyreslayer axes and smouldering. The one that had so very nearly accounted for Jordain was a glowing coal pile a few feet away, burning well in the fires contained within Gotrek's axe. The guttering flames threw the suddenly quiet wood into a nervy, unsettled light.

Jordain had not properly appreciated until that moment just how far beyond him Gotrek and the Fyreslayers were. He snatched his hand from the tree, suddenly convinced it was about to reach out and grab it. He had been a fool all his life to crave this. He was just a mortal man. What could an ordinary human like him offer to Sigmar in the fight against such monsters as these?

'You did all right, manling,' said Gotrek, with a consoling pat.

'Aye,' said Broddur. 'You nearly killed one.'

'Not bad for a first go, I say.'

'Didn't I say be quiet?' Uthan hissed, suddenly right behind them. Jordain almost jumped out of his skin, whirling around and going for his sword, but the necromancer had already scampered out of reach. He clutched a tree and glared around it with wild eyes. 'Didn't I say that the Charwood was restless? Didn't I? *Didn't I?*'

'I didn't see much of you during the fight, Uthan,' said Jordain, not quite ready to forgive the wizard for his fright.

'We had an agreement. *I* take you to the Burning Gate. *I* say the secret words. *I* guide you through Shyish. You and the duardin do the fighting.'

Jordain sheathed his sword. Uthan reluctantly crept out from behind his tree.

'They looked like Sylvaneth,' said Jordain.

'Mannish fool,' Broddur scoffed. 'This wood would've been scoured of its guardian spirits by Vulcatrix's fire.' The battlesmith's great bulk trembled with exertion, but it appeared to be due more to unspent energy than physical weariness. The runes in his body glowed with a vigour that caused the icon in his hand to alternately glower and brood. He was not even out of breath.

'And you know all, of course,' said Uthan snidely. 'Hoarding your wealth and your lore from on high while those below scrape amidst ash and bone. You are no better than Sigmar, safe in your mountain.'

Jordain drew an inch of steel from his scabbard. 'A man should be careful before insulting his gods. You never know who may be listening and take offence.'

Uthan's eyes, unnaturally large in his sallow face and flecked with glowing purple, bored into Jordain's as he shuffled back.

Although a minority creed in Edassa, the mortuary priests and necromancers of the Cults of Death had always been free to practise their faith there. That did not mean that Jordain liked them, any more than he did Gorkamorka's battle-mad barbarian priesthood or the enigmatic magi of Malerion. It was Sigmar alone who had taken the fight to Chaos and who strengthened those with the courage to stand beside him.

'If Sigmar cares not – and trust me, he cares not – then neither should you.' Uthan looked around. 'Do you see Sigmar here? Is Sigmar at Twinfire or at Hammerhal? Was he with you on the Great Ash Road when the servants of the Changer betrayed and slaughtered your countrymen? Is that the smell of his lightning on the air or is it ash and bone? No, boy, Sigmar does little here.'

'Sigmar was well known to the memory of the dwarfs, but he

was naught but a man,' said Gotrek. 'By what right does he claim to be lord of the gods in place of Grungni? And Gorka...' He trailed off with a grumble. 'That's the problem I see here. Everyone's forgotten the old grudges and had ideas above their station.'

'I think it's more complicated than that,' said Broddur.

'Indeed, battlesmith,' said Uthan. 'And we'd all be wise never to forget it. Here or anywhere. The Burning Gate to Shyish is close, and the power of Chaos waxes across this realm. Whatever Sigmar may wish to say of it.'

Broddur puffed himself up. 'I'll not be lectured on the lore of this land by some zaki–'

Charcoal sprinkled the roof of Broddur's crest as the slender but stupefyingly tall tree behind him bent its high trunk and stretched its branches. It looked horrifyingly like a man cracking the night's stiffness from his spine.

Everyone looked up. Broddur and the other Fyreslayers readied their axes. Jordain's jaw dropped. He had the horrible feeling that he knew now what had ripped that first Fyreslayer in half and dumped the pieces in his lap.

'Undead Chaos treemen,' Gotrek raged, stomping towards the awakening Treelord as though killing it would set some long-held wrong to right. His axe burned away the dark, drawing hisses from the lesser Sylvaneth lurking around the rousing titan's roots. 'And why not? It's not as though this world could get any stranger.'

'Gotrek,' Jordain warned, ripping his sword from his sheath and pointing it at the smaller spirits. 'The other Sylvaneth are returning too.'

'Good, it's a big wood and it'll spare my legs.'

'And they call *me* mad?' said Uthan. 'We must reach the Burning Gate *now*.'

'Who asked your opinion on it, liche?'

'He's right, Gotrek,' said Jordain. 'The realmgate is what we came for. There will be plenty of monsters for you to fight once we reach Hammerhal.'

For a moment it looked as though the Slayer was going to ignore Jordain as well as Uthan, but then he lowered his axe and bared his teeth. He snorted, apparently amused. 'You remind me of him you know, manling, and that's not *always* a good thing.'

'Remind you of who?'

'Never mind. It's not important. I hope you can run.'

Jordain did not need asking twice.

ELEVEN

Jordain was the last to burst from the treeline. The duardin were not fleet of foot by any measure, but their stamina was matched only by that of the undead creatures that pursued them. Jordain had imagined more than a few glorious ends for himself over the years. Surrounded by the heaped bodies of his foes, generally. Bloodied hand clasped between the quivering palms of a grieving maiden, often. Never had he dreamt that it would be with the taste of vomit in his mouth, acid in his thighs, and his sword dragging through the ground like an anchor.

'The Burning Gate!' Uthan Barrowalker called, raising a yellowed finger. 'There!' The necromancer dispatched the litter of slave spirits that had borne him through the wood, his body assuming solidity as he sank to the ground.

Jordain, meanwhile, had lashed himself bloody tearing through the Charwood's tangled branches, while Uthan was not even out of breath. *All right for some,* he thought, swallowing his annoyance and lifting his gaze to see where the wizard was pointing.

The realmgate was an arch of fire-blackened stone upon a low hill, haloed by a faint tingle of corposant flame. It looked as though it had once been the cornerstone of something greater. The ruins of an ancient fortress dotted the clearing, but only the gate itself remained. Rivulets of gurgling lava criss-crossed the site. Jordain could make out no clear path through or around.

'How are we supposed to reach it?'

'Stay here,' said Uthan. 'I will draw out the path.'

'Alone? That seems... uncharacteristically brave of you.'

'Not when you consider what's behind us it's not,' said Gotrek.

'I should be the one who goes,' said Broddur. 'If there's anyone here who can safely navigate a maze of fire and return, then it's a child of Grimnir.'

'No!'

Uthan flapped in the direction of some of the sturdier-looking ruins nearer the crest of the hill and the Burning Gate. Now that Jordain looked he could see that they had, in fact, been partially rebuilt and recently fortified. The heat coming from that part of the clearing was intense. Jordain could not hold it in his gaze for long enough to see any more clearly.

'Whatever this place was before the death of Vulcatrix or after, it is half in the possession of Tzeentch now. The paths through the lava are ever-changing. Duplicitous even. Home to the Seeing Legion of the Eye That's Seen. Alone, I can find a path. With nine blundering duardin and an Edassan prince-ling behind me, the Legion will come before we are halfway to the gate.'

'Subtlety is past being an option, liche.'

As if to demonstrate Gotrek's point, a shrivelled Sylvaneth exploded from the Charwood behind them. Broddur calmly split it in twain with a blow from his axe.

'Go with the necromancer, Lord Grimnir. The Unbaki'll hold

the Sylvaneth here, and maybe draw the eyes of the Seeing Legion while we're at it.'

Uthan looked peculiarly irritated given the circumstances, but relented. 'Fine then, but keep your distance and go only where I go.'

Gotrek hefted his axe and nodded. There were no farewells, no questions as to why the battlesmith would make such a sacrifice for a duardin who had treated him with nothing but disdain for as long as Jordain had known them both. He was reminded once again of how different humans were from the Fyreslayers.

'There'd better be something to kill up there or I'll be coming back,' said Gotrek.

Though it was hardly in character, and as backhanded as ever, it sounded to Jordain as if the Slayer was actually approving.

Broddur clashed his axe and his icon together and the Fyreslayer berzerkers erupted into cheers. 'Children of Grimnir, let the wood-kin feel the hew of our axes and the bite of our fire. Khazuk!'

'*KHAZUK!*'

'Khazuk-ha!'

'Are they all cracked, manling, or just those I attract?'

'I don't know,' said Jordain. 'These are the first Fyreslayers I've ever met.'

Gotrek looked briefly thoughtful. 'None in Edassa then?'

'No.'

'Maybe after Hammerhal, I'll go there.'

The first wave of Sylvaneth were already bursting out of the Charwood and onto the Fyreslayers' axes. The berzerkers sang joyously as they hewed at unliving wood.

'*Zon un gorl!*' Broddur roared.

'*Zharrdrengi angit!*' the Fyreslayers howled back.

'*Vorn un karak!*'

'*Zharrdrengi angit!*'

Jordain couldn't take his eyes away. A last stand was something he had played out often in his head. It didn't seem nearly so romantic to him now, either participating in it or leaving these eight courageous duardin to their dooms.

'They're the lucky ones, manling,' said Gotrek, misunderstanding Jordain's melancholy entirely. 'That's why you feel so.'

'Stay with them or come with me. Life or death.' Uthan giggled and clapped his hands, conjuring a typhoon of restless spirits from the soil beneath his feet that lifted him back into the air. His form became intangible, motes of fire drifting through him. Jordain quickly made the sign of the hammer. A useful trick, if an unsettling one. 'The choice is yours but make it now.'

'Sigmar protect me,' Jordain murmured, and settled on the lesser of two horrors.

The lava fields that surrounded the Burning Gate were a maze. Jordain was beginning to suspect that there was a malignant will behind it. More than once, Uthan had them doubling back as previously dry beds suddenly began to ooze with lava, or flows that had appeared fordable inexplicably swelled. Occasionally, Jordain spotted bare-chested warriors with eyeball shields and bird-like helms shadowing them, but never for long. The sounds of combat from the Charwood where Broddur and the Fyreslayers were still holding off the Sylvaneth drew them all away eventually. Gotrek paused to shake his axe at one such departing band.

'Come on then, bird men. My axe thirsts greatly in this heat.'

Jordain would have laughed had he not been so hot, tired and afraid. He was trapped in a lava field with the Seeing Legion, alone with a necromancer and a maniac. He should have thanked the Slayer for saving his life, bid him good luck on his journey to Hammerhal, and then turned straight back around. He sighed. But then he would never have learned of his cousin's treachery, and there could be no turning back for him now that he had. With five thousand troops disguised as reinforcements from Edassa, Osayande would be able to enter Hammerhal Aqsha unmolested and cause untold havoc. How long had his cousin spent plotting? he wondered. How had he not seen it?

'I should never have come here.'

'Hah! That's what he would have said.'

'And did *he* live to a splendid old age?'

Gotrek grumbled under his breath, but was spared from any further questions by the appearance of a band of Arcanites on the other side of the lava stream. They banged loudly on their shields and hooted like geese.

'Join us on the Nine-Forked Path, duardin. Or do you fear to lose your step?'

'You're the ones that set up home in a lava field, not me. Get over here before the manling wearies of the tedium and goes home.'

Jordain sighed. Was this all that fearlessness was, he wondered: being bored of horror? 'I'll take that as a *no* then, shall I?'

Uthan's spirit litter levitated him higher into the air, leaving Gotrek and Jordain behind as it swept him across a branch in the lava flow.

'Oi!' Gotrek shouted after him. 'We can't all float.'

Jordain tapped him on the shoulder, instantly regretting it as the belligerent Slayer rounded on him, and pointed. A string of stepping stones crossed the burping flow of rock. Gotrek grunted. He looked understandably less than keen. Jordain took a deep breath and decided he would go first. It was frightening, how quickly you stopped thinking about it.

He skipped across the roasting stones without once looking down, cinders erupting from the fissured earth on the other side as he stepped onto it with relief. The air tasted of molten lead. He brought his hand up to protect his eyes, though from what exactly he was not entirely sure. It was so hot that he could barely see twenty feet before the air wandered out of focus.

'Barrowwalker? Uthan, where are you?'

He looked around, but could make out no sign of the necromancer. The Burning Gate, however, was so close that he could feel its fiery emanations on the backs of his eyeballs. Charred black stones sticking out of the ground at all angles created a winding trail towards it.

A sudden whining noise made him look up.

Something blue blinked in the corner of his eye.

It hit him in the ribs before he had even turned around, a perverse knot of squirming muscle, crunching into his mail and knocking him back. He sprawled over the baking rocks and screamed, throwing himself over onto his back and cradling his steaming hands to his chest.

A massive warrior stood before him on a levitating disc. Thousands of eyes decorated his heavy plate. Their blinks sent rippling cascades of Change across the unholy champion, patterns that altered from moment to moment. Iridescent feathers sprouted from his pauldrons and helmet and fluttered in lieu of a cloak. The disc too was no biddable instrument but a malicious entity in its own right, a daemonic thing of barbed tentacles, suckered mouths and pink eyes shot through with evil blue veins.

'I am the Eye That's Seen, your doom a thousand times foretold. This gate is mine.'

Jordain scrambled to his feet as the disc swooped closer.

It seemed that he and Gotrek had achieved something that all the Stormhost chambers and Freeguild regiments of the Flamescar Plateau had been trying to do for decades: they had brought the Fatemaster of the Seeing Legion to battle. Jordain took precious little reassurance from the achievement.

The champion spun a heavy rod between his gauntleted hands,

as though it moved of its own volition and he was unable to make it stop. Although ornate and glowing strangely, it did not look like much of a weapon.

Jordain felt anger rise to subsume his fear. Hammerhal and Osayande felt a long way away from him just then, but the ultimate source of all the injustices that he had suffered since leaving home was before him now. Vengeance was a surprisingly potent motivator.

Hurt and weariness fell away from him as he raised his sword into a guard.

'You murdered my regiment.'

'I am the Eye That's Seen. Your doom a thousand times foretold.'

'I hope you've two in the back of your head!'

Gotrek landed in a geyser of hot sparks and steam. Flames billowed from his axe as if in riposte. 'For someone intent on waving a stick about and standing on a squashed daemon, you talk a good fight. But let's see how you fair against a dwarf.'

With a ripple of clawed fins and paddle tails, the Fatemaster's disc turned him towards Gotrek.

'I am the Eye That's Seen.'

'Valaya's queenly ankles, manling. Everyone here is mad but you and I.'

And then with a wild yell, as though this, when all the complications of time and place were stripped away, was what he lived for, the Slayer charged.

Still twirling his rod like a baton, the Eye emitted a burst of clicks and whistles that made Jordain's eyes water but which seemed to compel the daemon disc to sweep its rider high beyond the reach of the Slayer's axe. It pivoted back around as the Fatemaster swung his rod across his body. Dozens of yards separated the two combatants now, but as he swung, a phantasmal mace erupted from the end of his rod, shrinking the distance between them in the blink of an eye and striking the Slayer powerfully across the arm.

Gotrek stumbled, the flesh of his left shoulder hanging loose.

'Is that your best shot?'

The Fatemaster's mace winked back into the aether. His rod continued to spin. 'Your left side is unguarded. You are missing something there. As was foretold.'

'You hit like a halfling.'

The Eye was already zipping to a new position. He swung.

'Gotrek! Look o–'

This time the mace materialised from below, striking an uppercut that snapped Gotrek's head back and sent him staggering. He shook his head and growled.

'Fight me like a dwarf!'

The Slayer held his axe across his body like a shield, turning on the spot as the daemon disc darted about him. The Fatemaster twirled his rod until it blurred. Left hand. Right hand. Then let its bound weapon fly. Gotrek swung his axe to meet it, but it was like swatting an invisible fly with a gargant's hammer. The projecting mace bypassed the Slayer's axe by a hand's width and crunched into the side of his head. The mace ripped a clump of hair out of the Slayer's crest and thumped him to the ground. Gotrek spat blood. It sizzled on the rock.

Jordain had never seen two warriors so far beyond his ability. It was as though he had accidentally entered into one of the tales he had been raised on. Vandus Hammerhand versus Korghos Khul. Thostos Bladestorm versus the Everchosen.

Gotrek Gurnisson versus the Eye That's Seen.

'I know who you are, Doomseeker,' the Fatemaster taunted as his disc hovered closer. Jordain gripped his sword, willing Gotrek to get back up. 'I know from whence you came. I am the Eye That's Seen, and you are but a faded relic of a dead world.'

Gotrek drew his fingers into fists, clawing up two fistfuls of earth, but before he was able to push himself to his feet the ground beneath him shuddered. Jordain crouched back and shielded his eyes as the rock between the Slayer and him cracked and ejected fire. An eerie, splintered song carried towards them on the heat breeze. He heard what sounded like vast branches crackling over a fire. Jordain swore. In the madness of the ascent towards the Burning Gate, he had quite forgotten about the foe they had left behind.

'Gotrek, the Sylvaneth! The Fyreslayers have not been able to hold them.'

The Eye That's Seen turned towards the river of lava. His many eyes widened.

Clawing through the mist of cinders, a burning Treelord stamped through the molten river. As soon as its blackened bark touched the lava it caught fire, flames roaring up its gnarled trunk, but it carried on as though some impulse stronger than the pull of its own mortality commanded it. With a groan, the ancient Treelord took a staggering step onto more solid rock, but the flames had done their work. Almost immediately, it began to fall. Gotrek appeared to grin as the blazing tree-kin slowly pitched towards him, moving just quickly enough to grab the low-hovering Fatemaster by the ankle. Gibbering in panic, the daemon disc shot into the air like a discus from a catapult, dumping the Fatemaster on top of Gotrek.

'Not nearly so nippy now.'

'No!' Jordain screamed, as the burning Treelord crashed to the ground on top of Gotrek and the Eye That's Seen.

Whatever sorcery had animated the long-dead Treelord failed on contact with the ground. Jordain threw his cloak up over his eyes to shield himself from the eruption of ash and sparks. The initial wash of heat lasted no more than a moment. He dropped his cloak and shook off the burning embers clinging to the hem, coughing on the thick smoke of burning tree bark. The Tree-lord was nothing more than a smattering of burning logs strewn across a hundred feet of half-molten rock. To Jordain's disbelief, the Fatemaster was pulling himself out, delivering a tirade of clicks and squeals. From somewhere above them, the daemon disc answered, swooping through the scorched air to hover beside its master. It turned a blue-shot eye towards Jordain and emitted another excruciating squeal of sound. The champion turned as if noticing Jordain for the first time.

Jordain brought up his sword, all too aware of how feeble he must have looked to the Fatemaster just then. But he stood his ground.

'Soon, mortal. But first, I have grander skeins than thine to sever.'

'I'd like to see you bloody try! Come at me!'

Miraculously, the Slayer too was still alive, but pinned under the awesome weight of the burning Treelord's greater bulk. The only question was whether it would be the fire or the Fatemaster that killed him first.

Jordain closed his eyes and silently prayed to Sigmar for guidance.

What would Vandus do? What would Kyukain Hammer-Friend do?

How many times had he dreamed of this day?

'Lions of Edassa!' he roared, and charged towards the Eye That's Seen.

Somewhere beyond the choleric red sky, thunder rumbled.

TWELVE

'I'm coming, Doomseeker!'

Broddur powered through the river of lava, leaving his remaining brethren to hold back the Sylvaneth and sending hissing lumps of magma spraying. The rune of might embedded in his thigh could impart tremendous speed when called upon, even in the absence of a runesmiter to awaken the ur-gold fully, particularly when the heat of Vulcatrix was near and his own fires burned hot.

He slammed to a sudden stop as though hitting a wall. The world blurred back into place around him, the lava behind him slapping resentfully back into the channel he had cut through with his passing. He cast about for Gotrek, the Slayer's anguished cry still ringing in his ears, and gasped in relief when he found him alive and unhurt.

The Slayer was kneeling beside a nondescript lump covered by a red cloak. His back was turned towards Broddur. His huge shoulders shook with grief.

'Is he…?' Broddur asked.

'I never did see him fall, you know. A part of me refused to believe he could be dead, but he's dead, isn't he? Long dead. The manling was taken from me.' Gotrek squashed his nose under his fist and appeared to wipe his eye. 'Aye. Dead and gone. There's no way he could've survived what I left him to. And even if he had, how many years has it been? I was a fool.'

Broddur glanced down at the stricken princeling. It was difficult to bear the man enmity now he was gone, but he could not shake the feeling that he and the Doomseeker had somehow ceased talking about the same man.

'We're no company for mortal men,' he said.

The Doomseeker hissed in pain as he touched his torn left shoulder. 'You're right about that.'

While Broddur held a respectful distance, Gotrek unfurled the cloak from the broken remains of their former companion. Fyreslayers, too, would take time after a battle to examine the recently slain, particularly if they were not close kin. It was necessary to ascertain how many runes they bore and how difficult it would be to remove them before consigning the flesh to cremation. With a grunt of effort, Gotrek began wrenching the breastplate from Jordain's harness, his awesome strength peeling the iron plate from the man's chest as though it was a sheet of tin. As it came loose, Gotrek set it over his wounded shoulder. Frowning over it, he caught Broddur looking and scowled.

'Make yourself useful if you're going to just stand there. Give the thing a whack for me.'

'You want a shoulder plate?'

'That Chaos warrior was right. Until I find someone to watch this side, I'm going to have to do it myself.'

Broddur shrugged and began thumping Jordain's breastplate into shape while Gotrek held it in place over his shoulder. The

Slayer grunted with every blow, but if it hurt at all he did not ask for Broddur to stop.

'I thought… you… wanted… to die.'

'Do I look dead to you?' said Gotrek bitterly. 'If something wants to kill me, I promise it won't find me hard to hit.'

Broddur stepped back to admire his handiwork.

A black lion with a proud mane glared belligerently back at him from Gotrek's shoulder. It was hardly the worst bit of work ever carried out by an Unbaki battlesmith on the battlefield, but as far as Broddur was concerned it was a contender. Iron had many worthy qualities, but it had not a scratch on fyresteel or gold. He was glad that Skorun Firebrand was not here to see it. He thought of his kin in the Charwood and, overcome by a sadness of his own, looked away, catching a glimpse of something blue and blindingly swift. It flitted across the smoked wreck of the Aqshyan sky and was gone. Broddur paid it no further mind. It was heading away from them, racing in the direction of Hammerhal Aqsha.

'The Eye That's Seen has the same destination as us, if I'm any judge.'

'Then we'll settle this when we get there.' Gotrek rolled out his shoulder as he stood, testing his range of movement and the armour's strength. In spite of Broddur's professional misgivings, he seemed pleased.

'We're still going to Hammerhal?' Broddur asked.

'He's dead, storysmith, but what does that even mean in this place? He's been returned as I have, I know it. *I know it.* He waits for me in Hammerhal.'

'Jordain?'

'What are you blathering about now? The princeling is right there at your blundering feet. Of course not Jordain.'

Muttering and cursing and without a backward glance at the body of his friend, Gotrek picked up his axe and strode towards the infernal ring that the Burning Gate had carved out of the near distance.

Broddur could feel the energies it was casting out. His ur-gold shivered in response. It tasted of death.

'Come on, storysmith,' Gotrek barked. 'Before the blasted necromancer decides to leave without us.'

Maleneth Witchblade crept towards the dormant realmgate. She moved lightly, but only out of habit. The battle was long over, the combatants long dead. She stepped over the body of a Fyreslayer. His grotesque musculature was tangled with the thorny remains of what appeared to be a Sylvaneth Huntress. She paused to examine the body. He glowed faintly, the runes in his body still warm. He had fought his last battle mere hours ago. Not for the first time, she wondered how Fyreslayer magic worked. How was it that they could transform simple gold into objects that could grant them such appalling power? It was more than just idle interest on her part. She had been dispatched from Azyr to retrieve just such a rune, after all. And not just any rune, but the mightiest artefact of its kind ever produced by the Fyreslayer lodges.

'I count only seven duardin and the human,' she murmured to herself, tapping a long, dagger-sharp fingernail on the locket lying against her chest. 'Add the one we found in the Charwood, and that accounts for them all bar that obese hog, Broddur. If they left the bodies and their gold then I would say they were in haste.'

She pulled off a silk glove and ran her slender fingers down the stone dolmen of the gate. It was still warm. Her quarry had proven unexpectedly resourceful, not to mention fortunate, but no matter. They had only evaded her for a time.

The God of Murder knew every hidden pathway into the Realm of Death.

PART THREE

Here a Slayer Lies

THIRTEEN

It was dawn. A pale sun climbed over the Amethyst Fjords like a bloated corpse rising from the watery depths, chill and wan beyond the grave-mist that clung to the frozen ground. Broddur hugged his arms to his chest and shivered, his beard sputtering like a fire devouring its last coal.

'Put another bone on the fire, necromancer.'

The necromancer, Uthan Barrowalker, did as asked, reaching into his robes and tossing a small length of femur into the fire-pit. The spirits of men murdered by fire hungrily pulled the bone apart, releasing those bound within to roast anew.

'Mercy, oh wicked one!'

'Please, sir, I am innocent.'

Most simply burned with incoherent screams of agony. Broddur shuffled back from the ghastly blaze. It was no fire as he recognised it and gave no warmth that did not make his skin crawl, but this land that the necromancer had brought them to *was* cold.

'I swear my belly's shrunk a twelfth of a beard-length these last few days, just from shivering by your so-called fires.'

'If you will walk the Amethyst Fjords clad only in gold runes and a belt...'

'The fire of Grimnir inures me against the fiercest heat and warms me through the bitterest of cold.'

'And yet...' Uthan cackled. 'The chill of Shyish cuts deep, does it not?'

'You take a strange pride in your realm, necromancer.'

'As do you in yours.'

Broddur grunted, but acknowledged there was something in that. 'The wind's dropping off a bit at least.'

'It is nearly dawn. The damned rest their voices for another day.' Uthan poked at the fire with a bone-hilted knife.

'Nooooo! Pleeeease!'

Broddur looked away.

'Do the dead frighten you, Fyreslayer? Or is it the torment of the hereafter that makes you turn away?'

Broddur grumbled under his breath. Steam coiled about his mouth, hissing off his ur-gold runes to merge with the malefic dawn mist of the fjords. He did not answer. The Unbaki believed that a death in fire or battle bought a long sleep followed by a place at Grimnir's side for the final battle of Doomgron. It was uncomfortable to be shown that this was not true for everyone. And perhaps not true at all. Uthan shrugged, uninterested in his silence, the bone charms and soul catchers ornamenting his threadbare raiment jangling as he continued to stoke the flames.

'The Slayer's normally back by sunrise,' said Broddur, changing the subject.

'This is not Aqshy. Your realm is hot, febrile. Shyish is a place of introspection and disquiet. The ghosts of the past dwell uneasily alongside the souls of the present. Gotrek is a duardin with more than his fair share of ghosts in his past, I think.'

'I wonder what he does out there every night.'

Broddur looked out across the creaking vista of bone ice in the vague direction that the Slayer had taken. The weeks of hard travel, of complaints, even the death of his kinband at the Burning Gate, had not shaken Broddur's conviction that the strange duardin was the ur-Slayer, Grimnir, returned. Gotrek, however, had not been the same since that last battle. There had been no more complaints, less sarcasm. When he spoke at all it was to grunt his reply to an instruction that Broddur or Uthan had given.

'The Doomseeker hasn't been himself since the battle at the Burning Gate. Surely you've noticed?'

'I noticed his axe and his temper and choose to avoid both. The dead call me mad, but let no living thing call me stupid.'

'At first, I put it down to the death of the human princeling, Jordain. But now... Now I'm not so sure. Something about the Realm of Death wears on him.'

'Whatever a man seeks, vengeance on past foes, reunions with old flames, the wisdom of long-dead sages, he may find it in Shyish.'

'He seeks an old companion, I think. Some hero from the World-that-Was.'

'Perhaps Jordain reminded him of this long-dead hero?'

Broddur had wondered as much himself. 'He certainly died heroically enough,' he said bitterly. 'If that's what you call trying to single-handedly best a Tzeentchian Fatemaster in battle.'

'That is, indeed, what most people would call it.'

'You're both mannish. You share the same odd way of looking at things.'

'But Gotrek does too, does he not?' The necromancer leaned across his fire. It did not burn him, but it underlit his face eerily and made shadows stretch and bend across his haggard features.

'Is that what eats at you, battlesmith? That the Slayer does not see the world as you do? That he saw something in a young human prince that he refuses to see in his own distant blood? In you?'

Broddur growled. He did not care to admit that the necromancer had struck near to the mark. Uthan Barrowalker had never been the most pleasant of conversational partners. The attentions of the Khainite assassin who had plundered the Unbak vaults had driven him into the Fyreslayers' protection, but he was clearly a hermit by nature. He was abrasive, quite mad, and had grown increasingly short-tempered with his travelling companions as the Shyishan days had worn on.

'If the Doomseeker hadn't made me swear an oath to see you safely to Hammerhal…'

'Perhaps he has decided that he need not journey all the way to Hammerhal after all. Perhaps he seeks his old companion now in the Land of the Dead.'

Broddur shivered, the cold worming under his belly fire. He shook his head. 'No. The Doomseeker believes the warrior was fit for Sigmar's Reforging. He'll not find him in Shyish.'

With a scowl, the necromancer shrugged into his purple robes and stared deeper into his fire. 'Well, if that is what Gotrek believes, then surely it *must* be true. If I had known I'd have to put up with this incessant prattling then I might just have let the Khainite kill me.'

'Don't let the lack of a Darkling assassin stop us.'

The necromancer vehemently attacked the fire with his knife. A plume of cinders shot into the air. The wails of the tormented souls feeding the flames reached higher. Broddur decided to change the subject. Nothing good would come of killing Uthan Barrowalker here and stranding them all in Shyish without a guide.

'How many more days to the realmgate?'

Uthan sniffed and continued to poke sullenly at the fire. 'What does *Gotrek* believe?' He sighed and looked up, withdrawing his knife from the fire, which diminished to a low burn as if in relief at a torturer's departure. 'I do not truly know, but I will soon. Not every realmgate is to be found within a ring of stone, hewn from a mountaintop, or set within a mighty fortress. Most are little more than doorways, warrens that run from place to place. The way we seek is one such hollow from nowhere to not much. It moves with the ice floes on the Amethyst Fjords. I intend to confer with a fellow traveller in the next village who will know its present path better than I.'

'A village? Here?'

'There are those in the Mortal Realms who could not imagine life inside a volcano and yet that is where you choose to make it. For a recordist, you are surprisingly closed-minded.'

'Well, it'd better not be far. We've been too long in this realm already.'

Uthan regarded him archly. 'You fear the siege of Hammerhal will be over before we return?'

'Hardly.'

Broddur had no interest in the war. It was Sigmar's war, but Gotrek desired an audience with the Stormcast Eternals and if Gotrek desired it then Broddur was going to make sure he got it. If, after that, Gotrek wished to fight then Broddur would fight alongside him. If he wished to leave it to burn then Broddur would leave it to burn. The city, second greatest in the Mortal Realms though it was purported to be, was barely two centuries old. There were some Unbaki living under the mountain who wouldn't have noticed its being there and certainly wouldn't mourn its fall.

'Well fear not either way,' Uthan went on. 'Fear not. The war will outlast your stay in the Realm of Death.' His voice dropped. He stared into the fire. The hint of a smile appeared across his face. 'If you ever leave.'

'If you've got something to say, necromancer, then say it.'

'Nagash rules here, Fyreslayer. Absolutely. He does not idly permit the departure of souls from his realm. Particularly not the likes of the Doomseeker.'

'What about him?'

'You feel it too, don't you? His is an ancient soul, unlike any other in the Mortal Realms. Nagash is a jealous god. He will not allow Gotrek to pass freely from his realm and into the hands of another.'

Broddur was unnerved despite himself. He would fight any foe that his oaths to Gotrek demanded him to fight, but the God of the Dead? Unable to stay seated a moment longer, he tightened his grip on his axe and icon and stood, peering into the ghoulish winter. The wind moaned through his tall crest of hair.

'Wait. Do you hear that?'

Something outside the circle of burning souls crunched on the ice.

Broddur spun towards it, his imagination turning the blustering of unquiet spirits and freezing sleet into the glowing eyes and skull-faced visage of Nagash. He thrust out his icon in warding, his axe held ready to come chopping down.

Gotrek came stumping out of the chill towards him. Broddur was so tense that he almost dropped both weapons in relief. The Slayer simply glared at the out-thrust icon until Broddur lowered it.

'And here I thought I'd left a dwarfen warrior and child of Grimnir to mind my fire, not some elven fishwife to be startled by iron boots in the night. Put your axe down, storysmith, before you drop it on your head.'

'Sorry. I thought you were…'

He trailed off. Uthan chuckled.

'Someone else.'

Gotrek stared through him. There was a haunted look in the Slayer's eyes, deep bags of tiredness and depression hanging under them. Not even Gotrek could go on this way. Whatever dark nightmare or bitter hope it was that pulled him from their campfire each night, Broddur had to get him away. They had to get out of Shyish, and soon, before the Doomseeker lost himself to the Realm of Death forever.

'On second thoughts, leave your axe where it is. A good knock to the head might do you the world of good. And me. And him.'

Uthan laughed again.

'It's almost dawn,' Broddur said, determined to ignore his mockery. 'I was starting to get... Where have you been?'

'None of your business.'

'If you're seeking some sign of Jordain's passage, then Barrowwalker here thinks—'

'Leave me out of this, battlesmith,' said Uthan.

'I said it's none of your concern! If you wish to prise the saga of my life from these lips then come, let's see if that axe of yours is good for aught but cutting meat and pastries.'

Broddur recoiled. There was a rage in the Slayer's sleep-dulled eyes that even he, a child of the Unbak, had never seen outside of a Grimwrath Berzerker on the battlefield. He did not doubt that Gotrek would sooner kill him than hear another word on the subject from him. To his surprise, it was Uthan who spoke up in his favour.

'I'm sure the Fyreslayer meant nothing by it.'

'If he means nothing then he'd be better off saying nothing, and do us all a service.'

'Uthan...' Broddur hesitated over his dry throat, swallowed, and tried again. 'Uthan thinks we mightn't be too far from the gate.'

'I said *maybe*.'

'About bloody time,' Gotrek said with a scowl.

Broddur could not recall feeling so relieved. 'Everything'll look brighter once we're back in Aqshy.'

'The Realm of Fire, aye,' said Gotrek, with heavy sarcasm. 'Just what I've always wanted.'

FOURTEEN

The village was a dead thing, buried at the bottom of a steep defile. A mess of flat-bottomed fishing boats stuck out into the dark waters of the fjord like the swollen toe of a corpse. A crescent of incongruously colourful buildings clustered by the still water. Broddur could see no sign of people, neither on the shoreline nor on the boats. There was no smoke from cookfires. No hungry birds circled. Without Uthan to guide them, he doubted they would have discovered this place in a year of searching.

'Lively,' Gotrek muttered.

Broddur nodded.

'What? No anecdote about the Lands of the Dead to lift our spirits?'

'My ancestors never ventured this far from the Salamander's Spine.'

'I see why.'

'Do not let appearances trick you, Slayer,' said Uthan. 'Shyish is far from uninhabited. Nekroheim and Nulahmia are metropolises to rival Hammerhal, or even the great cities of Azyr itself, the living and the dead toiling side by side in serfdom to Nagash. This village is not as empty as it looks.' The necromancer threw Gotrek a loaded look. 'Just try not to slay the first thing you see here.'

'If they're already dead, does it even count?'

Uthan chuckled darkly. 'There are fates worse than death, Slayer, and underworlds where the living cannot tread.'

'We're not looking for a place to light our fires, Gotrek,' said Broddur. 'Grimnir was Wanderer as much as he was Slayer or Doomseeker. Once Barrowwalker's consulted the oracle he's looking for, we'll be back in Aqshy. The world'll look brighter from the walls of Hammerhal.'

Gotrek, however, looked anything but brightened by the prospect.

With Uthan in the lead, they ventured into the village. The buildings were covered in an icy lustre. To Broddur, they seemed strangely vibrant, as if the muted palette of this realm had sensitised his eyes to colour. Upturned boats and netting lay against houses, unused. Ice that varied in lustre from amaranth to aquamarine clung to the steeply slanted roofs, crunching underfoot and shimmering faintly from wheel ruts and potholes in the dirt track. The air smelled of fish, but it was faint, a distant memory trapped in the ice. Every so often the sound of a creaking door, a whining dog, a crying child, would pull Broddur's attention one way or the other, but there was never anything there. He heard gulls cawing and looked up, shading his eyes, expecting to see the hungry sea birds circling overhead, but the sky was empty. Just the turquoise swirl of an ice-laden wind.

'Strangers...' it seemed to say.

'Do you hear that?'

'Do I look deaf to you?' said Gotrek.

'Leave us.'

'This Slayer goes where he pleases,' Gotrek bellowed. 'And it'll take more than a wisp of spirit to make him do otherwise.'

'Does this village have a name, necromancer?' Broddur asked.

Uthan shrugged. 'Ullerslev. Vagenscrypt. Blöt. The dead live here and remember it by their own names. Few of them will have any sense that their home shares its ground with a hundred others. Only when Nagash or one of his Mortarchs summons the spirit hosts to war are they granted a glimpse of their true nature.'

'A cruel fate,' said Gotrek. He peered through the open windows and doors of the haunted dwellings as though hoping to catch sight of something familiar. 'But they met it, at least.'

'A fate that awaits most in the Mortal Realms. The companion you seek most likely resides in a village or a town like this one.'

Gotrek's grip throttled the haft of his greataxe. He glared at the necromancer for a long moment before visibly drawing himself back under control. 'And who says I'm looking for anyone?'

Uthan gave a knowing chuckle. 'For a duardin of your bulk, you're awfully transparent, Slayer.'

'*Slayer*,' said the wind, growing urgent. '*The Slayer is here.*'

Broddur turned into it fearfully. He was unpleasantly reminded of his talk with Uthan the night before, about the jealousies of Nagash and his absolute command of his realm.

'We should move on.'

'The dead know you,' said Uthan, still amused.

'Aye, well, so they should. I've sent more than my share to their rest in places such as this. Friends as well as foes. But not Gotrek Gurnisson, no. Not this Slayer. He will outlive this world as he did the last.'

An object that looked like a silver coin rolled out of a doorway and fell into a wheel rut in the path ahead, winking silver against the ice.

Gotrek sniffed the air.

'Ghoul.'

The prospect seemed to underwhelm the Slayer. He did not even raise his axe. Broddur looked up from the shiny coin to the house it had rolled from. Something bestial yet fleetingly humanoid issued a timorous growl and snuffled back out of sight. Broddur imagined that he could keep a pack of ghouls fat for a month, but he and the Slayer were clearly bigger game than this one was accustomed to trapping.

'Not very subtle, is it.'

'Shyish is not a realm where heroes are made,' said Uthan. 'It's where they come to die.'

'No,' Gotrek growled. 'It's where they come to fade.'

Uthan drew up the hem of his robe and stepped over the coin. He did not give their would-be stalker a second glance. 'Eaters of flesh. Suckers of marrow. Drinkers of blood. Where there is warmth and shelter there will be flesh-eaters, but this is a Nighthaunt kingdom. There is little sustenance for them here. They will not be numerous.'

'There's little here for us either,' said Gotrek. 'Let's get a move on, before we all end up just like them.'

Out of some perverse sense of sympathy, Broddur felt his own shrunken belly growl.

The path led them to a large structure on the shoreline. It was timber-framed with crisp blue wattling, round windows frosted with rough glass. A lawn of thin grass and shingle surrounded it, populated by nondescript wooden markers in remembrance of the dead. A salt-bleached picket fence snaked between it and the village. The quiet mutterings of a bell to no god drifted down from its small tower. There was nothing here that was living. Nothing at all.

'Whose temple is this?'

Uthan smiled as though the question betrayed something quaint in Broddur's thinking. 'It could belong to many.'

'Or maybe to no one at all,' said Gotrek.

'Maybe,' Uthan conceded.

Gotrek spat on the spiky tundra. 'I hate this place. More even than your Realm of Fire, storysmith, and I never thought I'd live long enough to be saying that. A rock should be a rock. A chair a chair. Make a thing be two things at once, and you're practically being elvish.'

The temple's doors were as characterless as the rest of the structure. Like everything else Broddur had seen of the Amethyst Fjords, they were glazed with iridescent ice. Some of it cracked and flaked away as Uthan took the handle. The dark wood underneath was carved with symbols that appeared fuzzy under the eye, as though several iterations of the same basic message had been overlaid until there was no meaning left at all.

'Aside from that ghoul in the village we've not seen a living soul since the Charwood,' said Broddur. 'Who're you hoping to find here?'

'And who said I looked amongst the living?' Uthan chuckled. 'Shyish is a realm of secrets. Of answers, even, if you are bold. There are oracles in every grave if you know how to find them, and how to appease them.' His glance alighted briefly on Gotrek and a smile pulled uncertainly at his thin blue lips. 'Somewhere in this realm there may even be someone who can guide you to what *you* seek, Slayer.'

'What happened to needing our protection to reach Hammerhal?' said Broddur.

Uthan raised his hands apologetically. 'Can I not have a weakness for lost and tormented souls?'

'I'll give you loss and torment if you don't get on with it,' said Gotrek.

'There is no need for threats, Slayer,' Uthan said, bowing. 'We both want the same thing. We do, we do.' He straightened, like a nervous bird drinking from a puddle, his expression suddenly becoming serious. 'It is important that you both wait for me here. Whatever you see or hear from within, do *not* come after me. Few amongst the Nighthaunt truly understand that they are dead. Upsetting them can have... unpleasant consequences.'

The necromancer turned the handle.

After all of his warnings Broddur had expected something dramatic. He was disappointed when the only discernible result was that the door it was attached to opened. Uthan was halfway through when Gotrek called after him.

'Middenheim,' he growled, speaking as though he was regurgitating a stone. 'The manling would have gone to a city called Middenheim. Do you know of any such place in Shyish?'

Uthan smiled and bowed. 'I can but ask.'

And with that, the wizard went inside and closed the door behind him.

He was an odd one and no mistake.

Gotrek sat down on a stump, apparently hoping to spend his time alone with Broddur staring at the ground in silence. Broddur frowned at him. Now he would do anything for the snide remarks and the incessant complaining that he had found so irritating during their journey across the Flamescar Plateau. Anything would be better than the lethargy that seemed to have possessed the Slayer since their arrival in Shyish.

'Middenheim?' he asked.

'I wasn't talking to you, storysmith. Mind your own affairs, and cease meddling in mine.'

'If it's a tale of the Land of the Dead that interests you then I could tell you a beard-curler of how Nagash betrayed Sigmar during the Nexus War and brought about the Age of Chaos?'

Gotrek looked up from his consideration of the ground. He regarded Broddur dangerously. 'What do you think?'

Broddur opened his mouth, then quietly closed it again.

The Doomseeker grunted, apparently pleased.

Looking out over the still, purple water of the fjord, Broddur made a half-hearted attempt at whistling the khazukhain, the traditional marching song of the Unbak Fyrd, but it soon petered away from him. There was something about this place that resented the intrusion of anything so lively as a tune. The feeling of Gotrek's scowl on the back of his head did not help either. Lips pursed, he stuck his thumbs in his belt and rocked on his heels for a bit before wandering on up the path to the temple. In spite of Uthan's grave and very specific warnings, he levered himself up onto tiptoes to peer through the window. The glass was too thick and crusted with salt damage to see much. He turned his ear to it and listened. At first, he heard nothing over the gentle lapping of the sea against the stony shore, but then he picked up on what sounded like a faint scratching noise, and the occasional high-pitched squeak that sounded like a wheel in need of oil. There were a few mumbled words that sounded like they could be Uthan's, but not enough to make out what he was saying, or to whom.

Broddur felt a prickling down the nape of his neck, and turned. He looked sideways. A furtive scuffling of thatch came from one of the neighbouring fisherman's huts. He shook his head. With so many half-heard sounds on the breeze, it was hard to be sure that he had heard anything at all. But there *did* seem to be an indistinct black shape dropping out of sight behind the angle of the roof just as he turned towards it. Broddur was ready to shrug it off as another roaming Nighthaunt or an inquisitive ghoul, but then he heard the noise again, an urgent *scrit-scratching* noise not dissimilar to those he had heard coming from inside the temple.

'Do you hear that?'

Gotrek grunted, but did not look up. 'Probably some fool lucky enough to have died ten thousand years before you were born. Ignore it, storysmith, and stop jumping at every shadow.'

Shortening his grip on his axe, Broddur walked a way back along the winding path towards the white picket gate to the village. He pointed to the hovel with his golden icon. 'It sounded like it came from over there.'

'A ghost or a ghoul then. Who cares? Sit still and leave me be.'

Gotrek looked reflectively at the grave posts sticking up out of the earth around him. He shook his head and muttered, throwing an angry gesture over the plain wooden posts.

'Look at these people, storysmith. No names. No record of their deeds. No honour in death or place in the memory of their descendants. Nothing. This is no way to treat the dead.'

'Is this still about the mannish prince you're mourning?'

Gotrek growled dangerously as he rose. 'I've had about enough of your insinuations and your talk. Is it not enough for a dwarf to lament the foul treatment of another's ancestors? What manner of dwarf needs more cause for despair than that?'

Broddur found that he was backing away. There was something in the Slayer's expression that he did not want to see up close. 'We Fyreslayers know how to honour our ancestors. We're children of Grimnir. But Jordain was naught but a mannish prince, the son of no–'

The words stopped coming as Gotrek grabbed him by the throat and choked them down.

'And you think him less worthy than you, is that it? You wonder why it is that I honour him and not you? You think me blind? You're no better than the liche, but where he dishonours the dead with grubby magicks you do with your petty words and your stories. I've known more men than most dwarfs, and some of them have proven themselves a far sight worthier than most dwarfs.'

'Stop… Doomseeker…'

'And why should I? What would I miss if you were gone from

140

my side? Perhaps I'd even look more fondly on you if you were dead. Isn't that what you've been wanting from me?'

'Grimnir...'

Gotrek shook him violently in his grip. Broddur could hear his own cartilage snapping. Darkness closed around his vision.

'For the last time, storysmith. I. Am. Not. He.'

Broddur thumped desperately at Gotrek's arm, but it was like an iron bar that had been bent around his neck. The runes in his biceps sputtered, but somehow could not overcome the strength that the Doomseeker carried in his own muscle and bone. His eyes roved over the graveyard and village, looking for a way out, his eyes slowly, very slowly, widening as it dawned on him that what he was seeing there were dozens of pairs of gleaming red eyes looking back. He tapped with even greater urgency on Gotrek's arm, trying to direct him towards the skaven night runner skulking up behind him using only his eyes.

'Behind... You...'

'Don't insult me, storysmith. No one ever fell for that one, not outside those dreadful plays that the manling once convinced me to read.'

Broddur made an incoherent choking sound and swung his icon. It cracked the snout of the skaven night runner, just as it had been preparing to pounce, dropping it like a stone. Gotrek's grip around his throat loosened as he looked down at it.

'Skaven!' he roared, giving Broddur's neck one last violent shake before letting go. Broddur gasped. He had never felt so hungry for the thin Shyishan air. 'Why didn't you say something? Most of the time it's all I can do to make you shut up.'

Realising that their presence had been spotted, black-clad skaven killers came pouring into the graveyard from all sides. They scrambled through windows, leapt off roofs and out from upturned boats, several even bursting out of concealed holes in the permafrost. Gotrek roared in surprise as a hole opened up beneath the stump he had been sitting on earlier, revealing a skaven night runner whose triumphant squeals soon became ones of terror as a furious Doomseeker fell in on top of it.

Before Broddur could come to terms with the suddenness of the attack, it was on him. Fist-claws, tail blades, knives, all of them smeared in soot to render them non-reflective, stabbed at him from every direction it was possible for a weapon to go. He parried the first flurry, but the skaven were too quick and kept on coming. He howled in pain as a skaven sank its teeth into his elbow. Another punched a steel claw into his shoulder. Tearing his arm free of the ratman's mouth, he hacked furiously into the seethe of fur and blades. A night runner shrieked as Broddur's blade clipped its tail. The rest of the pack twitched agilely out of reach. A beard-length of breathing room would have to do.

'Seven times did the axes of Grimnir carve the molten scales of Vulcatrix. Seven times did the ur-Salamander savage the god in return!' With a roar, Broddur charged.

The night runners slipped out of his way as he barrelled towards them, flowing into a circle, to surround and harry him: clearly the vermin were well practised in bringing down foes bigger than themselves. A single night runner skipped ahead of him, goading him further into his pack-mates' encirclement with whiplash strokes of his tail. But Broddur had no intention of slowing down.

'For Grimnir!' A sputter of energy from the rune in his thigh brought a burst of acceleration and a squeal of alarm from the night runner in front of him before it disappeared under his stampeding bulk.

He felt something crack against the side of his head. A pair of night runners swaddled in black silk from soft nose to pink tail tip were crouching on a roof with slingshots. The skittering of clawed feet on the loose ground dragged his gaze from the pair.

He swung his icon like a morning star, snapping the neck of the skaven that had been looking to jump him from behind and sending its body corkscrewing into a grave mound. Broddur could feel his runes starting to wake up. This land of stagnation and chill had made them sluggish. It was not the realm they had been forged to. The magic was different. But they were slowly giving up their strength.

'Runk-ha!'

Free of foes for the time being, he raised his arm to ward off slingstones and sought out Gotrek.

The Doomseeker was out of his hole and wreathed in the fire of his greataxe as though his body was breathing it. A mound of smouldering skaven dead littered the earth around him. The chaff of more still hung on the air like the spirits of the dead lingering about their killer. The Doomseeker hacked a darting night runner near enough in half. A breath of forgefire incinerated the squealing vermin into charred flesh and burning hair. It filled Broddur with battle-joy to see the Doomseeker so thoroughly enraged. He clashed his axe and his icon overhead and rejoiced.

'We are the scattered embers of Grimnir's fire. Never doused. Never quenched. We fight. We burn. Blood and gold! Khazuk!'

'Grungni's beard, do you never stop?'

'It's the same clan that attacked us in Karag Unbak, Gotrek. Clan Boil. I recognise the markings on their rags. What are they doing here in Shyish?'

'Who cares?'

'Kill-kill the Slayer. Quick. Quick!' An evil figure in long black robes was perched across the picket fence. It pointed a dripping blade towards Gotrek and Broddur. 'There are only two and you are lots-many. The lucky one who kill-stabs the Slayer will be rewarded by the Eye Not Seen and be greatly in the favour of the Grey Lord. He wants him dead. Yes. Very-very dead-dead!'

'Did he say Eye *Not* Seen?' Broddur muttered. He turned to Gotrek, surprised to find the Doomseeker frozen in place.

'Did he say *Grey Lord?*'

The skaven leader shrieked what sounded like a command and a chittering second wave of vermin came pouring into the graveyard.

'Grimnir, they're everywhere!'

'Shut your yap and get after the wizard,' Gotrek snapped.

Broddur cursed himself for forgetting all about their guide. The scratching, squeaking sounds he had heard while listening at the window: the skaven were clearly inside the temple as well as out!

Leaving Gotrek to hold off the night runners, which he did with a tremendous if grudging zeal, Broddur huffed back up the path. He tried the doors, but they wouldn't open. *Krutaz,* he thought. Barred from the inside. The skaven must have slipped the bolt across before springing their ambush, to ensure that no one came to the wizard's aid before it was too late. Well, they hadn't reckoned on a battlesmith of the Unbak lodge. And Broddur would sooner pet Vulcatrix's flaming nostrils than let himself and the Doomseeker be stranded in Shyish without their guide.

'I'm coming, Barrowalker!' he roared, as he dropped his shoulder and charged.

FIFTEEN

The doors exploded inward, and Broddur blundered through, eyes stinging, hacking up splinters, sweeping his icon ahead of him like a blind man with a staff. He felt a tickle in the back of his nose, like a sneeze that wouldn't come, as he scanned the temple's interior.

A group of figures had convened in the spot under the nave where several murky puddles of light merged into one. Uthan Barrowalker was one of them. He stood inside a ring of snarling skaven. They were all black-furred, which Broddur understood to be a signifier of ferocity and status in skaven society. The pack leader stood with a less pronounced stoop than its lackeys. It was also relatively well armoured, with bands of leather sewn with steel rings around its arms and chest. A weighted net hung off one hip. A silk rope wound around its chest and up the opposite arm like a protective snake. The paler flesh of paws, muzzle and tail was bound in black silk, its small armoury of bladed implements tinted and sleeved. Only its red eyes and bared fangs glinted evilly in the light.

'Barrowalker!'

Broddur's shout echoed through the timber-walled nave. Skaven and necromancer alike spun towards the interruption. In spite of the stark differences in anatomy, the expressions of surprise on their faces were surreally similar. Uthan pulled back the hand he had been holding out to the skaven leader, no doubt with the intention of annihilating the assassin with some necromantic spell, and cried out in relief. 'Battlesmith! Thank the Undying King for you. Help me!'

'But–' the assassin squeaked, before Uthan punched it in the chest.

The wizard's knuckles never quite connected with the skaven's body, but bound spirits typhooned down his wrist to erupt from the outstretched hand, lifted the assassin from its footpaws and carried it squealing across the hall.

'By Grimnir, Barrowalker. All this time we've been running after you, and you've been capable of doing that?'

But Uthan the necromancer had already slipped into a new incantation. A barrier of entwined spirits sprang up around him, human and inhuman faces locked in silent screams as they flickered and swirled like multihued flames. The necromancer drew individual spirits from the barrier as one would tame birds from a flock to sit upon his hand, sculpting them like origami creatures into spells to flay the flesh and fur from skaven bones or blast the living soul from their screaming husks. The night runners and their remaining leaders scrambled over each other to get clear of him, a foul odour of musk rising to fill the hall.

All Broddur could do was stare. He had never seen Uthan use his magic for anything other than cowering or fleeing. Seeing him unleashed was astounding.

'Blasted rats get everywhere,' Gotrek said as he stomped in through the open door. He was a scratched and bitten mess, covered in burns and dark skaven blood. His crest was askew and something had managed to pull out his nose chain, taking a lump of ear with it. He was also grinning savagely as he took in the scene inside. 'What in the blazes have I been missing out on in here?'

Broddur couldn't answer. He wasn't sure he knew himself.

'Hold the door for me, storysmith. I'll handle things from here.'

'Don't let any harm come to Barrowwalker.'

Gotrek snorted. 'As if I would.'

'I'm not finding my own realmgate to Hammerhal if he dies.'

'Don't *peck* at me, storysmith.'

Broddur rubbed at his nose again, and suddenly it dawned on him what the cause of his itch must be. Ur-gold. Only the rune-priests of the Zharrgrim had the gift to sift ur-gold from base, worthless gold, but all Fyreslayers were sensitive to it to some degree. One of the skaven in this temple was carrying ur-gold. Given that they appeared to belong to the same clan that attacked Karag Unbak, there was only one good explanation for it.

'The Master Rune, Gotrek. One of the skaven has it.'

'Which one?'

Broddur pointed out Uthan's first victim, the skaven assassin still steaming where he lay on the ground across the hall. 'I'd have to go with the leader.'

As Gotrek hacked his way through panicked ratmen, Broddur noticed something lissom and black detach itself from the ceiling beams and drop silently towards the Slayer. It was not a skaven. He could tell that immediately despite being unable to make out much else beyond its general shape and the mere fact that it was not screaming in terror towards the windows and doors. The night runners were creatures of shadow. This might have *been* a shadow. Were it not for the spirits being dragged gnashing and wailing from the walls to provide Uthan with yet more fuel for his spells, riffling across its black garb in an unholy gale, then Broddur might not have seen it at all until it was too late. And worse, Broddur thought that he knew exactly who it was.

'Doomseeker!' he roared, and Gotrek turned just in time to deflect the assassin's knives on the flat of his axe-blade.

'Not this time, Gotrek,' said Maleneth. 'This time the Master Rune is mine.'

'Did no one in these realms ever warn you about coming between a dwarf and his gold?'

'It is not yours.'

The Shadowblade and the Slayer traded blows faster than Broddur could follow them, blitzing their way across several dusty pews and the caryatid of an anonymous black-hooded god. They separated briefly, Maleneth panting heavily and hissing in annoyance at seeing her swords scrape harmlessly across the black Lion of Edassa that Broddur had helped the Slayer to fit over his shoulder.

'You wear armour now?'

'Just a little bit.'

'How irritatingly novel.'

'Stop toying with her and finish her off,' Broddur yelled. 'We can't let her out of here with the Master Rune of the Unbaki.'

'He thinks *you're* toying with *me*?' said Maleneth. 'Bless.'

And then they were away again, lost in a whirl of smoke, flying silk and knives.

Broddur felt his priorities cruelly torn. On the one hand, he felt obliged to let the Doomseeker fight his own battle as he saw fit, and die if that was his fell. But on the other, he was still a loyal son of the Unbak lodge who'd sworn to bring the Master Rune back home and make bloody examples of its would-be thieves. That second stipulation had been met in such a fashion as would satisfy even Runelord Krag's desire for vengeance, but his chances of seeing the rune safely returned to Karag Unbak could only be improved by ensuring Maleneth Witchblade's demise and the survival of Gotrek Gurnisson.

'Barrowwalker!' he yelled. 'The Khainite is here!'

Uthan turned immediately, hands half raised as if to defend himself and in the process of obliterating a pair of skaven night runners, who grasped the opportunity to scrabble through a window and escape. His jittery features settled into a snarl. 'Witch.' He drew his hands into an eye-achingly complicated sigil across his chest. A sudden gale blew. His hood blew back off his head, the mildewed tufts of his hair tearing free as the spirit hosts of Ullerslev and Vagenscrypt and Blöt answered his summons. The barrier around his knees roared to chest height as the dead of the Amethyst Fjords fed it with their souls.

'Noooooo...'

'Pleeease...'

'Let me reeesssst...'

The necromancer separated his clasped hands and drew them slowly apart. A crackling ball of malignant energy, a purple sun, appeared between his palms. The walls creaked, as though it was the spirits they had been harbouring that, ironically, had lent them their solidity. Even the temple's light seemed to bend towards the gravity of the purple sun. The edges of the hall fell dark. The wizard was no child of Grimnir, that was certain, but Broddur knew a battle-frenzy when he saw one. The power was in him, and he would destroy or be destroyed.

'Oi!' Gotrek barked, as Maleneth slipped out of reach of his axe.

'God of Murder! He will kill us all.'

A throwing knife left the witch aelf's hand. It flew unerringly towards Barrowwalker until, turned by one of the howling spirits in his barrier, it plunged hilt-deep into his shoulder instead of his heart.

'Blood of Khaine!' she swore.

'A flesh wound,' said Gotrek. 'Typically sloppy elf work.'

Uthan staggered a few paces back along the central aisle. Blood soaked his sleeve and he was visibly fighting to keep his spell under control. Broddur could see that it was already starting to unravel. Spirits strained against the circumference of the sphere, screaming faces with amethyst-glowing eyes manifesting from the churn faster than the mortal heart could bear. The howls of the spirit barrier rose and rose and rose, turning into a merciless shriek as the flames ripped free, and the purple sun detonated in Uthan's face.

'Yeeessssss!'

The spirits of the unbound dead raced from Uthan's grasp like floodwaters from a broken dam. They ripped up flagstones, tore the furniture to smithereens, blew the glass from the windows. Skaven night runners caught in their path were flayed alive, from silk, to fur, to skin, to muscle, and then finally to bone, stripped bare and strewn ahead of the cackling surge. Gotrek was next. The flood hit him side-on, one side of his face ageing a thousand years in the blink of an eye. It looked like it was melting, the eyeball bursting, dribbling down his face to where his beard burned like straw kindling. The Doomseeker managed to turn the good side of his face away, shielding it behind his hand as he bellowed in agony and outrage.

It was the last that Broddur saw of him before the flood caught him too, thousands upon thousands of delighted, hateful, bewildered hands lifting him up off the ground and propelling him irresistibly towards the open door.

SIXTEEN

Uthan Barrowalker dusted off his robes and walked out from the temple. He closed the door carefully behind him. Lying on the frozen grass outside, Broddur watched the necromancer in some confusion and then, with a groan, sat up. He had been expecting to find himself sprawled out next to a burning crater, surrounded by the detritus of the temple's destruction and skaven dead. While skaven dead were very much in evidence, the temple was disconcertingly unscathed. The temple's various bells tolled softly in the cold wind off the fjord. It was as though nothing had happened at all.

'How am I not dead?'

'Maybe you are,' said Uthan, in a voice taut with pain. 'This is Shyish, after all.' He turned to lurch down the dirt path and Broddur noticed that while the assassin's knife, too, had disappeared from the necromancer's shoulder, the wound it had left behind was very real. His left arm hung limp at his side, the purple sleeve stained dark with blood.

'The rune,' said Broddur, as his memories of events prior to his ejection from the temple began filtering back into his head. 'We have to retrieve the rune.' He groaned again, reaching out to steady himself as his head swam, then something else occurred to him. He looked around the eerily peaceful graveyard. 'Where's the Doomseeker? And what happened to Maleneth?'

'Pray on the name of every god you know that that Khainite *harpy* is shrieking on the wind with the dead this night. If a shred of her soul yet remains, I will find it. I will pick it apart with these very fingers and see that the pieces burn until the fires of Draco-thion falter and fall dark.'

Broddur stared, stunned at the human's passion and still, he admitted, more than a little dazed. The skittish old hermit he had been travelling alongside had a fiery heart he had not been expecting.

'You think she's dead then?'

Uthan shuffled to a stop a few yards shy of where Broddur was now solidly sitting and brought his hand to his injured shoulder. He closed his eyes for a long time, his pre-existing pallor becoming noticeably drawn and waxen. 'I don't know. What do you think I am? The spirits of this village will not talk to me now, thanks to you.'

'Thanks to me?'

'You were too slow.' He tutted angrily. 'You forced me to defend myself.'

'What were the skaven that despoiled my lodge even doing here with the Master Rune?'

'Are you asking me? I don't know. They caught me unawares, Fyreslayer, and doubtless fled with the trinket the moment the Khainite appeared.' The wizard hissed in pain and leant against a grave post with his good arm. 'By all the gods of Order and Ruin, Destruction and Death, that Darkling witch hurt me.'

Looking around, Broddur saw that Barrowalker was right about one thing at least. It was deathly quiet. No Nighthaunt whispered from empty houses. No malignant drifted in half-remembered life. Whatever false life they had borne with them unto death had been shocked from them by Uthan's magic. But he could still feel them nearby. There was an anger lying over the village like the pressure that built before a storm. Even the ghouls seemed to be lying low before moving in to feast on the glut of skaven dead. Broddur shook his head in a bid to uncloud his thoughts, blinking up at the pristine temple. There was something he was forgetting. Something…

He rubbed the back of his fist across his nose. It still felt as though it wanted to sneeze.

'I'm fine by the way,' came a foul-tempered growl from behind him. 'Don't bother asking.'

Broddur gasped as the Slayer stumped towards him.

Ever since his first encounter with Gotrek Gurnisson on the Caldur Bridge beside Az Skorn, Broddur had harboured the illusion that Gotrek was somehow indestructible. His screams as Uthan's miscast spell had mauled him had shattered that. The visage before him now ensured that it was not going to be restored anytime soon, if ever. The skin of his face had been withered and aged down one side. It was wrinkled and leathery, half of his orange-dyed beard now struck through with white hair. The eye was a blistered hollow. A length of black silk, taken from the body of a night runner, was stretched taut between his huge, scuffed hands. He was in the process of fashioning an eye patch. A shudder of pain ran through the Slayer as he pressed the bandage to his ruined socket and tied it off behind his head, but he did not make a sound.

'By Grimnir, you look… better than I'd feared.'

Gotrek gave a short boom of laughter, halted abruptly by a scowl of pain.

'My oath, Slayer! We'll wreak vengeance on the Clan Boil. Aye, and the temple of the Bloody-Handed God besides!'

'Calm yourself, storysmith, before you get a nosebleed. I've suffered worse from goblin arrows. If you'd told me before we left that volcano of yours that I'd be wearing manling armour on my shoulder and a skaven's sleeve over the ruin of my eye then I might have just tried to find my way back to the Realm of Chaos.' He grumbled under his breath as he finished tying off the silk bandage behind his head. 'Grimnir gave me that eye.'

'Being steadfast in the face of adversity is a trait of the Dispossessed clans, those duardin who lost all to the Ages of Chaos and Blood. It is not the way of the Fyreslayers!'

'It had better start becoming the way of this particular Fyreslayer. You're giving me a headache on top of everything else.'

Broddur gathered up his axe from where it lay on the ice. He pressed it to the palm of his hand until blood welled up around the blade. 'In word and in blood, in rhun and in gold, let vengeance be sworn.'

'What will it take? Tell me what will it take to SHUT... YOU... UP?' Adjusting his bandage, Gotrek turned to glower, newly one-eyed, at Uthan. 'Well? What've you got to say for yourself?'

'I was distracted,' said Uthan.

'Aye. I noticed.'

'I have strength enough left in me to wither your other half, if you push me.'

'Well ready it, liche, because you're about to get bloody pushed.' Gotrek closed on Uthan, who struggled to push himself back up off the grave post he was leaning on.

'Don't test me!' he hissed, baring his stumpy yellow teeth at the Slayer.

It was hardly the same man that Broddur had seen melt away from a Sylvaneth ambush and skirt happily around a battle with the

Seeing Legion. The Uthan Barrowalker that Broddur had thought he knew would never have dared stand up to Gotrek Gurnisson in this mood.

'You think a few extra years on my flesh worries me? I'm older than the rock I'm standing on, and I still look haler than my father did when he butchered your lot at Hel Fenn.'

Broddur hitched his axe to his belt and scrambled up to stand between them. Key chains and gold rings clinked as the movement splintered the ice that had frozen over his thighs.

'Cool your fires now, both of you. We came to this realm together and we'll leave it together. We vowed to protect you from the witch aelf, Barrowalker, and we did.'

'Barely.'

'And Gotrek, Uthan swore to guide us to Hammerhal in exchange, and so far he has.'

'I'm not so sure, storysmith. Has he? I'm not seeing these thousand-foot-high walls and moats of fire that the princeling spoke of. Are you?'

'I'll have you know that I...' Uthan swayed for a moment. He reached back for the grave post, catching it at the third attempt. 'That I spoke to my...'

'Look at him. *Wizards*. Little bit of real work and you'd think he'd just scaled Karaz-a-Karak.'

'She... told me...'

'Gotrek, he is looking very pale.'

'He looks like a ghost, storysmith. That's normal for him.'

'The battlesmith is right, I don't... feel... so...'

A sudden palsy ran through the necromancer. Broddur caught him before he could fall. He lowered the wizard quickly to the ground, the unfulfilled urge to sneeze threatening to make him drop the man. Pinching his nostrils and blinking, he backed away. Gotrek leaned in. His one eye glittered harshly in the glow of the soul ice.

'So, the dark elves of these worlds still like to lace their blades with poison, do they? That's good to know.'

'P-p-poison?' Uthan slurred.

Crouching down, Gotrek peeled the torn cloth of Uthan's robe sleeve from the wound in his shoulder. Uthan moaned in pain as it came away. Gotrek and Broddur both gagged at the smell. It was a miracle of endurance that Gotrek was able to remain by the wizard's side and not physically recoil. It was painfully sweet, like goat's milk that had been left three days by a forge to go sour. Gotrek prodded at the wound, drawing a louder cry of pain from Uthan.

'Unless there is some healing magic in those cloddish fingers, then stop touching it.'

'It's already starting to turn black,' Broddur muttered softly over Gotrek's shoulder.

'I say we leave him here,' said Gotrek, with considerably less tact.

Uthan's eyes rolled in seeming panic until they fixed on Gotrek. He reached out a hand, grabbing one of the dangling lengths of broken chain that hung from the Slayer's bracer. 'You must bear me to Hammerhal, Slayer. I have allies there, allies who can heal this kind of wound. You swore an oath to me.'

'*He* swore the oath to you,' said Gotrek, pointing a finger at Broddur. 'Not I.'

'You made me!' Broddur protested.

'I know the path and it is not far. Just a short voyage across the Amethyst Fjords.'

'You want me to get on a boat?'

'Your friend–'

'I've no friends here. Not worming liche-masters like you nor half-witted, thrice-bellied, short-bearded kin-botherers like him.'

'Not here,' said Uthan quickly. 'No. *No*. The human. The one you seek. He is in Hammerhal. The spirits told me so before the skaven interrupted me. Forgive me. Forgive me for leading you to doubt it. *Please.* Please bear me to Hammerhal.'

Gotrek's expression looked as though it were on the brink of shattering, before hardening into something else entirely. Something that Broddur had never seen before and did not recognise. It was pained, as though a broken bone had just been struck, and yet happy, as if the reminder that he was still alive and could feel pain was unexpected and surprisingly welcome.

He leaned in closer over the necromancer.

'He's in Hammerhal? The dead told you that?'

Uthan wound his hand around the Slayer's wrist chain until he was wearing several loops like a bracelet, as if forcing Gotrek to chop his hand off to be rid of him might actually prevent the Slayer from leaving him.

'Yes. Yes. *Felix is in Hammerhal.* Get me to Hammerhal.'

Gotrek straightened. He looked shaken by what Uthan had just said. 'I never told you his name. I never told anyone.' The Slayer got up, and was stomping off towards the water before Broddur could ask him what any of it had meant. 'Make haste, nugget forager. Or am I doomed to outlive another age here in the Realm of Death?'

Broddur rubbed his itching nose, then hoisted Barrowwalker over his shoulder.

Finally, he thought. *A little urgency.*

SEVENTEEN

There was going to be no sleep for Broddur that night, he knew. The sea was no place for a Fyreslayer at the best of times. It unbalanced his fires and made him feel queasy. And to make matters worse, the previous night's storm had risen again as soon as the pale sun had been interred for another long night beneath the horizon. It was the worst yet. The wind was a banshee, screaming and crying without relent, and battering the longboat with her fury. Glittering devils of soul dust, ripped from the floating plates of sea ice and glaciers and dancing to the winds' evil will, swirled up and down the helpless vessel.

'No place for a Fyreslayer,' he muttered.

'You whine like an elvish fish merchant,' said Gotrek. The Slayer had lodged himself and his enormous axe in the prow, finding some shelter there from the wind and spray, but he looked thoroughly sodden and miserable nonetheless. 'Shut your mouth, shut your eyes, and then go to sleep.'

Broddur obligingly clamped his mouth shut and wriggled up

against the gunwale, trying to hunker into a spot that would shelter all of him at once. It was hopeless.

'No place for a Fyreslayer...'

As though harkening to the summons of the wind, the sea too seemed to have awakened with the ending of the day. The pack ice had thickened noticeably since they had lain ahull for the night. It surrounded the boat now, embraced it, whispered to it in a shared tongue of creaks and splinters. Will-o'-the-wisps glimmered over the rowing benches like running lights, murmuring softly to one another, untroubled by the storm.

There but for the might of Grimnir, Broddur thought.

Uthan Barrowalker had been laid out between the ranks of spectral rowers, lashed to the mainmast with his head propped up by a bundle of netting. To Broddur's great envy, he was asleep, his breathing shallow. Aethereal nurses drifted back and forth occasionally. Their voices were so harrowing that Broddur found himself dreading their return.

'He's rallied well.'

'You mean he didn't perish before sunset as I'd said he would. Hardly praise, storysmith. Now go to sleep.'

'I suppose even Grimnir has it in him to be merciful. I don't think I'd want to be stuck out here without him.'

'That's it. I'm not going to lie here all night listening to this.'

The boat shifted as Gotrek left his berth and climbed overboard.

'Gotrek? *Gotrek!* You can't get out.'

The Slayer did not answer. Broddur heard his iron-capped boots landing in the thick ice and the stamp of his footsteps carrying him further into the storm.

'It's not as though we're smack in the middle of the Amethyst Fjords or anything!'

Respect for the Doomseeker's secrets warred with annoyance at his obstinacy. Gotrek's nightly flights from camp had become something of a routine, but that had been on land. Where in Grimnir's fiery halls could he be thinking of going out here on the fjords? Broddur had no doubt that had the mannish prince, Jordain, been aboard then the Doomseeker would have confided his purpose in him. But not Broddur, not his battlesmith, guide and oathsworn believer. Oh no. The two sides of his indecision settled into a kind of battle-weary curiosity that agreed to him peeking out over the side of the boat into the blighted gale.

'Who am I fooling?' he growled to himself. 'There'll be no sleep for this duardin tonight.'

Casting a furtive glance over the ghostly oarsmen, he bent to collect his axe and his icon, but then changed his mind. Coming from a volcano in Aqshy he did not have much experience of ice except that it was slippery and that he was liable to want both hands free. He left the icon in the boat and hitched the axe to his belt, then swung his leg over the side and dropped down.

He landed barefoot in the ice. The wind railed against him almost as soon as he was out of the boat. The cold nibbled at his toes. He crossed his arms against the mortal chill and stamped his feet to warm them, looking around until he found the Doomseeker's booted prints. They were being quickly filled in, wind-deposited motes of glowing soul-stuff tumbling over the sheet ice and into the depressions.

He had only followed them a short way before he started to hear voices.

Real voices.

'Didn't think you were coming tonight,' said one.

'Nothing better to do,' said another that Broddur immediately recognised as Gotrek's. 'Eight worlds they tell me, but is there a half-decent beer anywhere in them?'

A sigh.

'I'd kill something for a Bugman's. Even a Beardling's Best Effort.'

'You did once if Snorri remembers.'

'I was going to kill him anyway. The keg in his dungeon was a bonus.'

Narrowing his eyes against the wind and hugging his beard close, Broddur shuffled towards the voices until Gotrek came into view. The Slayer was sitting cross-legged on the ice floe. His back was to Broddur, his tattooed skin goose-bumped by the cold though the Doomseeker gave no other indication of suffering it as Broddur was. His beard and crest whipped about in the wind.

'You lost another eye,' said the other duardin. 'Looks like Snorri missed a decent fight.'

The Slayer ran his hand through his blanched beard. His hand came to his nose chain, one end flapping with the wind where it no longer pierced his ear. 'We've had better.'

'You're just saying that.'

Broddur turned to focus his attention on the duardin that Gotrek was speaking with. If anything, he looked even bigger and more brutal than the Slayer. Three coloured nails stuck out of his bald head. One of his legs ended in a lump of metal below the knee. His face looked as though it had been bent, torn and beaten one time too many. But despite that, or perhaps because of it, his expression was as bright as that of a flameling who had been allowed out of the karag and seen a flower for the first time. His body was tattooed in a similar design to Gotrek's, his beard dyed orange in similar fashion.

Broddur wondered if they hailed from the same Dispossessed clan. Could they be kin even? Some instinct advised Broddur to stay hidden and to approach no closer. The Slayer would almost certainly react badly to being followed, and he had no idea at all how this Snorri would react. If he was any relation to Gotrek then Broddur could expect it to be violently. But nor did he want to leave. One thing he knew for certain was that it was no flesh and blood duardin that the Slayer happened to have found waiting for him on the fjords of Shyish. Hunkering in behind what appeared to be a wave that had frozen solid, he resolved to remain where he was and watch.

'How do you always know where I'll be, anyway?' said Gotrek.

'Snorri doesn't know.'

'You're a fool, Snorri Nosebiter.'

The two duardin sat unspeaking for a time, as comfortable in their silence as old friends who saw each other every day. Snorri stared upwards, grinning childishly as wisps of spirit dust trailed across the stormy sky.

Broddur quietly shuffled on the spot while he watched. His feet were starting to freeze over again. How did these two not feel it?

'You've not seen anyone else round here, I suppose? Ulrika? Max? That mad fool, Makaisson?'

'Snorri thinks he saw Max and Ulrika once. Together. Long ago. A party, perhaps? He can't really remember. No parties any more. But not Makaisson.' The duardin brightened suddenly. 'Maybe he made it?'

'It's been thousands of years since Kazad Drengazi, Snorri.'

'Doesn't feel like it.'

'That's because you've not been able to count past fifteen since I cut your foot off.'

Snorri leant in towards Gotrek, beaming broadly. He tapped his squashed nose with a heavily tattooed finger. 'Snorri doesn't think you're really interested in them anyway.'

Gotrek looked at the ground. 'That wizard I told you about last night.'

'The necromancer?'

'Aye, I didn't think much of it at first either, but that's this world for you. No one does things the old ways any more.'

'Shame.'

'It is that, right enough. This *duardin* nonsense for instance, where did that all start?'

Snorri shrugged. 'Snorri supposes that *dwarf* was never our word anyway. It was just what the Empire men called us.'

'Huh. I got used to it. Too much time around men, I suppose.'

'You were talking about a necromancer?'

The Slayer stuck his tongue into the wall of his cheek, clearly reluctant. 'Aye. Well. He says the manling's not here, that he's in this place everyone keeps going on about called Hammerhal.'

'Never heard of it.'

'That's because you're an imbecile, Snorri.'

'Oh yes, Snorri forgot.'

'You think he could be there, alive after all this time? You think my oath to see him and his family well could be unbroken yet?'

'You said it's been...' There was a pause as Snorri creased his forehead in thought. 'Lots and lots of years.'

'And what of it? Grimnir may be dead, but the oaths of dwarfs are harder to break than gods.'

'Well, young Felix isn't here.'

'I had to ask.' Gotrek cleared his throat awkwardly. 'Fine. Well.' He stood up, stamping his boots on the ice. Broddur shifted position, waking up his frozen legs for the short dash back to the boat. 'Probably time I headed back. That storysmith gave me an earful when I got back after dawn yesterday. Almost like being married again.'

Broddur frowned at that.

There was an awkward silence before Gotrek spoke again.

'When you're next in the Ancestors' Hall, tell Bjorni and the others that I'm still looking for my proper doom.'

'That'll cheer them, Snorri thinks.'

'Aye, I bet it will. And I'm sorry about... you know.'

'Snorri knows. And Snorri thinks he earned it anyway.'

'Aye, Snorri did. But even so.'

'Probably best say goodbye now then. Snorri hopes you find young Felix, and your doom.' The duardin became sombre. 'Snorri doesn't think we'll meet again before you do.'

'What makes you say that?'

'You'll find the magic door tomorrow.'

'The realmgate, you mean?'

'That's it!'

'Anything you can tell me about it?'

The burly duardin scratched his head. 'There was something. But Snorri can't remember. Something about the door being in the fire. And something about that old Khemrian liche that decided to become a god.'

'Nagash?'

Broddur shuddered at the casual invocation of the name. He looked over his shoulder at the wind blustering around him, but if the spirits of the fjord had overheard then it seemed that they had not yet borne the message to their master.

'Yes,' said Snorri cheerfully. 'That's the one.'

'What about him?'

'Snorri... can't remember.'

'Wonderful help you are, Snorri. Just like old times. Nothing about this *Grey Lord*?'

'A grey what?'

'Never mind. I forgot. You never met him, did you?'

Sensing the conversation was drawing to its end and deciding that he had already risked the Slayer's wrath for as long as he dared, Broddur turned and hurried back to the boat.

Gotrek had already given him a lot to ponder on.

EIGHTEEN

'There it is,' said Uthan weakly. 'The Hammerhal Gate.'

The relief that Broddur felt at the utterance of those six small words bordered on the euphoric. Even having overheard Snorri's promise to Gotrek that they would find the realmgate today, he had not wholly believed it. The words of the dead were hardly reliable, and rarely did they have the best interests of the living at heart.

'Thank you, Snorri Nosebiter,' he murmured quietly. 'Wherever you roam now.'

'Did you say something, storysmith?'

Broddur flinched. The Slayer had ears like a bat when he wanted to.

'I'm just glad to be returning to my own realm. Shyish disagrees with me.'

'Five days without a hot meal is what disagrees with you, story-smith.'

Broddur frowned, but did not disagree. 'I don't see the gate yet, Barrowwalker.'

'Look harder.'

The necromancer pointed to a titanic berg of ice directly ahead of their boat. The ice sheet rose out of the sea the way a mountain rises out of the earth. A blast of cold spray doused them all, the ghostly oarsmen singing as their untiring efforts bore the boat on towards it. Despite the eerie, turquoise sheen and the way the berg creaked with the motion of the waves, there was something reassuring about its scale. Something familiar.

'It reminds me of Karag Unbak.' Broddur sighed. 'How I miss the home fires of my hearth forge.'

'No one asked you to come.'

'That's not the way I remember it.'

'As I already told you back in Twinfire Keep, I've no need of a rememberer.'

'Well, we'll both be in the Realm of Fire soon. Hah! To be warm again.'

'How do you plan on us getting up there, liche? I'm no sea-dwarf, but I've been on my share of boats and I see no good place to land.'

'I will show you.'

The necromancer spread his arms, like a crow with a splinted wing. The aether beneath each arm moulded into the gnarled form of a banshee woman dressed in the rags of healers. They took his weight between them, lifting him onto the litter of souls that formed below his feet. Broddur grimaced as he watched them bear the sickened necromancer from the deck and on towards the iceberg. The oarsmen rowed on, relentless, the boat riding up and down with the waves.

'I still don't like it when he does that,' said Broddur.

'I could make a list as long as your grandfather's beard of all the things I don't like.'

A few hundred lengths from the ice mountain, high above the longboat's masts, Uthan's spirit litter stopped. He gestured towards the gigantic iceberg.

'Kales. Uno. Stante.'

Pink fire flared about the wizard's outstretched hand, his hair and robes suddenly blowing counter to the wind, towards the floating mountain.

'Kales Uno Stante, Kales Uno Stante.' The oarsman chanted together, incorporating the wizard's spell into their rhythm.

Broddur felt his beard bristle as the magic built. His fires wavered. The sounds of cracking ice grew louder.

'Gotrek. The ice.'

'Stop fussing, storysmith. You're like a prospector staring into his last beer...'

'Kales Uno Stante, Kales Uno Stante.'

'... fretting over every tiny thing.'

'Rise, Okaenos!' Uthan screamed, reaching his hands towards the iceberg. 'Rise!'

'Rise, Rise, Rise.'

'Rise!'

With a calamitous shattering, the iceberg split up the middle, a blast of stagnant air and preserved grave stench blowing from its interior. The two halves sank under the water, the longboat rocking perilously as the waves unleashed by the mountain's sundering grew incrementally higher and harder. 'Rise, Rise, Rise.' The oarsmen rowed through the massive waves, even as those two shattered halves unfolded to become skeletal fins and flippers, the bones of some undead goliath entombed within the frozen plates. 'Rise, Rise, Rise.' A long, bony neck, each individual vertebra the length of their stolen boat, emerged from the glittering pall of obliterated ice. Its skull was an obscenity of mortal scale, crocodilian but many-fold larger, naked flames drooling through row upon row upon row of spiny teeth.

'Can't remember, he said,' said Gotrek. 'Snorri Nosebiter, you're still an idiot.'

'Behold Okaenos the Devourer, zodiacal godbeast of the Amethyst Fjords!' Uthan shrieked. His face was flushed with elation, horribly underlit by the two ghost-women who were helping him to stand upright. His hair streamed in the wind. 'At Nagash's behest, he consumed the Hammerhal Realmgate, devouring an entire legion of Khorne's daemons in so doing, and sparing the Realm of Death from the Blood God's incursion.'

Broddur ducked instinctively as the godbeast gave a mighty roar, fire boiling from its gullet and lancing across the amethyst-tinged sky. Gotrek merely drummed his fingers along the haft of his great-axe and watched the monster sourly. It was greater even than the ur-Salamander, Ignimbris, whom Gotrek had driven back into the Caldur Lake. The monster had perceived the Slayer as Grimnir returned, as Broddur had, and surrendered rather than fight him. Broddur doubted this undead titan would back down with so little bloodshed.

'So what is this, liche? Do we kill it? I'm not complaining, but a little warning would've been nice.'

'Where is the gate, Barrowwalker?' Broddur yelled up at the hovering necromancer. 'How do we enter it?'

The wizard laughed maniacally, obviously drunk on the power of his summoning. 'Can you not see what is right before you?'

The godbeast delivered another world-splitting bellow. Turning its serpentine neck around, it sent a blast of fire into the fjord, coring the water for a thousand beard-lengths down and enveloping them all in steam.

'The door is in the fire,' Gotrek muttered aloud. 'That's what Snorri was trying to tell me.'

'Those are the fires of Aqshy that you feel,' said Uthan. 'Drawn from the Realm of Fire and into Okaenos' belly. He was a true servant of Nagash, as once I was also. And for what? A tomb of ice in the Amethyst Fjords, an eternity of flame. And what then did the Lord of the Dead do with his sacrifice? He surrendered the Arc Gate of Gothizzar to Archaon, withdrew to the most secret underworlds beneath Nagashizzar. He hid, abandoned Shyish. Sigmar had already barred the gates of Azyr. Those of us left behind had to turn to other gods.'

'Oathbreaker!' Gotrek roared back. 'My world was destroyed too. My hold, conquered. My people, vanquished. My oaths, ash. My companions dead, or worse than dead, betrayed when I carried on living. Archaon the Everchosen swept across the world I knew and took it all from me. Do you hear me whining about it?'

Broddur decided it was not the time to answer that.

Reaching into his tattered and now sodden robes, Uthan withdrew something large and golden. As he held it up, vapours around him began to steam out of the air. This time it was Broddur's turn to gasp.

'Blackhammer's Master Rune! *He* had it! I knew I could still smell ur-gold.'

'I had originally intended to leave you both to die with your kin on the other side of the Burning Gate, but I underestimated Old World duardin tenacity. You took quite the toll on my brothers of the Seeing Legion there.'

'You're with the Legion?' Broddur asked.

Uthan laughed. 'I *am* the Seeing Legion.'

'And this Grey Lord the skaven spoke of?' Broddur asked.

'I know his true name, but even my esteem in the schemes of the Changer is not so great to have ever seen him in person. But he knows you, Gotrek Gurnisson. He knows you. And when he learned of your existence after your battle with my brother at the Burning Gate, my understanding is that he became quite... animated.' Uthan hissed, pulling up in pain. His hand went to his shoulder as his aethereal nurses made soothing noises around him. The rune went back inside his robes. 'But no matter. You have been true to your oath, Gotrek, son of Gurni.'

Gotrek looked positively incandescent. '*I've* been true to *my* oath?'

'You protected me from the Khainite and in exchange I have led you to the Hammerhal Gate. Each of our promises has been fulfilled to the letter. Never let it be said that a servant of the Changer is not always true to the word, if not the spirit, of his agreements. Go into your afterlife unburdened by shame and with the gratitude of the Eye Not Seen.'

'Get back down here onto this boat, liche, or Grimnir help me, I will throw this storysmith up there to get you!'

'What use is a Fyreslayer rune to you anyway?' Broddur yelled.

'It is of no matter to you now, is it? And with both the Shadowblade and the skaven dealt with, thanks to you, there is no one else left to interfere.' The necromancer turned fully to Okaenos, an insect hovering before the head of a godbeast. 'See me, Okaenos,' he called, making his voice boom, 'I who have summoned you. Traitor and apostate, am I. Spite your master one more time, as I would.'

The godbeast rumbled as it turned its great head towards the necromancer, its eye sockets flickering with restless intellect and malice. Its colossal jaws opened. Fire lit up the hollows of its neck, racing upwards vertebra by vertebra, to erupt from its maw like magma from a volcano.

Uthan Barrowwalker was consumed in it utterly.

His robes were blasted from amethyst to an iridescent admixture of pinks and blues, and then he was gone, ash, outlived by a few seconds by his own final, hysterical screams. His cremated remains hung in the air for a moment before Okaenos sucked them back in, its heavy jaws snapping over them like an avalanche.

Broddur stared, awestruck by what he had just witnessed.

'*Dreng Tromm!*'

'Still better than walking, I suppose,' said Gotrek.

The godbeast slapped back into the fjord, a titanic wave tossing the longboat aside like so much driftwood. Broddur grabbed hold of the gunwale as the world picked him up, spun him round, and dumped him back into the water.

'We have to turn back,' he bellowed, salt water spraying from his mouth. 'We can find another gate to Aqshy. We can–' He turned around. His words failed him.

The oarsmen were gone. The boat was empty save for himself and Gotrek.

'*Skrat,*' he swore.

They were stranded.

Gotrek, meanwhile, had mounted the bowsprit and was brandishing his greataxe furiously at the half-submerged godbeast. 'If there's one thing I'll say about these worlds, storysmith, it's that you do things big. When you make a monster, you make a *monster.*'

The boat rocked wildly as Okaenos' head erupted from the waves once again. It was some way behind them now, its neck so long that it had managed to encircle the boat entirely. Broddur looked up as it rose, water streaming through the cavernous ridges in its neck and the hollows in its skull.

'Don't make me get in there with you, godbeast,' said Gotrek. 'The water puts me in a foul mood.'

Okaenos opened its mouth, flames rippling.

Broddur sprinted across the deck to the bowsprit and slammed into Gotrek's back, throwing them both overboard and into the sea. There was a muffled explosion as Okaenos' breath annihilated the boat, the water above them roiling with orange petals.

Bubbles streamed from Broddur's mouth as he clamped down on the urge to cry out, and kicked for the surface.

He emerged with a gasp and a splutter of swallowed water. The Amethyst Fjords had been transformed into a vista from the

Flamescar Plateau. The water was burning, bits of wood and strips of canvas strewn across the trembling waves and turning the sky umber. Keeping a firm hold on the icon of Grimnir, he splashed around and yelled for the Slayer.

'You'll answer for that… storysmith. Didn't I just say that I… hated the water.'

Clinging to a piece of floating debris, the Doomseeker too appeared to be in one piece. His axe, Zangrom-Thaz, was underwater in his hand. The Unbaki forgefire between the two crescent-shaped rune-blades still burned there, bubbling the water around him as though he was drowning in a thermal spring.

With the natural grace of a Fyreslayer in water, Broddur paddled towards the Slayer.

'This would be… quite the doom… storysmith,' said Gotrek, the waves force-feeding him great gulps of seawater every time he opened his mouth to speak. 'But I'll not… accept it. Not while… other oaths… stand within my… grasp.'

'It's a godbeast, Gotrek. Such a creature slew Grimnir. Another, Drakatoa, entombed the greenskins' god, Gorkamorka, for an age until Sigmar dug him free. Behemat. Dracothion. Argentine.' Broddur shook his head violently. 'Such titans aren't for the blades of mortals.'

The Doomseeker regarded him scathingly. 'And you call yourself an heir to Grimnir? Any proper Slayer should leap at such a chance.'

Broddur felt his fires stoked by the Slayer's words and knew that they were true. Grimnir was Warrior and Wanderer, Oath-maker and Gold-Giver. He was not Builder or Maker nor even Chronicler, for such were his brother Grungni's interests.

'I *am* a descendent of the Shattered God. His might is here in the gold in my flesh. Aye! You're right, Gotrek. Aye! Let's fight this beast and die with a god's glory. Khazuk!'

The vast expanse of water immediately before their bobbing raft seethed as Okaenos' head broke the surface. It was indescribably huge up close, like watching a fortress rise up off its foundations.

'WHO. DARES?'

Its voice was a calamity, carving a bowl-shaped depression the size of a mustering hall out of the waves and briefly driving Broddur's head back underwater. Paddling and spluttering, Broddur struggled to keep his head above the swell. Fighting the godbeast felt suddenly very far from the forefront of his mind. He had expected Okaenos to be a thing of pure elementalism akin to Ignimbris or Drakatoa, or a passionless husk like any of the other creatures that could be found roaming the endless wastelands of Shyish. He had not been expecting it to speak. Suddenly, something that Uthan had said to the beast before it had consumed him sprung into his mind.

'I bloody dare, that's who!' Gotrek had let go of his plank and was treading water in order to wave his axe under the beast's colossal snout. 'My axe thirsts, and like any proper dwarf she doesn't care for water.'

'Wait, Gotrek. *Wait.* What was it that Snorri said to you last night? About Nagash?'

The Slayer glared at him, still kicking at the water. 'What was that?' His expression turned furious. 'Betrayal raised atop betrayal! You followed me. Is there naught in this world but elves and oathbreakers?'

'Never mind that now. Nagash wants all of our souls, but yours especially. Uthan told me as much himself. Well, Okaenos is no mindless puppet. He despises Nagash. Uthan as good as told us that too, that's how he knew he could use this realmgate to reach Hammerhal. The godbeast *wants* a reason to spite the Undying King, Gotrek. Give him one. My own death I could endure, Doomseeker, but not yours. Not until you discover why you returned to us.'

Gotrek scowled up at the godbeast and for the longest time, Broddur thought stubbornness and pride were going to win out and condemn them both to a fiery end and an eternity in the Amethyst Fjords. Then he raised his axe above the water.

'I am Gotrek, son of Gurni.' He spat into the water. 'And that's about as much as I care for you, your master, and all his so-called works in this world and in the last.' He shouted louder as he shook the water off his axe. 'Now come. Taste. My. Axe!'

Broddur looked on in horror as Okaenos unlocked its mighty jaws, teeth sliding over teeth, breath igniting in the bottomless depths of its gullet.

'Aye, that's right. This dwarf will ask no favours of you.'

'You couldn't have fed the flames just a little?' said Broddur, in disbelief. 'Lied?'

Gotrek chuckled. 'A godbeast like this one may have cowed Grimnir, but it'll take something bigger than this to make Gotrek Gurnisson beg.'

'Grimnir is mighty!' Broddur wailed as an apocalyptic blast of flame devoured them both.

PART FOUR

Blood and Gold

NINETEEN

'Felix! Oi you, are you Felix? No? Felix?'

The Doomseeker staggered along the miles-high red-stone wall of Hammerhal Aqsha, ale sloshing over the rim of his tankard. The wind was fierce and scented with ash and brimstone. Hordes of archers and spearmen frequently clattered by, striking up cinders with their boots, and Broddur hurried along behind Gotrek to make sure he didn't fall.

'You there!' Gotrek challenged a frightened-looking soldier in a kettle helm and an overlarge breastplate emblazoned with a fiery sun. 'I'm looking for a manling called Felix!'

'Perhaps you ought to step away from the edge, Gotrek.'

'And why should I? Seems like a perfectly good place for a Slayer to be. All the Chaos beasties he could wish for. Good stone underfoot.' The ramparts appeared in front of him, apparently unexpectedly, because he cursed as the last dregs of his beer went over the edge. He looked down, drawing a deep breath of the rising smoke. 'Aye.' He patted the flame-hued sandstone companionably. 'This all reminds me of the Siege of Praag. Except for the fire moat, of course, and those wandering castles, I suppose. Pah!' He belched loudly. 'Cogforts. Makaisson would've had a fit. Did you ever hear of such a thing, storysmith?'

'Actually, I–'

'You hear that, you lot?' Gotrek roared, leaning dangerously over the side. Broddur rushed to grab him by the waist. 'Gotrek Gurnisson stands on this wall. He fought the armies of Arek Daemonclaw, and then did the whole thing all over again for the armies of Aekold Helbrass when the old city finally fell.' Under Broddur's urging, he came back over the battlements, lowering his voice and becoming bitter as though feeling his long-awaited death slipping further away once again. 'And guess who's still bloody here.' He thumped miserably on his chest. 'That's right. *This* Slayer.'

Broddur rolled his eyes as Gotrek shrugged him off and tottered off along the wall yelling for 'Felix' some more. Of all the ways he had imagined spending his first night in the fabled Hammerhal with the Avatar of Grimnir, it was fair to say that this had not been among them. Incinerated by the godbeast Okaenos in the Realm of Death. Turned to ash. Drawn into the titan's throat and through to the realmgate in its gullet to be disgorged, horribly singed but somehow still alive, into the warren of dungeons that crawled beneath the foundation fires of Hammerhal Aqsha. The traitor and thief Uthan Barrowwalker long gone.

The creature-infested labyrinths and the near-limitless killing opportunities they represented had done little to assuage Gotrek's black mood. After several fruitless days on the necromancer's trail they had exited the catacombs into the cellar of an alehouse in the notorious Cinderfall District.

It had all gone rather precipitously downhill from there.

'Let's go back to that tavern you liked,' he suggested.

'There is nothing that I like here, storysmith. It is naught but the abode of elves and lies.'

Broddur left the Doomseeker to stumble on as he paused to look out. Smoke from burning siege towers and relentless cannon fire hazed the view. Ash and cinders blew across the walls like clouds over the shoulder of a mountain, buzzing against the Azyrite wards that studded the artificial cliff. Far below at the very bottom, a moat of living fire hissed and roared, carving the Flamescar Plateau between the combined hordes of Chaos *there* and the alliance of Sigmar *here*. Even from the battlements, Broddur could feel the heat from below. Even speaking as a proud Fyreslayer he wouldn't want to be the Chaos warrior having to charge across that.

'You there, the big one. You're one of those *Storm Cast Eternals* aren't you? Hey, storysmith, which side's the front?'

Broddur practically swallowed his tongue as he spun around to find Gotrek Gurnisson approaching a giant in sapphire-blue-and-gold plate armour. It was not true gold, of course, but the godly facsimile, sigmarite, but the way it shone set Broddur's pulse racing nevertheless. The champion's face was masked, haloed in yet more gold and with a crimson plume. The snarling face and mane of a lion extended the forehead upwards and merged with the sigmarite ring of his halo. The emblems of thunderbolt and hammer shone from his pauldrons and shield. The warrior of Sigmar looked up from his post at the wall.

'Are you addressing me, duardin? If so I would warn you to mind your tone. This is Sigmar's wall, and I ward it in his stead.'

Gotrek was clearly even drunker than Broddur had realised, for he ignored the Stormcast Eternal completely. He rapped on the warrior's breastplate as though he was knocking at a door.

'Felix? Are you in there?'

The golden mask was gloriously impassive, but the warrior seemed nonplussed. 'My name is Kyukain Hammer-Friend, Liberator Prime of the Flamescar Lions Chamber of the Hammers of Sigmar. I know of no Felix.'

'Please, Doomseeker, I'm *begging* you,' said Broddur, hanging well back. 'Leave the Stormcast be. You don't want that kind of trouble.'

'Lying wizards,' Gotrek muttered. 'Daemon dwarfs. Thieving elves. Gods that aren't. You're in there, manling, and I'm getting you out!' He dropped his greataxe, which Broddur took to be a good sign until the Doomseeker then grabbed the lip of Kyukain's shield and hauled the warrior in towards him. The Stormcast Eternal grunted in surprise, drawing back his hammer on instinct, but Gotrek already had fingers over the thick V-shaped gorget that projected from his armour between helmet and breastplate and was yanking him down to duardin height.

'Gotrek, what are you *doing*?'

'Enough!' Kyukain roared, cracking Gotrek's shoulder plate with the flat of his hammer. It made a solid *clang* as though he had just whacked an anvil. A spasm of lightning sprang from the struck plate to leap along the crenellations and zap Broddur's fingers. He recoiled with a bark. Gotrek appeared to shrug it off.

'This armour's come in handier than I'd thought it would,' said Gotrek. 'Should've worn some back in the day.'

'Whether you are intoxicated or simply driven to madness by the hosts of the Grey Lord, this ends now,' said Kyukain.

'Curse it, Doomseeker.' Broddur tugged on his belt as he charged in to the Slayer's aid, jingling his keys and gold and drawing his axe. 'Didn't I say you were asking for more trouble than you could want?'

The Stormcast Eternal struck Broddur with a backhanded swing that shattered his nose and beat him sideways into the battlements. He groaned, half-dazed, as he felt himself slide down the wall. A second blow struck him in the elbow.

'Arrgh!' he screamed.

The Liberator towered over him like an angry cloud, his face an implacable mask of golden sigmarite. Broddur waved his axe groggily and let it drop from his jangling fingers.

With a roar, the Doomseeker leapt on Kyukain from behind and dragged him back. Lightning arced through the Stormcast Eternal's straining armour as somehow, impossibly, the Doomseeker grappled the champion of Sigmar down to his knees.

'You are just a duardin,' Kyukain groaned. 'How are you this strong?'

'*Just* a dwarf? *Just?* Manling, what have they done to you?'

Holding the struggling Stormcast Eternal in a headlock, the Doomseeker forced the fingers of one hand through the eyeholes of Kyukain's golden helmet and pulled.

'Haha!' Gotrek yelled. 'I've found you, manling, I...'

The Stormcast Eternal's helmet dropped to the wall with a clang. Kyukain Hammer-Friend looked back at the Doomseeker with eyes that burned with the cosmic fires of Azyr. His skin was the colour of coal. His cheekbones were high, his brow flat, his chin strong. The hair that fell down his back was long and black and worn in thick braids, but with an actinic blue sheen as though every strand was a conduit for cosmic energies that Broddur could not fathom. Everything was too hard, too perfect. Some power innate to the warrior's mere existence made Broddur's beard kindle, the hairs standing on end.

'You're not... Manling?' Gotrek stumbled backwards and fell drunkenly to the walkway as the Stormcast Eternal picked up his discarded helmet and stood. 'Jordain. On my oath, you live.'

'Felix? Jordain?' The Stormcast Eternal shook his head. 'How many names do you mean to bestow upon me? I am Kyukain Hammer-Friend, of the Flamescar Lions.'

'Kyukain. Aye, I believe I know that name. You are Jordain's ancestor, the hero that founded Edassa a century ago? You are the bloody mirror of your thrice-great-grandson, you know.'

Broddur saw some internal struggle going on behind Kyukain's otherwise flawless countenance.

'Edassa?' The storm within him quelled, if only for a moment, as he searched his mind for a clue as to the emotions he appeared to be feeling. 'I have no memory of that place. I have… no memory of descendants.'

Gotrek frowned up at him. 'Nothing at all?'

'It is a small burden, too petty to complain over when held against the strength that Sigmar gives us to bear it.'

Gotrek turned away, his expression stubbornly hidden. 'Nothing at all…'

'Well, isn't this pleasing on the senses – pain, heartache… No really, do not stop for me.'

The voice had come from the battlements behind them.

Kyukain looked over, Gotrek's efforts at pulling his helmet from his head imparting a noticeable squeal to the movement of his shoulders. The aelf woman walking towards them was dressed entirely in black. A metal bodice enclosed her torso. Leather plates edged with ithilmar steel, each one sharpened like a blade, clad her forearms and thighs. A silk mask covered her nose and mouth, only her eyes left showing. A cloak of black silk rippled out behind her with the wind.

Broddur knew those eyes.

'Dark elf!' Gotrek spluttered, trying to stand back up, but managing only to grab a hold of Kyukain's leg.

'Maleneth?' said Broddur. 'You look… different.'

'Well, I would not be much of an assassin if I simply turned up outside your lodge looking like one, would I?'

Gotrek redoubled his efforts to climb up Kyukain's leg. 'Unhand me, Stormcast,' he growled, holding on tight. 'Can you not see there's a Darkling elf behind you?'

'Show the respect due to an agent of the Order of Azyr,' said Kyukain.

Broddur frowned. 'Order of... What, *her?*'

Maleneth turned her collar inside out to reveal the emblem pinned into the armoured lining. It was a twin-tailed comet. 'If I had tried to tell you before, would you have believed me? I did not have Kyukain Hammer-Friend and a city full of Stormcast Eternals to vouch for my claim when I was languishing in your dungeon. Hopefully even you two can see now that I am not your enemy.'

'You're a dark elf,' Gotrek repeated.

'*And* you violated the magma-vaults of the Unbaki!' Broddur said.

'I covered it with *dark elf*, storysmith. Anything more is mere dressing.'

The assassin glanced across to Broddur, then back to the Slayer, who was still grappling Kyukain Hammer-Friend's thigh. She shook her head pityingly.

'You assume a great deal, Gotrek, for a duardin who has walked out of the Realms of Chaos from a lost time. We were both their prisoner in Karag Unbak. I asked for your help then, don't you remember?'

Broddur remembered. He had been part of the fyrd that had first found the Doomseeker on the Caldur Bridge, addled and wandering unarmed over the lava sea of Karag Unbak. Gotrek had mistaken Broddur for a daemon and it had had taken Rune-son Forn's entire Auric Hearthguard to subdue him and drag him to the Hall of Censure.

'Aye, you did,' Gotrek conceded. 'But it's better to cut your own throat than hand the knife to an elf. Who could say what *they'd* think to do with it.'

'Is no one going to ask me why the order wants Blackhammer's Master Rune?'

'No,' said Gotrek.

Maleneth sighed. 'The Unbak lodge are yet to declare for Sigmar in this latest war, and they have sided too often with Chaos to be trusted with such a weapon.'

Gotrek gave a harsh bellow of laughter. 'Pull the other one, elf. Left in this world may well be right, dwarfs may live in the sky and elves in the heavens, but *this* you can keep in your vault and hold sacred forever – no dwarf would take his coin from Chaos filth.'

Maleneth turned to Broddur. A smile pulled on her silk mask, her eyes gleaming like amethysts. 'Is that so, Broddur? Would a duardin really never pledge his axe to the Ruinous Powers in exchange for their gold?'

Broddur crossed his arms and huffed dismissively. 'It's not about picking sides if that's what you're angling at. It's about taking ur-gold from those as have ur-gold and doing proper honour to Grimnir. If Sigmar wants the aid of the lodges, then he knows how to get it, and I suspect he can damn well afford it.'

Gotrek's face had turned the colour of lava. 'Honour to Grimnir? Honour to… Hah! Here, elf, take my axe. Better to die now with the disgrace of being on my knees before an elf than live in a world that holds such dwarfs as I see now.'

Broddur hurried to Gotrek's side. The Slayer misunderstood. He had had the truth twisted by the cunning words of a Darkling aelf. He had to explain. The Fyreslayers did not pick sides. They fought only to restore the lost might of their Shattered God. And who could better convince him of the truth than a battlesmith of the Unbak? He squatted down beside him, ready to explain, but Gotrek ignored him. He turned instead to Maleneth.

'What do you want from me, elf? Since you've not yet stabbed me in the back in the traditional elvish manner of greeting, I take it you want something.'

'Your help finding the Eye Not Seen, of course. He is loose behind the walls of Hammerhal, and with a terrible weapon at his command.'

'We looked,' said Broddur, staring disconsolately at Gotrek, who refused to meet his eye. 'After being sucked down Okaenos' throat and through the realmgate we found ourselves in the labyrinths beneath the city.'

'A lot of creatures down there,' Gotrek muttered. 'I liked it. Reminded me of Karak Eight-Peaks.'

'There's a thousand ways a necromancer could lose himself down there.'

'So we got drunk instead.'

'You travelled with him for days,' said Maleneth. 'He let nothing slip? No hint of his plans? What the rune he stole might actually do?'

Broddur felt the eyes of all turn towards him and he shrugged. He felt angry and betrayed. He wanted nothing other than to throw the witch aelf over the battlements and be rid of her, but he thought that this might actually make things look worse in the Slayer's eyes so he fought the impulse down.

'It does nothing. Until beaten into a Fyreslayer's living flesh it is naught but metal.'

'Even for a duardin, you are thick-headed,' said Maleneth. 'I held it briefly in my own hand. I know its power. The Eye Not Seen would not have carried it across two realms and aligned his cause with allies as untrustworthy as the skaven if he did not have a means to use it.'

Horns cried from the killing grounds below, and Kyukain Hammer-Friend left them for a moment to look over the walls. Broddur tore his gaze from Gotrek and Maleneth to see what had drawn his attention. The horizon wobbled like a heat haze over a lava sea, but Broddur's eyes were well adapted to heat and he easily picked out the ant-like swarm of soldiers running towards the nearest gatehouse. *Ash Hammer Gate,* he thought, recalling his drunken ramblings through the district with Gotrek. His immediate instinct was to dismiss it as yet another assault. Hammerhal was vast, sprawling across several continents and through the Stormrift Gate into the realm of Ghyran. It had a hundred gates, a dozen of which seemed to be under concerted assault at any given time. But something here was different. Their commanders were screaming up at the garrison, blasting furiously on their trumpets and waving their banners at the walls. Broddur noted the heraldry on the flags.

A black lion rampant on a red field.

'It is not an assault, my lady,' said Kyukain, after an unhurried moment of consideration. 'It is a regiment from one of the free cities beyond the Charwood. Someone has made it through.'

Gotrek shoved Broddur roughly aside and glared down. 'That banner they fly. It looks passingly familiar.'

'It is the exact same motif as the armour plate on your shoulder, you witless oaf,' said Maleneth. 'Were you always this observant or was it your better eye that you left behind in Shyish?'

'I still have one eye, elfling. Were I to cut out your tongue then I doubt you'd be talking half as well as I now see.'

'It is no wonder that the Eye Not Seen was able to fool you for as long as he did.'

'A black lion rampant on a red field...' Kyukain mused.

'You remember it?' Gotrek asked hopefully.

Kyukain paused. 'No.'

Gotrek looked disappointed.

'It's Jordain's Edassans,' said Broddur. 'Barrowalker was honest about one thing, at least. Time did pass more slowly in Shyish. We got here ahead of them.'

Horns blasted from the Ash Hammer Gate and the gates began to grind apart.

'I think I might be drunk,' said Gotrek.

'You do, do you?' said Broddur.

'I see flying Stormcasts.'

'Prosecutors,' said Broddur.

As they watched, Stormcast Eternals in gold and silver and glittering jade flung themselves from the cliff-like walls, spreading wings of power to hurl themselves towards the Chaos hosts like leaves on an autumn gale. Javelins of bound lightning blasted into the warriors' grips and then the storm descended, lightning bolts blitzing the enemy warriors and casting the charred armour and bones of the survivors to the wind.

'The warriors in gold and silver are of my own Stormhost, the Hammers of Sigmar,' said Kyukain, pointing to the skies. 'Those in jade are the Emerald Wardens, from Hammerhal Ghyra. Hammerhal Aqsha is garrisoned by two dozen chambers, and many hundreds of Freeguild regiments.'

'Tell me, duardin,' said Maleneth, urgently, 'what have the Edassans to do with the Eye Not Seen?'

'You don't know? Where were those oh-so-sharp elf eyes on the Great Ash Road? Or at Twinfire?'

'They're imposters,' said Broddur.

'What?' said Maleneth. She looked genuinely alarmed by the prospect.

'Silence, Chaos-lover,' said Gotrek. 'Tell her nothing. The dark elf clearly needs no help from us and I've other things to be about. Two dozen chambers of Stormcast Eternals sounds like a lot of Stormcast Eternals. Felix is here somewhere, I know it.'

'And what if he is?' Broddur yelled back, quite ready to lose patience with the Doomseeker and his mood swings and his *judgement*. 'Hammerhal Aqsha is huge. It has a hundred gates spread across an entire continent. And that's without even considering Hammerhal Ghyra beyond the Stormrift Gate.'

'What do you intend to do, Slayer?' Maleneth added. 'Line them up and take off their helmets one by one?'

Gotrek gave a threatening growl. The Doomseeker was being

drunk and unreasonable and he knew it, but he was never going to admit that or compromise.

'And what then, duardin?' Kyukain asked softly. 'If you did find him, what then?'

Gotrek thought for a long while, and then sighed. To Broddur's surprise, he backed down.

'I suppose there are newer oaths that can be honoured first. I did swear to Jordain that I would avenge him on his traitorous cousin.'

'Don't forget that thieving swine Barrowwalker,' said Broddur.

'And the Grey Lord.' Gotrek chuckled blackly. He seemed to have come back to his usual, violent self. He had entirely forgotten to insult Broddur or Maleneth as he stroked the rim of his blade with his callused hands. 'I owe him a long-overdue reckoning from the days of old.'

Maleneth extended a hand to each of them. 'Help me to kill them all,' she said.

'Very well, dark elf, since you put it like that. Let's get down there.'

He did not, Broddur noted, come anywhere close to shaking her hand.

TWENTY

Adjusting the golden mask that the Edassan Lioness from whom she had borrowed it no longer had a use for, Maleneth stepped into the flow of soldiers.

Upwards of a thousand blood-drenched and desperate fighters were forcing their way through the barbican of Ash Hammer Gate into the safety of the courtyard. Their cries echoed sweetly through the tunnel, steel scraping on steel and clanging on the red stone. Paladins in the verdant heraldry of the Emerald Wardens strode imperiously against the flow, as if against a crimson-and-black river, determined to be amongst the Chaos forces on the other side of the tunnel.

It seemed to Maleneth like an awful lot of pain and effort for the sake of getting a few hundred soldiers into a city of millions. Not that Maleneth was averse to pain and effort, providing it was other people's, but this was excessive. Why? What did the Eye Not Seen have planned for the Edassans?

Seeing the carnage spilling across the courtyard from the gate,

Maleneth wondered if this had been the traitor Barrowalker's plan all along: to simply seize a gate through which his forces could enter. Maleneth dismissed it at once. It was too simple. The minions of Tzeentch and the skaven both delighted in complexity. To them, the merits of a scheme could be judged by the insane number of its convolutions. This one hardly justified the crossing of realms and the theft of an Unbak rune. And Hammerhal was huge. A dozen gates would have to fall at once for the city as a whole to be remotely compromised. *That* would have been a more appropriately intricate scheme, but Maleneth had seen no signs of attacks at other gates.

No, whatever the Fatemaster had in mind for his Edassan imposters and the Master Rune it would be grander in scope.

Ensuring that her mistress' pendant was tucked under her lion-skin cloak, she altered her gait to that of a cloddish human warrior with too much armour and an inelegant sword and ventured into the carnage. Where she walked, Edassans found themselves mysteriously tripped as they tried to flee, or nudged into the path of axes swung by screaming Bloodreavers. She thanked Sigmar for being so generous when it came to doing Khaine's work, but otherwise she kept to the role she had made for herself. She was an Edassan Lioness with an important message for her general. But humans *were* clumsy.

She found her mark almost immediately. He was holding the barbican with a small knot of well-armoured bodyguards while the last of his soldiers streamed through. He was wearing a thin circlet of gold around his short, greying hair. There was a black lion stitched into his red cloak.

Mimicking the Edassan battle cry, hardly the most sophisticated of disguises given that it amounted to opening one's mouth and yelling loudly, Maleneth pirouetted through the melee and thrust her Lioness greatsword into the neck of a Chaos warrior. He had been about to bludgeon the Edassan general into paste with a flail comprised of sixteen spiked and flaming skulls. The tainted blood that came gurgling down the fuller of her borrowed weapon did its clumsy appearance no harm at all.

'My gratitude…' The general took a moment to study her, trying to ascertain whether she really was the elite Edassan warrioress that she appeared or just another imposter in a mask. 'Lioness,' he finished. 'But you should not be here. I ordered everyone back from the gate.'

'I bear a message from the Eye Not Seen, Manezomo Osayande. He awaits us. He is impatient to reveal his designs.'

'As am I,' said Osayande. 'The Grey Lord's armies push harder than I had thought they would. We are supposed to be on the same side.'

'A necessary deception,' said Maleneth, improvising quickly.

She was almost enjoying herself.

'Is it truly beyond the Fatemaster's guile to have them hold back a little? We are the ones who are going to break open this city, not these rabid berserkers.'

Maleneth would have liked to allow the Edassan to talk for longer, but prying out his secrets was currently of lesser import than following him to his master. There would be time for that later.

'He would have you join him in the agreed-upon place,' she said.

Osayande gave her another long, probing look.

Lightning flashed from the far end of the barbican as the Emerald Wardens took the fight to the pursuing forces of Chaos. The tunnel became a strobing zoetrope of electrocuted daemons and flailing, inhuman skeletons. The stink of fulgurised mutant flesh breathed back through the tunnel. The Edassan soldiers around Osayande looked as though they wanted to vomit. The general himself merely frowned.

'As you say, Lioness,' he said, sheathing his sword and allowing his relieved bodyguards to usher him away from the fighting. 'Let us go and put an end to the war that Sigmar has brought upon the Flamescar Plateau. Once and for all.'

The bloodied and wearied column of Edassan soldiers – or whatever it was they were supposed to be under their disguises – trooped through the ever-narrowing streets of the Ashlands District. The residences were abandoned, the shopfronts boarded over. The occasional crater in the rows of tenements told why. The evidence of fire and artillery and Chaotic magic was everywhere Broddur looked.

'Running *away* from the battle of a lifetime, chasing a band of Tzeentchian turncoats on the off-chance of finding a liche-in-hiding, all on the lying say-so of an elf,' Gotrek muttered to himself as they jogged after them, complaining as usual. 'There are days when I miss the Realm of Chaos.'

The district was crowded in spite of everything. Lean-tos played host to temporary stalls doing a brisk trade from the masses of scavengers, salvagers and soldiers. Urchins and vagrants and men too badly injured to stand on a wall with a spear fought over the best spots to beg. Priests and priestesses of Sigmar and Alarielle and countless other faiths, greater and lesser, chanted over the ruins, seeking the protection of gods that, as far as Broddur could tell, had left them to their own devices long ago. Freeguild infantry packed every road, swarming around their horses and wagons and sedan-borne generals and monstrous Ironweld engines that trundled through the crowds under their own steam. Thousands of soldiers marched on Ash Hammer Gate at any given time. Thousands more marched the other way, relieved or redeployed, piling up in long, frustrated columns of men and beasts and war machines as the lords of Hammerhal moved their pieces between the innumerable barracks and billets and garrison forts contained within this one district alone.

A thousand times a thousand mortal soldiers held the Twin-Tailed City for their God-King. The Edassans were quickly disappearing into the mass.

'Would you look at all these people, Doomseeker. I've never seen so many in one place.'

Gotrek didn't answer.

Realising that he had been walking the last few hundred paces alone, Broddur glanced back. The Doomseeker was some way behind, peering hard at a priestess in white-and-blue robes with a tall mitre and crescent moon staff, bedecked with the symbols of Hysh.

'I think I've just discovered what's gone wrong in this world,' said Gotrek.

Broddur hurried back to look for himself.

He did not see anything in particular that stood out. Just a priestess tending a small maze of succulent greenery and a modest marble shrine to Teclis, God of Light. Gotrek did not seem to be in the mood to elaborate.

With a scowl, he left the Hyshite shrine behind. 'Come on, Gotrek. We'd better hurry.'

'I have eyes, storysmith. I have *an* eye.'

'Have it your way, but they're getting away.'

'Maybe that's what you and your dark patrons want me to think.'

Broddur swore under his breath, but at least the Doomseeker was moving again.

Gotrek had been in a particularly sour mood since their run-in with Maleneth and the Hammers of Sigmar. He did not think it was the beating, nor even his belated education into the mercenary leanings of the Fyreslayer lodges. It was something that Kyukain had done or said. Or rather, something that Gotrek had hoped to find in him and failed to. He tried to put it from his mind and concentrate on the task of retrieving the Unbak Master Rune and saving Sigmar's city. The Doomseeker was as prone to inescapable depressions as he was to blind rages. This would pass, Broddur knew, and Gotrek would be furious about something – and someone – else soon enough.

'Stop lagging, Chaos worshipper! I'm not about to lose the Edassans and let the dark elf accuse me of tardiness just because you're fat and slow.'

Broddur jangled a few seconds behind the Slayer's determined trot. 'I'm no Slave to Darkness and I wish you'd stop saying it.'

'Tell me that every word out of the elfling's mouth was a lie. Swear it on your oath and I'll believe it over the poison of a dark elf's tongue any day.'

'On my oath?' Broddur sighed and shook his head. 'I can't. There's no love spared between Sigmar and the Fyreslayer lodges, I'll not deny. It's no secret. Sigmar could've fought Vulcatrix himself, but no, not high and mighty Sigmar. He bade Grimnir go in his place. We don't resent the Man-God that. Grimnir was indebted, and Sigmar entitled to name his price, but if he expects the same devotion from us as from the warriors he forged with his own thunder, then he's more a fool than Grungni.' Broddur thumped his bare chest, jangling the various keychains and bracelets he wore about him. 'Blood and gold, we say, and it's blood and gold we fight for. The kin of our lodge and the remnants of our Shattered God. Why should we care where it comes from?'

'I'll kill this Osayande and his band of oathbreakers because I swore I would. I'll kill the liche because he wronged me. Oaths and vengeance, storysmith. That's all that really endures in the end.'

Broddur bowed his head as they ran. 'Maybe I was wrong... If you can't understand, then maybe you're not Grimnir after all.'

'If Grimnir were here then he'd disappoint you no less than I. Don't fool yourself on that.'

Rather than answer, because he could think of nothing more that needed to be said, Broddur focused on the Edassans ahead. If nothing else, there was still the Master Rune to be reclaimed. The regiment appeared to have become mired at a crossroads. A company of Anvilgard heavy cavalry, arrogant-looking aelves in thick black plate mounted on hissing drakespawn, had been moving in the opposite direction at the same time as an impatient convoy of men and duardin had been trying to lead their armoured wains across. He and Gotrek had gained on them a little.

Without turning, he waved for Gotrek to slow down.

'Don't flap that hand at me. Not if you want to keep it, and pass those rings on to your descendants.'

'Someone up there might recognise us from the Great Ash Road, or even the fight for the Burning Gate. We shouldn't get too close.'

'Hurry up. Slow down. Bah! Let's just have them now and be done with it. How many of them are there anyway? Five hundred? Six? Barely enough to work up a thirst.'

'And give Barrowalker the chance to escape?'

'I hate it when you talk sense, storysmith. Fine. We'll do it the dark elf's way.' He made a face, as though he had unwittingly taken a mouthful of some poor grot's shroom lager. 'I can't believe those words came from my lips.'

Gotrek grumbled on a bit more but made no further argument.

Broddur had known Fyreslayers who could hold a grudge. Skorun Firebrand had been able to recall his former apprentice's every misplaced nick in every bead-book, but the Slayer had turned the notion into his personal and inviolable code. Broddur would gladly put an axe in Uthan Barrowalker and his kin for what the necromancer had put him through, but he had no doubt that Gotrek would put himself through fire and misery and walk barefoot to Realm's Edge and back to have his satisfaction.

His ways were strange and no mistake. They weren't Broddur's ways.

A sudden change in the air called him back from his reverie. A burnt acid stench tickled his nostril hairs. A scratching, grinding ghost of a sound whispered from just the other side of the wind. It was a sound and a smell that Broddur had encountered before. In the Unbak Khaz of Karag Unbak.

Gotrek sniffed the air, then scowled. 'I know that smell.'

'Skaven!'

Even as Broddur yelled the warning, explosions of poisonous gas were going off amidst the packed blocks of men. He saw one dirty glass orb come tumbling through a savage tear in the air and shatter under the Anvilgard regiment. Thick yellow-green clouds of poison gas billowed across the road. Huge, reptilian drakespawn gasped as their lungs filled with acid, crushing the heavily armoured aelven knights underneath them as they fell, sparing their riders the same cruel death at least. Goggled ratmen wielding spinning mechanical grinders leapt into the street through those same rips in the air. Scores and scores of skaven warriors came pouring after them, squealing excitedly, even as the poisonous fog began to clear.

Broddur saw a few companies forming up, offering resistance, but most simply broke. The skaven chittered mercilessly as they chased them down, every man they slew adding to their confidence and their glee.

'Don't forget this dwarf, vermin! I've supped already this day, but my axe has not!'

The Doomseeker charged towards a pack of skaven Stormvermin that had, until then, been enthusiastically butchering the remnants of a Hammerhal Ghyra skirmish infantry regiment.

Their enthusiasm over facing the Slayer was noticeably lesser.

His firestorm greataxe, Zangrom-Thaz, hacked off a skaven arm and torched the stump. The skaven squealed in panic as Gotrek shouldered it to the ground. He looped his axe around in a series of flaming figure-of-eights, sent a Stormvermin scurrying away minus one leg below the knee, gutted another and immolated its insides. Barbecued entrails piled up about his feet and still he killed. A sword nicked his bicep, driven more in terror than aggression. Its former wielder practically threw it at Gotrek as, squealing in terror, it turned tail and fled.

'What's this?' the Doomseeker yelled after them. 'You'll fight a band of half-dead manling soldiers wearing flowers, but not one dwarf!' A gasping Ghyranite officer tried to thank him, but Gotrek shrugged him off with a scowl. 'More! Bring me more!'

Strange and no mistake, Broddur thought, quickly taking in the anarchy that had descended over the crossroads.

Thousands of skaven had already emerged from their realm-burrows and more were pouring into the city all the time. A block of duardin longbeards and a couple of human handgunners held the wreckage of an artillery wain over at one corner of the crossroads. The broken remnants of the Anvilgard cavalry loped stubbornly away from the fray, the Drakespawn Knights flatten-ing those skaven foolish enough to come between them and safety. A motley assortment of choking Freeguild infantry and dazed Ironweld engineers fought to escape the slaughter in their wake. Everywhere else, skaven ran rampant, congregating over the bodies of the dead like crows.

Broddur recognised the drab russet colours and unique glyphs that the skaven warriors wore. It was Clan Boil. The same vermin who had defiled the magma-vaults of Karag Unbak, stolen the greatest work of the lodge's mightiest living runemaster, and conspired with Uthan Barrowwalker to kill him and Gotrek in Shyish.

'More!' he heard the Doomseeker yelling as he set about butchering a freshly arrived pack of Clan Boil clanrats. 'More!'

Leaving Gotrek to his own devices, Broddur pointed himself at an entirely different pack of clanrats and charged. They were patchily armoured and armed, half with their snouts already buried in the gassed corpses that littered the road. A twitchy, one-eyed rodent in a mail vest wielding a warped metal shield and a mace looked up sharply as he came. Broddur lifted the icon of Grimnir high. Gotrek may have disappointed him, but he still had his faith where it counted.

'Unbroken! Khazuk-ha!'

The skaven clawleader reacted with verminous speed, swinging up its shield as Broddur's axe came down. It caught the blow sweetly, turning it aside without allowing Broddur's greater strength to shatter every bone in its scrawny paw, and then buried its mace in his gut.

'Ooof!' Broddur doubled over.

The ratman chittered excitedly, but duardin were thick of skin, dense of bone, and the ur-gold runes studding Broddur's flesh had strengthened that durability considerably. He flexed, the muscles buried deep under his belly fat spitting the mace back towards its astonished wielder with nothing more than an angry bruise and a few pinpricks to show for the impact.

Broddur brained the formerly triumphant clawleader with his icon pole, sending him sprawling as he pivoted on his heels, chopping his axe into the wooden shield of another clanrat and hammering it to the floor. The ratman turned and squirmed away on its belly before Broddur could do to it what he had done to its leader.

'Despoil the magma-vault of a Fyreslayer will you? Hah! I'll tell a tale of Unbaki vengeance in the blood of your clan, upon the cheapest gold known to the metalcraft of the Dispossessed!'

The skaven were the ancient nemesis of all duardin races – with the exception, perhaps, of the sky-faring Kharadron – feeling as they did the same draw to the deep places. Broddur had read bead-books twice the length of the Firebrand's beard filled with tales of skaven perfidy and every one of them came to him now. 'For the Kaldun Deepings!' His ears filled with the hiss of boiling blood, and with every ancestral wrong he smote a skaven warrior. 'For Aven Wyr! For Barak Izor! For Az Skorn!' Runes of might glowed bright and hot, molten strength filling his arms, so that even as he fought his vigour did not diminish but heightened. The fury and fire of the karag blazed from his eyes and set his beard ablaze.

As one particularly gnarly looking ratman went down beneath his axe he caught a glimpse of Gotrek. The Slayer had slaughtered a path through the second pack of clanrats and, leaving a long trail of dead skaven and hastily abandoned tunnelling equipment behind him, had gone and bludgeoned himself into a third block of vermin several score deep.

A strange, smoky sensation filled his belly.

Faith.

'Doomseeker!' he roared, shaking with rune-powered aggression.

'I'm fighting, storysmith, believe it or not. Just because I prefer to do it without shouting about it doesn't mean I like it any less. Blood is for spilling. It's for feeding the soil with, not singing about. Hah! If you'd read the tales that had been written of me, the blood that's soaked this beard, then you might find that enthusiasm dampened just a little. Now watch me, storysmith. Watch how a real Slayer of the Old World greets his doom.'

Broddur watched, as asked, as Gotrek joyfully butchered his way through his third pack of clanrats. Broddur frowned. He'd not have his efforts shamed, even by the Doomseeker.

'Anything you can do...'

Attempting to yank his axe-blade from that last skaven's neck, his rune-bolstered strength accidentally sent the scrawny creature flying over his shoulder. Scenting the opening it had been waiting for, a skulking clanrat tittered and stabbed at his exposed side with a notched dagger, only to explosively disintegrate as a bolt of lightning struck its pot helmet.

The blast knocked Broddur onto his heels and he looked up, open-mouthed, as the Angelos retinues of the Hammers of Sigmar swept overhead.

The Prosecutors' wings hummed as they carried them over the melee, blitzing the crossroads with uncannily accurate lightning strikes. The skaven, however, were already breaking for the cover of the Ashlands District, tails waving through shopfront windows and sewer grates as they disappeared. The Prosecutors, realising that their stormcall javelins were too indiscriminate to give chase through urban areas, wheeled off to engage more open quarry. Horn blasts and pounding drums from the neighbouring wards declared the infantry patrols and watch militias hunting broken skaven through the back alleys.

'Fired up yet?' Gotrek asked as he stomped disappointedly through the carpet of dead skaven towards him.

Broddur did not know what Gotrek wanted to hear, so he simply grinned through his panted breaths. The Doomseeker looked up as a flight of Prosecutors in golden war plate swooped in low, obliterating a swathe of road with arcing bolts of stormcalled lightning.

'These Stormcast Eternals are impressive enough, I'll give them that, but if they were real warriors they'd be down here on the ground getting their beards wet with the rest of us. You'd never catch this dwarf accepting a pair of wings. Not for any god.'

'Do we go after them?'

'Aye, let's…' The Doomseeker's expression turned grim again, as if he had just remembered something he was ashamed at having forgotten. 'No, wait. Over there!'

Through the cloud of pulverised paving slabs and routed skaven warriors, Broddur caught a glimpse of black and red.

'The Edassans. They're making a run for it.'

'The poison wind attack must have been a ruse to clear the path. The ambush after was just to throw off anyone that might've been following. Well, they didn't count on this Slayer. Come on. We can still catch them.'

The two duardin ran for the crossroads. Despite his considerable girth, Broddur was still the quicker of the two. He was first to the crossroads, Gotrek huffing angrily some way behind. He looked in the direction that the Edassans had departed. The highway had descended into smoke and confusion, as had clearly been their intention, screaming civilians and muddled soldiers filling it. He looked ahead, then right, left again.

'*Thaggaz!* They're gone.'

Taking a deep, rattling breath, Gotrek drew up alongside Broddur. With hands on hips, he looked around. His eyes narrowed as he caught the glint of something metallic lying on the road between them both, reflecting the lightning-storm of the Emerald Wardens above. He crouched beside it.

'A fyresteel dining knife,' said Broddur, joining him on his haunches. 'It's…' He slapped his hand to his belt in surprise. 'Wait, that's *my* dining knife.'

'Just the sort of sloppiness I've come to expect around here.' Gotrek snorted. 'Can't even keep an eye on your own cutlery? For shame. Ranald himself couldn't pick the pocket of a real dwarf.'

'I'll drag her all the way back to the Hall of Censure myself,' Broddur muttered. 'Stealing my knife…'

'Forget that now, storysmith. Hark at where the blade is pointing.'

Broddur did. It was pointing towards an alley.

The Doomseeker grinned nastily.

TWENTY-ONE

Arcanite cultists in Edassan garb filled the old building. It had been a storehouse. The occasional kernel of embergrain was still trapped between the flagstones. Maleneth had seen several buildings like it in this quarter, abandoned in the early days of the siege after the Grey Lord had demonstrated how far beyond the city's walls his sorcery and siegecraft could reach.

Those true Edassans that Manezomo Osayande had not left on the Great Ash Road to feed the Charwood Sylvaneth watched their Arcanite brethren with apparent disgust. Their lips moved with the cadences of the sorcerers' chant, their eyes alarmed, as though the unclean words demanded repetition and they were only now realising that their lips were mere vessels for that need. Even Maleneth had to bite her lip to prevent herself from doing the same. She reached surreptitiously for the reassuring lump where her mistress' pendant lay under her cloak. The magic that preserved the old Hag's blood and bound her spirit provided her with some protection from hostile sorcery. She was glad that the Lioness mask concealed her discomfort from Osayande.

'I hate magic,' Osayande murmured, apparently to himself, but Maleneth's sharp aelven hearing caught the sentiment as though it had been whispered into her ear. 'It is a tool by which the weak and the powerless seek parity with the strong.'

'Then you have made a curious choice of patron.'

Osayande turned to her. 'Such are the twisted ways of the Nine-Fold Path, no? I did not seek out the Eyes, Lioness. They sought me.' He gestured to the Arcanites who appeared to make up the majority of the congregation. 'Not as these damned souls did.'

'Can you feel it though? The way it makes you want to speak its words.'

The general looked away. 'I hate magic.'

At the far end of the storehouse's main floor was a raised platform and an oriel window, boarded over, accessible by a set of wooden steps. Standing upon the platform, overlooking the Arcanites and Edassans that he had summoned here, was a man. A wizard. His hair was long, spidery grey, webbing his hollow cheeks, straggling down past the shoulders of a ratty gown of iridescent purple. Maleneth had seen this wizard before, though he had been different then, a harmless dabbler unfortunate enough to be at crossed purposes with an acolyte of Khaine. It would be churlish of Maleneth, given the circumstances, to not doff her cap to a good disguise. The man she saw now was none other than the Eye Not Seen, twin brother to the Fatemaster of the Seeing Legion, the hidden guile behind his blade.

Uthan Barrowalker spread his arms in welcome. The chant of the Arcanites seemed to rise in reply.

'Today, my brothers and sisters, we take one step further along the Nine-Fold Path.'

The wizard withdrew something from the ragged folds of his gown. It was unnaturally heavy, appearing to drag on his hand as he held it forth. It was a thick plate of gold larger than the

Fatemaster's palm. Maleneth tightened her grip on her mistress' talisman as she recognised the Unbaki's Master Rune. The unusually complex arrangement of Fyreslayer motifs looked like a pair of runic numerals denoting the name Grimnir, topped by a crown. The *throb* of something old and potent pulsed behind her eyes as she stared. She blinked quickly and looked away, breaking contact. The heartbeat faded into the chant.

Maleneth took a long breath out.

'Beautiful as only an ugly thing of gold can be,' said Osayande dismissively. 'Why do you all gasp as though one of the nine Honoured Guests has just appeared before you?'

'Bound here,' Uthan went on, 'within the ancient runecraft of the Fyreslayers, is a weapon. One with the power to break this great city in twain.'

The Arcanites hooted and cawed, but the Edassans, Osayande included, looked rather less pleased. Maleneth supposed that a weapon of mass destruction was a delightful toy to throw at a distant battlefield, but a little too thrilling to be in the same room with.

'But the duardin are cunning in their works. Only through implantation into the flesh of their own can it be properly harnessed, for it responds to their fire and their faith. Only through proper ritual can such a bonding be achieved, and only with the proper phrases can its full potential be invoked.'

'And you know the proper phrases?' Osayande called out.

There were so many sharp intakes of breath at the interruption that for a moment the air felt heady and thin. Osayande tilted his jaw and looked up at the platform, unperturbed. Maleneth smiled behind her mask. Betrayal of the God-King and the entire Pantheon of Order aside, she actually rather liked Prince Osayande. She admired a little arrogance in a man. She would not spit on a thirsty beggar in the street if he were not prepared to murder four thousand countrymen and his own cousin for the privilege. Standing beside him now, a sword's length from the centre of everyone's attention, she could see why so many otherwise good people had chosen to follow his lead into damnation.

Uthan bared his teeth at him, wide-spaced and yellow like a skeleton's. 'You must be Osayande, First Sword of Edassa and would-be wearer of the crown. My brother has told me all about you.'

'He told me next to nothing of you.'

'Such are the ways of Tzeentch.'

The Fatemaster held out the rune in his hand. The shadows about the boarded windows deepened and grew heavy as though taking on something of the golden rune's mass, causing the walls to creak, all light in the room bending towards the artefact in the wizard's hand.

'Tirazen rhun – bryndal!'

At the command 'bryndal' the rune ignited.

Maleneth grunted and had to turn away, masking her face behind her hand as light and heat blazed through the Fatemaster's fingers. It was as though he had just reached into the sky and robbed heaven of one of Sigmar's stars.

'He did it, mistress,' Maleneth whispered to herself, lowering her hand from her eyes to stare into the golden blaze in disbelief. 'You had better be nearby, Gotrek.'

With or without the irksome Slayer's company, this needed to end soon.

'The Order of Azyr has played their part in the Great Game well,' Uthan went on, and Maleneth froze, certain that he had been looking directly at her as he said it. But then his gaze swept on. 'They have purged this city of our brothers in duplicity, which is why I required outside aid in carrying our great scheme forward. I need a volunteer.' His eyes settled on Osayande and he smiled. 'Perhaps even you, manezomo?'

Osayande placed his hand upon his sword hilt. He did not dare answer.

Uthan laughed.

'Then again, perhaps not. I require a warrior of conviction *and* faith. One in whom the Great Conspirator might find favour, one who is prepared to make of themselves a vessel for his implement of Change.'

Maleneth looked over the subdued gathering with a smirk. She had seen the same thing a thousand times in the armies of the enemy. Cometh the hour, even the most fanatical became circumspect. No one spoke up to volunteer.

Maleneth raised her hand and stepped in front of Osayande.

'I will volunteer!' she said. 'I will prove my god's favour!'

The Fatemaster extended a hand to her, the sleeve of his voluminous robe hanging from his emaciated arm, and beckoned for her to join him. 'Welcome, daughter of fortune. Come closer. Stand before me and receive his blessing.'

She ascended the steps.

The silence and attentiveness of the cult deepened with every step she took towards the waiting Fatemaster. She had no idea what she had just volunteered herself for, but the opportunity to get close to Uthan Barrowalker without having to fight her way through five hundred screaming cultists was a gift she would not pass up.

At the top, the wizard bowed to her.

'Tzeentch thrives on questions, and on challenge,' he said softly, for her ears alone rather than the congregation below. 'He is uncertainty. He is Change. You will make him a worthy offering, I think. Yes. And with the might of Krag Blackhammer bound to your flesh, like a tretchlet to the body of a curseling, you and I will break this city asunder. You will be the usher of Change such as you cannot imagine. A fine gift for the Grey Lord, worthy of the great schemes that made it be. Give me your sword, sister.'

Maleneth drew the Lioness greatsword. It was huge and unwieldy, yes, but strangely beautiful now that she was made to part with it. Lions rampant ran up and down the length of the blade. The hilt was clawed and golden. It was heavy, but also deadly in expert hands.

After a moment, she turned it and proffered the hilt to Uthan.

The wizard examined it. 'A crude weapon. So unlike the subtler methods that our god would have us master.'

'My god is indeed subtle, Fatemaster,' Maleneth replied, returning the Fatemaster's earlier bow and offering the weapon up to him. 'When he chooses to be.'

Taking the blade, the Fatemaster turned to address the congregation. He held the long Lioness greatsword up between his hands.

'To take a life is to know power. To take a life freely given is to wield power. To take a life with the giver's own blade...' He cackled then, something of the old Uthan that Maleneth had stalked through the Charwood, not even knowing what he truly was. 'That is to bring great pleasure to Tzeentch. Have you any valediction for your brothers and sisters, Lioness?'

'Only one,' said Maleneth.

Head bowed, she pulled the concealed knife from inside her lion-skin cloak and rose, grabbing the Fatemaster by the forehead as she drove it between his shoulder blades. She stabbed him several more times in the back before letting his body tip over the edge of the platform.

It smacked wetly to the wooden floor below.

The congregation had fallen deathly silent. Osayande was staring up at her with something between outrage at this betrayal, relief the wizard was no more, and terror that his treachery had been unmasked. Maleneth grinned as she ripped off her mask, raising the dripping knife high above her head for the dumbfounded crowd below.

'My god is called Khaela Mensha Khaine, the Bloody-Handed, the Widowmaker, the Lord of Murder, and I thank you, Eye Not Seen, for inviting me to share his blessings today.'

TWENTY-TWO

'That's the signal then, is it?' said Broddur. 'Pushing Barrowalker off the platform?'

'I'm not waiting on another,' said Gotrek, pushing through the storehouse's neglected front door and throwing off the mouldy tarp that he had draped over his head as a disguise. It would not have fooled a short-sighted troggoth, but the Arcanites had been too fixated on the performance on the platform to notice.

And quite the show it had been too.

'Your doom is here, Chaos filth!' The Doomseeker cackled as he hacked his axe into a cultist's back and then destroyed his spine wrenching it out. 'It's coming for you as once it came for Arek Daemonclaw, Loigor Goldenrod, Waldemar Lichtman, and greater champions of your worthless god than any I see before me now. Turn and face it if you dare!' He laughed as he cut his way through a dozen more before they had time to draw their curved swords. He laughed cruelly. 'Some things you just never tire of. You'll learn that, storysmith, if you ever get to outlive the world you're living on.'

Those cultists not trying to get up the stairs to Maleneth – barely recognisable in her plate leather armour and swinging a broadsword that looked almost as heavy as the Doomseeker's axe – turned instead towards Gotrek and Broddur. They came in a rush, armed and armoured like Edassan soldiers but attacking like madmen. Gotrek and Broddur beat them back, two rocks side by side in a maelstrom of black and red.

'I notice the way you said *if*,' Broddur yelled.

'Too many years travelling with a poet. I learned to pick what words I mean.'

'Would this be the human you're looking for? Felix? Do you really think a mannish poet would be chosen by Sigmar?'

'He slew a Chaos dragon, storysmith. Have you ever done that?' Gotrek growled in Broddur's face before quickly returning to the fighting. 'He followed me to the darkest places in the Old World, all the way to the Chaos Wastes and back, all on the strength of his oath alone. Twenty years, we travelled the world before I released him so that he might go home and have a family as I once did. And even *then* he managed to be beside me at the very end. If there's a hero amongst the Stormcast Eternals worthy of polishing the manling's mail then I'll cut an inch off my beard and give it to them. You, storysmith, aren't yet up to speaking his name, not until you've notched yon blade on a Chaos lord or ten.'

'A-aye,' said Broddur, taken aback by the onslaught of words.

'Watch your side, storysmith!'

Gotrek gave a savage cry and cut the Arcanite down. 'I had him!'

Broddur parried an incoming sword on his axe, winded the swordsman with a blow to the gut with his icon, then buried his axe in the roof of his skull. 'Unbak-ha! Should we go help Maleneth, Doomseeker?'

'Aye, she owes me a liche.'

'Grimnir, does it matter who took the finishing blow?'

'Are you cussing, beardling, or have you started calling me Grimnir again?'

'Cussing!'

'Good. And yes it bloody matters. How am I to say proper vengeance was properly done if some Darkling elf got in there first?'

'Maybe Barrowalker's not totally dead yet?'

'You're just saying that to cheer me up.'

'Servants of Chaos aren't always easy to kill. And he was once a necromancer too, lest we forget.'

The Doomseeker looked genuinely thoughtful as he hacked off an Arcanite's sword-arm, shinned him, then beheaded the warrior to his left on the backswing. 'Cease your prattling, then, and follow me. I'm having that Master Rune. This may be a world of godbeasts and Chaos treemen and beer you can poach your eggs in, but I'll be taking that much vengeance from his sorry, finally dead hide.'

With a bludgeoning roar, Gotrek shoved his way into the crowd, hacking himself a path as he went.

Broddur held his icon aloft and his axe short, shepherding the Slayer's progress with economical blows to left and right. Slivers of golden light beamed occasionally through the crush of bodies from where Uthan's body lay, blinding in their intensity, and arriving generally in the short intervals between Gotrek hacking someone down and some other fool taking their place.

'If you're going to guard a side, storysmith, then at least pick the one with the eye patch.'

Broddur panted. He may have been able to outrun the Doomseeker on open road, but keeping up with him in battle was exhausting. 'I thought you'd appreciate keeping the one you've still got.'

'I can almost see the liche on the ground there. He looks dead to me.' The Doomseeker sounded enormously disappointed.

'Just follow the rune-light. It looks as though the Master Rune is still burning.'

The walls around them shuddered suddenly. Wood and stone creaked as if a giant hand had closed over the entire building and was squeezing it. Broddur glanced up into the trickle of dust from the ceiling, distracted just for a moment as Maleneth hurled another flailing Edassan from the platform. By the time he'd blinked the dust from his eyes, an Edassan swordsman had cut across and raked an ornate longsword over the Doomseeker's bicep.

Gotrek grunted as the warrior drew his sword back into a perfect guard, blood trickling down the angled fuller towards the golden lions on its hilt.

The Edassan's mouth was a thin line. He was tall and black-skinned, a native Edassan then, with a golden circlet upon his brow. His armour, though distinctly lacking in metal, was a master-piece of the leathermaker's craft. He was a living fresco of red and black and gold, creaking like a well-minded forge bellows with every step and shift in posture. A red cloak bearing a black lion rippled behind his back.

'So,' he said. 'You bleed like any mortal.'

'More than any mortal if I ever got my way.'

'My name is Osayande. Manezomo of the armies of Edassa. First Sword of the Lion. First cousin to the crown. And I will not be defied.'

Gotrek's one good eye narrowed. 'Osayande, is it? I know you. Oathbreaker, I call you. *Kinslayer*. This is for Jordain!' The Doomseeker launched himself at the Edassan lord, driving the swordsman back before a flurry of devastating blows.

'Yes, I killed Jordain.' Osayande flowed from block to parry to block again, desperately at first, but with increasing fluidity as he weathered the initial onslaught. Deflections became interspersed with loops and feints, feeding into dazzling combinations that left the Doomseeker bloodied and reeling. 'I killed Jordain with the stories of heroism I read to him as a child. If I had raised him on the truth, of Sigmar and his warmongering and the death he sows, then he need not have died.'

'If we started killing men for being idealistic fools then we'd never get round to those who actually need killing.'

The Doomseeker's axe trailed flame as he struck it towards Osayande's chest. The Edassan leapt back and nudged it almost casually aside on his sword. Broddur had to concede that Osayande hadn't been boasting. The human was a superlative swordsman.

'The Queen of Edassa is old and weak. Just like her son.'

'You don't know your cousin half as well as you think you do.'

'And you do?'

'Aye, you didn't quite manage to kill him on the Great Ash Road. I'd say he had more to him than you thought.'

Osayande threw himself into a ferocious sequence of attacks that the Doomseeker did not even try to defend himself against. It was not that Gotrek lacked for any skill of his own, but rather that he did not seem to care how often he got cut. He fought the way a battering ram fought with a gate.

The Edassan laughed, though it sounded tired and strained. 'How have you managed to live this long?'

'You'd not be the first to ask that question. Nor the last.'

'Edassa *needs* me.'

'It needs Chaos as well, does it?'

'A means to an end, and with the Eye Not Seen now dead, Edassa will be no one's vassal. Not Sigmar. Not the Grey Lord.'

Finally seeming to run out of clever swordplay, the Edassan threw everything into a direct lunge for Gotrek's face. The Slayer met it with a contemptuous swipe of his greataxe, a hammer-blow across the flat of his twin blades that cracked Osayande's sword and wrenched the arm out of its socket. Osayande screamed, dropping to his knees and clutching at his dislocated limb. His useless sword clattered to the ground.

In an awesome feat of brawn, Gotrek dragged the enormous axe back across his body. Flames broiled from its captive forge-flame like a comet's tail as he swept it back, up high, and then sent it down. Osayande looked up, refusing to look away as the Doomseeker's axe split his face down the middle. The sacred fires of the Unbak blasted out from his throat and his ears, cooking his eyeballs from within until they popped and ran down the charred ruin of his face.

Gotrek grinned.

'Jordain is avenged,' he said. 'And it felt better than I thought it would. Perhaps there can be a place for me in these worlds after all.'

Another fierce groan shook the building, like the one before it but it was louder and went on for longer. Broddur was compelled to lower his axe to balance. The Arcanite Edassans around him swayed as the ground shook. The light streaming from Uthan's body fluctuated. It brightened, a tremble rippling through the floor beneath him as a wave of force knocked down the nearest cultists. Broddur crossed his forearms over his face and braced. The blast hit him like a tsunami of molten gold, but duardin were built strong and broad, and he held his ground while Arcanites were tossed aside like gravel.

'Your arms are glowing, storysmith!'

'It's the Master Rune. It's awakening my runes!'

Krag Blackhammer's Master Rune had split the earth where it had fallen from Uthan's grasp. Light and power blazed from it. Whatever Barrowwalker had done to ignite its power, it had not been undone with his death.

The surviving cultists began to pull themselves away and run for the doors. One last lingering clash of steel drew Broddur's gaze upwards.

Maleneth was still on the platform, dancing like a trapezist around a pair of Arcanite cultists and employing her enormous broadsword with consummate ease. She swayed gracefully as the earth tremors emanating from the Master Rune caused the platform to pull against its moorings, waves of power slowly disintegrating the staircase's timber frame. The Arcanites, heavier on their feet, fell into one another, and from there down the stairs.

'Get down from there, elfling,' said Gotrek. 'Trust an engineer, that shoddy human carpentry isn't going to stand much lo–'

Maleneth leapt clear of the platform just as the entire wooden edifice came crashing to the ground, burying the screams of the Edassans and Arcanites still scrambling down from it under a cairn of kindling wood. She landed on the storehouse floor in a crouch.

'That's just showing off,' said Gotrek.

Throwing down her broadsword and shrugging out of her lionskin cloak, she ran to join the two duardin over the blazing Master Rune.

'Why have you stopped?' she said.

'Everyone's dead, thanks for asking.'

'The Master Rune is still awakened, you ignorant duardin fool. Unless we find a way to quieten it again then Uthan may succeed in destroying this city yet.'

'I didn't know you cared, elfling.'

'Indiscriminate death brings Khaine some amusement, but little glory.'

The Doomseeker snorted in mirth. With his one eye half shut against the glare of the rune, he gave Uthan's body a kick. 'I knew it. He really is dead.'

'A knife in the back will do that.'

'Some liche he was.'

'Are you even capable of focusing on the matter in hand?'

Gotrek made to spit on Uthan's body, only to see the gobbet of saliva evaporate mid-fall.

'We should try and move the rune,' said Maleneth. 'If we can bring it to Kyukain's Lord-Veritant or to the Collegiate Arcane then maybe they will be able to reverse whatever the Eye Not Seen has done.'

She bent to pick up the rune from the crater it had blasted for itself out of the ground, only to recoil with a high shriek and a *hiss* of scalded flesh. Clutching her still-smoking fingers, she kicked her discarded lion-skin over the rune, attempting to smother it that way, but the skin immediately caught fire.

'Well, that worked well,' said Gotrek.

'At least I am trying!'

'Well stop now. The thought of you shedding any more layers is making my stomach turn.'

'It's like trying to pick up a hot coal.'

'No,' said Broddur, with a snarl of frustration. 'It's hotter by far. I could pick up a hot coal.'

'Can *you* move it?' Maleneth said, turning to look at him.

Broddur shook his head. 'No. It was meant for Aruk-Grimnir or one of his runesons. It can't be moved. It'll have to be quenched before it breaks itself apart. And takes Hammerhal Aqsha down with it.'

'Typical,' said Gotrek. 'First place in this realm where you can get a half-decent beer.'

'*Quenched*,' said Maleneth pointedly. 'How?'

'I know only one way…'

The runecraft of the Fyreslayers required a Fyreslayer's flesh to balance its power. Broddur stared at the Master Rune until he could see it writ red even with his eyelids shut. Part of him did long for it, to reach out and touch the hand of Grimnir. To feel the power of the Shattered God channelled through his mortal flesh and bones. Yet he was fearful to. Such a weight of ur-gold would drive even the greatest of warriors mad, and he knew that he did not stand in that company. His beard was short. His runes were few.

He was also the only Fyreslayer here.

Gotrek had made that painfully clear.

'Here goes, Doomseeker. Blood and gold!'

Broddur plunged his hand into the Master Rune's halo and grasped the burning metal.

The face of Grimnir exploded in his mind. Callous. Joyous. Cruel. Gold rained before his eyes and became blood. Then fire. It burned. The laughter of the gods echoed, countering his screams. He heard his own voice screaming, but could not make out the words and had no awareness of speaking them. A vision of Grimnir flashed before him, like a city revealed by lightning. The Berzerker God bled from a thousand mortal wounds. His muscles were the sinews of the earth. His beard was molten rock. His glorious bulk was covered in tattoos not unlike the Doomseeker's, every swollen muscle straining in that captured moment against the red-scaled coils of an ur-beast greater than Ash Hammer Gate.

Vulcatrix.

The moment of Shattering.

'Let go of the blasted thing, storysmith.'

'Not yet.'

The vision ran from him, like blood running down a mountainside, his screams descending into a gargle of insanity as his hand suddenly caught fire. Instinctively, he tried to let go of the Master Rune, but it was too late. It had burned through the flesh of his hand and deep into the bone. He could no longer drop it.

'It burns!' he screamed in a voice that was no longer entirely his own. 'Hotter than the end of the world!'

The rune detonated in Broddur's hand like a piece of pyroclastic rock, obliterating meat and bone as far as his elbow and spinning him halfway across the storehouse floor.

The rune slammed to the ground.

'Storysmith!'

Broddur heard the Doomseeker's cry, but it was from a desperate distance away. An age later, when he opened his eyes, Gotrek's image was wavery and blurred. It was as though they were once again drowning under the Amethyst Fjords of Shyish. He cracked a smile. He could almost hear the Realm of Death call to him from somewhere. The voices of Snorri Nosebiter and all of Gotrek's former companions in his Hall of Ancestors were a whistling burr in his ears.

Blood burbled up from between his lips as he tried to answer them.

If it made a sound then Broddur did not hear it.

'Leave him, Gotrek,' said Maleneth, from equally far away. 'The only reason he is not dead already is because duardin are too stubborn to die quickly. It is time that you and I followed the Arcanites' example and got out of here.'

The Doomseeker, however, was staring at the rune.

Broddur tried to sit up and scream 'no', to remind Gotrek that only an heir to Grimnir could own the Shattered God's power, but he had no breath, no strength left even to move his lips. He made a painful attempt at movement and failed. His attempt to claim the Master Rune had taken it all.

'Don't wait for me, elfling.'

'You heard what he said. Only a Fyreslayer can absorb that kind of power.'

'And much good his lore did him.' Gotrek bent down and closed his fingers around the fallen rune. 'This Slayer chooses doom.'

A pink steam billowed from the Doomseeker's hand and swallowed him whole, but he held the awakened Master Rune in his grip regardless.

'Grimnir's Halls, that hurts. Worse than my head the morning after the wedding in Karak Kadrin. Worse than Krell's axe!'

He bent into his clenched fist, teeth bared, muscles bulging, as though the rune weighed more than the Anvil of Power upon which it had first been struck. And yet he lifted it. His one eye flared briefly golden, thousands of years of visions passing across his half-dead face in an instant. He gibbered as though the electric fury of Dracothion's breath was running through his spine.

'Grimnir... damn it... I'll... regret... this...'

With a roar of pain, the Doomseeker pushed the Master Rune into the muscle of his chest. His body tensed and shivered and appeared to swell. The white lines that Barrowalker's purple sun had struck into his beard flashed golden. And golden they stayed.

And slowly, like the pulsing of an artery that has been spent, the light began to diminish, power that had until that point been spiralling out of control earthing itself in the meat and tissue of duardin muscle.

'I think that's the... the worst of it.'

Gotrek peeled his roasted hand from his chest. Muscles continued to twitch and flex at random, but the Master Rune now blazed from his chest. Golden fire streamed from his hair and from his eyes, as well as from the rune itself. The Slayer dropped to his knees with a thud, steam rising off him with the smell of burnt flesh.

Broddur forced himself to hold his eyes open a little longer.

The Master Rune had transformed into the angular, runic likeness of a face. He glanced to where his icon lay upon the floor.

'Storysmith...' The voice came from far away. So far. *'Storysmith!'*

Broddur closed his eyes again for the final time. A smile stretched the blood caked over his lips.

'Grimnir,' he breathed.

And then stopped.

He had never truly doubted.

Not even for a second.

Your Celestial Highnesses,

I apologise for the inexcusable delay since my last correspondence.

After the explosion in the Ashlands District it became necessary to lie low for a few days, lest unwanted attention fall upon the order. I was able to bribe a guard to slip us across the Stormrift Gate into Hammerhal Ghyra and it is from here that I write this letter now.

Gotrek has been consoling himself on missing out on the siege of Hammerhal Aqsha by, or so it looks to me, re-enacting its bloodiest battles across the seediest taverns of the Stranglevines. Loath as I was to keep him from pickling himself to death, offending the wrong ogor, or simply falling off a bridge while blind drunk, I made arrangements with an Admiral Hradsson of the Golden Skies to bear us to Thyria and the nearest realmgate to Azyr.

Imagine my irritation then, on paying off yet another set of guards to pull my dog-haired companion out of another dungeon reeking of ale, to discover an idea of his already lodged in that quaint excuse for a head. Gotrek had already abandoned his previously mooted quest to find this Felix character (who, from what I gather, was unfortunate enough to have endured the Slayer's acquaintance over many years) and I had hoped he would forget this new one before the day was out, but to no avail. His latest obsession is for the recovery of a pair of axes which, he claims, were originally forged by Grimnir himself in the dawn of the World-that-Was.

If he wasn't so obviously still drunk then I might concede such a quest to be a worthwhile diversion but I confess that, at this point, it does not matter a jot what I say or think. Not to you, and certainly not to Gotrek Gurnisson. Where he goes, I will follow, and do my best to hasten along the death he so obviously craves.

Preferably before the Golden Skies *departs for Thyria.*

Your most loyal and faithful votary,
Maleneth Witchblade

PART FIVE

Armour of Winter

TWENTY-THREE

'Winter in Ghyran? I really am cursed. Or could I simply be that unlucky?' Maleneth shivered, fiddling with the silver amulet under her woefully inadequate corselet of silk and leather. What next? she wondered. Snow on the Flamescar Plateau? A noonday sun in Hagg Nar?

'You could always try keeping your mouth shut for a bit, elfling. It'll keep the warmth in. And who knows, that grisly keepsake about your neck might even answer you if you give it half a chance.'

Maleneth let her hand fall away from the amulet. She did not like the idea of Gotrek knowing that it was there, or overhearing what she said when she spoke to it. Until then, it had not occurred to her that he had done either. It was at times like these that she wondered whether Gotrek's disposition as an obnoxious, beer-soaked misanthrope was not part of some elaborate ruse to dupe her out of the Fyreslayer rune in his chest. She dismissed the nagging suspicion. No one could be that subtle.

'We could have been in an *airship* now.'

'You think it would be any warmer up in the clouds?'

'Perhaps not,' she muttered under her breath, safely below the duardin's range of hearing. 'But my suffering would have been briefer.'

They had entered the rugged hills of the Nevergreen Woods several hours earlier. The great emerald sprawl of Hammerhal Ghyra spread out beneath them, as vast as an ocean, but largely occluded now by the dense woodland and occasional flurries of snow.

'That's always been the problem with you elves – naught but pasty skin on your bones.'

Maleneth glared at the duardin's broad, tattooed back as she struggled after him up the steep trail. His burly physique and apparently bottomless reserves of stamina seemed ideally suited to the cold hills. His strong fingers dug out handholds from the snarled roots and frozen earth that hers would never find. He did not even appear to feel the cold, for all that he would periodically complain about it, declaring it moderately bracing compared to a spring day in Karaz-a-Wherever that no one cared about any more but him. It would be sad if it were not so irritating, and if Maleneth were not damp, filthy and chilled to the bone. She could practically taste the cold.

'One day soon, Gotrek son of Gurni, I am going to cut out your heart and–'

Her toe-hold slipped. Maleneth screamed as she slid downhill. Her body bashed against trunks and tree roots and it was only her sturdy leather armour that protected her from more serious harm. She stabbed a vambrace into the frozen bole of a tree as she slid past. The sudden brake almost yanked the arm out of its socket. She hung there for a moment and let out an angry breath. It steamed the cold air in front of her face.

'What was that, elfling? I failed to catch that last bit on account of your girly screaming.'

Maleneth pulled herself up and patted the bits of torn moss and snow from her leather. She reminded herself that, had Gotrek listened to her from the beginning, then they could be in Azyrheim already, dining with the Grand Theogonist herself, instead of freezing to death in this embittered corner of Verdia.

'Explain to me again this wonderful plan you had while sitting in a cell, drunk.'

'If a dwarf wishes to speak with a sacred tree about his missing axes, then I say that's his own business. Being an elf as you are, I would have thought you'd approve. And besides, no one asked you to come along.'

Maleneth sighed. Gotrek had somehow got it into his head that this Ancient Hruth'gael could point him in the direction of his missing axes. The noble spirits of the Sylvaneth were said to be very old, the most ancient of all holding ancestral knowledge going all the way back to the last days of the World-that-Was. According to whoever had spoken to the Slayer last, at least. Her instructions, meanwhile, were much more straightforward: she was to return the Master Rune of the Unbaki to her superiors in Sigmaron as expeditiously as possible. Truth be told, however, with the rune now firmly embedded in Gotrek's chest she had little appetite to return empty-handed. Her patrons were powerful, but enemies were many and the streets of the Eternal City were infinite and often dark.

She had not left the Khailebron Temple on the best of terms. No one *left* the temple. Not on any terms but Khaine's. So until Gotrek could be steered into the path of an adversary bigger than even his boasts, or she stumbled upon a poison equal to his constitution, it looked as though they were stuck with each other.

The duardin's boots crunched in the frozen earth as he came back down the slope for her. Maleneth seethed at the indignity.

'Look at the state of you, elfling. You're going blue.'

'It was summer when we left Hammerhal Ghyra. Mountains, yes, but this is still Ghyran. I did not dress for snow and ice!'

'I thought bitterness ran in your people's blood, the Land of Chill in your bones.'

'I was born in Executioner's Row, in Azyrheim, under the same stars as a million others. I never even saw another realm, much less this *Land of Chill*, until the Lady Witchblade sent me to Chamon to end my first life for the God of Murder.'

Gotrek took an enormous breath in, pumping his arms as if to create the space for a little more. His nose chain tinkled like some mad berzerker's weirdly cherished wind chime. A sprinkling of snow fell from his tall, absurdly orange crest and settled across his shoulders.

'Well, I like it. It reminds me of the high slopes of the Everpeak, near to the source of the Skull River, where I was a beardling.' He growled as he looked around. 'Except for all the bloody trees, of course. Cut them down, I say, quarry some stone from yonder hill for a hall. Raise some goats.' He paused, nodding to himself, as though there was an actual thought at large somewhere behind that one, bloodshot eye. 'You could almost picture a hill dwarf clan here. Poor old dirt-grubbers and shearers, aye, but respectable.'

'This winter is *unnatural*, Gotrek.'

'Pah! You elves. You'll watch two hogs pissing on the same scrap of grass and see it as an omen. It was the lava channels through the Stormrift from Aqshy that made the city clement. It fooled you into thinking the year younger than it is.'

'Is a walking relic of the Mallus really going to lecture *me* on the workings of the realms?'

'I was an engineer, girl. Once.' He took another long, thoughtful breath as he beheld the cold, forested hills. 'Maybe I'll have to be again.'

Maleneth tried to imagine her surly companion building a clock or caring for a goat.

'The changing of the seasons is not a casual occurrence in Ghyran. It is a change in the mood of the Radiant Queen that will garland her entire realm in spring flowers or lock its kingdoms in ice for a generation. It is something you *notice*, wherever you are.'

Gotrek turned to stomp back up the trail. Resigned, Maleneth followed him.

'It was six thousand years before my birth that Erat Osthensson left Snorri Whitebeard's golden hall to circle the globe on a dragonship of Ulthuan.'

Maleneth idly wondered if it was too late to catch Hradsson's ship after all. A slow and agonising death at the hands of a gloating Khainite assassin or a witch hunter of the order could hardly be worse than listening to another of Gotrek's interminable tales.

'Over twenty years he visited Tor Achare in the north, Arnheim and Dawn and the Tower of the Sun, and Tor Elithis in the far south to measure the size and tilt of the world, its distance from the sun and from its moons. It took ingenuity, elfling. Daring. It was my father's tales of Osthensson's adventures that first made me want to become an engineer.' The duardin growled unhappily. But then, when was he ever happy? 'Is the movement of great spheres through the heavens not elegant enough for these worlds? Must all rise and fall by the whims of the gods?'

'The last time winter came to Ghyran was during the Realmgate Wars, when Chaos waxed fullest and Alarielle had retreated to the Athelwyrd.'

'Alarielle.' Gotrek scratched his chin on the back of his firestorm greataxe. It was a wonder the oaf did not burn his own beard off. 'The name is familiar, though I know not from where. Another queen of elfkind who cheated death in exchange for godhood, I suppose.' He gave a sour laugh. 'Though I'm one to talk.'

'It *was* summer in Hammerhal Ghyra, Gotrek. I would swear it on the Sword of Khaine.'

A cold wind knifed through the forest. There was a music to it that made Maleneth shudder. Every creaking bower, every scraping branch, even the differing notes of the wind as it was funnelled through the hills was part of the forest's ensemble. Maleneth turned to regard the trees. They shivered and swayed, clad in frost and needles.

'Do you hear that, Gotrek?'

'Naught but wind.'

Maleneth shook her head. 'It is the Life Song of the forest. It has changed.' It appeared as though the guardians of the wood had taken note of them at last. It had taken them long enough. She had assumed that Gotrek's blundering, not to mention the furious power of the rune in his chest, would have had them howling from their glades long before now.

She surreptitiously took a step back from him, and just in time too as a pack of woody, half-frozen figures lurched from the treeline onto the narrow trail.

They resembled human women draped in holly, mosses and briar, their slender bodies shaped by knots of bark. They moved stiffly, as though their limbs were fused and their splayed feet rooted, but some cold determination drove them on regardless, chilly moans escaping from their hard lips as they stumbled towards Gotrek. Maleneth raised her hands from her sheathed daggers and put a few more steps between herself and the duardin.

'Dryads,' Gotrek spat. 'And here I was hoping for a fight.'

'*Awake, my sisters,*' the spirits moaned in chorus. '*Awake. Though winter's songs cool your sap and freeze your heartwood, the horn of Kurnoth sounds.*'

An eerie note sounded from the forest as though in answer. Maleneth did not think that it had been made by the wind.

'*A Wild Hunt is called.*'

Maleneth cursed under her breath. It would seem that Gotrek's presence had riled the old spirits of the wood more than she had bargained for. She wished she could blame them. It was, however, just possible that she had bitten off more than even the Slayer could chew.

'What's going on, elfling?'

'If a Wild Hunt has been called then every Sylvaneth great and small is going to be coming for us soon.'

'Good,' said Gotrek, stepping forward and driving Zangrom-Thaz into the head of a tottering dryad as though he was splitting a log. Fire roared through it. It flailed briefly, issued one final moan, and then collapsed into lumps of crisp, white charcoal that littered the ground around his feet. 'It's chilly on this hill and we could do with the firewood.'

Before Maleneth knew it, the Slayer was surrounded by burning figures. He was a bonfire in which the ugly wooden effigies were inexplicably desperate to throw themselves in. But he was one duardin in a large forest. Already, Maleneth could see a dozen more lurching stiffly from the trees either side of the trail. She backed away, but the revenants had her surrounded.

The nearest dryad swiped at her with long, crooked talons. The blow was so predicable that, had it come from one of her many rivals in the temple, she would have assumed they were mocking her. She beat it out of the way and struck back, drawing a knife and then crying out in pain as it bounced off the Sylvaneth's rock-hard bark. The ice had frozen the dryad's natural armour solid. Gotrek had made killing them look so easy.

With a roar, Gotrek hacked the dryad down from behind. She stumbled on for a pace or two, still grasping for Maleneth, before the flames of the Unbak ripped through her. Her fiery demise added a moan of rage and anguish to the song of the others.

'Killing dryads is axe-work, elfling. Listen to how they simper and weep at the sight of a little honest flame.'

'Careful, Gotrek. The Sylvaneth are connected through their song. What one feels, all feel.'

Gotrek cackled mercilessly. 'Good.' He shook his firestorm great-axe at the encircling spirits. 'Is this the best that this great wood has to offer me? A fierce enough wind may ruffle this dwarf's beard, but the cold concerns him not. He has wintered in the Troll Country of Northern Kislev, and travelled Black Blood Pass to the frozen wastes beyond. He has slain yhetees in the mountains of Norsca, and felt the chill of the grave itself. So blow your worst. You'll not freeze this dwarf's bones, nor turn his beard any whiter. Not unless you've claws to back up your moaning. Ice will shatter and frozen wood yet burn, and even a Kislevite wind will falter before scarring this dwarf's face!'

Another eerie blast on what sounded like some manner of horn caused the trees before them to thrash. As if in distant answer to the Slayer's ill-judged challenge, they bowed aside for what, on first impressions, was another tree. Superficially, she resembled the dryads already on the trail except for the insignificant detail of being three times their size. Her bark was darker and thicker, hard outgrowths emerging from the head, shoulders, and various random joints like antlers. Whorls in her bark created unnerving symbols, pulsing an unsettling, living green with the jade energies within. The wooden sword in her hand looked twice the weight of Gotrek's axe. She lowered the curling ivory horn from her lips as she strode from the treeline.

'Who brings fire into the hearthglades of the Cueth'nhair? What hunted thing is so foolish as to cross the trail of Kurnoth's Huntress?'

Gotrek looked up and whistled. The fool was never happier than when presented with some appalling new monster wishing him harm. 'You never told me that dryads came so big these days, elfling. This one's mine.'

'By all means, Gotrek. Do not mind me.'

'Good of you, girl.'

The Sylvaneth champion's woody body appeared to vibrate, the surrounding woodland groaning in sympathy as it became the focal point of the Sylvaneth war-song.

Their heartwood is warm.

It harkens of spring.

But the Everqueen sings of winter and war.

Kill them, sisters. Kill them both. Let ground frost chill their sap.'

'I am Druanthael, Huntmistress of the Free Spirits, and I offer your carcass to the soulfather. May it please him, and rouse the Living Queen to lift her winter from the Cueth'nhair.'

Gotrek roared as his axe-flames charred the towering Sylvaneth's sword. Maleneth tried to keep their duel in sight, but her own need to evade the hordes of cold-hardened dryads soon took precedence. *By the bloody cauldrons of Máthcoir,* she thought. Even *if* this Druanthael creature could kill Gotrek for her, this was not going to end well. She could outrun these dryads easily enough, half-frozen as they were, but a Kurnoth Huntress, an avatar of the Wild Hunt? No. She could not risk leaving the Master Rune in the claws of a creature such as her and expect to see it again.

Ducking between a pair of lurching dryads and fending off the talons of a third with her knives, she turned to yell at Gotrek.

'Use the rune, Gotrek!'

'I need no advice from you, elfling, and I need no aid from *him* either.'

Gotrek battered Druanthael back towards the trees in a fury. The brazier in his greataxe burned hotter, the great Sylvaneth's chest beginning to darken as its flames reached beyond her sword. The Master Rune blazed in his chest as though awakened by fire, throwing shadows past the battling Sylvaneth that clawed at the stark, glittering wood of the trees beyond. Maleneth heard a voice in her mind. It was the molten hiss of lava as it devoured solid rock, the *clang* of glowing iron as it sparked under a blacksmith's hammer.

Dum. Git a krutkhaz, frurndar. Dum. Grimnir or Grimnir, or an af dum.

She was horrified to realise that the voice was coming from the rune.

It had never *spoken* before.

'No!' Gotrek roared, and some of the Master Rune's golden fury receded into the metal. 'You have as much of this dwarf's flesh as I will allow you.'

Druanthael appeared to shrink into her own writhing shadow as she backed away. Her breast was blackened and her sword was smouldering.

'What unnatural union of flesh and fire are you?'

Gotrek pressed his advantage, but Maleneth could see that he was holding back. His teeth were gritted, the Slayer putting as much effort into restraining the Master Rune as he was into destroying the Kurnoth Huntress.

'Kill her, Gotrek. Use the rune!'

'The hunt does not end,' Druanthael wailed. 'Not until its quarry is boned and gutted and displayed on Kurnoth's table. Leave this wood, duardin, or be crushed beneath the hounds and hooves of the Wild Hunt. I care not who you are. The Everqueen sings the song of winter, and your fire will be permitted no nearer the hearthglades of the Cueth'nhair.'

Sounding a blast on her hunting horn, Druanthael broke. The dryads that were not already dead or burning turned and fled, disappearing into the trees like snow on wet ground. The wind played its song through the trees and hills, mocking, haunting, and if not for Maleneth's panting breath and the piles of burnt sticks around Gotrek she might have convinced herself that she had imagined the entire battle. Quickly sheathing her knives, she hurried towards Gotrek.

'You don't need to say anything, elfling. I'm not going in there after them. You think me mad?'

'Do you want that answered?'

'Anyway, my legs ache from climbing.'

'I was actually just going to ask if you had the faintest idea what the Kurnothi was talking about.'

Someone cleared their throat behind them.

Maleneth whirled as a rugged, white-bearded duardin in a mail coat and red cloak crunched out of the forest with his hands up. How a walking armourer's dummy like that had managed to sneak up so close behind her *and* evade a Wild Hunt, she did not know. The duardin gave them both a big, white-bristled smile when she did not kill him straight away.

'She was telling you that you'd best get a shift on,' he said.

Maleneth ran at their unexpected guest, leaping at the last minute and thumping the flats of her feet into his chest. The old duardin lost his breath in a *woof* of air and went down under her with a crash. Maleneth rode him all the way to the ground, ending up straddling his chest with a knife against his hairy neck.

'Whoa there, *elgi*. Mind the beard.'

'I was actually going for your throat. Nicking your beard will simply be to add insult.'

'Now there's no need for–'

Maleneth pressed her knife further into the duardin's beard, cutting him off. 'Give me one good reason why I should not feed your life's blood to Khaine.'

The duardin's eyes rolled towards Gotrek, who was frowning disinterestedly over her shoulder.

'Did you somehow arrange for the Sylvaneth to waylay us?' Maleneth went on. 'Or did you simply know that they would, knowing what Gotrek carries? What are you, a Fyreslayer in common garb, come to claim the Master Rune for your own? Or another servant of the Grey Lord sent to deceive us?'

'Now hang on a–'

Maleneth raised an eyebrow warningly.

The duardin shut up.

'That's enough, elfling,' said Gotrek. 'Leave him be. You think every snotling and its half-cousin is after this blasted rune.'

'And I thought that we had come to an understanding that, after your experience with Uthan Barrowwalker, you would allow *me* to decide whom you can and cannot trust.'

'And I told you never to utter that name in my presence again.'

'If you could just put the knife away, I can explain,' said the white-bearded duardin.

'Have you been following us?' Maleneth demanded.

'Following you? There's a cheek. I didn't have to follow you. I knew where you were going, didn't I.'

Maleneth blinked. 'What?'

'There you go, elfling,' said Gotrek. 'Now you can get off him. We've a tree to find, and this is no way to treat an elder.'

'I swear,' said Maleneth, 'if someone does not tell me what is happening here then I will start slitting throats and see where it leads.'

'This is Witromm, girl. Or *Wyr Tromm* as it used to be said in old Khazalid, as opposed to the bastard version spoken today. White beard.'

'Is that supposed to mean something to me?'

'He's the longbeard I was telling you about. The one I met in that dungeon in Hammerhal Ghyra.'

Maleneth stared at her companion in disbelief. He had, quite typically, told her nothing of the sort. 'And you just *invited* your fellow drunkard along on our quest for a weapon of the gods?'

'When I told you about Ancient Hruth'gael and the sacred grove of the Cueth'nhair, I honestly thought we were going together,' said Witromm. 'I was truly put out when the Freeguild let me out of that cell and I found you'd gone without me.'

'You're always so suspicious, elfling. That's your problem.'

'*I'm* not the one who chose to wallow in a Fyreslayer dungeon rather than believe the world was real.'

'And why should I have believed it real, elfling? The whole thing is ridiculous.'

Maleneth looked down at Witromm. The old duardin smiled up at her. His teeth had been yellowed by ale. His breath smelled of tobacco. In spite of his situation, pinned to the ground under a Shadowblade of Khaine, a position that few living souls could relate to, he seemed more tickled than flustered. That alone was reason enough for Maleneth to be distrustful.

'What reason could you have for following us into the Nevergreen Woods?'

'For the adventure, lass. One last hurrah in the saga of Witromm. And maybe a snifter of gold to go with it.'

'Gold?' said Gotrek, suddenly interested again.

'Well...' Witromm shrugged. 'There's always gold isn't there. Somewhere along the way. With you after your axes and her after...' He turned his eyes to Maleneth and hesitated. 'Whatever it is she's after, it'd be a shame to see it all go begging.'

'You swear it on your father's beard?'

The duardin became sombre. 'I swear.'

'Let him up, elfling.'

'You cannot be–'

Taking her by the leather collar, Gotrek hoisted her off the other duardin as though she was a child playing in a bloody puddle.

'He swore it on his father's own beard, elfling. Let that be the end of the matter.'

Witromm sat up and patted himself down. 'I've no interest in taking that rune from him, elgi, I'll swear on that as–'

'If you so much as *think* about the Master Rune I will cut out your eye. And that will be your last warning before I take your heart. Are we clear?'

To her surprise and irritation, the duardin merely smiled. Before she could impress on the fool that she was not joking, Gotrek gave a bark of laughter.

'The Darkling elves are infamous practitioners of the sadist's arts. This one's preferred implement of torture is that acid tongue of hers. Best thing's to ignore it.'

Maleneth drew a sharp breath of annoyance. It was one thing for Gotrek to be impossible to threaten. It was quite another for him to ruin her ability to strike terror into everyone else that their paths crossed as well. She looked on in disbelief as Witromm proceeded to unpack a pipe and stuff it with dried leaves from a crumbling roll of yellowed paper.

He lit it.

'It's chilly out here,' he offered up on a plume of pipe-smoke by way of explanation.

'There are still Sylvaneth in these woods, you know,' Maleneth sighed.

'Don't worry, lass. I'm here to help.'

'How?'

'It just so happens that I know Hruth'gael from way back.'

'You know the Treelord Ancient?'

'Aye. Didn't I say?'

Maleneth regarded him suspiciously. 'No.'

Witromm shrugged as though this were neither here nor there. 'I helped him out once, back when all this was swamp. The domain of some plague champion stretching from Greywater Fastness to the freshwater seas of Quogmia. Algur, I think his name was.

Elgin. Algon. A big deal back in the day.' He drew thoughtfully on his pipe. 'It was a little thing, really, but the elder Treelords aren't so unlike us duardin, they remember their debts.'

'It's good to see someone in this world who still does,' said Gotrek.

'Well, I still do not trust you.'

The duardin smiled around his pipe in that infuriatingly knowing way. 'Goes with the Darkling blood, I'm afraid, lass. Anyhow.' He turned to Gotrek. 'Hruth'gael had an outpost of sorts in the woods around here, but you're a way off track. Must be all this snow.'

'Unless it is the intention of the Sylvaneth to lead us astray,' said Maleneth. 'I have heard tales of Sylvaneth singing new paths into a forest to lure intruders into traps and ambushes.'

'After the Wars of Life, the forest folk of the Nevergreens came to an accord with the Hammerhalians. I don't know what madness has befallen these woods of late, but Hruth'gael's a reasonable sort. We'll get a hearing with him at least. Or we will if I'm there to speak for us, anyway.'

'Convenient,' said Maleneth. The finger of one hand tapped the hilt of her dagger. The other rested on the blood talisman at her collar.

'How far to this outpost?' said Gotrek, gullible as ever when it came to monsters and treasure and people he met whilst drunk.

'Oooh, I'd say it's about…' Witromm bit down on the stem of his pipe and looked around. Picking a spot apparently at random, he waved his hand towards it. 'Over there.'

'Could you be any more vague?'

'It's like I told you, elgi. This was all swamp when I was here last.'

Somewhere in the distant woods, a horn sounded its hunting call. The trees about them whispered and Maleneth did not like to think about what they were saying. She ground her teeth. She thought less and less of the Nevergreen Woods with every passing moment, but it did not appear as though she had much of a choice but to venture deeper into them.

'Best crack on then,' said Gotrek, speaking for the both of them. As usual.

TWENTY-FOUR

Maleneth cursed for the hundredth time as, for the hundredth time, a whipping tree branch managed to scrape her freezing white skin. She threaded her way between the trees as delicately as she could, telling herself that the pair of blundering rhinoxen ahead of her would be suffering worse, but to little avail on either count. The cold wood appeared to stir a little more, the deeper they ran. The trees rustled and sang, a brittle melody that touched something buried in her aelven soul. It made her want to run, far from this place, to bury her head and hide until the trees sang no more.

'I think it is even colder here than it was on the trail.'

'This winter's the work of the Everqueen,' said Witromm. Maleneth cast Gotrek an *I told you so* look that bounced off the Slayer's back unheeded. 'I fear that as we near the Cueth'nhair hearthglades we're inadvertently approaching the heart of it.'

'Why would she lock one of her own kingdoms in winter?' asked Maleneth.

'Who knows why the gods do anything? Are you going to ask them, lass? I'll not be.'

'Which is probably why they imagine they can get away with it,' Gotrek grumbled in typically gnomic fashion.

The sounds of hunting horns rang through the forested hills. There were several of them now, and from all around, ahead of them as well as from behind. Maleneth was more accustomed to being the one set loose onto some terrified quarry's trail, but she knew what it was to be hunted. The dryads were closing off their routes of escape, herding them ever further uphill towards their hearthglades. It would not be long now until they attacked again, this time in over-whelming force.

'Can we evade them?' she said, panting. 'The Huntress, Druanthael, offered Gotrek the chance to leave. If we were to follow the slope downhill, then perhaps we could let her believe we are fleeing back to Hammerhal Ghyra.'

'I'd sooner set fire to my own beard than have some tree harpy entertain any such thought.'

'Who cares what she thinks, Gotrek, so long as we are alive?'

'It's too late for that now anyway,' said Witromm. 'You heard her. The hunt's been called and it doesn't end until we're dead.'

'Still glad you came along?' Maleneth asked.

'Better to die in the woods in half-decent company than in some Hammerhalian gutter.'

'I *liked* the gutter,' Gotrek muttered.

'Hmm,' said Maleneth suspiciously.

'Any chance you could up the pace a little, lass?'

Maleneth let out a breathless laugh. 'I do not think I will be able to keep to *this* pace for much longer.'

'No stamina, you elves,' said Gotrek. 'I bet you couldn't even run up a small hill without stopping for breath.'

A horn sounded close by. Something in the snow-laden branches moved, a shadow too stealthy even for Maleneth's sharp eyes to follow. The trees shivered, less with cold than with anticipation. Maleneth moaned in frustration and ran faster. She refused to die on a hillside in Ghyran because Gotrek Gurnisson was as stubborn as an Ymetrican longhorn with its head down.

'Don't be so quick to discount the aelves' qualities,' Witromm huffed as he ran, his pipe still firmly clenched between his teeth. 'They may surprise you with their worth.'

'You've spent time with them, have you?'

'I once counted a prince of the Darkling aelves amongst my dearest friends.' His voice became wistful. 'A long time ago now.'

'Not *so* long ago. In my day, no dwarf worth his beard would countenance such a thing.'

Again, that infuriatingly knowing smile. 'No? I suppose not.'

Maleneth felt like screaming. Here she was, barely able to breathe and half-frozen, and the two duardin were chatting like a pair of labourers at lunch. 'How much farther to the hearthglades?'

'I'm not certain,' said Witromm.

'Witromm!'

'Too far, lass.'

Arrows whistled from the trees. Maleneth jinked on instinct and a shaft *thunked* into a frozen trunk. It was a single, crooked twig with young green leaves sticking at irregular intervals, as though some tree had nurtured it before freely offering it up to the Sylvaneth for this purpose. It should never have been able to fly straight and yet somehow, by the will of the wood, it did. Maleneth sprinted on as dozens of arrows hummed after her, hammering into tree trunks all around her. She hurtled past Gotrek, who turned and growled, hefting his axe.

'No more running then.'

'Not now, Gotrek! Even you can't kill an entire wood.'

'Watch me!'

'We'll find sanctuary in the high grove of Hruth'gael,' said Witromm. 'We've just got to run a little farther.'

Gotrek scowled, lowering his axe, and then turned to pound after Maleneth. 'If we're going to run then let's bloody *run*. Before I change my mind!'

Maleneth watched helplessly as the great tattooed lump overtook her, a huge arrow sticking out of his shoulder that he did not seem to have felt. She opened her mouth to gasp something appropriately scathing, only to scream in alarm as Witromm hoisted her up by the waist and flung her over his shoulder.

'What do you think you are doing, you fat hog? Put me down.'

'Hush, girl. A little indignity's fair exchange for your life, don't you think?'

'I most certainly do–'

Her protestations were cut rudely short as the duardin started running. Maleneth scowled as she was jounced against his back like a sackful of loot from a dungeon he was now having to hastily vacate. She looked up and almost wished that she had not. The forest behind them seethed with angry spirits.

'They are gaining on us!'

'Of course they're gaining on us. You don't outrun the forest folk in their own wood.'

'Then loath as I am to echo Gotrek, but why are we running?'

'They can gain all they like, lass, provided they don't *catch* us.'

'You could always try spitting out that blasted pipe.'

Witromm grinned around the offending item, but continued to blow out smoke as though making a point.

'Do you think it is only Gotrek they are hunting?'

'Thinking of leaving him?'

'Surprised?'

'Only that you've not suggested it already.'

Maleneth bared her teeth. She would have gladly served up both duardin to Kurnoth herself if the artefact her masters demanded of her was not embedded in the Slayer's flesh.

'Just shut up and run.'

'Watch out for the trees!' Gotrek yelled from several yards ahead.

One of the trees did indeed appear to be moving, and Gotrek turned his axe towards it with an eager look flickering in the firelight across his ruined face. Maleneth saw almost immediately however that it was not the tree that was moving and that Gotrek was facing entirely the wrong way to meet the gargantuan Treelord that had just pushed the trunk aside to step through. She took a deep breath to shout a warning, only to think better of it at the last minute and did nothing as the gnarled elder spirit struck Gotrek with a fist the size of a wagon. The blow lifted the Slayer off his feet, but he did not fly far. He slammed face first into a tree and Maleneth could not help but smirk. Regardless of whether the Sylvaneth meant to kill them all or just Gotrek, ensuring that Gotrek died *first* would do her own chances of returning home to Azyr no harm at all.

'Ungh,' Gotrek mumbled. 'Is that the best you can do?'

'Hold him, Silver Birch,' the Treelord sang in a deep, deep voice as it advanced. 'Hold him for me.'

The branches of the tree that Gotrek had fallen into twitched at the Treelord's song. They whipped around the Slayer's ankles and wrists until he was held fast to its trunk. Gotrek struggled, but succeeded only in sending blood running down his arms and spattering from the bottoms of his feet.

'Get your branches off me, you bloody *tree*.'

'This glade falls under the protection of the Radiant Queen,' said the Treelord. 'In my slumber the Huntmistress calls to me – you are not welcome here.'

'Is it Hruth'gael?' Maleneth yelled.

'No, lass. One of the younger Treelords would be my guess. And he's not alone.'

Maleneth looked in the same direction as Witromm as a familiar giant strode through the forest towards them. A sword, either brand new or miraculously healed of its burns, was in her hands. An army of rustling, frost-clad dryads capered stiffly at her back.

'All children of the woodland realm heed the song of the Everqueen. All but the maddest of spite-revenants answer the call to the Wild Hunt.'

'That's enough, Witromm.' Maleneth patted furiously on the duardin's back. 'We're surrounded. Let me down.'

Witromm set her down. She drew her knives.

'You've a plan?'

'Cut off the Kurnothi's head. Make of it an offering to Khaine.'

'I've heard worse.'

Witromm unshipped his axe. Maleneth took a moment to admire it.

'A fine weapon for an old duardin.'

'It was left to me by a very distant ancestor.'

'Well, just try to keep up.'

With a cry to the Bloody-Handed God, Maleneth leapt into the melee that had developed around Gotrek. A dryad lunged for her. Maleneth dropped to the ground and rolled under her outflung arm. A second made a beeline. Maleneth sprang out of her roll into a flying kick that knocked the dryad back into a third, dazing the pair of them for the split second Maleneth needed to sprint between them.

'There is no victory for you here, daughter of shadow,' said Druanthael. 'Your god was slain and broken, where mine lives and breathes and guides my hunt through her song. In the flowering of her anger has the might of the wargrove been marshalled, and no river of blood shall slow its march. You will be crushed, your heartwood rent asunder, your sap spilled to nourish the Cueth'nhair's soil.'

'Khaine is not dead, Huntress. He lives and will live again. Every life I take in his name nourishes his iron heart. Ignorance does not exempt you from the punishment Morathi demands for suggesting such a thing.'

Maleneth leapt through the screen of dryads in a whirl of knives. A dozen killing blows in as many seconds struck off the Kurnothi's hard wooden armour. Druanthael shivered in song and chopped at Maleneth with her sword. Maleneth leapt over the swing and thrust her blade deep into the spirit's mouth, cursing as she did greater injury to her own hand. Leaving the knife embedded in the Kurnothi's hard palate, she drew another and flipped backwards, pulling a somersault and landing on her spread feet before the Huntress could throw her off herself. Druanthael pulled the knife from her mouth and tossed it away as though repulsed by the touch of metal.

Maleneth wondered what she had been thinking. Gotrek had not been able to land a telling blow on the Kurnoth Huntress and she was nowhere near as strong as he was. She had fought him twice now, and come close to killing him on both occasions, but that had been before he had absorbed the powers of the Master Rune. That was why she had been compelled to encourage the drunken braggart to kill himself.

'Maleneth!' Witromm yelled, still chopping his way through the dryads behind her. 'Behind you – the Slayer!'

Gotrek continued to struggle against the branches that were restraining him, even as the approaching Treelord shook the earth underfoot. Maleneth saw what had alarmed Witromm. The Master Rune in Gotrek's chest was burning.

Dum. Git a krutkhaz, frurndar. Dum. Grimnir or Grimnir, or an af dum.

Dryads flailed in panic as the voice of the rune impinged on that of their war-song. Several broke and ran screaming for the woods. Only the greatest spirits, Druanthael and the Treelord that had cornered Gotrek, remained entirely steadfast in the face of it. Even they seemed distressed by the metallic voice shouting its rage into their heads.

'I said,' said Gotrek, and took a deep breath, the sound like that of liquid gold being poured into a mould, until his voice was as deep and hot and furious as the power speaking through him. 'UNHAND ME!'

The rune burst into flames, but Gotrek betrayed no pain. The voice that wore him bellowed like a dragon as the fires spread outward from his chest to consume his shoulder and went from there down his arms, up his neck, until his entire torso was aflame.

'COME AT ME, HUNTRESS, REVENANT, DAEMON OF THE FROSTLING WOOD! FAR INTO THE NORTH I WALKED TO FACE MY DOOM, INTO CHAOS ITSELF. AND BEYOND! *AZ-DREUGIDUM!* THE FEARLESS, THEY CALLED ME. PRO-TECTOR OF THE DWARFS OF OLD!'

The tree that had been restraining him went up like a bonfire. The Treelord recoiled with an unexpectedly high-pitched and lilting scream, and with a wrench that Maleneth felt in her heart the war-song faltered altogether.

Druanthael looked around with what Maleneth could only assume to be an expression of horror.

'He thaws the wood! Silence his song, my sisters. Silence it quickly before it is too late!'

In place of the rustling war-song, Maleneth began to pick up on the croak of birds, the buzzing of insects, and the slow *drip-drip-drip* of snowmelt trickling through naked branches. A foul reek from absolutely nowhere filled her nose and mouth, like being plunged head first into a midden. She gagged. It reminded her of her first years as an acolyte of the Khailebron, cleaning the draich-masters' cells, only a hundred times worse.

She covered her mouth, trying not to be physically sick as, with a *plop* like fresh manure being dumped into a pile, a diseased warrior appeared out of the thaw.

He looked like a man hours away from becoming a corpse, but there was a burning vitality about him that even death could not safely come near. His skin had a greenish pallor and shone with fever sweat. Strings of hair clagged his scalp under a tricorne hat struck through with a drooping feather. One eye was a milky white while the other was wide and giddy.

'Ahhhh.' The man took a deep, rattling breath and beat on his chest, disgorging a swarm of fat, foetid flies from under his mouldy brocade coat. 'Do you smell that, Jaro? 'Tis the odour of bounteous Ghyran in full and fecund bloom.'

A tiny nurgling in a pot helm gave a wet fart of agreement.

'Indeed, dear Jaro. Indeed. 'Tis good to be home, surrounded by the flatulent reek of growing things once more.'

'Algur Threefingers,' said Witromm, trying to speak with a handful of beard held over his mouth. 'As my beard grows white, he lives.'

''T'wouldst appear we are remembered, Jaro. Pray stretch thy rancid fingers – playeth a tune to match my good cheer.'

The nurgling picked up a fiddle the size of a matchstick and proceeded to strike out a jaunty tune. Maleneth felt dizzy just listening, catarrh building up in her throat, behind her ears, her forehead growing hot.

'And to thee, sir duardin, I bow.' The warrior swept off his tricorne and bowed. 'Sir Algur Threefingers, Leper-Knight of the Order of Despair, at thy foetid service. This cruel winter hath held my blight at bay, but this thaw hath set it free. It is the Grandfather's work thou doe'st here, and I applaud you for it.' Resetting his hat on his head, Sir Algur clapped quickly and the nurgling dutifully increased the tempo of his playing.

Maleneth moaned, her eyes so sore she could barely see, barely care, as slouch-shouldered daemons of disease and despair squelched into the forest all around her.

'*Flee!*' the forest sang in despair.

'*Retreat to the hearthglade!*'

'Avast and avant, ye bearers of plague, ye one-eyed drudges of the lord of flies!' Sir Algur declared happily. 'The Everqueen casts off her mantle of frigidity and welcomes thee to her bosom warmth. Where art thou, Alarielle? Though thou playeth hard to get, the Grandfather desireth thee still!'

Maleneth recalled the Lady Witchblade once telling her of how, over the long centuries of the Realmgate Wars, all of Ghyran had locked winter at the Everqueen's command. She saw now why that had been so, and why the goddess had invoked the same spell again over the Nevergreen Woods. It was her last defence against the incursions of the Plague God, Nurgle. No wonder the Kurnoth Huntress had been so determined to drive Gotrek and his fires from her lands. Desperate enough to summon a Wild Hunt.

Towering over the fleeing dryads, Druanthael strode towards Sir Algur. Her body growled with the violence of a song that she alone now could still hear.

'For Kurnoth and the Everqueen, your head is mine, Rotbringer!'

'Who is this Kurnoth, this unruly cur? Most assuredly he is a consort unbecoming of so fecund a queen. But fear not, my magnificent lady, fear not. The Grandfather shalt gift unto her a cage of most tarnished silver, that she might sing sweet lamentations as he brews the filth to inundate this realm.'

The diseased knight drew a slender épée with an absurd flourish. It was rusted brown, and had no edge that Maleneth could discern.

'Is it then to be single combat, a bout between worthies for the hand of thy radiant lady? Know thee that I suffer neither fear nor pain, and that as Leper-Knight of the Order of Despair I am a swordsman without compare in the Mortal Realms.'

An explosion from the vicinity of Gotrek shook the entire hill. The flames that had already consumed him roared higher as Gotrek tore his limbs from the burning tree, setting about plague-bearing daemons and routed Sylvaneth with an indiscriminate killing fury.

'MY AXE THIRSTS!'

Az, or az a guz! the rune echoed in Maleneth's head.

What could throw back the protective winter of a god, Maleneth wondered, but the shining wrath of another god? Khaine help her, she was starting to think like that wide-eyed cretin Broddur. But it explained why everyone was so eager to lay their hands on the Unbaki rune.

Sir Algur gave a mucous cough. 'Forgive me, my lady, but I see thou art indisposed with company.' He bowed quickly to Druanthael. 'Another time, perhaps.' He turned to his disgusting fiddler and snapped, '*Enough*, Jaro.'

The nurgling lifted its fingers from the saggy strings. The tuneless screech whined to a migraine-flaring halt. Sir Algur doffed his hat, just as the pair of them dissolved into two heaps of maggots, one of them very large and one very, very small, which retained their humanoid shapes for a moment or two before slopping down into two squirming puddles that wriggled off into the forest floor.

'All the gods of Mount Celestian,' Maleneth gasped, one hand over her nose and mouth, the other held firmly to the side of a tree lest her spinning head cause her to fall.

'He's got the right idea, elgi,' said Witromm. 'We *really* want to be a long way from here very soon.'

'What about Gotrek and the rune?'

Witromm dragged her into the woods. 'You don't understand, lass. It's Gotrek we're running from!'

TWENTY-FIVE

Maleneth fled through a forest that seemed to be rotting before her eyes. Plaguebearers and Sylvaneth fought running battles between the trees. From somewhere blessedly far behind her, the occasional earthquake spoke of Gotrek still rampaging through both sides with abandon. *Just another day in the company of Gotrek Gurnisson,* she thought bitterly.

'Not so fast, elgi,' said Witromm. 'The forest is turning to quagmire as we speak and we can't all have your lightness of step.' The ground slurped at his boot as he turned to hack open a Plaguebearer. His face had turned as white as his beard. 'You wouldn't think it possible, would you? These daemons smell fouler dead than they do living.'

Dryads swarmed the way ahead. Maleneth looked left and right, but neither way was any clearer. She could see the spirits darting from tree to tree.

'Bloody Hag. Why are they still so determined to kill us while daemons stalk their wood?'

'The winter was all that protected their forest from Nurgle's Rot,' Witromm explained.

'Until Gotrek thawed it.'

As if on cue, a fiery eruption turned the sky beyond the tangled branches red. A moment later, the ground trembled.

'DIE, DAEMON!'

Uzkit dumrhun!

Maleneth launched the knife in her left hand, then one in her right. Both thudded into bark, but the two dryads lurching onto the path ahead kept on coming. She swore, drawing two more. She had never been in danger of running out of knives before *Gotrek* had come along.

'Now the blight runs rampant,' Witromm went on. 'I fear it's driving the treefolk mad.'

'Khaine!' Maleneth yelled, accelerating into a flying leap that carried her across a stagnant pond and into the body of a Sylvaneth. Her kick sent it crashing to the ground. 'Perhaps I cannot bleed you, but you fall like any clumsy fool I have ever known.'

The dryad groped for her from the ground. Maleneth stamped on the creature's head; she finally heard wood splinter beneath her heel and it stopped. She almost wished her mistress could be watching: fighting barehanded against the daughters of Alarielle! The Lady Witchblade had always despaired of her appetite for a real challenge. Maleneth smiled at the thought. But then, the Hag had had so many appetites that Maleneth had found equally distasteful.

'You take the Sylvaneth, Witromm. Leave the Plaguebearers to me.'

'It'll be just like old times, elgi.'

Maleneth had not the faintest clue what he was talking about.

'Ho-ho,' a Plaguebearer gurgled merrily, slogging through the waist-deep mire. 'What pale delight doth this tallyman uncover he– *Arrrgh!*'

Maleneth pulled her knife out of the daemon's one eye, watching with considerable satisfaction as it dissolved into clumps of steaming flesh. That was more like it.

With great care, she wiped the blade clean on her thigh. Forged from celestium and kissed by the envenomed lips of the Hag of Azyr herself, it was lethal even to things that could not be conventionally killed.

She had been saving it for someone special.

'MY AXE THIRSTS!'

Az, or az a guz!

'Come on, elgi,' said Witromm, squelching back with a beard full of mud and splinters to grab her by the arm. 'We've got to keep moving.'

'But Gotrek–'

'Is taking care of things quite handily by the sound of it.'

'It is not *Gotrek* whose wellbeing concerns me. If I leave without that rune then I can kiss goodbye to the faint hope of ever seeing Azyr again.'

Another fiery blast shook the treetops, but it sounded fainter this time. As though the worst of the rune's fury had been spent and it was simply throwing out wild, earth-shaking tantrums while it settled.

'Have bloody at you!' Gotrek roared.

The voice was almost his own. Maleneth waited, listening, but there was no metallic echo in her mind. Whatever power had possessed him, it seemed to have receded back into the rune.

'The Cueth'nhair hearthglade is this way,' said Witromm, still pulling her on behind him. 'That's where Algur Threefingers and his daemons'll be headed, the last bastion of winter in this wood. I sent Gotrek here, don't you see? This is all on my beard.'

There was a squelching of mud as something rustled its way out of the dry foliage behind them. Maleneth slithered her arm free of Witromm's grip and swung her knife towards it.

She lowered it again.

'Hag of Azyr! Gotrek?'

'I turn my back for two minutes and you're both going on without me?'

'What happened to you?' said Maleneth.

'I don't want to talk about it.'

Maleneth touched Gotrek's arm. If he was about to die then she wanted to be ready to cut the rune off him and run. 'My gods, Gotrek, you are freezing.'

'Nonsense. The day this dwarf so much as shivers while an elf prances about in a skimpy bit of leather is the day he shaves his beard and calls himself a… a…' Gotrek sneezed loudly. 'A goblin,' he finished miserably. 'Wicked sorcery, I'd expect. Ice magic. Aye. Or more foul necromancy.' He paused to blow his nose in his hand, looking blearily into the trees ahead. 'Do I see daemons of Nurgle fighting a bunch of dryads?'

'You do.'

'I thought so. Whose side are we on?'

'Neither. We are getting out of here. If you are going to die at last then the least you can do for me is to do it far away from this battle. If my superiors did not want the Unbak to have their Master Rune then we can be sure they would not want this Algur Threefingers *or* Druanthael to find it on your corpse.'

'No, elfling! We came to this damnable wood for my axes. I will learn what I need from the longbeard's old tree if I have to wring the knowledge from its bloody branches.'

'This way,' said Witromm.

'Gotrek, you can barely stand,' said Maleneth, exasperated.

'Allow me, lass.'

Witromm unbuckled his red cloak and threw it over Gotrek's shoulders. Almost at once, the chill left the Slayer and colour returned to his cheeks. Gotrek, who had been about to protest that he needed no wet nurse, or words to that effect, looked at Witromm in shock.

'That's no ordinary cloak.'

'Another old gift. This one from a lady.' Witromm regarded Gotrek pointedly. 'So I'll be wanting it back.'

Gotrek shrugged it off and handed it back, masking his reluctance behind his usual scowl. 'This way, you said?'

'Aye.'

'The forest is rotting around us,' said Maleneth. 'How can you still be certain this is the right way?'

'I told you, didn't I? This was all swampland the last time I was here. Well, it's starting to look awfully familiar.'

Gotrek started off, looking only slightly less likely to keel over and die than he had a moment ago. Maleneth sighed and followed. She had only gone a few steps when she realised that Witromm was no longer with them. She turned. The old duardin was up to his knees in mud and struggling to pull out one of his feet.

'I'm stuck!' Witromm called to her.

It was worse than that. Judging by the occasional bubble rising to the surface and popping between his legs, the duardin was definitely sinking. Maleneth silently debated with herself whether it would do her any good to tell him.

'Stop fidgeting,' said Gotrek.

'That's easy for you to say,' Witromm snapped back.

'You're only making it worse.'

The Slayer squelched in until he was almost as deep in the mud as Witromm. Maleneth felt a moment's panic that Gotrek was about to carry the Master Rune with him to the bottom of a swamp, but then she saw the fierce care the Slayer was taking over every step and was reassured. When he had got as close to the stranded duardin as he could, he took hold of an overhanging branch, pulled on it to assay its sturdiness, and then stretched his arm out towards Witromm.

'Have my hand, longbeard.'

Witromm swung up an arm and, on the third attempt, managed to hook his fingers around the tips of Gotrek's. Muscles bulged along the length of the Slayer's arm, mud squelching and oozing between their fingers as he tried to pull the other duardin out by the fingertips.

'Is that the best you can do, Gotrek?' said Maleneth.

'I'd like to see you do better!'

'You once threw an Anvil of Power at me.'

'It's that bloody rune. It took something out of me.'

'I think I'm sinking,' Witromm belatedly realised. 'Pull harder!'

'I'm pulling as hard as I can.'

Maleneth hopped onto the opposite side of the bog. 'Give me your other hand, Witromm.'

'I don't need your help, elfling.'

'Pride, Gotrek? Really? Now?'

'I've got this.'

'Let her have the damned hand!' said Witromm, a note of panic entering his voice.

There was a gentle creak as a long, wooden limb extended across Maleneth like a branch.

Witromm's eyes widened as Druanthael took his hand in hers. Gotrek took a moment, but did not so much as blink his one good eye. Maleneth supposed that so many things had tried to kill him down the centuries that he no longer took such attempts personally, nor as permanent states of affairs.

She had tried, and look at her now. She was *still* trying.

It was not a pleasant thought.

'On three then, tree-kin,' Gotrek muttered. 'One.' He strengthened his hold on Witromm's fingertips.

Druanthael silently tightened her grip.

'Two. *Three...*'

TWENTY-SIX

Maleneth looked around with interest. She had heard stories of the spirit paths that the Sylvaneth used to traverse the great distances between their glades, and to evade the assassins that were sometimes sent to kill them, but she had never expected to see one. They were open only to the Sylvaneth, and only the Sylvaneth could navigate them safely.

It resembled a forest path, but Maleneth could never have mistaken it for a real one. The leaves were the brightest green she had ever seen. The sky, on the occasions that it appeared above the canopy, was too intense to look upon. The scent of tree sap and wildflowers was so sweet it was intoxicating. Every twig that snapped underfoot, every leaf brushing against a piece of clothing, every merry twitter of birdsong, was but a single note in the great song of Ghyran.

Um afrhun nu elgram. Wanrag um krutdammaz?

'Speak at least in a language all here can understand,' said Gotrek, thumping irritably at the rune in his chest. 'You sorry excuse for a rune of power.'

Anustrolha a kazak a krutdamaz!

'Shut up!'

'Now I think of it...' Maleneth mused. 'I believe I have heard the rune whispering before. But only for brief spells after you had drunk yourself unconscious. I have never heard it speak aloud.'

'Gods,' Gotrek muttered. 'They love the sound of their own voices. Especially the dead ones.'

'It'll be these spirit paths,' said Witromm.

'You sing true, Oldwood,' said Druanthael. The Sylvaneth walked ahead with a band of Kurnoth Hunters armed with greatswords and bows. They moved with a stiff yet eerily graceful stride, their long limbs allowing them to cover great distances with ease. 'The life-song of the goddess speeds our travel on the root paths. The power this one bears in his metal responds to hers.'

Gotrek leered down at his chest. He tapped on the golden rune like a drunk trying to wake up a pet. 'You like that, oathtaker? You're singing for an elf-witch?'

Grimnir or Kazakaz. Or gorlrik. Or Az-Dreugidum.

'I didn't think so.'

'Thanks again for your help, Huntmistress,' said Witromm.

'The forest heard your regret, Oldwood. Friends we are not and the season of reckoning will come, but we share an enemy now.'

'Well, I'm obliged all the same. I don't think I fancy being another ornament in Nurgle's garden.'

'Are we there yet?' Gotrek complained, apparently growing bored with tormenting his god.

'Almost,' said Druanthael. 'The Realm Roots allow us to travel with great haste.'

'Good. All this green is making me dizzy.'

'It looks like Gotrek,' said Maleneth. 'But it whines like an acolyte snatched from his cell for the morning sacrifice.'

Elgi a elgar.

'You can shut up too,' said Gotrek, but Maleneth felt he was speaking to the rune rather than her.

Maleneth could not tell right away that they had left the spirit paths behind. She crunched through dry leaves until slowly, very slowly, they became mulchy underfoot, the sweet smell became sickly and the chill returned to nip at her skin.

'This is the place all right,' she murmured, shivering in the sudden cold.

The trees here were huge and regally spaced, kings of the wood sharing counsel, but had the delicate, brittle appearance of ice sculptures in some Azyrite noble's winter garden. This had to be the source of the enchanted winter. The hearthglade of the Cueth'nhair. Perhaps even the abode of Ancient Hruth'gael and the end of Gotrek's ridiculous quest into the Nevergreen Woods.

Hiding herself behind a fan of frostbitten green foliage, Maleneth watched as coughing, retching, sneezing, dolefully cheerful Plaguebearers hacked at the ice cladding the frozen trees.

'Come out, come out, mine feculent queen.' Sir Algur paced back and forth past the wheezing gangs. 'I know that thou doth veil thy doe-eyed beauty within the bark of this frozen glade. Such modesty. Such chastity. Thy feminine virtues doth inflame me, my goddess-to-be. Breaketh the ice, my fine fellows! The doxy doth hide within one of these ancient trees, but I would bear her forth, and look but once upon that lady's verdant countenance before making of her an offering to the Grandfather.'

'For the Grandfather!' the daemons hacked and spluttered.

'For the Grandfather, indeed!'

'It looks as though all their attention is on the sleeping Tree-lords,' Maleneth murmured. 'I do not even see any sentries. If we are quiet we could–'

'Oi!' Gotrek yelled, striding through the intervening foliage like a steam tank through a hanging basket. 'Over here, you rancid gargoyles, you vomit-breathed, flake-skinned, drip-nosed crusts of filth from the unwashed nether reaches of Gazul's under breeches! Wipe the pus from your eyeballs. Never let it be said that Gotrek Gurnisson is a difficult dwarf to find when there are trees to be felled and axe-work to be done. He's right here! So come and taste the fires of Zangrom-Thaz if you've an appetite for it.' He laughed, drawing the smouldering brazier to his own cheek so that the fire sparkled in his one good eye. 'For if not then I'll be forcing it down your gristly little necks!'

'He hears the War Song of Alarielle,' Druanthael sang approvingly. Maleneth rolled her eyes. They were all mad.

The Plaguebearers did not respond at all to the Slayer's challenge. Either his appearance had stunned them utterly or their rotten brains really did just process their reactions that slowly. Gotrek stood there, amusingly disappointed and increasingly annoyed as Druanthael sounded a blast on her horn, her Kurnothi kindred striding elegantly past him into the glade.

'Awaken, Glath'nhair,' Druanthael sang, gesturing with long, stiff fingers towards a frozen tree. Its trunks shivered at her summons, sheet ice splintering off and falling in a twinkling shower from its branches. 'Awaken, Khuron'laer. Awaken, Lord of the Emerald Bowers and Shield of the Chestnut Thousand. Alarielle commands a Wild Hunt. The Everqueen commands you awaken.' She hacked a Plaguebearer into two dribbling halves with a mighty swing of her sword. 'Cast off the armour of winter and fight. Awaken.'

'What is this?' Sir Algur demanded. 'Intruders upon mine lady's grove? A pox on them, I say!'

The Plague Knight drew his rusted steel with a sound like a bread loaf being grated and proposed a highly theatrical *en garde* to the oncoming Sylvaneth giants. The man gave every impression of being a buffoon, but everything he had wrought on the Nevergreen Woods over the past few hours told Maleneth otherwise.

'Jaro! Playeth a melody to stoke my choler.'

The little minstrel scrunched its face into something appropriately angry, launching into a screeching, screwball melody as its foppish lord tore cheerily through the Kurnoth Hunters.

'This one's mine,' said Witromm.

Maleneth said nothing. If the duardin expected her to try and dissuade him then he was going to be disappointed.

'He's mine!'

Gotrek plunged through a waterfall of draining ice water, emerging on the other side sopping wet but still furious, swinging his steaming greataxe for the knight of Nurgle.

The fiddler arrived at a nails-on-chalkboard crescendo just as Gotrek's axe hammered into Sir Algur's flimsy-looking sword, sprinkling the top of the Plague Knight's hat with flakes of rust.

''Tis the Fyreslayer,' Algur said, betraying no hint of the monstrous strain that had to be involved in holding Gotrek's axe at bay one-handed. 'And worse too f'r the wear.'

'I'm no Fyreslayer.'

'Thou lookest half-dead already from chill. Yield to me now. The Everqueen's accurs'd winter shall not touch thee when Nurgle claims this garden.'

Gotrek swung again, but some miasmic aura of despair about Sir Algur robbed the blow of its ferocity. The minstrel, Jaro, plodded around the duelling fighters with over-heavy feet in exaggerated slow motion. The tempo of its fiddling dropped to a snail's pace that left Gotrek struggling to raise his axe for another swing. Maleneth could barely get herself to stand up. Elsewhere in the glade, she could see Witromm, Druanthael and the Kurnoth Hunters still fighting, but moving as sluggishly as the Plaguebearers, who chortled at the prospect of sharing their misery with fresh souls.

'Yes, Doomseeker. 'Tis the very act of shivering that reminds thee thou art bitter cold. Warmth cometh from acceptance.'

The knight delivered a darting thrust. Gotrek blocked it sluggishly.

'Other Slayers used to mock me, you know.'

'For shame,' Algur said, and flicked a cut across Gotrek's brow. The Slayer barely registered it.

'Worse. They used to *pity* me. Said I was unlucky. Said I was cursed. Gotrek Gurnisson, the Slayer who couldn't find his doom. Maybe when this winter passes I'll go back to that hill beyond the walls of Hammerhal. Quarry that stone. Raise that hall. Get some goats. Cut down those bloody trees.'

'Do not fight it, duardin. I see the makings of a Leper-Knight in thee, a fine convert to the Order of Despair.'

'Gotrek!' Maleneth yelled, but the Slayer did not even hear her.

Nothing good, she decided, would come of Gotrek dying here.

Maleneth struggled to raise her knife for a throw, but the arm felt stiff, the joints swollen and painful, the knife as heavy as a Kurnothi broadsword. It was that minstrel and its infernal instrument. Tears streaming down her face from the pain and effort of turning her neck, she looked towards it. The nurgling had perched on the toe of its master's boot, intense concentration causing it to dribble as it struck one painfully off-key note very slowly after another.

Her thoughts began to feel heavy. Why had she been trying so hard to get back to Azyrheim? she wondered. All this blood and scheming, and for what? For a home filled with enemies and a handful of fair-weather friends all waiting for the chance to spurn her, and all dependent on the pendulum swing of Gotrek's mood? What would it have mattered if the Master Rune had stayed in Karag Unbak, or ended up in the hands of the Eye Not Seen? Who would have cared? Would it not be so much easier to just sit down in this pleasant forest and wait for the end to come? Or better yet, take the knife and cut her own throat with it, take the easy way with one last offering to the Bloody-Handed God…

She looked at the knife in her hand, trying to move it to her neck, and almost cried when she found that her limbs were too sore even to do that. The blade had been forged from celestium, kissed by the envenomed lips of the Hag of Azyr herself.

It had been meant for someone special.

With a scream, she drew her arm back and threw it.

Maleneth never knew whether she was aiming at Algur or at Gotrek himself, but she missed both targets, the blade plunging instead into the tiny nurgling minstrel, which gurgled and fell over with a whine of broken strings and a splat.

'Jaro!' Sir Algur wailed.

Gotrek blinked and seemed to regain his focus. 'You'd use sorcery to get me to lie down and die, would you? Make me throw down this axe? If I desired such an end I'd have taken the elfling's advice and drunk myself to it in Hammerhal Ghyra. Give me blood. Give me gore and entrails, broken bones, lumps of meat stuck in trees and slaves to the Dark Gods weeping for their mothers!'

The Slayer hurled himself at Sir Algur and this time it was the Leper-Knight struggling to keep up.

'There art as many ways to surrender as there art for the body to die and maketh new life. No god understands despair like Alarielle, Fyreslayer. No god fears it so. No other hast been to yonder ledge and jumped. Why else would Grandfather desire that lady over all others?'

'For the last time, I am not a Fyreslayer!'

Gotrek stove his axe through Sir Algur's sword. The blunt tip went spinning off into the wood and Algur's arms milled as they tried, and failed, to keep him from tripping and falling backwards onto his rear. His demeanour remained one of resigned good cheer throughout. Like a dinner host coming to the end of a long but thoroughly worthwhile evening.

'Calleth on the power of thy god once more, Fyreslayer,' he said, and smiled. 'Destroy me. I welcome it, for acceptance is the highest virtue in mine master's eyes. Allowest me only to tell the Grandfather it is an equal that sends me to him.'

'Grimnir does no favours, poxling,' said Gotrek, swinging his greataxe up overhead. 'Not to you.' His shoulders bulged. His face became volcanic. 'And sure as hell not to me.'

His axe struck through Sir Algur's upturned face to the base of the neck, halving it like a rotten fruit and splattering his beard with maggots.

'And I'm *not* a bloody Fyreslayer.'

A groan of lament went up from the Plaguebearers in the hearth-glade as the body crumbled, a new and bellicose song shivering from Druanthael and her kin to which the slumbering trees thrashed and swayed in time. *Now what?* Maleneth thought. Algur and Jaro had been slain, but she still felt as though she had been dragged from her sickbed for Death Night. She did not think she could survive any more excitement.

'My queen,' Druanthael sang. 'She comes.'

The ice around the greatest tree in the glade exploded, twinkling bits of ice transforming and taking wing before Maleneth's eyes, a host of beetles shaking off their winter coats and swarming joyfully around the glade. Where they encountered a Kurnoth Hunter they billowed around them, trilling and singing and glimmering for all the world like a million tiny flecks of emerald. Where they fell upon a Plaguebearer they did so without mercy, rendering them down in moments to pools of fertile sludge from which fresh millions burst into exuberant new life. At the very centre of it all, Gotrek bulged over his axe, daring so much as one beetle to flutter a wing against his bloody crest.

Maleneth watched in awe as a portion of the swarm separated itself from the rest, swirling over Gotrek's bristling head into the titanic form of a woman.

'Khaine, spare my beating heart. She is so beautiful. Never did I think my service to the Bloody-Handed would see me standing before a goddess.'

'Aye,' Witromm mumbled. 'Get on your bloody knee, Gotrek.'

'Pfft.'

The Radiant Queen hovered before them on a million sets of wings, buzzing with life, her appearance rippling and shimmering with the individual movements of the creatures within her. Her voice, when it came, was all that Maleneth might have imagined it could be. Beautiful and terrifying. Ancient and new. Arising from every leaf and creature and tremble of wind in this glade, in this forest, in this realm.

'You do not bow before a goddess?'

'I thought about it,' said Gotrek, after a moment's consideration. 'But if I bow to you then who else is going to expect the same. Teclis?'

The Slayer spat on the ground. Maleneth was horrified, but to her astonishment the gestalt apparition before them appeared to smile.

'He'd bloody well like that, wouldn't he? To this lot you're a goddess, and it's only right and proper they show respect. But to me?' He shook his head sadly. 'If I'm to be honest then I'm not sure what to make of either of us, yet.'

'This forest is a part of me,' said Alarielle, and her voice now was the sound of roots and vines tearing through rock. 'These mountains are a part of me. We are worlds apart, Gotrek Gurnisson. I could end your life with a verse of my song.'

'Maybe,' Gotrek conceded.

Witromm cleared his throat nervously. 'We've come looking for Ancient Hruth'gael, m'lady.'

'But some of us are more than happy to whet their axe on a goddess if the opportunity presents.'

'Not *now*, Gotrek,' Maleneth hissed at him. He was shameless. Absolutely shameless.

'I know of your quest, Slayer,' said the Everqueen. 'I know what you look for, and what you seek, and know too that they are not one and the same. Hruth'gael is departed, which is how his hearth-glade was allowed to fall, and why I was forced to bury this seed of myself in its soil and cloak it in winter ere his return. He left on the same errand that brought the return of Algur Threefingers. The Silver Tower of Xer'ger'ael, the Tyrant of Eyes, appeared in my child's kingdom at the same time as the Grey Lord began his siege of Sigmar's city in Aqshy.'

Alarielle and her buzzing drew closer.

Maleneth had never been more terrified of anything in her life, but she could not look away. She could not even blink. She was as captivated by the Everqueen's beauty as she had been by the plague minstrel's song of despair, and it was no more pleasant an experience.

'Druanthael.'

The Kurnoth Huntress was already on one knee. She stiffly lowered her head. 'Your heartwood and your song, my queen.'

'You will guide the Slayer to the Silver Tower. There you will seek out Ancient Hruth'gael, to return him if he lives and requires aid, to retrieve his lamentiri and avenge him should my child have fallen. Let her lead you, Slayer.'

The immense, multifaceted green face turned to Gotrek. He turned his chin belligerently towards it.

'I cannot promise you the weapons of my fallen ally, Grimnir, but follow my Huntmistress into Xer'ger'ael's tower and you will find what you need.' She drifted back. 'Consider this my gratitude for the slaying of Algur Threefingers, and my warning – do not ever return to my woods.'

With that, the goddess exploded into her constituent creatures, millions of individual beetles released from her will and swarming upwards into the trees, carrying the voice-song of Alarielle further and higher onto the wind.

'Gods,' said Gotrek. 'So bloody *dramatic*.'

'Your will is mine, my queen,' said Druanthael, head bowed and rocking slightly on her haunches. From a creature as formidable as the Kurnoth Huntress, it was an unsettling sight. 'I will seek out the Silver Tower of the Tyrant of Eyes, and learn the fate of Ancient Hruth'gael.'

'Aye. I'm sure you will.'

'A Silver Tower…' Witromm muttered fearfully.

Maleneth was forced to agree. Both the sentiment, and the eloquence. Only a goddess would think so little of sending a group of mortals to such a place.

'I begin to think my life would have been easier had Khaine simply taken me as a bride.'

'It would have been shorter,' said Witromm.

'That might be preferable, where we are going.'

'So,' said Gotrek, inexplicably amiable again now that his goal was further away than ever and the promise of more monsters to battle had been dangled over him. 'What's a Silver Tower, then?'

PART SIX

The Everlasting Oath

TWENTY-SEVEN

'I'm not one to complain, as you know,' said Gotrek as his great-axe splattered through a giggling, pink-skinned monster.

After several days spent following Druanthael through the Realm Roots, as well as more conventional forest paths, they had passed the very edges of the Nevergreen Woods, many hundreds of miles from Hammerhal Ghyra. It was here that, according to Everqueen Alarielle, a Silver Tower of Tzeentch had manifested within the goddess' kingdom.

The trees there grew in odd formations and appeared almost crystalline, diffracting light and sound and even, sometimes, thought, so that it felt more like being inside a hall of disturbing mirrors than a wood. If anything, it was worse than the rot and despair that Algur Threefingers had brought to the hearthglades. Evil was *supposed* to be rancid and hideous. It should be foul-smelling and rankly warm. The body should be able to know it and immediately reject it. This crystal grove was altogether too beautiful.

It could have been the gibbering horde of daemons of course, or the bellows of a mad duardin impairing her senses, but one thing that Maleneth felt reasonably sure of was that there was no citadel of sorcery and Change hidden behind the bushes.

'Yes, Gotrek,' Maleneth sighed. 'That was one of the first things I noticed about you in our short time together.'

Gotrek wrenched his flaming axe free, his brutal face clenched into an expression of extreme distaste as the Pink Horror split into two grumbling blue ones. The smaller daemons ran in opposite directions around him until he managed to stamp one underfoot. It deflated with a miserable-sounding whine and a sulphurous stench, only to split again into a pair of yellow creatures so shrill with rage that there was smoke rising from their tiny backs.

'As Grungni is fond of metal and Grimnir is a lying swine, I despise these monsters.'

'No? Really?'

Sarcasm, as always, was wasted on the Slayer.

'It is as though they taunt me, elfling, for no matter how many I kill there will always be more, and no matter how many there are–'

One of the miniscule brimstone Horrors belched fire over Gotrek. The Slayer gave it a look as though he had just been puked on by an infant: more fed up than angry.

'No matter how many there are, there are never enough of the bloody things to kill me.' He growled and turned towards Maleneth, who was doing her best to keep well out of it. 'On top of everything else, I think this Fyreslayer rune insulates me against the daemons' fire.'

'That's a… pity?'

Gotrek struck his axe through one of the brimstone Horrors. It exploded with a final expletive-laden screech, dousing the Slayer's leg in fire.

'I hardly even feel it.' He shook his axe fiercely. 'You hear that, you rubber-limbed daemon jackals, don't be shy now! You're going to have to try harder if you mean to tell your infernal master how you brought down Gotrek Gurnisson.'

With that, Gotrek gave a roar and charged into the tainted grove where the mass of gibbering Horrors was still thickest. Maleneth let him run ahead. She sighed. She did not even need to *try* and get the fool killed.

Or so one would have thought.

'It is not here,' Druanthael moaned as she strode through the kaleidoscope of Horrors, searching. The gigantic Kurnoth Huntress towered over the sea of pink and, increasingly, yellow and blue daemons, sweeping the creatures clear with her wooden sword.

'I am so glad to have one of the fabled scouts of the Sylvaneth as our guide,' said Maleneth.

'The Silver Towers exist outside of time and mortal dimensions,' said Witromm. Like Maleneth, the old duardin was doing his utmost to avoid the fighting. Unlike Maleneth, he was sitting on a tree stump with his cloak folded up under his behind, supping amiably on his pipe while he watched Gotrek and Druanthael work. 'It might just as easily have made itself small enough to disappear into the forest. Or tucked itself into a fold in the aether.'

'It has not done either of those things, though, has it?' said Maleneth.

'Apparently not. Look out behind–'

Maleneth spun, drawing a knife and hurling it. It went through a tuberous, free-floating creature that had been dribbling pink fire from various orifices before Maleneth's knife severed its main hose. It exploded spectacularly. Maleneth covered her eyes.

'If you wish to help, then you could start by getting up off that stump.'

'Preserving my strength, lass.' Witromm gestured grandiloquently about him with his pipe. 'You don't get to grow a beard this long by exerting yourself too early.'

'The Silver Tower was here,' Druanthael sang out. 'The Ever-queen would not guide us astray.'

'You have not been long with us, Huntress,' said Maleneth. 'But if a daemonic horde is not evidence enough of a Chaos incursion upon the Mortal Realms then Gotrek's good mood should be.'

The Slayer gave a delighted hoot as he put paid to something particularly large and unpleasant.

'Oh well,' said Witromm, sliding off his stump and beating cobwebs from his hands on his trousers. 'It was a good effort. We gave it our best swing.'

'So quick to give up?' said Maleneth.

'It could be anywhere in the Mortal Realms now. Or beyond. It's a Silver Tower, it's what they do.'

'No, it is more than that. The Silver Tower frightens you even more than the Everqueen. Why?'

The old duardin did some suspiciously evasive grumbling.

'The Silver Tower is not here, but I hear it yet.' Druanthael strode back towards them, leaving Gotrek to mop up the last belligerent Horrors amongst the crystal trees. 'The Life Song of those it has stolen from my queen's forest calls out to me still.'

'I thought Alarielle's song didn't carry so well over the barriers between realms?' said Witromm. He glanced at Maleneth and explained. 'I've met treefolk from Shyish to Azyr, in Aqshy even, if you can imagine it, but seldom more than a handful in an enchanted forest here and a forgotten glade there. They've never been what you'd call properly adjusted.'

'It must have moved only recently,' said Druanthael, after a moment's consideration. 'Being here in this grove is like walking through goosegrass. The Silver Tower has left tendrils of life energy and unsettled magicks that I can perceive.'

'So where is it?' asked Maleneth.

Druanthael tilted her head towards the shimmering canopy,

emitting a low woody creak from somewhere deep within her chest that Maleneth was certain she felt the ground beneath her answer. 'I see a forest, lush and green, but unlike those of Ghyran. I see stalking things, biting things, killing things. Rats that scurry. I see poisonous serpents and lurking reptiles and plants that snare and eat what birds dare visit their flowers.' She shuddered and turned back to Maleneth and Witromm. The emerald glow returned to her deep eye sockets. 'It is a cruel perversion of my lady's realm.'

'It sounds as though it could be somewhere in Ghur,' suggested Maleneth.

'Ghur?' Gotrek bellowed. He was surrounded by smoke-belching Horrors, his face flushed from the effort of killing them all, but the Slayer had ears like a bat when it suited him. 'I've not heard of that one yet.'

'You will like it, Gotrek,' Maleneth yelled back. 'The Realm of Beasts.'

Gotrek stomped back, panting, the last of the brimstone Horrors a charcoal stain up his shin. 'Pathetic creatures. My arm is barely even warm. But what's this, elfling? There is a whole Realm of Beasts?' He puffed himself up as though no duardin in the Mortal Realms had ever been so wronged. 'Why am I only hearing of this now?'

Druanthael delivered another barrage of clicks and groans and sing-song wooden creaks. The forest around her responded in kind. It was like listening to something vast and green extending itself around them. Even discounting the state of the trees in this part of the Nevergreens, it was far from a pleasant experience.

'The forest knows of a realmgate to Ghur. It is not far from here.'

'It's speaking of Ohlicoatl,' Witromm said quietly. 'The Realm-serpent.'

Something about the way the old duardin said it sent a shiver down Maleneth's back. 'You know of it?'

'The Maw of Sotek? Aye, you could say that. For if jumping into a fire wasn't dangerous enough you can always bathe yourself in oil beforehand.'

Druanthael, however, was already striding purposefully away.

'Where are you off to?' Gotrek called after her.

'The Everqueen bade me to seek out the Silver Tower and recover the lamentiri of Ancient Hruth'gael. You may follow or you may not, but my way is clear.'

Gotrek grumbled about being ordered about by a 'tree-witch', but was soon stomping off after her. Maleneth watched them both ruefully. As a young acolyte, she had used to enjoy tormenting the captives in the cells before the ritual sacrifices. There had been a look on their faces that she had particularly appreciated on a superficial level, but which had also proven deeply fascinating in the smaller hours of quieter nights: a combination of resignation and utter dread. Watching Gotrek disappear into the woods after the Kurnoth Huntress, Maleneth wondered if she was not wearing the exact same expression.

'What is a little extra danger, Witromm? If we are lucky then maybe Gotrek will get himself killed before we even reach the Silver Tower.'

The Slayer was close enough to laugh.

'I don't think she's joking,' said Witromm.

'Good.' Gotrek grinned back at them both. 'Nor am I.'

TWENTY-EIGHT

The prayer candles flickered, arranged across the huge black altar in a twelve-pointed star. Lightning charms crackled in their sconces. Beyond the thick walls of the Stormkeep's austere chapel, a battle raged. Jordaius Lionheart bade himself to ignore it. He knelt before the altar in his armour, eyes watering as he stared unblinking into the image of the High Star painted in candlelight, and prayed.

'All my mortal life, such as I recall of it, I dreamed of being a hero in your armies. I wish only to serve you now.'

Dum. Git a krutkhaz, frurndar. Dum. Grimnir or Grimnir, or an af dum.

He closed his eyes, the twelve-pointed star, Sigendil, still glowing against the backs of his eyelids, and endeavoured to ignore the echo in his thoughts. Its voice was harsh and metallic, not his own, as though the Mask Impassive of his helmet was trying to speak with him.

'God-King. Please. If I have failed you in some way then I beg you, tell me. Show me how I might make amends.'

Dum.

'What is this voice that speaks to me when you do not? What tongue of the Mortal Realms does it speak?' He waited. There was no answer forthcoming. 'Answer me, Sigmar!'

The door behind him opened. Jordaius hung his head as the clank of heavy boots on stone advanced down the chapel's nave towards him. He felt the hair on the backs of his hands and neck rise in response to the approaching warrior's lightning aura.

'Would you address Lord-Castellant Ansiris Oathforged thus, Prosecutor Jordaius?'

Jordaius looked up, but did not turn around. He stared into the candles on the altar. 'Lord-Relictor Sekrus, forgive me. I did not mean–'

'Sigmar has it in his power to forgive. You and I, however – we are merely his servants. Answer the question, Prosecutor – would you demand such answers from your Lord-Castellant?'

'No, Lord-Relictor.'

'Then what makes you think to do so of Sigmar Heldenhammer, God-King of Azyr, foremost of the gods? Is it because Sigmar is not here with you in this sanctum as I am, or out there defending the walls of this Stormkeep with Ansiris? Do you think that means he does not hear?'

'I do not know, Lord-Relictor, but I...'

Jordaius hesitated. It felt shameful even to speak the doubts aloud, as though he was confessing to a flaw that everyone could already see but him. He had thought that the Reforging would bring certainty and strength. The God-King had lifted him up from the Mortal Realms at the brink of death, granted him the power to stand against foes who would before have slain him in a heartbeat. He had lent him wings that he might carry that power wherever such defiance was needed. And yet, where there should have been faith and conviction, he felt only doubt.

'But I fear it. I feel as though my destiny is not wholly my own.'

'You carry a spark of the Storm Eternal within your soul, Jordaius. You have no destiny that is not now bound eternally to Sigmar's, and that is a great gift.'

'I know it. But I feel...' He paused again, trying to put words to the feelings of a soul. 'Torn. As though another contests the God-King for some part of me. Who was I in life, Sekrus? What manner of being could lay a claim on my soul even now?'

He turned then, seeking the reassurance of a human face only to be confronted by the brooding skull mask and jagged golden halo of the Lord-Relictor. The blue eyes staring out through the pin-hole slits were almost as cold. The Lords-Relictor of the Stormcast chambers were charged with the spiritual wellbeing and purity of every warrior under their charge. As the souls of those warriors were immortal, destined to be reforged again and again, returned to new bodies with each death and sent back into the Great War, there was no more vital task. Jordaius had not been taught these things. There had been no books or tutelage to prepare him for this new life. The knowledge he had been deemed to require had been beaten into him on the Anvil of Apotheosis, even as his recollections of his life before fled from him like sparks under the Smith's hammer.

The Lord-Relictor was there to offer strength, not comfort.

'You are young, Jordaius,' said Sekrus, with a heavy sigh. 'Recently slain and newly forged. You have died and been remade as an Anvil of the Heldenhammer. Doubt is natural. But you have been chosen. Remember that. Hold it to that place where a living heart once beat. You have been chosen to serve beyond death in the Stormhosts of the God-King where untold others have been left to fade into the underworlds of Shyish.'

'A voice speaks to me when I pray, Lord-Relictor. It speaks in a language I do not remember ever hearing, but it is no human tongue that speaks it.'

He closed his eyes and struggled, as he would often find himself doing, to unearth just one more scrap of memory from his mortal past. *A city in the desert. A lion on the wind. Black and gold. The same colours I wear now.* A coincidence? Or fate? He remembered a mother, an uncle, comrades, but they were all nameless, shades, existing in a different world to that which Sigmar had for some reason chosen for him. But stare long enough into that fog, and one broken recollection always emerged to push aside all others.

'It is a duardin. A Fyreslayer, I think. His hair is red and struck with gold. His axe burns. He calls to me from beyond the Cosmic Storm. His name is…' He concentrated hard. The answer was right there at the back of his mind. It felt as though Sigmar himself was willing him to grasp it. 'His name is…'

'Enough, Jordaius, no more. We all had lives before this one, but they are gone now, shed like the shrouds in which our mortal remains were buried. The Hallowed Knights may record their memories in the Sepulchre of the Faithful, and I am told that the Astral Templars deliberately seek out mortal servants from their old cultures to remind them of past deeds and glories, but we are the Anvils of the Heldenhammer. We are dust and bone, our glories long buried beneath the sands of time. We do not speak of such things. You should have learned this already, before you were permitted to depart the Mausoleum of the Lost in Sigmaron to join us here in Ghur.'

Jordaius averted his eyes. He turned back to the twelve-pointed star upon the altar.

'My desire is only to serve, to emulate the great heroes of old. But these questions… I have to share them with someone or I fear I will lose my mind. Who can I talk to if not the Lord-Relictor charged with the sanctity of my soul?'

Sekrus laid a gauntleted hand on Jordaius' pauldron. Lightning snapped and crawled between the metal plates. 'You may confide in Sigmar, Jordaius,' he said softly. 'And no other.'

'Yes, Lord-Relictor.'

Sekrus withdrew his hand and took a step back from the altar. 'For now, however, you may attempt to praise him in battle. Ansiris' need for you is greater.'

'You mean…'

The Lord-Relictor nodded once and Jordaius felt a thrill go through him, more potent than Sekrus' lightning.

'It is time for you to don stormshield and Mask Impassive, and to take up your javelin in real battle. Against my better judgement, it is time for you to leave this cloister and face the enemies of Sigmar alongside your new brothers.'

TWENTY-NINE

Gotrek hummed tunelessly as he hacked through the thick foliage. The forest ahead was filled with flapping wings and the screeches of terrified animals, and for once, Maleneth did not think that Gotrek was the cause of it. The air carried a faint shimmer, motes of star-dust that trembled with the crashing of something truly monstrous in the trees up ahead. Maleneth bared her teeth in annoyance. Monstrous things had started cropping up *up ahead* with alarming frequency since she had shackled herself to the Slayer.

'Enough, Doomseeker!' Druanthael said as Gotrek cut himself an opening through another criss-crossing tangle of vegetation. 'They are but saplings. Can you not hear how they cry out?'

'If you can't leave a few dead trees behind you then what's the point of traipsing through a bloody forest?'

Maleneth looked up, mouth falling open as a colossal spectral tail rose up above the forest canopy. It hung in the sky like a small moon before crashing back down, shaking the earth and flatten-ing a swathe of forest. The horizon turned briefly green.

'Hag of Azyr,' Maleneth muttered.

'It's the Realmserpent,' Witromm yelled over the thundering commotion.

'You think?'

'It's not usually this violent. Something has it angered.'

'Gotrek has that effect on the best of us.'

The Slayer snorted with laughter as he went about upsetting Druanthael by killing some young trees. *Khaine help me,* she thought. Gotrek was actually starting to *like* her.

'There's got to be something up on the other side of the bridge,' said Witromm.

'Something like a Silver Tower?'

The old duardin shrugged.

'Are we supposed to just climb onto its tail? Look at the size of it! It would be like trying to catch a passing comet.'

Foliage tore as the great tail rose again. Druanthael cried out at the destruction. If the Sylvaneth had been flesh and blood rather than hard wood and sap then she would have been on her knees weeping.

'Gah, it's going up again,' said Gotrek.

'It'll be back down,' said Witromm darkly.

'It's moving away. Come on!' The Slayer attacked the foliage with redoubled aggression.

'I said *enough!*' Druanthael's body groaned and shuddered, emitting a throbbing, woody song that elicited the trees and bushes directly ahead of her to quiver to attention. 'Part, little saplings. Pull up your roots. Shed your coats of earth and stone. Part.'

The undergrowth shuffled aside, pushing a narrow but clear path into the wood ahead.

'Now that is where a Kurnoth Huntress comes in useful,' said Maleneth.

'You could have just done that from the start instead of crying on about it,' Gotrek complained.

'The life here is fragile,' said Druanthael. 'It suffers under the cold light of Azyr. To command it in this way is to weaken it further, but you give me no choice.'

'Azyr?' Gotrek looked accusingly at Maleneth, as though everyone was now trying to trick him into Sigmar's city. 'You promised that this realmgate led to the Realm of Beasts!'

'Ohlicoatl was a Star Titan,' Witromm explained. 'He fell from the heavens to Ghyran and found a glade here in the Nevergreen Mountains, where the walls between realms were thin. He bored through, meaning to find his way home, but Sigmar by then had barred the ways to his realm.'

'You seem to know an awful lot about it,' said Maleneth suspiciously. Indeed, Witromm seemed to know an awful lot about everything.

Witromm shrugged. 'I'm old, lass, and I've been around.'

'The Star Titan found itself drawn instead to the jungles of Ohlor, in Ghur,' Druanthael went on. 'He has been trapped between the two realms ever since. Not a portal but a *bridge*. A bridge of the Realmserpent's own body.'

'Not all realmgates are as easy to walk as the Stormrift of Hammerhal.'

Gotrek grunted in agreement, apparently recalling some traumatic journey of his own that Maleneth had not been privy to.

She hoped it had been awful.

'But the Star Titans are true immortals,' said Maleneth. 'It should have died and returned to Azyr to be reborn long ago.'

'Devouring the energies of Ghur must have prolonged its life,' said Witromm. 'As well as filling its back with every beast imaginable to duardin, aelf and Sylvaneth too, I'd wager.'

Gotrek chuckled. 'Good.' The Slayer broke into a plodding excuse for a run along Druanthael's path as, with a terrible, yawning inevitability, the Realmserpent's tail came crashing back down. 'Come on! The last one on that thing's back is a beardless halfling!'

THIRTY

The black stone walls of the Mortisrock, Stormkeep of the Anvils of the Heldenhammer, stood as a bulwark against the savage jungle. Trees pressed against the ramparts, lush green foliage thrown over the top like ladders, climbing a little higher each night, drawn by instinct to devour it all and claim the ground it stood upon for their own. And today, it was not only the jungle that those walls struggled to hold at bay.

Jordaius looked down into the Stormkeep as Sekrus led him from the chapel onto the uppermost battlements. The wind caught the night-black plume in his helmet, his wings creaking as the gust passed through the unlit harness.

Stormcast Eternals, his brothers and sisters, battled the skaven invaders for the walls, for the mausoleum streets, for the skies. The children of Ruin were everywhere, crawling over his god and master's walls like the vermin they were. It made the storm in him thunder like a second heart.

'How many times did I dream of this day?' he murmured,

wondering at where the words came from and the strange longing they brought to his heart.

'The Mortisrock was raised two centuries ago by Lord-Castellant Ansiris, to hold the Ghurishside of the Ohlicoatl Realmbridge.' Sekrus' gauntlets crunched down on the battlements. His skull-faced gaze swept the battles below like that of the God of Death himself, selecting who would fall and who would soar. 'To honour the oath he made to Starmaster Zectoka in exchange for the Seraphon's aid against the armies of Khorne – to guard this gate until the end of time.'

'A warrior must honour his oaths.'

'That he must. And he–' Sekrus turned to him, sensing something unsettled behind the Mask Impassive. 'What is it, Jordaius? You are distracted.'

'I… I do not know, Lord-Relictor. This talk of oaths and debts, I…' He shook his head as if to clear it of unwanted thoughts. 'It is nothing. Forgive me.'

'Then look now to where the outer walls of the Ward of Stars once stood.'

No one in all of Sigmar's mighty Stormhosts could have expressed such loathing with a pointed finger as Lord-Relictor Sekrus mustered then, and nowhere else in the Mortal Realms could it have been more richly deserved. Jordaius felt the weight of its presence before he saw it, a curse upon his very soul.

The Silver Tower of Xer'ger'ael. One of the Damned Nine, Gaunt Summoner of Tzeentch, and slave of the Grandmarshal of the Apocalypse, Archaon Everchosen himself. The so-called Tyrant of Eyes. The daemon's abode defied simple description. Words were inadequate to it. Its outer dimension and materials of construction changed with the hour, with the moment, with the mood and identity and darkest secrets of whoever beheld it. Jordaius feared to look upon it, uncertain whether its appearance would be used to test him or tempt him and unwilling to find out. Sekrus had commanded him to face it, however, and so he did, limiting himself only to the battles spilling outwards from its iridescent gates.

'It is a splinter of the Changer's accursed domain in the skin of Sigmar's blessed Order,' Sekrus intoned. 'Is there some malign intent that causes it to manifest within a Stormkeep consecrated to the God-King? Or does its daemonic castellan simply taunt us with our impotence at its incursion? I know not, but every guise of evil in this realm has been drawn to its gates, and hence through us. Were it up to me I would cede the Ward of Stars to them entirely and withdraw to the Maw of Sotek. Our oath binds us only to defend the gate. Let these vermin murder one another over their prize. I would whisper no prayer for those trapped forevermore with the Gaunt Summoner therein.'

Jordaius looked up. A thunderous battle passed overhead, several retinues of Prosecutors harassing a flotilla of rickety skaven sky-barges and war-balloons. A shiver passed through the Mortis-rock as some of the crossfire earthed itself in its lightning rods, feeding that energy back into the wards that crackled across the outer walls.

'Have I your leave, Lord-Relictor?'

Sekrus looked reluctant, but nodded once. 'Fly, Jordaius! Join your brothers and sisters. Fly, and fear no death.'

Jordaius made a fist in the sign of the comet and clanged it to his breastplate. 'Fear no death, Lord-Relictor!' Heart pounding, a storm raging in his immortal chest, he threw out his wings, lightning flaring from the starmetal frames as his soul soared.

How many times had he dreamed of this day?

With a terrific *clap* of thunder, he beat his wings and felt the Mortisrock fall away beneath his feet. Leaving it all behind, as he had been forced to do to his mortal life, he turned his face towards the melee, picked out a lurching skaven blimp, and climbed towards it.

The thing was massive. The balloon was made from the stitched-together skin of some Ghurish monster, braced with corroded metals and leaking a hellish green glow from whatever poisonous gas the skaven had devised to inflate it. A metal basket swung underneath it on chains. Compared to the balloon it was tiny, but it was crowded with enough Stormvermin to take a small castle, jezzail teams and ratling gunners restricting the Stormcast Eternals to hit-and-run attacks.

Shots whistled past Jordaius' ears, the occasional projectile pranging his armour as he flew nearer. He ignored it. He watched out of the corner of his eye slit as one of his fellow Angelos warriors took a mortal hit. The warrior's body dissolved into energy even as it fell, blasting back into the sky on a bolt of lightning bound for the soul mills of Sigmaron. The armour of the God-King was strong, but not inviolate, and the inventions of the skaven – though as dangerous to the wielder as the target – were deadly.

Jordaius raised a hand, summoned a stormcall javelin to his grip, and cast it at the balloon. The weapon broke apart into spasms of frustrated energies, turned by the deceptively cunning wards scratched into the balloon's skin. The shrill voices of the skaven jeered him as he swept across their machine.

'Sigmar, give me the strength and I will tear this abomination from your skies!'

Git a krutkhaz, frurndar.

Jordaius beat the heel of his now empty palm against the side of his helmet, but the echoes of the voice lingered.

'Not in battle, too…'

With a shake of the head, he dismissed the voice from his thoughts and summoned a second stormcall javelin. It was not a weapon designed solely for use at range. If they could not bring the skaven down from afar, then they would have to do it in close.

Dum.

'I serve only the God-King!' Jordaius roared, drowning the voice out with his own, strangling it with his faith.

'Board them!' someone was yelling, and Jordaius was the first to obey.

Skaven weapon teams filled the air with warpstone pellets, roasting it at shorter range with gouts of warpfire and zaps of green lightning so powerful they caused the basket to recoil against its chains and all aboard to shriek in terror. Jordaius judged the swing and pulled up his knees, rocketing over the basket's metal parapet and landing amidst a pack of heavily armoured Stormvermin. Two immediately went down under his boots. His javelin exploded from the back of a third, the Stormvermin going rigid and kicking as the energies of the War Storm burnt through its nervous system. A fierce backhand sent another flailing over the parapet, its squeals getting fainter and fainter as it plummeted towards the Mortisrock.

There was a heavy thump and another strenuous yaw on the chains as one of Jordaius' brothers landed beside him. The scarlet trim on his bone-white tabard and the golden beastmarks on his vambraces identified him as the Prosecutor-Prime, Vultar Carrionwing. Jordaius had met him only once, after his arrival in Ohlor, before his sequestration to the chapel.

'Welcome to the Oathforged, Prosecutor!' he said, laying into the swarming vermin and halving their numbers in a matter of moments.

'Thank you, Prosecutor-Prime. This is my first battle.'

'In this life, perhaps. You would not be here in black and gold if you were not a hero of many.'

'I appreciate your faith in–'

A flock of brilliantly feathered aetherwings billowed up from below before Jordaius could finish, swarming the basket with enough vigour to drive the remaining skaven to the forward and aft ends of their listing basket. Vultar cocked his head as the birds twittered urgently in his ear, the dark eyes behind his Mask Impassive becoming darker still.

'What is it?' Jordaius asked. The Smiths had not blessed him with the knowledge of the aetherwings' tongue.

'Skaven war machines strike at Sotek's Maw.'

'Do warriors not hold the realmbridge portal?'

'A Thunderhead Brotherhood of the Oathforged led by the Lord-Castellant himself,' Vultar hissed through the narrow mouth slit in his mask. 'I fear that Ansiris has underestimated this Grey Lord greatly. He is not here solely to drive us from the Ward of Stars and claim the Silver Tower. He means to slay Ohlicoatl and destroy the bridge to Ghryan.'

'Why? What purpose could it serve him?'

'The skaven are wretched cowards. They would have been wiped out millennia ago were they not devious. Be assured that they do nothing without reason, even if it would appear as madness to you or I.'

'Is such a feat even possible?'

'Ohlicoatl is a Star Titan and a god-killer. Were he assailed by any other warlord, I would say no, but as I tried to warn the Lord-Castellant, one underestimates this foe at their peril.'

Vultar reignited his wings, allowing the winds of Azyr to catch them and sweep him clear of the war-balloon's basket. Jordaius leapt after him, lighting his own wings at the first pull of the ground on his weight. He swept after the Prosecutor-Prime, the disbelieving squeals of the reprieved skaven crew disappearing behind them both. It hurt Jordaius deeply to leave them at large above the Mortisrock, but he could only have faith that whoever had dispatched the aetherwings had their own plans for dealing with them.

'Withdraw to the Maw,' Vultar yelled, raising his voice for all to hear. 'The Everlasting Oath will not be forsaken this day. Prosecutors, to me. Fear no death!'

'Fear no death!' Jordaius roared in return, as the Prosecutors broke off from the skaven's balloon armada, seen off by jeering skaven and a desultory hail of jezzail fire. The sounds of individual battles rose and fell below them as the Prosecutor retinues swept in formation across the Stormkeep's embattled wards.

No castle stood at the centre of the Mortisrock. There was no structure the Lord-Ordinators could design that could possibly have survived it. The energies of Ghyran leaked through the rift between the realms, the most potent fertiliser known to the gods, the essence of life itself, spilling into the heart of the Mortisrock and bringing it into savage bloom. Predatory flowers filled the air with scents that would have driven an ogor to insanity. Trees of a thousand species thrust themselves higher than the walls and towers that surrounded them, heavy with succulent-looking fruits that were invariably poisonous and, in most cases, outright carnivorous. Each day, Devastation Brotherhoods would scorch the growth back to the lip of Sotek's Maw, but with the Grey Lord's incursions their attention had been demanded elsewhere. After only two days of unattended growth, the vigour of Ghyran coupled with the predatory drive of Ghur had made for a rapacious combination.

In amongst the towering, saw-edged trees, the aethereal head of Ohlicoatl the Star Titan writhed in pain and hunger. The colossal serpent dwarfed the Mortisrock itself, caught betwixt realms for untold centuries and unable to tear itself free.

Jordaius had seen Dracolines and Stardrakes, the storm gargants that guarded the Thunder-Gates into the heart of Sigmaron, and even, once, the God-King himself, but he would never have thought that a creature as vast as this could be. It was as though Dracothion himself chewed through the wall of the realm to consume them all. Could even the engines of the Grey Lord hope to injure such a titan of Azyr?

Ohlicoatl delivered a roar that set an entire cohort of Prosecutors spinning away from it like sycamore seeds in a storm, even before spitting out a lightning bolt that blasted a skaven war-balloon from the sky. Prosecutors and Knights-Azyros darted amongst the fleet of skaven ironclads and war-balloons that had laid siege to the realmbridge, dozens of them returning to the lightning every moment Jordaius spent watching under the sheer volume of fire.

'The skaven are too many,' Jordaius yelled. 'Their weapons are too powerful.'

'Fear no death!' came Vultar's fearless retort. 'Scatter them to the gravewinds of Shyish!'

'For Sigmar!'

Grimnir or Grimnir, or an af dum.

'*Sigmar!*' Jordaius yelled again, louder.

Wallowing at the centre of the skaven armada's massed formation was a floating battleship of immense proportions. It was so big that it might have registered as a pinprick in Ohlicoatl's vast pupil. Three tattered sails yanked at its masts, each one bearing a variant of the skaven deity's horned symbol. Grinding engines turned the creaking paddles that gave it motion, and waves of artificially generated and harnessed electricity flowed through copper coils to feed the guns that bristled along its great length.

Jordaius would wager Ghal Maraz itself that he was looking at the flagship of the Grey Lord.

Why the skaven warlord, so mysterious that no one even knew his real name, had abandoned the siege of Hammerhal Aqsha and the Chaos warbands it had managed to unite, to turn its attentions to the Ohlor Jungle, Jordaius could not say.

The Silver Tower, perhaps? It had to be.

But it was not his place to wonder.

'A just and righteous cause,' he murmured, as he followed the flight of his brothers towards the Grey Lord's armada. 'To fight in a battle that mattered. This is everything I have ever wished for. I know it.'

'Sigmar remembers,' came an echo in his thoughts, a voice that reminded him of his own, how his own might once have been before the God-King had filled him with thunder.

'Does he now?' The gruff voice of a duardin. *'I wonder.'*

'Why then do I wish for more?' Jordaius screamed into the sky. In the thunder and lightning of battle, it went unheard. 'Why does my heart draw me to some place other than here, where it belongs?'

'I should have said thank you very much, bid you good luck on your journey to Hammerhal, and gone straight back to Edassa to count my blessings.'

'Aye, that's what he *would have said.'*

'And did he, *this manling you keep alluding to, live to splendid old age?'*

'Who are you?' Jordain felt tears of frustration tracking down his face beneath his mask. 'What destiny animates the soul of this duardin, this stranger, that even the fury of the Forge Eternal cannot strike every last trace of it from mine?'

'Life is full of such disappointments, manling, great and small. Don't be so quick to welcome death, though. It has eluded me thus far.'

'I am Jordaius Lionheart. A Stormcast Eternal. That life is over!'

'You remind me of him, *manling, and that's not always a good thing.'*

'Who is "him"?'

Umgi...

The voice of metal was almost welcome after the sounds of his own.

'Sigmar! Why must I always hear these voices instead of yours?'

'What would Vandus do? What would Kyukain Hammer-Friend do?'

In his mind, men and woman roared like lions, while all around him in the skies of Ohlor demigods returned to the storm in shrieks of death and thunder.

'Am I alone in my doubts?' he cried, but this time no one answered.

'We are the Oathforged and we are their doom,' Vultar Carrion-wing was yelling from somewhere very, very far away. 'Bring it down, my brothers! Bring it down!'

Dum.

And then a voice called from the thunder.

'JORDAIN!'

Jordaius' head snapped towards the crackling heart of the storm that was the head of the Realmserpent. Its teeth were lightning bolts. Its eyes were comets. Every scale on its head was the size of a dragon, wreathed in the fury of the Storm Eternal. Its maw was a vast pit, fathomless as the dark gulfs beyond the boundaries of Azyr. Contemplating it was like contemplating the surface of another world.

'Doomseeker,' he breathed, uncertain yet what that word meant, only that it meant something *to him*.

Another oath pulled on him, one that was older and, somehow, more powerful even than that he owed to the God-King. It was impossible, surely, and yet he felt it. A spark of Sigmar's Storm Eternal animated his soul, allowing him to live even though he had died, and so if he had doubts, if he felt himself called to some other battlefield, then it could surely only be because it served Sigmar's will for him to pursue them. It was the only answer that allowed him to reconcile his faith in the primacy of Sigmar with the feelings in his heart.

'Forgive me, my brothers,' he said, too quietly for any of his embattled brotherhood to hear as he angled away from them, leaving the battlefield behind him as he swooped towards the mouth of the realmbridge. 'But a warrior must honour his oaths.'

THIRTY-ONE

The Realmserpent was almost as difficult to stand on as its tail had been to leap onto in the first place, constantly bucking, twisting, flexing to one side or the other, and all through a wheeling void of *wrong*-looking stars. All of Maleneth's natural poise and considerable training went into keeping her balance while she fended off a pair of terrified grots in feathered hats desperate to get past. Druanthael was screaming and had not stopped since they had left Ghyran behind. Witromm had actually spat out his pipe in order to concentrate. Why it had ever occurred to her to cross the Realmserpent while every monster in Ghur seemed intent on coming the other way genuinely escaped her now. Gotrek, naturally, seemed to be enjoying himself.

'It's like killing zombies in the Reiksfort, beastmen in the Drak-wald, goblins in the underdeeps of the Eight Peaks, only all at the same time! It reminds me of the Realm of Chaos.'

'We are between realms here, Gotrek. The stars boil and the very ground beneath us is a living thing wishing us ill. The similarities are greater than you think.'

'Not a bad place for a Slayer to while a millennia or five, then.'

Maleneth winced as Druanthael's screams went up an octave. It almost caused her to misjudge the thrust of a grot's spear. The tip scraped across her leather breast panel before she stabbed the little greenskin firmly in the eye. Maleneth was a student of pain and, although she could not understand the cause, she could see that Druanthael was suffering greatly.

'What is that tree-banshee wailing about now?' said Gotrek. 'She hasn't let up since we climbed onto this beast.'

'I'd wager this is her first trip beyond the borders of Ghyran,' said Witromm.

'I cannot hear her!' Druanthael cried in panic. 'I cannot hear my queen! She sings, but I do not hear!'

'Protect her, Witromm,' said Maleneth. 'She is the only one who can track the movements of the Silver Tower.'

Witromm duly fell back to defend the Kurnoth Huntress. Her occasional lashings out were still accounting for greenskins by the score, but there were thousands of them out there, and those swings were far too wide and careless for Maleneth's tastes. It was infinitely preferable to leave Witromm looking after her.

'If you ask me, you all put too much stock in the mutterings of those you call gods,' said Gotrek. 'Aye, I shaved my head and tattooed my skin, but if you think I ever chased after *this* greater daemon or *that* dragon's horde because *he* told me so then you're madder than a night goblin with a head full of madcap brew. Follow gods and prophecies and you're apt to end up like Snorri Nosebiter, a head full of nails and thin air, and disappointed come the end.'

'Remember, Gotrek, that we are supposed to be *crossing* the bridge.'

A little further behind now, Witromm gave Druanthael a slap in a last attempt to rouse her. A vain attempt, surely, on that woody face.

'Is this how the flesh and blood races live?' she screamed. 'In silence? Nothing but the spirit-echo of their creator-song in their breast. Take my hand, duardin. Take it.' She forced it onto Witromm, practically crushing the old duardin's hand in hers. 'Feel how my heartwood trembles.'

Heedless of anyone's travails but his own, Gotrek laughed as he forged his own way into the sea of beasts, like the bowsprit of some thuggish but indisputably hard-wearing ship of the line.

'I see beastmen, centaurs, squigs, and something beyond that horde of orruks that looks like a zoat.' He gave a mad giggle. 'I thought them an elven myth, a foolish legend of Old Ones, elementalists and tree-hugging lizards. Hah! And what's that I see? I think I once killed something with that many legs in the Cursed Marshes west of Marienburg! I see chimeras, hydras.' He drew a huge breath in, careless of the fact that both nostrils were gummed with the blood of a dozen species each. 'I can almost smell the spilt beer and the meat roasting for me in the Ancestors' Hall. Well, fill your tankards, carve a platter, and spare the juices for dipping stonebread – Gotrek son of Gurni will soon be banging on your gates and he's a terrible thirst for ale!'

The Realmserpent gave a rumbling hiss, a warning passed along the length of the entire world before the titan bucked wildly. All fighting ceased, all thoughts of fighting ceased, as Maleneth and her unwanted companions and every creature on their stretch of Ohlicoatl's back was flung into the air. Maleneth landed in an ungainly sprawl and amidst a pile of groaning ungors, several yards from where she had started.

'Shards of Khaine.' Maleneth stabbed one of the gangly beastmen in the back of the head, using it to help lever herself back up. 'It is not just the beasts of Ghur we fight, but the Star Titan itself.'

'Ohlicoatl is angry,' said Witromm. 'I fear there'll be no crossing the realmbridge with the godbeast in such a fury, even if Druanthael was in any shape to lead us.'

'What do you suggest?'

'Shelter. If Druanthael's going to pull herself together then it's not going to be out here.'

'We are on the back of a Star Titan, trapped in the gulf between two realms. What makes you think such a place even exists in– Wait!' Maleneth peered ahead. The undulations of the titan's back warped her sense of perspective, making distant objects appear close and hiding closer ones entirely in its coils. 'Do you see that, Witromm?'

'I see nothing, but I'm not blessed with the fair eyes of a Darkling Shadowblade.'

'If Ohlicoatl could just stop writhing for a moment. I have seen grots that hold up better under torture...'

Witromm wisely said nothing.

'It is a tower... I think.'

'Who in their right mind would build a tower on the back of a god-snake in the void between Ghur and Ghyran?'

'Nothing that we have encountered here so far, that is for certain. I am willing to find out, however. We can shelter there and regroup, perhaps even see the serpent's head from its summit.'

Gotrek gave a joyous bellow of the kind that invariably betokened unpleasantness on the near horizon, and Maleneth looked up sharply, realising that she had entirely lost track of the Slayer. He took only a moment to find. All she had to do was locate the largest monster in sight.

The beast in question looked as though someone had crossed a Chaos gargant with a kharibdyss, and then mated its offspring to a minotaur. Gotrek charged towards it, smoke and fire trailing from the head of his axe. It swung its club. Maleneth could not say for certain whether the flexing of the realmbridge threw the Slayer off balance at the wrong moment or whether he was simply not paying close enough attention, but the blow cracked the side of his head and sent him flying.

'Gotrek!' Witromm roared.

'The rune!' Maleneth shrieked at the same time, near hysterical with glee as she dodged and vaulted clumsily attacking greenskins, bounding towards the spot where Gotrek had fallen.

The large monster that had accounted for Gotrek gave a confused grumble and swung for her. Its club sailed overhead as Maleneth ducked, sliding between the monster's legs and grinning as she rolled onto Gotrek's body. She had been starting to worry that, against all the odds, he would never actually die. Finally, she could cut the rune from his stubborn hide and get as far away from the insanity he had led her to as a realmgate to Azyrheim could take her.

With a considerable effort, Maleneth heaved Gotrek onto his back. She hissed in annoyance. Somehow, he was still breathing, the golden Master Rune riding up and down on that huge chest.

She shrugged and raised her knife.

'I told you that one day I would cut out your heart and eat it. Luckily for you I have to make this quick and will have to content myself with the Master Rune. Please, Gotrek, do scream for me. You owe me that much.'

Instincts honed in the murder yards of the temple tingled a warning and Maleneth threw herself to one side, at the very instant that an armoured fighter mashed into the ground beside her like a cometary strike. Lightning arced. The ground shuddered under the impact. Maleneth rolled into a fighting crouch, a knife ready in each hand, just as a storm-cloud writhing with golden flecks and lightning exploded towards her again. A spearhead crackled from the storm like a lightning bolt. She was fast, but she was not nearly that fast.

Ideally, she would have dodged a blow like that altogether, but the best she could achieve was to cross her blades in front of it and brace.

The impact threw her back, tearing up the hordes of greenskins like the blades of a rusty plough, the energy discharge turning both her arms to jelly.

The Stormcast Eternal unfolded his wings as he straightened. He was a dark god, haloed in sparks, towering over all he surveyed.

'I am Jordaius Lionheart, of the Oathforged,' he said in the richest voice that Maleneth had ever heard, amplified somehow by the mask that covered his face. 'You will have to go through me, Daughter of Khaine.'

Maleneth stared at the warrior in disbelief.

What cruel fate had dispatched one of the Anvils of the Heldenhammer to this place? Would Sigmar really frustrate her at the last, condemn her to a slow death on a covenite blade or, worse, an even slower one shackled to Gotrek's primitively tattooed ankle?

She would not accept it.

Maleneth bared her teeth and sank once more into an easy fighting stance.

The temple and the Stormhosts were technically allies but the Lady Witchblade had always thirsted for the day she would be called on to bring one of their kind down. She had prepared her daughters well.

'Stand down, Darkling, if you are truly a servant of Order. Turn your murderer's knives on the beasts that would kill us all.'

'No!'

'I will kill you if I must.'

Gotrek stirred and sat up, rubbing at his bruised head. 'I know that voice.' He turned towards the Stormcast looming over him. 'Jordain?'

The Stormcast Eternal banished his javelin to the aether and reached up to remove his helmet. The face underneath was black-skinned and dreadlocked, a long set of parallel scars, a mauling from some manner of beast, across his face from temple to chin.

His features were human, but the scale of them was not. He was a man carved upon a mural, too large, too perfect, diminishing all who stood before it simply by existing.

'Yes,' he murmured softly in that same, deep voice. '*Yes*. That was my mortal name. You remember me!'

'Of course I bloody remember you,' said Gotrek. 'It's only been a few months, manling. There isn't the five-armed beast-giant in these realms that can knock my head that hard.' He narrowed his eye. 'Although as I recall you died, so perhaps I do the monsters of this place a disservice.'

'I remember you as well. *Gotrek*,' the Stormcast said, after a moment's effort. 'Gotrek Gurnisson. I remember the adventures we shared. And that plate on your shoulder, I...' His brow furrowed. 'The Lion of Edassa. My home.'

'How can this be?' said Gotrek. 'You lot are supposed to forget everything. That's what Hammer-Friend told me, and what I saw with my own eye in Hammerhal Aqsha.'

'It is true, Gotrek,' said Maleneth. The one thing she needed even less than an Anvil of the Heldenhammer watching the Slayer's back was a beloved former companion putting notions into his head that did not involve him giving up this pointless quest and returning with her to Azyr. 'The memories of a mortal life cannot survive the fury of Reforging. A little may remain, but every subsequent death and remaking costs them a little more.' She sneered towards the Stormcast. 'This is not Jordain.'

'And yet I remember. Either Sigmar made me remember for a reason or *you are* the reason. Either way, I had to discover why.'

'But if *you* remember...' The Slayer appeared inexplicably crestfallen. He no longer even noticed the monsters still screaming around them. 'Maybe *he* still will. Could it be that I abandoned my search of Hammerhal Aqsha too soon?'

'You've all picked a fine time for a sit down,' Witromm puffed, interrupting before Maleneth had a chance to, hoisting Druan-thael along over one shoulder whilst hacking a way through frantic grots with his free arm. 'There are still beasts about, in case you– Is that a Stormcast Eternal?'

'Are you friend or foe, duardin?' said Jordain, Jordaius, or what-ever he claimed his name to be.

'That's still to be decided,' Maleneth hissed. 'For now, let's run. We make for the tower.'

'The Startower of Temekzuqi?' said Jordaius, a note of surprise in his voice that made Maleneth immediately wary.

'You know it?'

'It marks the centre of the realmbridge. I have never been there, for the Oathforged are sworn to eternal stewardship of the portal's Ghurish side, but I know of it. We will find sanctuary there.'

Jordaius offered his hand to Gotrek, and the Slayer, to Maleneth's unexpectedly deep annoyance, took it, allowing the Stormcast Eternal to help him to his feet.

'As I recall you once reminding me, Doomseeker, there is killing work to be done.'

THIRTY-TWO

The slender needle of celestite and obsidian rose from the back of the Star Titan. The wall around the startower was a ruin, something accidentally cleared out of a jungle, the crumbling rocks overgrown by vegetation that Maleneth had seen nowhere else on the Realmserpent. She could not look at it for too long. The stars wheeling behind it made her feel nauseous. It was as silent as a forgotten shrine. Elsewhere over the realmbridge, the hordes of Ghur trampled one another to reach the Nevergreen Woods, but here it was unnervingly peaceful.

An energy barrier ghosted across a half-collapsed arch adorned with golden hieroglyphs. There was no other obvious way through the strange vegetation.

While Maleneth studied the place as thoroughly as she would any strange castle that she might need to escape from in a hurry, Jordaius stepped unhesitatingly across the barrier. Celestial energies crawled across the Stormcast's armour, probing it, probing *him*, but did not otherwise impede his entrance.

Maleneth sniffed. There was suddenly a smell of burnt hair and ozone on the air.

'What was that *shimmer* you just walked through, manling?' Gotrek asked.

Jordaius turned. Now that he was through, Maleneth could not even see the field. It was entirely transparent and she saw the Stormcast clearly.

'I imagine it is the barrier, rather than these walls, that keep the beasts of this plane from the startower. The magic of the Starmasters is powerful. Even the mightiest of evil creatures would be unable to pass such a barrier unhindered.'

Maleneth smiled sweetly. 'Nervous about having the purity of your soul tested, Gotrek?'

'I'd invite Sigmar to step down off his high bloody pedestal to ask after its purity from within reach of this axe.'

Maleneth took a deep breath and stepped through after the Stormcast.

There was a prickle as the boundless fury of Azyr walked across her skin. She emerged on the other side a little more quickly than she had gone in, pushed out, repulsed by the field's energies and walking in short, hurried steps to slow down. She turned back, spreading her arms and bowing, as she would have done for her mistress after a particularly lethal display of acrobatics.

Sigmar saw no fault in her soul.

'I admit to being surprised,' said Jordaius.

Maleneth offered a poisonous curtsey. 'Always happy to disappoint.'

'I should have greater faith in your choice of companions, Doomseeker.'

'Not so hasty, Stormcast,' said Gotrek, waving at Jordaius to be patient. 'It probably just takes a moment.'

'You wound me, Gotrek. When will you accept that I am on the side of the heavens?'

'Maybe when I accept that this heaven of yours has a place for a murderess like you.'

'Oh, Gotrek,' said Maleneth, her smile sharpening. 'You would be *amazed* at what the God-King has found it useful to tolerate.'

'Would you two stop dithering up there,' said Witromm. 'I'm carrying a Kurnoth Huntress here.'

'Dwarfs don't dither.' Gotrek eyed the door suspiciously. 'I've never trusted magic. And if there's one thing I hate almost as much as elves or trees, then it's lizard people.' He blew his breath out as though steeling himself for something distasteful. 'But never let it be said that Gotrek Gurnisson wavered at a cliff edge where others leapt.'

He stepped through.

There was the same spasm of energy that Maleneth had observed from Jordaius' passage. The rune fizzled and popped, like water dropped into hot oil and angrily resisting everything about it, continuing to burn a little more brightly than it had going in.

Okurt, nuf git, said the voice in all their heads.

Gotrek chuckled. 'I don't think the rune liked that. Maybe I'll go through again.'

Grimnir or Grimnir.

Maleneth could not help but be disappointed. She had been vaguely hoping that the energies of the Cosmic Storm would burn the maudlin relic to ash and spit the Master Rune out the other side for her to pick up. She had lately given up on the idea that there was any justice left in the Mortal Realms.

'It would appear that you are not *entirely* anathema to Azyr either,' she said.

Gotrek grunted, as though she had offended him on purpose, which perhaps she had. 'It tingled.'

Witromm and Druanthael staggered through together.

'The stars,' Druanthael half-sang, shivering like a once proud tree with a high fever. 'They sing. But their voices… their voices are so cold.'

'Maleneth,' said Witromm, his arm around the Sylvaneth's waist, looking up at her with concern. 'See if you can find somewhere to set her down.'

'Aye,' said Gotrek. 'A nice inn with a stout roof and a roaring log fire would do nicely.'

Maleneth looked around. There was not much more to see. The courtyard was stone and weeds. Vines hung over the ruined walls, slowly crushing them into the rubble that dotted the ground. A flight of crumbling stairs made a half-spiral around the startower's base. There was a doorway there, but no door. Faded hieroglyphs on plates of gold picked out the occasional brick, no pattern to it that Maleneth could see.

'Shoddy work,' said Gotrek, no denunciation greater.

'The startower was built in the last days of Myth by Starmaster Zectoka,' said Jordaius. 'With the Seraphon's aid, Lord-Castellant Ansiris Oathforged conquered the jungles of Ohlor in Sigmar's name. In return, the Starmaster demanded the Oathforged raise a fortress of their own, the Mortisrock, over the Maw of Sotek, and hold it for all time.'

'He doesn't ask for much then,' said Gotrek sourly. 'You're sure he's not a god?'

'It is a debt we repay gladly,' said Jordaius.

'What are you doing here then?' said Gotrek.

The question seemed to catch the Stormcast off guard. 'I… I mean… I needed to…'

'Well?'

Maleneth wished she could have watched the self-righteous paragon squirm for longer, but the rustling sound of something large pushing its way through the jungle growth, alas, drew precedence. She whirled, knives out, as a hulk of nightshade-blue scales and thick golden armour dragged its heavy tail into the court-yard. It was taller than Jordaius, even with the muscular hunch to its shoulders, and broader than Gotrek. The mace it carried was solid stone. Its eyes were two chips of obsidian, cold and reptilian and utterly unblinking.

'Lizardmen,' Gotrek spat, squeezing the haft of his axe as though to force an extra flicker of heat from its blades.

'It is all right, Gotrek,' said Jordaius, holding out a hand. 'It is the Eternity Warden of Temekzuqi, one of the Fangs of Sotek under Starmaster Zectoka. They are allies of Sigmar, and brothers of the Oathforged.'

'Indeed, Brother Jordaius. We all play our parts in the Great Plan.'

Maleneth had been given no inkling that the other Seraphon had been present but, as if its words had unmade its own spell, there the creature was, halfway up the steps to the door to its tower and draped in a cloak of multicoloured feathers. Where the saurus guardian was solid and brutal, the little skink would have made the grots streaming over the realmbridge feel large. Where the warrior regarded Maleneth and her companions with cold-blooded indifference, the master's eyes were bright with calculation.

'You stray far from your path, Old Blood.'

Gotrek sniffed. 'Is he talking to me?'

'Temekzuqi, I presume?' said Maleneth.

The skink gave a reptilian chirp that Maleneth took for an affirmative.

'On the beards of all our ancestors!' said Witromm. He had laid Druanthael against the wall, but the huge Kurnothi was starting to seize, spasmodic jerks defying his efforts to hold her down. 'Can we sort out who's on whose side? Druanthael needs help.'

There was a twinkling of starlight, a suggestion of movement and a rustle of feathers, and suddenly the skink was no longer there. Witromm swore as Temekzuqi appeared in front of him.

The skink crouched over Druanthael, sinking into his long cloak, translucent membranes flickering across his eyes as he studied the ailing Sylvaneth. Another enigmatic chirp caused the wattle hanging from his neck to swell and vibrate.

'The Grey Lord assaults the mouth of Ohlicoatl, and now the Old Blood attempts his crossing. It is all as Zectoka foresaw when he first dreamt of my existence.'

'The Mortisrock stands yet,' said Jordaius. 'As long as the Everlasting Oath binds us, my brothers will hold it.'

Maleneth looked at the Stormcast slyly. 'And where are your brothers now, Jordaius?'

'I...' Jordaius looked downcast. 'I left them, it is true.'

Gotrek regarded him stonily. There was no reading his mood, which, given his emotional range went from outraged berzerker to melancholy misanthrope, was a remarkable achievement on Jordaius' part.

'To find *you*, Gotrek,' Jordaius hastily explained. 'When we return they will understand that what I did was Sigmar's will.'

'I am sure they will.' Maleneth gave Jordaius a pat on the pauldron. '*You* understand don't you, Gotrek?'

The Slayer had to grind his teeth apart in order to speak. 'Our oaths are the rock upon which all else is built, manling. If a god had the power to tell you that you need serve your king no longer, or that my shame could be expunged by more than my death alone, then what would be the purpose of such immutable vows? The Everlasting Oath, you called it? Pah! I know what both of those words mean, manling, and perhaps they mean less in this world than they did in mine. Here the gods make the sun rise and the seasons turn, and they cull the ranks of the honoured dead for warriors that, with eight worlds to plunder, they cannot find abundantly enough amongst the living. Forgive me, manling, if I am unimpressed by you, your oath, or your so-called god.'

Maleneth clapped her hands together and laughed lightly. That would teach the prig to show up at the eleventh hour and steal her mark.

Jordaius ignored her. 'It is not like that.'

'The elfling was right. You're not the Jordain I knew. I saw that man die. Felix Jaeger too is long lost to me, or so I should hope if you are the example of what he will have become in the millennia since we parted.' Gotrek turned to Temekzuqi, sheer stubbornness dismissing the eight-foot-tall demigod from all notice. 'Can you help us or not, lizard, before I tear that feather crown from your head and choke you with it?'

The saurus made an angry noise, but Temetzuqi placated it with some soothing clicks.

'There can be no passage. Not yet. Ohlicoatl is too enraged. That is the motive I glean behind the Grey Lord's purpose – to keep the Old Blood from following him into the Silver Tower. To escape the realmbridge now you would need to kill Ohlicoatl, and that I cannot allow, even if the feat were not beyond you. If it could be done then Zectoka would have done so an age ago, returned the titan's spirit in peace to Azyr and spared Ansiris his long duty.'

The jade light behind Druanthael's deep, deep eyes wavered slightly as the Sylvaneth looked up at the skink crouched over her. He bared his pointed teeth in an apparent smile. She reached out tentatively, as if to be certain that he was real.

'My eyes see you, Seraphon, but I hear no life beat within you.'

'Can you mend her?' Witromm asked.

The skink turned to his guardian. They engaged in a brief dialogue of clicks and chirps that concluded with the burly saurus setting his mace against the wall and bending to gather Druanthael off the ground. The Eternity Warden lifted her as easily as if she was hollow.

Whatever the starseer had in mind for Druanthael, Maleneth

hoped that she could rely on it taking some time. Not just because this was the first genuinely safe place they had come across since leaving Hammerhal Ghyra, nor because it reminded her more than a little of her home in Azyrheim, nor because the skink's talk of *Old Bloods* and *Grey Lords* and *Great Plans* involving the Silver Tower all sounded deeply disturbing.

The dejection on Jordaius' face as Gotrek turned his back on him soothed her like a bath in warm blood, and Maleneth wanted to soak in it for a long, long time.

THIRTY-THREE

The Startower of Temekzuqi was a sliver of the Celestial Realm in this liminal plane. The stones were smooth and cool to the touch. The furnishings were comfortable, lavish without being gaudy. The light sang the hymns of the stars. There could not have been an environment better suited to salving the ache in Jordaius' spirit, and yet he felt more torn than ever.

He had left the battle at the Mortisrock because he had known in his soul that the Doomseeker had a hold on it that preceded Sigmar's. Took precedence over it even, as blasphemous as that sounded even in the confessional of his own mind. He still believed this to be true, and that such a geas could only have been left on him with Sigmar's full knowledge and, thus, his will. And yet, in following it, he had led the Doomseeker to shun him.

Jordaius closed his eyes, listening to the mutter and trill of Starseer Temekzuqi weaving his spells on Druanthael, the occasional low bass chirp of the Eternity Warden, the pointedly jarring *scrape-scrape-scrape* of the Darkling sharpening her knives.

'Don't worry, lad,' said Witromm. 'I get the feeling Druanthael's in good hands.'

'It is not the Kurnoth Huntress I pray for.'

'Is he listening, do you think?'

Jordaius opened his eyes. 'I believe he is.'

'What does he say?'

'He does not answer my prayers with words...' A smile began at the corners of his lips, expanding its borders tentatively into his cheeks as he realised that something *had* changed since his departure from the Mortisrock. The voice in the metal was gone. He gave a relieved sigh. 'He answers them with silence.'

'You seem pleased about it.'

'More than you can know.'

Witromm sat across from Jordaius around a circular table of thin obsidian. Jordaius was not sure what to make of the venerable old duardin. Although Jordaius was immortal he was also, in some indefinable way, *newly* immortal. He was young, where the word that could most meaningfully be ascribed to Witromm was *old*. There was a depth to his pronouncements and a weight of thought behind his eyes before making them, as though he had seen more of the Mortal Realms than he could possibly speak of if even he wanted to, and had done more than he could freely share. The ease of his disposition in spite of that was inherently reassuring. For if one who had seen *everything* could retain genuine humour in their smile, then things could not truly be as bad as they appeared. Maleneth did not trust him, and there was that in his favour, and the care he had showed to their Sylvaneth companion was obvious.

The duardin brought a stone tankard to his whiskers and slurped on the frothy ale.

'A passable interpretation of Grustangle's Owd Nasty,' he declared, clapping his lips thoughtfully. 'How a Slann Starmaster from the age before ages stumbled upon the memory of it is a riddle for whiter beards than mine.'

'You seem unperturbed by the strangeness of our surroundings. You must be as well travelled as you claim.'

Witromm took another appreciative sip of the ale that Temekzuqi had conjured for him. 'You could say that.'

Starlight shone from the corner in which Temekzuqi worked. Jordaius winced as the pure note of his High Magic turned shrill. Druanthael creaked within the dodecahedral wards that the skink had set, a tree with no room to grow. She shrieked, arching her back off the floor only to be restrained by unseen hands and celestial bonds.

Maleneth hissed, dropping her sharpening stone to cover her ears. 'What in the heaven's name are you doing to her? I did not think it was possible to inflict that level of anguish on a Sylvaneth.'

'I am exposing her soul to the heavens,' Temekzuqi calmly explained, bobbing around the writhing Sylvaneth. 'I cannot recreate the absent song of her queen, but there is peace in the quiet between stars.'

The Starseer resumed his chant. The off-key note in the magic quietened and Jordaius felt his spirit relax. Druanthael's suffering, too, noticeably lessened. Maleneth tentatively drew her hands from her pointed ears and grimaced.

'Am I the only one who can still hear that buzzing?'

Witromm chuckled over his ale. 'Aelf ears, lass.'

With a glance at the Eternity Warden, staring coldly at them all from its corner of the star-shaped chamber, Jordaius set his elbows on the stone table and leant forward. 'Do you think Temekzuqi will try to prevent Gotrek from battling the Realmserpent?'

'If that's what he said, lad. For a race of star-blooded dream figments, the Seraphon are terrible liars.'

'Why do you whisper?' said Maleneth, speaking overloudly as

though to compensate for the discomfort in her ears. 'Are you afraid that our reptilian hosts will overhear you? Or is it Gotrek whose opinion troubles you? Well, you need not worry on that score. I suspect he is still pacing the grounds like a troggoth that struck its head and cannot remember its way home. Even if he was sitting where I am now, I doubt he would notice your concern over his own complaining.' Her scowl deepened, her voice coarsening as she adopted a remarkably adroit Gotrek Gurnisson imperson-ation. 'Lizardmen were more opaque in my day.'

Jordaius smothered a smile. Witromm laughed so hard that ale spurted from his nose.

'No wonder this tower has fallen down after just one Age. What do you expect if you build from stardust and dreamstone?'

Witromm wiped his nose on his sleeve, crying.

Maleneth shrugged, but there was an unpleasant smile on her face that suggested she was pleased with the appreciation as she went back to sharpening her knives.

'I am not *afraid*,' said Jordaius.

'Of course you are,' Maleneth replied. 'You are not Jordain. You are Broddur. You wonder if Gotrek will insist on throwing his life away against Ohlicoatl, and worry that you will have to choose him over our hosts.' She rested the point of her already sharp knife on the table. 'Aww, what is the matter? Second thoughts? How long has it been since you turned your back on your last friends? A day?'

'I am sure it is easy for you, Darkling,' Jordaius answered coldly. 'To glide from master to master without regret or consequence.'

He had used to think that questions of *purpose* and *loyalty* were the simplest to answer, but he had learned since that they were not. There was evil, but there was no one clear good. If anything, the questions had become harder to answer since Sigmar had reforged him with the immortality and strength to truly ask them of himself. By leaving his brothers to aid Gotrek, did he turn his back on Sigmar? Or was this a part of *his* plan also, for reasons he could not share with Starmaster Zectoka, or even with Jordaius?

'I am not some paladin of storm and flesh, *we...*' His hand waved back and forth to encompass Maleneth and himself. 'We are not automata like those that serve his wayward ally, Nagash. We must think for ourselves. Whom do you really serve, Darkling, beyond yourself?'

'And why must I serve anyone?'

'If we are not serving willingly then we are being used unwittingly. Is that not right, Witromm?'

The duardin grunted in surprise, raising his eyebrows, but was spared from picking a side of his own by Druanthael's sudden, piercing scream.

'My queen! You are so far away!'

Jordaius made to rise, to help in whatever way a warrior of Sigmar could, but a look from Witromm dissuaded him. He sat back, and almost at once, the Sylvaneth's anguish broke, her screams turning into exhausted sobs that sounded like the kind of peace that falls after a bloody battle.

'I am an isle of harmony in a sea of bitter solitude,' she murmured. 'I hear the echo of her song within me, but she is so far. So far.'

'As far as Sigendil from the lands of the realms. Or the constellation of Sotek's Fangs from this tower.' Temekzuqi bared his translucent fangs in an approximation of a human smile and patted the back of the Sylvaneth's hand. 'Yet they shine all the same.'

Witromm puffed out his cheeks and took a relived draught of his ale. 'She's back. There's a relief. There's an outside chance we'll find the Silver Tower without her, but I wouldn't rate our hopes of finding Hruth'gael on our own. Now, once the Realmserpent calms down, we can all get out of here.'

A second saurus warrior, armoured in thick white stone rather than the Eternity Warden's shining gold, entered the chamber then. Its scales gleamed as it passed under the field of stars towards the Eternity Warden. Jordaius listened to their growling conference. It was difficult to escape the conviction that the news it conveyed was not good.

Maleneth was evidently of a similar mind.

'What are they saying?' she hissed.

'I do not know.'

The Eternity Warden swung its monstrously powerful jaw to Temekzuqi and clicked a brief summation. The Starseer looked up from Druanthael in dismay.

'The Old Blood is gone?'

'Gone?' said Jordaius, rising from his chair. 'Gone where?'

'He will not get far,' Temekzuqi trilled angrily. 'Ohlicoatl will force him to turn back. The rest of you must remain here until–'

Jordaius blinked in surprise as Temekzuqi suddenly halted mid-flow, his shock no less than that of the Starseer, who looked down to find Maleneth's sharpened knife in his chest.

'I am sorry, Temekzuqi,' said Maleneth, with no sign of remorse. She was standing by her chair, arm still outflung from the throw. Jordaius had not even noticed her move. 'But if Gotrek is about to get himself killed somewhere, then I am afraid I simply do not have the time to linger.'

Temekzuqi took a staggering step, neck wattle trembling in dismay. His scaly body was already fading into stardust, nostrils aquiver, drawing breath for one last syllable of crucial guidance towards the Great Plan only for his dissolution to reach his lips before he could speak it.

The skink shimmered one last time, and was gone.

Surprise finally penetrated the saurus' cold-blooded reserve as they bellowed in outrage.

Witromm set his beer down and sighed. 'I was hoping to finish that.'

'What did you do!' Jordaius yelled.

'Time to decide whose side you are on.' There was a large star-crystal window behind Maleneth. It overlooked the grounds below. Before Jordaius could react or the Seraphon could reach her, she hurled herself through it, pieces of star-crystal clinging to her like a halo as she fell.

Jordaius could only stare.

To set aside his oath for a greater one was one thing. To leave his brothers in the midst of battle aggrieved his sense of natural justice and martial pride, but the path to a greater purpose lay before him and he had faith enough to walk it. But this?

'I am confused, Witromm,' said Druanthael.

'I wish I could say I was, lass.'

'Do these Seraphon keep us from Ancient Hruth'gael?'

The duardin sighed heavily.

The Sylvaneth issued a warlike shudder as she sat fully, thorns sprouting from her tough bark and broadening her shoulders until she loomed over even the saurus warrior and the Eternity Warden like a vengeful oak.

'That is not the Everqueen's wish.'

Nor is it Sigmar's, Jordaius thought, and knew it to be true.

But he refused to turn the gifts of the God-King against servants of Azyr.

Screaming in frustration at being driven to this, he threw himself through the shattered window after Maleneth, wings flaring, bearing him up by Sigmar's will, and once again left the sounds of battle to fall away behind him.

THIRTY-FOUR

'There you are, Doomseeker.'

Jordaius arrowed through the monster-infested skies, darting sharply to avoid the harpies and the direflocks and the chomping squigs that would occasionally flap into reach. He could not believe that Gotrek was actually fighting the Star Titan, and by the sounds of things, he was holding his own as well. Ohlicoatl would take a bite out of Sigmar himself if he was enraged enough to do so.

How did the World-that-Was ever fall to Chaos, he wondered, with heroes like Gotrek Gurnisson to stand before its armies?

At the head of the Realmserpent the energies of Ghur were pre-eminent. The void in which the titan writhed was shaded amber, the hoots and snarls of apex predators echoing through tears in the weakened aether in submission to the angry hisses of the titan.

Ohlicoatl's immense, spade-like head hung over them all like another realmsphere forcefully nudging its way into the sky of this one. Great storms raged in its eyes. A forked tongue limned with static charge flickered between mountainous teeth, appearing to do it slowly only because it had such a vast span across which to travel and thence return.

Gotrek was an insignificant speck in comparison. The duardin stood with his feet firmly planted to the Realmserpent's back, brandishing his axe as Ohlicoatl twisted its neck to gaze down.

'Sigmar, lend me courage!' Jordaius screamed, as Ohlicoatl lunged.

It moved as swiftly as any striking serpent, as unstoppably as any falling mountain. The furious hiss of its breath summoned a storm that blitzed the scales around Gotrek's feet with lightning. Comets materialised out of the air behind its head, dragged into its wake like debris around a falling star. The star hit, an apocalypse of rock, fire and lightning that blasted through the light from Jordaius' wing-frames and sent him screaming through the air like a leaf in a cosmic gale. After a few desperate seconds of prayer, his wings reignited. They snapped, catching the air, as he swooped back around.

Somehow, the Doomseeker was still standing, a flea pecking at a dragon's lip as he battered at the Realmserpent with his axe. Jordaius could hear him rage and curse, even from there, flickers of flame accompanying every golden pulse from the rune in his chest.

'Come face my axe, you legless dragon. Bring me my doom or prepare to meet yours!'

Dar ek elg-ha ong tusk bin Gotrek Gurnisson!

That voice…

Jordaius saw now why Sigmar had wished for him to cross the Maw of Sotek and witness this for himself. The voice of Gotrek's rune was the very one that Jordaius had been hearing in his prayers. *The voice of Grimnir.* It all made sense now. He understood. This was why he had been haunted by memories of a past life and of oaths made to another. It may even have been why Sigmar had taken and reforged him in the first place: for his bond to the Doomseeker as opposed to his deeds. If that was so then Jordaius could not resent it.

Had any warrior of Sigmar been set with a greater task?

Not since Thostos Bladestorm retrieved Ghal Maraz from the Realm of Metal.

'Down, godling,' Gotrek growled down at his shining chest. 'Back into your cage of fire and gold. I will fight this beast mortally or not at all.'

Jordaius summoned a javelin and hurled it at the Star Titan as he flew a swift, dangerously close orbit around it. The javelin flew true and he could not have missed, but it merged ineffectually into the star-matter of the serpent's scales without so much as a flicker. He could not fight a creature made from the same essence as the God-King himself. It would be like trying to douse a fire by pouring on oil.

'This is my fight, Stormcast,' Gotrek snarled up at him. 'Flit off.'

'Embrace the power of your rune!'

'I will not! This Slayer will yield himself to no god, and certainly not to that one. Without me this rune is but a poor likeness of a dead god. Without *it* I am still the dwarf that left a good portion of the Old World dead at his feet and outlived it all. You did not know what this rune took from me, manling, what it cost me, and may cost me yet. You did not see how it thawed the winter of the Everqueen and allowed the foul hosts of Nurgle to invade her realm. I will fight and prevail, by my strength and my strength alone, and hope one day soon to die in the same manner. To do otherwise would be an insult to my oath.'

'Then why wield an axe at all, Gotrek? Why wear the Lion of Edassa on your arm? Why not fight the Star Titan naked and with bare fists? If you want no part of the Fyreslayer's god then why not let the Darkling have her rune and take its strength from you? I do not believe it is because you fear the pain of her knives.'

The titan reared over Jordaius. He did not know what made him so certain that its attention had fallen on him for it filled the heavens: it reared over them all without the need for wilful action on its part.

A torrential rain of lightning bolts struck Jordaius from the sky as the tongue of a chameleon skink would snatch at a fly. Agonising arcs crawled over the surface of his armour, fingers seeking a way through and finding it, overloading his wings for the second time in quick succession and delivering such a revelation in pain that he did not even notice his impact with the ground until he regained consciousness to find himself on it a moment later. His eyes felt as though they had been melted shut. With a groan, he opened them. Stars whirled across his vision, specks of light and dust compacting into hunks of ice, a fresh system of deadly satellites forming around the titan's head.

He tried to get up, a spasm of electrical energy causing his limbs to jerk and dumping him onto his back.

'Do they not teach you to *duck* in the Gladitorium?'

Maleneth was looking down on him with pursed lips, as though even here he found ways to slight her. The stars wheeled above her head in the throes of a tempest. The ground under Jordaius' back trembled.

'What have you done with Gotrek?' she demanded.

'The way is clear,' Druanthael sang, arriving alongside the witch aelf before Jordaius could fumble his tongue into answering. Her voice was strident as she swung past with a confident stride, battering at cometary fragments with her huge sword. 'I sense it keenly now! The Silver Tower and the life it harbours are just beyond us. If the Realmserpent will not yield then it must fall! My queen demands it.'

'Aye,' said Witromm, huffing breathlessly up behind. 'No way back now anyway.'

'Where is *Gotrek?*' Maleneth hissed.

They were all here. Jordaius struggled to get up, but he could not even unclamp his lips. He gestured with his head to where he had last glimpsed the Doomseeker hacking ineffectually at Ohli-coatl's bottom lip.

'Wait here, Stormcast. Watch the rear, or something.' Maleneth stepped over him. There was absolutely nothing Jordaius could do to stop her. 'I will take care of Gotrek from here.'

After decades of Death Night revels, dodging a handful of comets was child's play. Maleneth leapt, danced and spun her way through the rain from the heavens, keeping her eyes firmly on the golden glare that was Gotrek Gurnisson and her other senses painfully alert. The Slayer was locked in what must have constituted the most one-sided struggle in the Age of Sigmar, hacking away at its bottom lip like a miner who had sworn a drunken vow to single-handedly excavate a mountain. A runic barrier muttered and shimmered around him. Flashes of gold and fire deflected the worst of the titan's lightning even as it turned his skin black and forced him ever further towards his knees. If it was a glorious death at the hands of the mightiest foes that Gotrek sought, then Maleneth could, perhaps, understand why he looked so pleased with himself now. If, on the other hand, his stated ambition was to reclaim his god's axes then he had found a remarkably self-destructive way of going about it.

'You do know that it barely even realises you are there!' Maleneth screamed to him.

She had not expected the Slayer to hear her over the apocalypse coming down on his head, but he looked up from smiting the Star Titan's chin to at least recognise that Maleneth was there.

'I don't know my god-snakes as well as you, elfling, but I don't think it's liking this very much at all.' He waved his axe up at the oblivious Realmserpent's head. 'Get yourself down here, lizard. There's plenty more of you for me to hit.'

Maleneth would have torn her hair out, had she not been so occupied courting death. Gotrek's spiral towards self-destruction had brought her some measure of solace and occasional amusement over the months she had spent in his shadow, but as Sigmar Heldenhammer and the Bloody-Handed were her witnesses she was putting a stop to it now.

'Summon the strength of Grimnir and *kill* this thing!'

'I have bested godbeasts before this one without godly aid.'

'As I understand Broddur's tales, Ignimbris mistook you for Grimnir and fled, while Okaenos burnt you both to a crisp and spat you out. Hardly the most *stellar* of records, Gotrek.'

'Aye, but who's still standing? Not bloody Grimnir!'

'Use it, Gotrek! If you do not then you may as well have gone into this battle intending to die. Is that what this is, Gotrek? Will suicide by godbeast be enough to erase whatever idiotic shame you cling to from your dead world?'

Gotrek hacked at the Star Titan in fury.

'You don't understand, elfling. The axe I seek, it too had a destiny. It wanted me to find it. And ever since I took shelter in the cave that harboured it, it has been guiding my fate to suit its own. I had not yet taken the Slayer Oath then, but somehow it knew. It must have known, or shaped my fate to its purpose. Helga. Gurna.'

His voice broke up as he spoke names that meant nothing to Maleneth, even as the fire of the rune turned the silver in his hair golden and caused his muscles to bulge.

'I had a daughter once, elfling. Did you know that? My little Gurna.' His sorrow blackened into anger, the golden flames that had already spread across his shoulders licking higher. 'And Snorri.

Damn his idiotic grin and his head full of empty dreams for what he made me do. The axe knew it all, or helped make it be. For what was the weapon of the first Slayer in the hands of a father with a home on the Skull River? No. Only a Slayer would do. Only the greatest Slayer to walk the World-that-Was since Grimnir himself sought his doom! *It* made me what I became. It made me into *this*. So understand, elfling, that I'll not make such a bargain again. I'll not see my destiny forever wed to Grimnir's.'

'Cry me a river, Gotrek! Your destiny is tied to a god's while I am stuck with you. So summon the power, or by Khaine's red hand, I will stab you in the back and take my chances with the Star Titan alone.'

Gotrek roared his defiance. Of Maleneth. Of Grimnir. Of the world he professed to hate, but could never just leave to its fate. It became laughter, low and bitter, but rising to a fiery gale that combined with the volcanic rumble of the Master Rune as it wreathed the Slayer fully in its flames.

For the first time, Ohlicoatl appeared to recognise that it had a challenge.

'HOW DO YOU LIKE THIS, REALMSERPENT? WHEN WAS IT THAT YOU LAST FACED AN EQUAL?'

Maleneth tried to follow what happened next, but it was as though her eyes were not big enough for what they were seeing. The earth became fire, the air became lightning, and the elements went to war. Neither held back. Maleneth watched for as long as she could before the tempest blasted her vision to white.

Her last thought, before unconsciousness took her, was that if Gotrek survived this, it was going to be up to her to somehow kill him.

THIRTY-FIVE

Maleneth woke to the hoots and screeches of the jungle. She carefully opened her eyes.

The sky was amber-tinged, flocked with birds and thickly hazed by clouds of insects. It smelled of smoke. Nodding leaves with blood-splattered blades and margins that were serrated like teeth grew amidst the ruins of a stone castle. Looking at it all hurt. She wondered if she had been hauled back to the Startower by Temekzuqi's Seraphon. What punishments would the infinitely patient Seraphon have devised for the aelf who had murdered their Starseer? And was that a guilty little part of her that would welcome the torturer's offer to just lie down and stay there? But this did not feel like the Seraphon jungle on the realmbridge. The air tasted wrong. It was humid and warm. Sweaty, even. The ground rumbled digestively beneath her.

Ghur.

By some miracle, they had made it to the Realm of Beasts. This was not quite the welcome she had been expecting from Jordaius' Stormhost.

She heard what sounded like Witromm and Jordaius and turned her head towards them.

'The realmgate…' Jordaius murmured. The Stormcast Eternal was on his knees before a jumbled cairn of black stone rubble. His wings were folded around him as if to offer comfort, or, knowing him, to better hide his shame from the heavens. 'It is closed forever. My oath is no more.'

'It's all right, lad.' Witromm patted the Stormcast on the back. 'I should have been here.'

'Aye,' came Gotrek's dry croak. 'You should have.'

At the sound of his voice Maleneth sat up, earning herself a warm smile from Witromm, but she disregarded it, and him, in favour of the one true source of all her woes.

Gotrek was looking a little charred, she would go so far as to say shaken, but depressingly none the worse for his duel with a Star Titan. The rune simmered quietly in his chest. Dormant again. Maleneth suspected that, whatever the source of its powers, it was spent for the time being.

'Sigmar forgive me,' said Jordaius.

'Gods aren't the most forgiving sorts,' said Gotrek. 'But they do live long. Odds are he'll forgive you before I do.'

With long, creaking strides, Druanthael left the others behind. She approached a low parapet of smashed-up stones. It overlooked some kind of a depression or vale, and beyond it the raucous din of the Realm of Beasts. Maleneth could not see it from behind the wall where she lay, but the hungry sounds and warm smells were threatening enough. A predatory vine snaked through the cracks in the parapet and lunged for Druanthael's neck. It had teeth in place of thorns. Bits of what appeared to be skaven fur were stuck to its hairy sides. Druanthael caught it one-handed. It sawed furiously in her grip, unable to chew through her tough bark. She regarded it for a moment before tearing it by its root, sending loosened stones tumbling towards the hidden vale.

It spasmed, flicking its bloody root ball, and then died.

The Sylvaneth clearly had no compunction about ending *this* life.

'The Silver Tower of Xer'ger'ael,' she said, casting the vine aside. 'It is here.'

Maleneth closed her eyes and shivered. Even after everything, she had been entertaining the hope that they might fail.

'Let's go then,' said Gotrek.

He set off, crunching through the rubble of the realmbridge towards a destiny he claimed to not want. With varying degrees of willingness, Witromm, Jordaius and Druanthael followed.

Maleneth tapped the amulet at her neck with a long, sharp fingernail and gave serious consideration to letting them all go on without her. She entertained the pleasant daydream for all of a moment, and then sighed.

'No, really,' she muttered to herself. 'There is no need to help me up.'

'Behold, boldest and most fierce of skaven warriors!'

The Grey Lord stood upon a teetering metal platform, hastily erected over a matter of hours for the sole purpose of elevating him as high above the adoring masses of skavendom as his achievements demanded. Large and noisy machines of superior skaven design toiled away to clear the jungle and admit more of his horde into the former Stormkeep, spitting out gnawed logs and, very occasionally, the gnawed body of a clanrat pushed too close by the masses around him.

'Behold the–'

It dawned on the Grey Lord that the din of the logging machines was preventing his majestic squeaks from being heard. He made a mental note to have stern words with the warlock engineer in charge once he was finished. Reaching into his grey robes for his snuff box, he brought it to his snout and took a long, hard sniff. The electric thrill of pure magic burned its way up his nostrils. His eyes widened, his fur bristled, his tail went rigid. His brain inflated like a balloon and sparks flew from his whiskers. He tittered as he pointed his staff towards the closest of those infernal sawmills and obliterated it with a blast of warp lightning.

'Behold the Silver Tower!'

Skaven warriors squealed, almost certainly with adoration, as bits of machinery rained over them. They were certainly listening now.

As well they should! Who but the very greatest of skaven could have matched wits with a Gaunt Summoner and foreseen the Silver Tower's passage so deftly? And one who had weathered such wanton treachery as he had to boot; who had suffered allies as hapless as the man-prince Osayande and the Eye Not Seen. After his plans to undermine Hammerhal Aqsha had been unwittingly foiled – again! – the alliances he had assembled from the warbands of the Great Parch had predictably fallen apart. He, however, had seen the wisdom of a tactical retreat and fled to Ghyran before the Chaos army had been crushed.

His loyal rat ogor bodyguard had, sadly, not survived its encounter with the vengeful Emerald Wardens. He would replace it in due course, but for now his plans were grander than ever! In his eagerness to atone for his many failures, the Eye That's Seen had revealed to Thanquol the secret of the Silver Tower's great treasure, and this time not even the orange-fur would be able to stop him. Not after he had cunningly collapsed the realmbridge behind him. The Clans Skryre engineers – blinkered by small minds and petty jealousies, all of them! – had insisted that it could not be done, and yet look! The titan was not simply injured, as he had hoped for, but dead!

As the storm-things were all dead.

As the orange-fur, one day very soon, *would be dead.*

'Dangers there are still ahead,' he squeaked, voice pitched loud and manically fast by the dose of warpstone snuff. 'Yes-yes! Most assuredly! Traps there will be, and monsters, and tricks, and ruses aplenty, but you, brave warriors of Blight City, are the equals of any creature lacking the superior skaven intellect. From your elite ranks have I assembled a party to brave the perils of the Gaunt Summoner's pathetic mazes and return to me the prize that I desire. Galg Steamclaw of the Clans Skryre!'

A scrawny-looking skaven with singed fur flinched as the Grey Lord pointed his malefically glowing staff towards him.

'Snark Bolgwrack of the Moulderclan!'

At the mention of its name, a muscular brute swung its drooling muzzle towards the stage and looked up with semi-intelligent eyes.

'Naoto Deathskweel of the Eshinclan!'

There was a pause. The Grey Lord peered down, but of the Deathmaster there was absolutely no sign.

'Filth Croor of the Pestilensclan!'

A Plague Monk in dingy robes blew his nose.

'Four brave adventurers!' the Grey Lord went on. 'The cream of skavendom and the equal of any adversary. And yes! The magic of Xer'ger'ael is formidable. But it was nothing compared to the mystic might of I, *Thanquol*, supreme amongst sorcerers, deadliest of diviners, most magisterial of all mages, and *I* will be leading your every step' – he thumped the butt of his staff upon the platform between his footpaws – 'from *right here*, where my insight and intellect will surely be of greatest benefit to you all. So go now, brave skaven. Go! Bring me the great treasure of the Silver Tower!'

PART SEVEN

The Silver Tower

THIRTY-SIX

Jordaius watched the battle from above.

The Silver Tower was a game of dimensions, played without rules. Ceilings and floors were interchangeable, depending wholly upon where one stood. It should not have been possible for any wall to physically link them and yet they did, flexing from near-infinite heights to the most furtive of dimensions in the blinking of an eye, often conspiring to hold both scales at once and all between. Entire worlds floated in the empty spaces that the ever-shifting perspectives left in the eye, and in the mind. They gleamed like golden cities, mirages of hope, wealth and destiny above an abyss of nothing, always there while achingly out of reach. Corridors crossed them, leading nowhere, everywhere, more often than not to their own beginnings to be crossed again.

His companions were strung out along the daemon-infested gallery below him. Gargantuan statues that had been carved, or perhaps summoned, into the snarling likenesses of greater daemons belched fireballs at random. Druanthael strode ahead of the group with Maleneth a blur of knives and bitterness fighting to keep up. Next was Witromm, with Gotrek determinedly fighting the bloody-fleshed Khorne Bloodletters pouring after them.

They had been trapped in the Silver Tower for what felt like weeks, but it was difficult to be certain. There was no day or night inside the structure. They did not tire, or grow hungry. Gotrek had resentfully pointed out that even his beard had stopped growing. They had spent most of that time wandering, lost, from one vicious battle to the next, and yet Gotrek seemed far from sick of it.

'Willingly I walked to my doom, into the pit of the Prince of Shadow and the darkest hell of the World-that-Was, but my thirst for senseless bloodshed remains as it ever was.' Gotrek laughed harshly. Bloodletters swarmed around him and fell by the dozen, fires boiling from his axe's runic brazier to leave burning contrails behind his swings. 'The fires of my axe burn bright, and though my beard falls nearer the floor than once it did, the heart of a true dwarf of old beats in this chest.'

'Come *on*, Gotrek,' Witromm yelled back. 'I don't think even Maleneth's going to persuade Druanthael to wait for you now.'

'The spirit-song of Ancient Hruth'gael calls to me from the passage beyond,' the Kurnoth Huntress sang, a hundred yards on and partially obscured from Jordaius' view by smoke and cinders. 'It is the sound of falling leaves in my mind, autumn's splendour and winter's distant threat. He is not far.'

'Of course,' Witromm went on. 'She's been saying that for days now.'

Gotrek laughed maniacally, slaughtering the last of the Bloodletters still in reach of his axe. 'Killing daemons is like eating vegetables. No matter how many they pile onto your platter, it's never enough to fill your belly.' Looking disgruntled at having nothing more to kill, the Doomseeker gave in to Witromm's urging and turned around to resume running. 'This place is a labyrinth, longbeard. As devious as any maze concealing the treasures of my ancestors. As lethal as any glamour conjured by the heartless cunning of the elves.'

'I only wish there *was* some treasure in it.'

Jordaius turned to look ahead as Druanthael lengthened her stride to leap over a gurgling stream of lava that split the gallery in twain. She landed easily on the other side, crunching the dae-monic stonework under her woody mass.

'Khaine's cold iron heart,' Maleneth cursed. 'We do not all have the long limbs of a Kurnoth Huntress.' The Darkling ran at the sluggish flow and then leapt, hitting the other side and rolling. Panting, more relieved than she was letting on, she turned back. 'Gotrek, can you make it across?'

'Hah! There is nowhere an elf can run that a dwarf can't follow.'

'Speak... for... yourself,' Witromm wheezed.

'Stop your whining, longbeard. It's not so wide.'

One of the statues sent a tongue of fire licking across the gal-lery, just as Witromm prepared his run-up. Jordaius swept around, ready to dive down and pull the duardin out of the flames, but Witromm stumbled short on his own, coughing and patting out loose flames in his cloak and beard.

'I swear those statues have a will of their own,' he said.

'A little fire,' said Gotrek, brushing flames off his skin. 'I barely feel it.'

'Behind you, Gotrek,' Jordaius called down.

Without once acknowledging the voice above him, Gotrek turned his back on the lava channel, shifting his balance from foot to foot and readying his axe eagerly. Another pack of Bloodletters was advancing down the gallery. Their eyes burned like coals. Skinless muscles shone wetly as they marched under the glow of the lava. They were coming much more cagily than Jordaius had come to expect from lesser daemons of Khorne. Even they, it seemed, had learned to respect the Doomseeker's appetite for killing.

'Haven't we banished them all yet?' Witromm sighed.

'*We*, longbeard? If you mean to start bandying around words like *we* then that axe of yours will want to drink a little more deeply of daemon ichor than you've allowed it. I will gladly banish every last one that lurks within this Silver Tower. Do not expect its madness to cow me. The halls of the Changer hold no terror for a true Slayer.' He cackled with murderous expectation. 'Scream to your gaoler, daemons! Scream the true name of *Xer'ger'ael* and pray he heeds. We will see which of us outlasts the other – the daemon slave of the God of Change, or the thirst for vengeance of the last of the *dawr tromm!*'

The Bloodletters delivered a cacophony of bestial, semi-lucid shrieks and charged.

Jordaius had no doubt that Gotrek and Witromm could handle any number of lesser daemons without help, but not without the risk of losing Druanthael, or getting bogged down in an endless wave of attackers. The Doomseeker would not thank him for getting involved, he knew, but it was time. With a hum of Azyrite energies, he folded his wings and dropped.

He hit the ground like a bolt from a Celestar Ballista. The force of his impact knocked Bloodletters to the ground and fouled their charge, arcs of electricity spraying out to incinerate several more. From his crouch, he thrust out with his stormcall javelin, impaling a Bloodletter with a clap of thunder. He ripped the weapon free. Daemonic blood smoked off the sigmarite blade as though it had been pulled from a stove. Taking it two-handed, he swung it, messily decapitating a second as it charged him from the side. Marking a third, he rounded on it, only to feel rough hands yanking him off balance. He threw out an arm, his elbow passing harmlessly through Gotrek's crest as the Doom-seeker pulled him back and stepped across him to bury his axe in the daemon.

Witromm's axe accounted for the last of them.

'I need no aid from you, Stormcast,' said Gotrek. 'Nor do I wel-come it.'

Jordaius shook his head in disbelief. 'Can we not come to some kind of peace, Gotrek? You have barely spoken a word to me since the Mortisrock.'

'And do you expect the animosity of a dwarf to abate over a mere handful of days? Do you think a hundred years more will see it fade? You are immortal now, but you think as a man still.'

Gotrek brushed him off and strode determinedly towards the gurgling stream of lava that had cut the gallery in half. Maleneth beckoned to them from the haze on the other side.

'The Silver Tower is influencing you, Gotrek,' said Jordaius.

'Bah!'

'You are right that I am no longer a man,' Jordaius called after him. 'I am a Prosecutor of the Celestial Host and I *see* the dark-ness of this labyrinth. I see how it wraps itself about us, seeking to influence and corrupt us, and you, I think, most of all. With all the power you bear can you not feel it also?' He smiled grimly. 'The Doomseeker I remember was no hero, not of the kind whose deeds fill the Great Library of Sigmaron, and for whom the Bell of Lamentations tolls, but he was not one to spit on an ally or dis-miss an oath earnestly given.'

Gotrek swung back from the path. 'Allies? Oaths?' For a moment, Jordaius felt certain the Doomseeker would attack him as he had the daemons, but then he laughed. 'How little you know me. The things I have done. The innocent folk I have killed or allowed to die on my quest for glory and fame. I should not be surprised, I suppose, for we are strangers, you and I. The manling who followed me from the Great Parch is dead. *Both of you are dead.* I will accept no less. For if I were to find that he has been remade as you are, as anything less than he once was, then I would feel obliged to end that darkening of his memory myself. And then my axe would be turned on those who dredged an honourable soul from its well-earned rest in the Gardens of Morr and forced it into the broken likeness I see before me now.'

'You are mad,' Jordaius breathed. 'You are mad and you do not even see it.'

'And he would not be the first,' Gotrek went on, ignoring him. 'Nor the best friend that fate put in the way of my axe.' Turning his back, he stomped on towards the lava flow.

Jordaius watched him go. He felt lost for words.

'Well, I for one am glad you're here,' said Witromm, walking up behind him and patting him gratefully on the back.

'He is as stubborn as the Khazalid kings of legend. Does he not realise I forsook an oath to Sigmar to follow him?'

'Aye. I think he realises. One day he may even understand.'

It was the influence of the Silver Tower, Jordaius told himself. The Doomseeker's fearlessness, his recklessness, were virtues elsewhere, but here the tower twisted them, turning them into the weakness that would destroy him. That was how the Gaunt Summoners amused themselves in spite of their enslavement by the Everchosen. Jordaius feared that Gotrek was forgetting he was not here to find a doom, but to claim the new purpose promised him by the Radiant Queen.

Perhaps that fear was to be his own undoing.

He shook his head. Or perhaps it was the doubt.

'Come, Witromm,' he said. 'Before we lose our guide.'

He took the old duardin by the collar of his cloak and beat his wings hard enough to lift his feet off the floor. Witromm kicked out in surprise, but Jordaius' wings were strong enough to carry them both down the gallery, bearing down on Gotrek's back. With his free hand, he reached for the Doomseeker.

'What are you…?'

Jordaius snatched Gotrek up as he flew past, dragging both duardin with him over the lava channel. Witromm looked down, making a sound that was half scream, half terrified laughter.

'Not much farther,' said Jordaius.

'You can't carry two dwarfs, you fool,' said Gotrek.

'It is by Sigmar's power and his will alone that I fly. Even in this dark place there are no limits to what faith in the God-King allows.'

Jordaius set both duardin down on the other side, their boots a little cooked but otherwise none the worse for having crossed a river of lava.

'Solid ground.' Witromm knelt down to touch it. 'By all the gods of Order.'

'Come on,' said Jordaius, already striding off. 'The last I saw of Maleneth, she was attempting to break the seals on the door to the next chamber.'

'Waiting on a dwarf's aid, I'd wager,' said Gotrek, hurrying along beside him without any obvious awareness that that was what he was doing. 'Not that she'd ever ask for it, mind you. Best lead me to her, Stormcast. The elf will as likely kill herself and all the rest of us to boot as actually crack one of these daemon-tainted locks.'

THIRTY-SEVEN

Galg Steamclaw charged the warp lightning cannon riveted to his right gauntlet. The impressively large and potent weapon drew energy until the reactor cage bolted to his chassis' steel spine rattled alarmingly. With an excited squeak, he swung the cannon towards the horde of red-skinned, horn-headed, blade-wielding devils and zapped them into steaming puddles of oblivion.

'Die-die, daemon-things. Die! Die! *Die!*'

He delivered several successive blasts, each one arcing a considerably shorter distance from the emitter claws and obliterating fewer daemons than the one before.

'Gagh!'

He smacked at the hot barrel. The capacitor coils were depleted. Well, no matter.

Shrieking with laughter, he opened up with the ratling gun built into the left gauntlet. He swept the arm from side to side, spraying the daemonic hordes with warpstone as though he was dousing a laboratory fire started by some careless underling.

Almost unnoticed by rat or daemon, Naoto Deathskweel sat cross-legged on the floor, manipulating the stone keys of yet another fiendishly complicated puzzle.

'This is not the Life chamber that you squeak-promised, Steamclaw.'

'A detour, Deathskweel. A scenic scurry.'

'Hssss, now.' The Deathmaster raised a claw for quiet, as though ignorant of the battle being fought to keep the daemon-things off his tail. 'The riddle that bars this door is complicated. I need to focus.'

The ratling gun clicked empty.

'Graaagh! Thirteen Curses of the Great Horned Rat!'

Days, they had been trapped in this accursed Silver Tower. Weeks. Months! All of his weapons suffered for lack of ammunition, maintenance, and a steady supply of slave-meat prepared to stand still long enough to reset the targeting rig.

Galg Steamclaw rued the day his scurrying path had crossed that of Grey Lord Thanquol.

'Stop fussing over your own tail and help me.'

Deathskweel sighed. 'If your wish is to fight them then yes-yes. I can help. If, instead, it is to run-flee and claim the Grey Lord's prize so we may leave this place, then leave me to open this door.'

With a gratifying *clunk*, the ratling gun accepted a fresh magazine.

'Hyah! Better!'

The barrels started spinning again, obliterating Bloodletters in puffs of red before they could get close.

'The wise rat is miserly in times of plenty,' said Deathskweel calmly. 'He would not want-wish to run out of bullets.'

'We will not be here that long. No. No. The portals that link the chambers of the Silver Tower may appear to function at random, but there is a pattern. Yes. Yes! A triskonometrical repeating series perhaps. Or even, yes, yes, a derivation of a thirteenth base logarithmic. Yes, yes, *yes!* It is a riddle worthy of a Clans Skryre warlock, one that my genius will soon unpick. We will find-scurry our way to the Life chamber. The next portal, most assuredly. Or the one after. Maybe. Maybe. Yes. I am sure of it. Almost completely sure.'

'The tower infects you too, I think. It was a mistake to let you take charge when Bolgwrack...' Deathskweel hesitated. '*Stepped down.*'

The hulking Master Moulder bellowed nearby, flattening Bloodletters by the score with each swing of his muscular arms. 'Kill-kill! Kill-kill more! Bolgwrack is hungry!' The Bloodletters surrounded him, but still he held on to one frenzied daemon in the third arm that shared a shoulder with his left, pausing between blows to tear another bite out of it.

Steamclaw swallowed.

He hoped that the Master Moulder would stop when he ran out of daemon-things.

Just then, Steamclaw's clanking harness coughed up a wad of smoke. Fingers of green lightning walked across the frame of his shoulders, an alarm warbling tinnily from the loudsqueakers mounted on a pole on his back. The warp lightning cannon must have malfunctioned again. He raised his other hand to bash it.

'It is the farsqueaker,' Filth Croor gurgled. The Plague Monk was watching the fighting. The Bloodletters seemed to find Bolgwrack and Steamclaw far more appealing targets, but every so often the Plague Priest would cough in the direction of one that got too near and giggle as the muscles sloughed off its bones. 'The Grey Lord makes contact.'

Bolgwrack roared again. He ripped the head off a Bloodletter and ate it.

Steamclaw tried to ignore it.

'Does he not know-smell the time is bad?' said Deathskweel.

'Hold them off, Bolgwrack, while I speak-squeak with our great leader.' Steamclaw picked up the clunky metal receiver from his armour and held it to his ear. A mindless howl of static, an insane blending of daemonic gibbering and damned wails, forced its way through the receiver and into his sensitive ear. He winced in pain. This was all Deathskweel's fault. The assassin had been too slow solving his puzzle, practically demanding that Steamclaw drain his reactor blasting daemon-things, and now the Grey Lord could not get through. Well, Steamclaw would make sure that Thanquol knew who to blame. 'Quick-quick, Deathskweel. Crank-turn the handle.'

The assassin snarled as he looked up from his puzzle. 'A rat can be of two minds, but can only wish for three paws.'

'Quick-now! Or I will have Croor do it and tell the Grey Lord it was your laziness that kept him waiting.'

It was an idle threat. Steamclaw would not let Croor touch him if he was sleeping through a gnawtunnel collapse and the Plague Monk was the only one around to warn him. But it was clearly enough of one to make Deathskweel get up and scurry around behind him. It occurred to Steamclaw that having the assassin behind him was almost as unpreferable as being breathed on by Croor. No sooner had his musk glands clenched, however, than he felt a paw on his back as Deathskweel cranked the handle to manually top up the warpstone reactor. The machine hummed and shuddered as it built back its charge levels, Deathskweel already panting as Thanquol's tinny voice emerged from the farsqueaker.

'Do you hear me, most malign and terrible of seers?' Steamclaw squeaked loudly into the handset.

'Why do you shout, fool-meat?'

'Apologies, most merciful of masters.'

'The mystic might of the Gaunt Summoner is rightly legendary, much feared by those whose mastery of the arcane is less than my own. But be assured, brave and fearful minions of the Great Horned

Rat, that the sundering of time and dimension and the most devious wards of the God of Sorcery are no impediment to one such as I. I, who first mastered his art when your thousand-times-great-litter-mother was a blind pup.'

'Yes, most pre-eminent one. I mean no. I mean...'

'I would speak-squeak with Bolgwrack.'

Steamclaw looked up as the Master Moulder bludgeoned a pack of Bloodletters to death with the half-chewed leg of another.

'Snark Bolgwrack is engaged with... er... important matters.'

'Good-good. Your lack of failure and slow, moderate successes reflects most positively on my leadership in this venture.'

'Yes-yes, Grey Lord. Yes-yes. I have many theories as to the nature of this maze that I am sure you would–'

'Do not burden me with details, Skryre. My thoughts, by necessity, must scurry through larger mazes than yours.'

'Give me the farsqueaker,' Deathskweel demanded.

'No-no.' Steamclaw hugged the handset to him. 'This is a most complicated and delicate piece of–'

Deathskweel snatched for it. The pair of them struggled over the receiver before the assassin, deeply versed in many arts of unarmed combat, prised it out of Steamclaw's fingers and pressed it to his muzzle.

'Grey Lord. This is Naoto Deathskweel, do you hear me?'

'I hear you, Naoto Deathskweel.'

'There are lots-many enemies here. Foe-meat beyond counting. More even than the much vaunted sagacity of Grey Lord Thanquol saw fit to mention before procuring my blade for this task. I have stalked Khaine's Daughters through the shadowpaths of Ulgu, and hunted mages through fortresses that change as I scurry them. But the Silver Tower is madness itself. Its ways are tangled, warded by puzzles to test the most knotted of skaven minds.'

'Forgive the Eshinclan, Grey Lord!' Steamclaw squealed over his counterpart's shoulder. 'He lacks the blind faith in your leadership that I–'

'With your great power, Lord Thanquol, could you not scry-sniff for us the proper path? Or bring your terrifying magicks into the tower to lead us in person?' Deathskweel bared his teeth in a snarl whose target, not coincidentally, would be unable to hear. 'Could you not open this door?'

A shrill burst of static hissed through the receiver. Steamclaw and Deathskweel both recoiled with pain.

'What was that, Deathskweel... failing... hear you... wind it harder... make me come in there... fool-fool...!'

Deathskweel took a deep breath. 'I said–'

The farsqueaker gave a cough of smoke and died. The static faded. The alarm klaxon issued a last drawn-out note and then fell silent.

'Grey Lord?' Steamclaw snatched the receiver back from Deathskweel's unprotesting paw and banged it on his armour. 'Thanquol?'

Typical bad luck on his part. That the farsqueaker should inexplicably act up *just* as the great Thanquol was about to flex his vaunted power and join them in the Silver Tower. He glared at Deathskweel as he set the handset back into its slot with exaggerated care.

'Back-back to work on that door,' he hissed. 'I squeak-told you it was delicate.'

THIRTY-EIGHT

Maleneth glanced over her shoulder as Gotrek, Witromm and Jordaius battled their way towards her through the Bloodletters flooding the promenade. She sighed heavily and turned back to the puzzle in front of her. Druanthael had been holding the daemons off her perfectly adequately, and the puzzle was fiendishly complicated enough already without having Gotrek yelling 'advice' in her ear.

The door she was attempting to open was inset into the wall at the corridor's end. It was recessed behind two uprights that had been carved from stone to resemble winding thorns. She could see why Druanthael had led them to it. Set in front was a pedestal bearing a stone tablet. The tablet, in turn, displayed several hundred ivory tiles about the size of Maleneth's thumbnail. Each one carried a hieroglyphic fragment and could be shifted around the tablet to assemble into whole words. Presumably a password of some kind.

'Despite what you appear to think, Gotrek, I do not need any help from you. There is more to being a Shadowblade of Khaine than knowing where to find a man's throat. Believe it or not, most people with a Death Mark on their soul lock their doors at night.'

'Here.' Ignoring her completely, as was his custom when dealing with absolutely anybody, Gotrek reached across her to slide one of the rune-inscribed stone keys into a new slot.

Maleneth slapped his hand away and slid it back. 'I have this, Gotrek. Go and kill something.'

'What did you do that for? That key clearly bears the klinkerhun sign for "unlock".'

'Do you never tire of pretending to know what you are talking about. It is clearly the ancient Abhorashi word-glyph for "unmake".'

'Pffff. You made that up.'

'Do you know how many languages I speak?'

'And what do I mean when I say "Af eru drengrodd ekthag a naibolg un nuftromm"?'

Maleneth looked away primly. 'I would rather not say.'

Druanthael strode from the battle towards them. She had been fighting for several long minutes and was well due the chance to hand duties over to Jordaius and Witromm. For all that, though, she did not look tired. Quite the opposite, she appeared restless. As if she would resort to hacking through the door, and Maleneth too, if necessary, if she could not get it open.

'Why is the way not yet open?'

'Aye,' Witromm barked over his shoulder. 'Even a Stormcast Eternal can only keep this lot at bay for so long.'

'It would be done by now if Gotrek could leave well enough alone.'

'Bah! I'm simply undoing the damage.'

Gotrek swiftly repositioned a number of the keys while Maleneth watched on in panic.

'*Darath'nhair!*' she swore. 'Blessed murder, Gotrek, what do you think you are doing?'

An ominous rumble shuddered through the stonework. Gray dust cascaded from the ceiling.

'Is that the portal opening?' asked Jordaius. 'Are we clear?'

The thunderous din of stone scraping over stone grew louder as the door that had been blocking their escape from the fire chamber ground slowly up into the ceiling. Gotrek brushed dust off his brawny, work-callused hands and cackled.

'What...?' Maleneth mumbled, staring at the puzzle keys in disbelief. 'How...?'

'Easy as flying a pedal gyrocopter,' said Gotrek. 'You only have to fall out once.'

'The way opens,' Druanthael sang, immediately moving forwards. 'I am coming, Hruth'gael. We come.'

The door concluded its ascent with an almighty slam, the dust it shook loose causing everyone to cough, with the exception of the unbreathing Sylvaneth. A round of curious squeaks and mirroring splutters sounded from the other side of the pall.

'*The portal is opened, Skryre.*'

'*Good-good. I had full faith in your ability to–*'

The speaker trailed off as the dust dispersed. It eyed Maleneth. Maleneth stared back in shock. Its red-eyed gaze left her in a squeal of its powered fighting armour, tracking upwards in favour of a gigantic Sylvaneth bristling with thorns and the lightning-wreathed Stormcast Eternal behind her.

'Minions of the Grey Lord,' Jordaius cried in a voice like thunder.

'Skaven?' Gotrek demanded.

'Orange-fur,' drooled something huge and impossibly well muscled.

'Impossible,' hissed the first skaven. 'Impossible! Thanquol kill-killed the realmbridge!'

Gotrek's face turned a colour that Maleneth had never seen. 'Thanquol?'

'Kill-kill?' The muscular, half rat ogor brute pushed its way to the front.

'What? No, Bolgwrack. I did not mean–'

The giant gave a slobbery roar and pounded its three paws on its chest. 'Kill-kill!'

Jordaius strode forward to intercept it, his obvious fury causing lightning to turn the stone underfoot to fulgurites.

'A debt of blood is owed, creature. For Sekrus. For Ansiris. For the Mortisrock.'

Gotrek turned his furious expression onto Maleneth. 'What are you smirking at, elfling?'

'I *knew* it was not you who opened that door.'

'Is something happening up there?' Witromm shouted.

'Wait for me, Stormcast,' Druanthael sang.

'And me!' Gotrek roared, taking up his axe. 'If the mangy old grey seer is back there, then he's mine.'

'Oathforged!' Jordaius roared, thrusting a stormcall javelin at the one called Bolgwrack, just as the skaven swung a boulder-like fist at him.

A wall of Chaotic energies flared off between them.

The pair of them grunted in pain and separated. Jordaius staggered back into Druanthael and Gotrek. Bolgwrack drooled and snarled, beady eyes looking around in confusion.

Maleneth blinked the unpleasant after-images from her eyes.

'What just happened?' said Gotrek.

'A barrier of some kind protects them,' said Jordaius, just as the skaven engineer appeared to be explaining something similar to Bolgwrack.

'It shall not protect them from my queen.'

Druanthael strode up to the invisible barrier and swung. The surge of counter-force hurled her back. She crashed to the ground near to where Witromm continued to hold the Bloodletters from the portal.

The barrier spasmed and chuckled, the echoes of Druanthael's fall morphing into that of a daemon's mirth. Maleneth twisted around to look for the source, but it was coming from everywhere.

Welcome, heroes, it said in a voice like crumbling paper and sour wine. *You have travelled far, overcome many obstacles, driven by desires only the master of the Silver Tower can grant, brought together by naught but the pull of fate. Some of you have come to slay me.* The walls laughed in mockery of that. *I am Xer'ger'ael, the Tyrant of Eyes. Within the walls of this tower I am god.*

'God, are you?' said Gotrek belligerently. 'Show yourself then, if you think yourself so mighty. Or are your boasts so hollow that you fear this dwarf's axe?'

The chamber trembled with Xer'ger'ael's laughter. The skaven squealed in terror, all four paws to the floor, ears flat to their heads, as all around them the last of the Bloodletters burst into flames and disappeared in puffs of smoke.

'He banished the daemons,' Witromm shouted in amazement. 'Just like that.'

'One does not *fight* one of Archaon's Nine, Gotrek,' Maleneth hissed.

The Darkling is wise. Do you know how many berserkers I have choked on their own fury? Could you count the unbested champions I have paralysed with narcissism and envy?

Gotrek ground his teeth as power shimmered across the rune in his chest. Maleneth watched, appalled. It looked as though it was not only flesh, blood, and heartwood that was being affected by the evil of the Silver Tower.

Rork or gromrhun. Krutkhas dumrhun, ek orf or drung.

The Slayer beat on the side of his head.

'Get out of my head. Both of you. My destiny will be my own.'

Not yet, Gotrek son of Gurni. Not yet. I alone will decide when this ends. There was a pause and, though there was no obvious speaker, Maleneth had the sense that the Gaunt Summoner had dismissed Gotrek and was now addressing them all. *Your efforts so far have amused me, but the game grows stale. I have allowed you a glimpse of what awaits you. You know now that you are not alone in your quest. The first to find my sanctum will be rewarded with all they desire and more. The other party... will be snuffed from existence at the snap of my finger.*

Gotrek answered the threat with an ugly leer, but Maleneth felt herself go cold. She grasped the talisman around her neck, but found little reassurance there.

Not just dead, but *gone*, forgotten by Khaine. Could the Slayer have brought her to a worse fate?

'The light of the God-King is not yours to extinguish,' said Jordaius, with a confidence that Maleneth wished her mortal soul could share.

'It does not matter,' Druanthael hummed. 'We will be first.'

The terrified skaven party squeaked over one another as though refuting the Sylvaneth's assertion of victory was half the contest.

Let us see how you contend with a new maze, and a new set of rules.

The voice slipped into a language that poisoned the air that Maleneth breathed and drained the light from the room before it could make it to her eyes. It was the Dark Tongue, spoken by the servants of Chaos, and Maleneth felt her heart race as, with a terrific rumbling and wrenching of stone, the entire chamber was bidden to tear loose from the adjoining corridors. She saw the terror in the warlock engineer's eyes, so like her own, the skaven's screams falling into the distance as their chamber too was whisked away.

'Everyone hold on to something!' Jordaius yelled.

'Trust me, Stormcast, I am bloody holding on!'

Maleneth clutched on to the solid stone pedestal housing the now meaningless puzzle keys as they fell into darkness.

'What is he doing?' she screamed.

The answer echoed from everywhere.

Let the real challenge begin.

THIRTY-NINE

'Wait, Deathskweel,' Steamclaw panted, clanking in pursuit of the boundlessly energetic Eshinclan. Bolgwrack plodded along behind him. Whenever Steamclaw turned he found the Master Moulder staring at him and salivating in a way that he found particularly disquieting. Croor, meanwhile, he could hear wheezing from the rear. That position was typically reserved for skaven leaders, but in this instance Steamclaw was prepared to let the Plague Monk have it. He felt about as comfortable as he was going to get right there in the middle. 'Wait-Wait!'

'You heard the daemon sorcerer as well as I,' Deathskweel chittered. 'The last to reach the sanctum of the Summoner will be killed-slain. Well, it will not be I. Not Deathmaster Naoto Deathskweel of the Eshinclan.'

'Do you even know-smell where you are going?'

Deathskweel whirled around with a scrabble of polished claws on stone and a menacing *swoosh* of night-black cloak. 'The nose is keener than the mind, Steamclaw.'

'What does that even mean?'

'It means I know-smell where I am going.' The assassin sniffed and turned away. 'Even if I do not *know* I know-smell where I am going.'

Steamclaw sighed as the assassin scurried on as before. They needed to stop and think, to scratch-gnaw at this problem and solve it with superior skaven intellect. *That* was how they would beat the furless heroes to the Summoner and claim his reward. Not by scurrying witlessly like still-blind whelps through his maze.

'Permit me, at least, to calibrate the aetholocator and take a sounding. It will be the work of a–'

'No.'

'I am in charge here, Deathskweel!'

Bolgwrack growled in his ear, making him yelp.

'I am second-in-charge!' he corrected. 'We should at least attempt again to contact Grey Seer Thanquol. While it is quiet-calm. He will want to know-hear that the orange-fur is here with us.'

'Orange-fur...' Bolgwrack snarled.

'No time,' Deathskweel hissed, scampering ahead until only the pale skin of his tail was waving at them from the darkness.

Steamclaw turned to Bolgwrack with a frustrated sigh. 'Say something, Master Moulder.'

Bolgwrack licked his lips in deep thought. 'Hungry.'

Steamclaw looked ahead. Suddenly, a little haste did not sound like such a terrible idea.

'Wait for me, Deathskweel!'

'A fork in the path,' said Gotrek, somewhat superfluously as the Slayer had no monopoly on eyes.

The straight corridor they had been walking down for the better part of an hour split in a Y-shaped fork. Gusts of wind and the occasional deeply unnerving echo emerged from one branch or the other. Maleneth cocked her head and listened, taking a moment to sample the air from each passage as it brushed across her face. There was nothing that would make her favour one path over another.

'You didn't think the Summoner was going to make it easy for us, did you?' Witromm dumped his pack on the ground and sat down. He proceeded to take off his boots and his helmet, grunting in something between pain and relief as he massaged his thumb into the soles of his socks.

Apparently, he expected to be there a while.

Walking past them all to the front, Druanthael planted herself at the fork, looking one way and then the other.

'Can you feel the correct path, Huntress?' asked Jordaius.

'Pffft!'

'Shut up, Gotrek,' said Maleneth.

Ignoring them all, the Kurnoth Huntress sank her roots deeper into the flagstones and emitted a shuddering tree-song. Maleneth held her breath, and even Gotrek bided the wait in silence as the echoes of her song returned. They sounded warped and terrible to Maleneth's ear, chuckling from both passages in a voice horribly reminiscent of the Tyrant of Eyes'. Maleneth felt almost ready to give into despair. The Gaunt Summoner was toying with them. If they could no longer rely on Druanthael to guide them, then she was not sure what advantage they had, or if they still had one at all.

'I am… uncertain,' Druanthael murmured softly.

'It happens to us all,' said Jordaius, with a glance at Gotrek. 'From time to time.'

'Not to me,' said Maleneth. 'Never to me.'

'Nor to me,' Gotrek said, scowling.

'Oh, please–' Maleneth began, the Slayer's shameless misremembering of events she had been all-too-present for just about pushing her over the edge. She took a step towards him, for some reason reaching for her knife, only to pull up with a hiss of pain.

Her hand went instead to the sudden agony in her shoulder.

'You're wounded,' said Witromm.

Maleneth peeled her hand away and looked down. There was a bloody stain in her silk shirt, masked by the black colour, but leaking through to the outer layer of leather padding. One of the Bloodletters must have stabbed her without her realising it. She tried to lift the shoulder and almost passed out from the pain.

'It is just a scratch,' she lied.

'Sit yourself down, girl,' said Witromm, standing himself back up and clicking his fingers for Maleneth to sit down in his place.

'I will not be the one to slow us down.'

'Well, you're in luck then, since we don't seem to be going anywhere just yet. We'd *all* be advised to rest up for a moment.'

'The leaves do not fall when the days do not shorten,' said Druanthael, her first experience of indecision rendering her melodic speech sharper than usual. 'The flower does not lean when there is no sun. I do not tire.'

'Nor I,' said Gotrek.

Maleneth scoffed again.

'Now that I think of it, that does strike me as uncanny,' said Jordaius. 'After the days we have spent here and the battles we have endured, I am not weary. Nor am I hungry or thirsty.'

'The master of the Silver Tower wants to see us fight,' said Witromm. 'Naught but a violent end in the heart of his labyrinth will satisfy him. Where do you think this unnatural vigour comes from, lad? Where if not from the Summoner himself?' The duardin patted the stone floor underfoot. 'I prefer to sit. As nature intended.'

'Very well, Witromm,' said Maleneth, leaning back against the wall and wincing as she slid down until she was sitting. 'You may look at the wound. But *only* until Druanthael finds her way.' She looked up at him suspiciously. 'And I will be watching you.'

The old duardin unfastened his cloak and threw it over her lap like a blanket. Maleneth shivered as a sense of warmth went through her, a pleasant ache replacing the pain in her shoulder. It was the feeling of warming cold hands before a fire, or stretching a muscle after heavy exercise, of draping herself in the physical embodiment of warmth and comfort. She had seen Witromm's cloak bring Gotrek back from near death after his first encounter with the Plague Knight, Algur Threefingers, but experiencing its magic first-hand, it still felt miraculous.

'The cloak was a gift, you say?'

The duardin's brow creased into a smile. 'From a lady.'

While she sat with Witromm fussing over her, feeling her body mend itself, Jordaius walked ahead. Sparks flared up around his black sigmarite boots every time they struck the floor. He passed Druanthael. Her murmuring song continued, unabated, as he stopped to study the fork in the path.

'Where are you off to, Stormcast?' said Gotrek.

Jordaius brushed moss and cobwebs from a stone bust that the state of the corridor had concealed from Maleneth until then. It sat in an alcove, in the narrow stretch of wall between the two paths.

'It's not about to breathe fire is it?' said Witromm, only half in jest.

Jordaius stared for a moment, as though struggling over something in his head. 'Kyukain,' he murmured. 'Hammer-Friend. Yes… Yes, I remember his likeness. It was on the back of every coin, and in bright mosaic on the wall of every public building in Edassa. His statue stood bestride the Heroes' Gate, his hammer raised to Sigendil where it shone down upon the Realm of Fire, and his shield…' He stopped himself, looking at the statue anew.

'What?' said Gotrek.

'We should take the right-hand path. We should follow the hammer.'

'We should, should we?'

'It directs us on the path to the heavens. Don't you see, Doomseeker? It is a sign. A clue for us to follow.'

'Strikes me as a little thin, Stormcast. And obvious.'

'Maybe,' said Witromm. 'But then again maybe not. The Silver Towers, for all their challenges, are designed to be beaten.'

'Why?' Gotrek asked.

'Because the rewards of the Gaunt Summoner are more often than not what they always wanted to hand out anyway, and not what anyone of sound mind would ever ask to receive.'

'Then why did you come?'

With a non-committal grunt, Witromm ripped the cloak from Maleneth's lap like a stage magician unveiling his final trick and sent it flaring back over his shoulder. 'There.' He refastened the buckle and grinned warmly down at her. 'Good as new.'

'Thank you.' Maleneth stood up tentatively. She rolled the shoulder and, even having felt the magic of the cloak at work, marvelled at how completely it had healed. She felt the way her mistress had always looked when she emerged from her Cauldron of Blood on Death Night – not just healed but restored, *revitalised*. No wonder the old duardin had been able to keep up with her and Gotrek, and maintain such good spirits throughout. Still, she could not help herself from adding an icy 'I suppose' to take the edge off of any implied gratitude.

Witromm smiled, regardless, as Maleneth brushed past him to join Gotrek and Jordaius at the fork.

'Strange,' she said. 'I do not see this human hero of yours.'

'What do you see, Darkling?' Jordaius asked.

Maleneth stared as though she could not look away. An Avatar of Khaine: a great sword in one hand, a bleeding heart in the other.

'Does it direct you in any particular way?' Jordaius pressed.

'The heart,' said Maleneth, pulling her eyes away and turning her head to the right. She nodded down the right-hand fork. 'I agree with you, Jordaius. We should go that way.'

'I agree also,' said Druanthael.

'Do you hear the Treelord's song again?' Maleneth asked.

'The lingering echo of his life's lament is on these stones. I... I believe so.'

'Sounds like we're in agreement,' said Witromm.

'I say we go left,' said Gotrek.

Maleneth threw up her hands. 'Now you are just being contrary for the sake of it.'

'What do *you* see when you look at the carving?' Jordaius asked.

Gotrek growled and muttered, the way he did sometimes when asked to play with others. 'I see a dwarf who once made a poor choice.' Without further explanation, he turned left and started walking.

'Where do you think you are going, Gotrek?' Maleneth called after him. 'We have not made a decision yet.'

'Yes we have.'

Druanthael shook her head. 'I am going this way. The geas of the Everqueen draws me.'

'Bah!' Gotrek turned, gesturing angrily towards the Sylvaneth. 'We've been wandering this maze, following this song of yours, for what feels like days. Go your own way, tree-witch, and I'll go mine and we'll see which of us is the first to solve the daemon's maze. Your once-elven queen asked only that I let you lead me here, and lead me here you have. You have the gratitude of Gotrek Gurnisson, as does she, and may consider me duly in her debt, but your bond to me is done.'

'This is the Gaunt Summoner's tower, lest we forget,' said Witromm. 'Let's not for a moment think it chance that the sign he leaves here for us divides us as it does.'

'Well, I'm still going left,' said Gotrek.

'I must go right,' said Druanthael.

Maleneth and Jordaius shared an agonised look. She turned to Druanthael. Maleneth had never particularly warmed to the Sylvaneth. She was too detached, too different for Maleneth to ever really understand, but she would have danced with Druanthael through the gates of the Varanspire if it meant avoiding another moment in the company of Gotrek Gurnisson. She cursed the Master Rune and the fate that had bound them together. She considered abandoning him, and it, and following the Kurnoth Huntress. It was remarkable how one's entirely justified and reasonable terror of the Order of Azyr and the vengeful Khailebron could evaporate after a few days at the pleasure of the Tyrant of Eyes. If Maleneth could only get free of this maze, and Druanthael surely represented her best chance of that, then she would quite happily deal with whoever came looking for her from Azyr afterwards.

For a sweet, delicious moment, she imagined what genuine freedom might be like, but it was only for a moment. She had not joined the Order of Azyr *only* for their protection from her Khainite sisters. She did feel some crumb of loyalty to them and took her duty to Sigmar seriously. She could not leave a weapon as powerful as the Unbaki rune in the clutches of Xer'ger'ael.

'Forgive me, Huntress. As much as I think you are right, I have no choice.'

Jordaius simply nodded.

There were no farewells. Once the decision had been made and given, the Sylvaneth simply turned to her own path and took it. Maleneth watched her go, a part of her still wishing she could be going with her.

'Wait!' Witromm shouted after her. 'The last thing we should be doing is splitting up!'

Gotrek, with no greater acknowledgement of the parting than the Sylvaneth, stomped off in the other direction. Jordaius gave Maleneth another pained look, and then trailed after him.

Witromm's shoulders slumped. 'Well, that was particularly stupid.'

'It could be worse,' said Maleneth.

For the life of her, though, she could not think how.

Rats skittered through the dank chamber, feasting on the aftermath of the orruk ambush. It had not gone well for the greenskins. Steamclaw did not know where the lesser vermin came from, only that they seemed to be drawn to Bolgwrack. They squeaked and scurried around the lumbering Master Moulder like pups competing for the protection of an obscenely fearsome litter brother, chittering aggressively as they gnawed on the big, tough corpses left behind after the battle. Steamclaw wondered if the orruks had ventured into the Silver Tower as they had, become lost as they had, some interminable time ago. He tried not to think about it. He was not some stupid green-thing!

He wondered if the rats had got into the Silver Tower the same way. He found it reassuring to know that they infested this place just like they did everywhere else in the Mortal Realms. Perhaps it would not be so bad, he allowed himself to muse, to find a quiet corner of the Silver Tower to slink away to and hide. Forever.

With a sigh, he raised his weapon claw to the orruk that Death-skweel had taken alive and dialled the kill setting down to one claw-scratch mark.

'Let me rip green-thing's arms off,' Bolgwrack snarled.

'No-no. We need it to tell us the way to the Summoner's chamber.'

'*If* it knows,' said Croor.

'One arm then. I eat-eat as it watches.' The huge Master Moulder licked his lips. 'Then it squeak-talks.'

Steamclaw grimaced. Now the Master Moulder was making *him* hungry.

He fired a short pulse of warp lightning into the wounded orruk. Even with the cannon on its lowest setting, the brute roared, almost biting through its own tongue as electricity coursed through its muscular frame. Steamclaw chittered excitedly. A little more, perhaps. Yes-yes. Just a *little* more. He dialled the power setting up to two claw-scratch markings, delivering a longer zap and an ever so slightly louder scream.

Green smoke rose off the orruk. Filth Croor took a disgustingly long sniff.

'You get carried away, Steamclaw,' said Deathskweel sullenly. 'This is your clever scheme? What makes you think the green-thing even knows the way to Thanquol's prize? Most likely it is trapped here just as we are.'

Steamclaw chose not to mention that he had been thinking something very similar himself. 'Better than scurrying in circles, Eshinclan!'

Bolgwrack issued a warning grumble.

The rest of them looked up to find the Master Moulder with his nose raised to the air.

'Do you smell something, Master Moulder?' said Steamclaw, ready to acquiesce to Bolgwrack's superior nose.

'Wood,' he grunted. 'Sap. Itches in noses.'

'Life magic?' Steamclaw asked hopefully. They never had found the Life chamber, which Thanquol seemed to believe lay at the centre of this maze.

'Something comes through the portal!' Deathskweel squeaked. 'Hide! Quick-quick!'

The four skaven scrambled to hide themselves away behind

statues and pillars. Bolgwrack burrowed under a mound of orruk corpses until his bulk was entirely concealed and difficult even to smell. Steamclaw shivered at the thought of having the Master Moulder lying in wait for him in a dark burrow.

The portal through which they had, just a few moments before, emerged to find themselves beset by orruks spasmed with energy. Steamclaw covered his mouth with his gauntlet lest he breathe too excitedly. The tall Sylvaneth from the orange-fur's party stepped through and looked around, issuing a few creaking, groaning bars of tree-gibberish like a realmborer machine taking an echo-sounding. Steamclaw waited, mouth shut, expecting the Storm-cast and the orange-fur himself to step through at any moment, but then the portal snapped shut behind her.

She was alone.

Showing no interest in the still-warm bodies of the orruks or the swarms of rats devouring them, completely failing to notice Bolgwrack concealed amongst them, she strode off.

'The Sylvaneth,' Steamclaw whispered.

'The Kurnoth Huntress,' Deathskweel corrected. Steamclaw bit his tongue.

'Does she seek what we seek?' Croor wondered aloud.

'If what I know of her kind is true,' said Deathskweel.

'Does she know the way?' Steamclaw asked.

Deathskweel looked down his snout at Steamclaw. 'Better than we do.'

'Does our crossing paths here not mean we were *on* the right path, Deathskweel? Yes. Yes. I think it does. Did I not squeak-say that skaven intellect would sniff out the shortest scurry-hole to success?'

'I hear you, Hruth'gael,' the tree-thing's creaking voice sang to them from the far end of the chamber.

Steamclaw muffled his chittering laughter with his paw.

'Not far,' she said.

Not far.

'Can you follow without her sniff-smelling you, Deathskweel?'

The assassin looked offended. Steamclaw grinned eagerly, and gestured for him to do so.

The reward of the Gaunt Summoner, and the gratitude of Grey Seer Thanquol, would soon be theirs.

'Finally,' said Gotrek, stomping towards the softly rippling portal at the corridor's end. 'I was starting to think this corridor went on forever.' He rapped the butt of his axe on the stone ring that framed it.

'As was I, Doomseeker,' said Jordaius.

'I ask no one to follow me, Stormcast. That they choose to do so anyway reflects poorly on the choices *they* have made in life. Do not seek to blame me for them. I carry shame enough for a hundred lifetimes without adding the burden of an immortal's to my own.'

'I do not blame you. You are a comet, Gotrek, dragging stardust in your wake.'

'Not too late to run after the tree-witch.'

'It is far too late for that, and you know it,' said Maleneth, in no mood to indulge this special moment. Frankly, it no longer troubled her in the least that Jordaius might supplant her in Gotrek's – *ahem* – affections. They could encourage one another to whatever bizarre and outlandish grave they chose, so far as she cared. 'I am afraid that we are all stuck with one other until we find and kill the Gaunt Summoner or, more likely, die.'

Maleneth should not have been so astonished that Gotrek took that as a cue to cheer up.

'Now you're looking on the bright side, elfling.'

Maleneth scowled and turned to find someone sane.

'Any indication where this one goes?' said Witromm, looking up, tracing the pattern of runes around the stone ring with his eyes. 'Anyone feeling anything?'

'No,' said Jordaius, and if the Prosecutor sensed nothing then no one would. 'As far as I can tell it is just a doorway.'

'Only one way to find out.'

Before anyone could stop him, Gotrek stepped through the portal. Maleneth resisted the urge to call it *good riddance*.

'I have faith,' Jordaius said, and stepped through behind him.

Maleneth wished she could say the same. She found herself thinking back on what Jordaius had said to her in Temekzuqi's Startower: what exactly *did* she believe in? While she hesitated, Witromm approached the portal. He seemed noticeably less keen than Gotrek and Jordaius had been.

A faint, eerie laughter rang through the hall. *I know who you are, Wanderer,* it seemed to say. It was coming from the portal.

'Do you hear that?' said Maleneth.

'Hear what?' said Witromm, with a strained nonchalance that, had they been anywhere else, Maleneth would have been quicker to challenge.

The laughter faded away, and Maleneth almost convinced herself that she had imagined it. She shook her head. 'Never mind.'

'Quickly then,' said Witromm, huffing up his chest and squaring up to the portal. 'Before the portals shift and we lose Gotrek and Jordaius as well as Druanthael.' He glanced over his shoulder, smiling at Maleneth in a manner that made her think of the father she had never had, or the mentor that the Lady Witchblade had never been.

She prickled. 'What is it?'

He smiled, a trace of sadness buried behind his whiskers, and for a moment, it looked as though there was something more he wanted to say. But then he shrugged and turned away.

'Nothing important, now I think of it,' he said, and disappeared through the portal.

'*Duardin*,' she muttered to herself. Something about growing old made them act as though they could be both talkative and tight-lipped at the same time. With a last look back, she stepped into the portal and splashed into shallow water.

The portal had carried them into a small chamber. It reminded her of an Azyrite bathhouse, with tiled walls and more water pouring in through spouts moulded into elaborate pelagic displays. The floor was flooded. It was so humid it was hard to breathe, and neither Gotrek's burning axe nor Jordaius' lightning aura were helping in that regard. Maleneth was so occupied by the change in environment that she almost walked straight into the Stormcast's back.

'Jordaius? What are you…?' She felt a stab of panic at the sight of him in front of her. 'Where is Witromm?'

'Is he not behind you?' said Jordaius.

'He entered ahead of me!'

Maleneth turned and splashed back to the portal, only to find it inert, a lifeless stone ring, partially submerged at the base. 'Witromm!' she yelled, pounding at the portal's stonework. Jordain came to join her. He grasped at the stone ring with his big, sigmarite-clad arms as though he might lift it from the ground and reveal a hidden door beneath, probing the seams with his fingers and achieving nothing.

'He's gone, elfling,' said Gotrek.

'No!'

'I don't seem to remember you being all *caring* when I fell over the realmbridge. No, it was all knives and cackling.'

'I…' The appalling realisation of what she was about to say made her pause. Like all unpleasant truths, it found its way out, regardless. She sank to her knees, submerging them in lukewarm water, as panic turned to despair. 'I *liked* Witromm.'

'The Gaunt Summoner picks us off one by one,' said Jordaius, not ominously at all.

'Which of us will be next, I wonder?' said Gotrek. 'Best beat the daemon's little maze, and find the elder tree we came for, lest we need to find out.' The Slayer splashed on ahead, apparently scanning the architecture for a way out.

As though the old duardin was already forgotten.

Maleneth wondered why she cared so much. It was Gotrek who had brought him along. She would have slit his throat and left his carcass for the Wild Hunt of the Nevergreen Woods if it had not been for the Slayer. She should be celebrating the loss of one more unwitting living shield between her knife and Gotrek's back, but she was not. Was it the obvious hopelessness of the task before them that made her crave a useful warrior beside her? Or was it, perhaps, because Witromm was the only one with a word of kindness for her, even though she had done nothing to ask for it?

Was she really that weak?

'Gotrek,' Jordaius mused. 'How high was the water when we first entered this chamber?'

'I don't know. Why?'

'I am certain it was to your hips. Now, it is almost past your waist.'

Maleneth blinked, wiping the sting from her eyes, and looked up. 'He has moved further in,' she said. 'The chamber must be on a slope.'

Gotrek looked down. The bottom of his beard was definitely underwater. 'No, elfling. It's flat as a year-risen stone bread. Trust a dwarf.'

'The water is rising!' said Jordaius.

'It's coming in from those spouts up in the corners,' said Gotrek.

'Our arrival must have triggered them somehow,' said Maleneth, drawing back towards the portal as if that might reverse the effect. 'Pressure plates under the floor perhaps?'

'Magic, more likely,' said Jordaius.

'Bloody tower,' said Gotrek. 'There must be a pump or a mechanism hidden up there somewhere. Can you reach it with those wings of yours, Stormcast?'

'I will try.'

Jordaius leapt out of the water from standing, wings igniting before he was fully clear, water streaming from his greaves as his wings carried him the short distance to the corner of the ceiling. There, wings still humming, he clung to the elaborate stone carvings like a climber to a rock face. Water gushed into his face as he repositioned himself over the spout to reach his arm in and feel inside.

'There is nothing in here, Gotrek,' he spluttered.

'There must be. Water doesn't just pump itself.'

'This is a Silver Tower, Gotrek,' Maleneth reminded him.

'So people keep on saying.'

'It is up to your chin now, Gotrek.'

'Aye, elfling. I noticed when my lip got wet.'

'Wait!' Jordaius cried, turning his head out from the thumping water. 'I see something else.'

Maleneth covered her eyes. Between Gotrek's splashing about and Jordaius putting his body in the way of the spout, the air was rapidly filling up with spray. She saw what Jordaius was gesturing towards. A number of circular panels in the wall, just below the ceiling.

'They look as though they could open onto doorways,' she said.

'How in the name of Grimnir's hairy arse are we meant to get up there?'

'We wait for the water to lift us.'

'What?'

'Can you not swim?' said Maleneth.

Gotrek gave her a look that would have made a troggoth turn and walk away. 'Can you not walk on water?'

'Then *float*, Gotrek.'

'Float?' the Slayer sputtered. *'Fl–'* The water rose to cover Gotrek's mouth. His response, quite typically, was to fume and thrash about as though he was wrestling with a Nighthaunt.

'It means lie still and stop flapping.'

'I'm familiar with the bloody concept, elfling!'

Maleneth sneered, turning from him as she heard what sounded like something large scraping through a narrow, water-filled passage behind the walls.

'Something comes,' said Jordaius, drawing back from the ceiling.

Gotrek struggled to raise his axe high enough to brandish it above water. 'The Summoner toys with us yet, elfling. Well, he'll find this Slayer good and ready for him.'

One of the doors in the wall opened. A torrent of water gushed through, followed by a large, grey-skinned sea monster, saddled and harnessed and ridden by a pair of pallid, hairless aelves in sea-green scale.

'It's a shark,' Gotrek growled. 'Trust an elf to try and ride a shark.'

'It is called an allopex.'

'Looks like a bloody shark to me.'

'Slay the duardin,' said the aelf in the saddle. 'But keep the Darkling. I would have her soul.' The second aelf, standing on a platform behind the saddle, aimed a harpoon that would have made a gargant's eye water.

'Duck!' Maleneth yelled.

Gotrek ducked his head and the harpoon hummed past, smashing into the stone behind him.

'My thanks, elfling. Being skewered by a sea-elf harpoon would be a poor way for a Slayer to die. Grateful as I am, I was under the impression you wanted me dead.'

'*After* we are free of the Tyrant's lair.'

More of the high doorways ground open, spilling salt water and more pale-skinned aelves into the rapidly flooding chamber.

'Idoneth Deepkin,' Maleneth gasped. 'The fallen children of Teclis.' She had thought them legends.

'They have bows,' Jordaius called down.

'Bah! What are they going to hit? They don't even have eyes.'

The archers loosed their volley.

Maleneth blew as much air from her lungs as she could release in haste and dropped beneath the surface. Arrows plunged after her. A few, guided by something more than just aelven aim, even hit her leathers, but their sting was much reduced from entering the water and all scraped off without doing harm. She pushed herself back off from the bottom, resurfacing to find Gotrek in the unlikely situation of brawling with an allopex and both of its riders whilst fiercely treading water.

'Trust...' he said, punching the allopex in the long snout. 'That particular elf...' He ducked the swing of the Idoneth's sword. 'To think that making a bunch of shark-riding...' The allopex reared its mouth wide, only to jerk back, taking the outraged aelf noble with it as Gotrek punched it in the tonsils. 'Water-breathing...' Another punch. 'Sea-elves...' And another. 'Was the sort of thing a god should be doing.'

'I said *float*, Gotrek!'

The Slayer hewed his axe through the allopex's hugely thick neck. Its runic enhancements coupled with Gotrek's own prodigious strength saw it almost all the way through, but not quite. The allopex writhed for quite some time, turning the water red and thrashing it up to foam as Gotrek tried and failed to touch the bottom with his toes.

'Looks like a shark. Dies like a bloody shark.'

The aelf with the harpoon had been crushed to a red smear against the walls by the sea monster's death throes, but the rider rose from the crimson waters. With a cold fury, it pointed a sword made of coral at Gotrek.

'You are mine, duardin.'

'Give it your best try, elf.'

While Gotrek and the Idoneth knight duelled in the water, Jordaius, still hovering just below the ceiling, summoned a javelin to his hand.

'Allow me to take care of the archers.'

'Wait!' Maleneth threw up a hand so sharply it was a miracle it did not fly off her wrist. 'Do not start throwing lightning bolts into a pool of water while Gotrek and I are still swimming in it.'

'Sigmar...' Jordaius clenched his gauntlet, snuffing the javelin out. 'I did not think.'

'*I* will handle them.' Maleneth hurled her knives, accounting for two of the blind Deepkin archers and ducking behind the inert stone portal before the return volley could rattle towards her. '*You* find us a way out of here before we drown.'

'The Deepkin entered through these hatches in the walls,' said Jordaius. 'It would stand to reason that there must be a way out that way.'

Maleneth drew another knife, peeked around the side of the portal ring and threw it. Another archer fell on its back with a loud splash and a knife in its neck.

'This is a small chamber. I see no other way.'

Jordaius tried to force his armoured frame into one of the passages, but the force of water gushing out was too great, even for the strength of a Stormcast Eternal.

'You'll have to wait for the floodwaters to rise enough to cover the outlets, Stormcast,' said Gotrek. His eyes were locked on his foe, rasping with the effort of matching a Deepkin aelf in water, but still managing to snipe from the back seat.

'Will the water not continue to flow?' Jordaius asked.

'Trust an engineer.'

Gotrek and the Idoneth knight continued to douse each other

in spray. Maleneth gave him a moment before hurling a knife. It struck the Idoneth in the side of the head, killing her instantly. Gotrek would have stared with even greater fury, had the rising floodwaters not been so intent on submerging his face.

'I had that, elfling!'

'I am *very* bored now, Gotrek. Let us leave.'

The water had covered the portals now. It was almost to the ceiling.

'I still can't swim,' said Gotrek.

'Take my hand.'

'I will not!'

'Is drowning that much better an end than a Deepkin harpoon?'

With a tirade of grumbling that was rendered largely wordless by the water overflowing into his mouth, the Slayer slapped his hand into Maleneth's. He deigned not to crush it in his grip, for which Maleneth was both surprised and grateful. The water was slapping against the ceiling as Maleneth took a deep breath and ducked back under the surface. The liquid distorted sound, but amplified it too. She could hear the roar of running water, the hum of Jordaius' storm-energy, the heart-breaking language of the Deepkin as they cut through the water like fish. The blind aelves seemed more intent on looting their dead masters than on finishing the fight they had begun and Maleneth was relieved to be able to ignore them for now.

She surfaced with a gasp.

Gotrek spluttered like a torture victim who refused to talk.

'Where's that blasted Stormcast? There must be half a dozen of those exits that I could see.'

'Did you not hear it, Gotrek? His aura lights the way like a celestial beacon. He knows we will be able to follow it even in pitch darkness. How long can you hold your breath?'

'Don't fret over me, elfling. I'll not perish gulping down water that some soggy sea-elf has just swam in. I'd sooner die of the shame.'

Maleneth took another deep breath and this time Gotrek did the same and followed her under. She could see the doorway that Jordaius must have swum through. The circular opening in the stone was limned with the ghost of his presence and the faint glow of Azyr shone from within its depths. She swam towards it, grabbing the stone lip of the channel and pulling herself in. She turned around to see Gotrek fighting with a pair of blind aelves, bubbles streaming from his lips in his fury.

Gotrek! She tried to scream, only to surrender bubbles of her own, but it somehow got the Slayer's attention. He turned his back on the two aelves and kicked clumsily after Maleneth.

The tunnel went in, down, deeper into the wall, narrowing to a point past which it was impossible to believe Jordaius had been this way at all but for the trail he had left to guide her, a light that no daemonic sorcerer could falsify.

She crawled rather than swam, pulling herself along what might have been ceiling or floor for all that it mattered. The portal was ahead of her. She could see it! It was a shimmering skein of light, like water that existed discrete from the water around it, rippling with a power and a logic of its own. Her breath was turning to acid in her lungs. Her pulse thundered in her ears. But Maleneth was no keener on leaving her soul to wander the Gaunt Summoner's labyrinth than the Slayer was.

She resisted the urge to draw breath for one torturous second more, stretching for the portal with one claw-fingered hand.

FORTY

'A forest?' Deathskweel chittered softly, lifting his silk-wrapped snout and sniffing around. 'Inside the Silver Tower?'

Following the Sylvaneth tree-thing at a safe remove, Steamclaw had brought them to what looked like a forest, or someone who had never seen a real tree's weird dream of what one should look like. The other skaven stood around, dumb and gawping. Crystalline leaves rustled amongst real ones, like a breeze in a glassmaker's workshop. Strange creatures croaked and called, sharing secrets that Steamclaw longed to hear, but never once did he catch their scent. Gesturing frantically for the others to do the same, he hunched down.

The tree-thing crunched over glass towards the great tree at the chamber's centre.

'The Life chamber. It has to be.'

'The Sylvaneth tree-thing has found it,' said Deathskweel.

'Did I not squeak-say she would?'

'Do you forget whose skills allowed us to follow her?'

'Which was *my* idea.'

Bolgwrack made an impatient chewing sound that quietened the argument. 'We farsqueak the Grey Lord?'

'No,' said Steamclaw.

'No-no,' said Deathskweel.

'Not *yet.*'

'The slave does not wake the master to tell him he still looks for his lost token.'

'Yes-yes. *No.* We still have not found that which the Grey Seer craves. I would not want-wish to anger him.'

'Accuse us of wasting his invaluable time,' Deathskweel added.

'Or the farsqueaker's power.'

'No.'

'No-no.'

'But soon,' Deathskweel suggested.

'Yes-yes,' Steamclaw agreed.

'Very soon.'

A rumble passed under the floor. The trees tinkled and chimed and Steamclaw threw out his paws in a panic. The Sylvaneth seemed to be shaking in response, her arms outstretched towards the big, central tree and emitting some manner of keening tree-song of her own in response. The initial quaking grew even more vicious. Steamclaw squealed in fright as the shuddering threatened to throw his war-frame off balance. He had given no consideration to how he would get it up again if it fell. He had designed it to be so powerful and terrifying that it *did not* fall!

'Sshhhh,' Deathskweel hissed.

'She rouses the forest!'

'Do not be a coward-meat, fool-fool. Can you not hear-smell? These trees are false.'

With a grinding of metal joints and a belch of steam, Steam-claw pointed to the big tree that the Sylvaneth had stopped in front of. Its trunk was wider than all four of the skaven together could have reached around, and it stretched all the way to the ceiling. As far as Steamclaw could tell, its sleepy green canopy *was* the ceiling. All of the other trees that Steamclaw could see were gathered around it. They seemed to be faced towards it, inasmuch as that could be for a tree, their crystal forms reflecting its colours even as they fell well short of mimicking its appearance.

To Steamclaw's horror, it started to move.

It was just a bend in the trunk at first, as if against a wind that Steamclaw could not feel yet, but then it was struggling, a dreamer tangled in blankets, pulling on roots that had become locked in stone, and Steamclaw could no longer wish away the reality of what he was seeing.

The Sylvaneth was waking it up!

'It moves! It moves!'

'*Sshhhh!*' Deathskweel hissed again.

The assassin set a claw across his lips, then turned pointedly towards the Sylvaneth.

'I hear the confusion in your song, Ancient Hruth'gael.' The tree-thing laid a woody paw on the monster's bark and to Steamclaw's eye the thing seemed to settle. The shaking in the ground ceased. 'Do not struggle. You are rooted too deeply.'

The tree, Hruth'gael apparently, groaned drowsily.

'Rooted...?' Its voice was the creak of old timbers beneath a skaven's footpaws. 'How...? I do not recall...'

'Even as the storm blows, be still. I will clear this unclean stone from your roots.'

The Sylvaneth proceeded to hack at the flagstones with her sword, trying to lever up the tree's roots. Steamclaw watched her disdainfully. A sword was a terrible choice of tool for digging.

'One moment I was exploring the Silver Tower,' Hruth'gael went on. 'Seeking the Summoner. To slay him. To rid the Cueth'nhair hearthglades of his tower's taint. And the next...'

Steamclaw stifled another squeak of alarm as the entire chamber shook again.

'The next...' The tree rustled, settling, like an old rat accepting the diminishment of his powers and inevitable usurpation by lesser vermin. 'I am so weary. As if the sky has swallowed the sun and the earth beneath me has turned barren.'

'Alarielle bound me to find you,' said the tree-thing.

'The Everqueen sent you? Herself?'

'Even she could not see into the Silver Tower for what had become of you. You are her child, as am I, and she feared you lost.'

The tree issued a long, slow groan of despair. 'I am lost.'

'No. Our lady's song may not pierce this darkness, but she reaches for you through me.'

'I will never leave this grove.'

'Speak no more, Ancient. This is no grove.'

'For time beyond reckoning I have stood, my roots going deep in the bedrock of the Nevergreen. I remember how Ghyran once gleamed, still wet with creation's dew and the first words of the goddess' song, but now, I fear, I must be brief. If Alarielle herself sent you then she too has become ensnared in Xer'ger'ael's web and must be warned. I must speak to you of the realmgate.'

'Realmgate?' Croor mumbled, starting awake.

'Sshhhh!' said Deathskweel.

Steamclaw leant forward. It could only be referring to Thanquol's prize.

'What realmgate do you speak of that could be so important?' the tree-thing asked.

'It goes to a place that no other in all creation can reach. The Gaunt Summoner thinks I do not know, or perhaps he does not care that I do. I am naught but the lure.'

'You are a Noble Spirit of the Cueth'nhair!' the tree-thing sang defiantly aloud.

'Since before my soulpod was planted in Ghyran's soil by the tender hand of the Radiant Queen, Xer'ger'ael has held this realmgate for his master. It has brought them both much enjoyment, but the end of their game approaches.'

'Did it say "realmgate"?' Croor said again.

'Yes-yes,' said Deathskweel. 'It did.'

'It knows where it is,' Steamclaw added excitedly.

'Kill-kill now?' Bolgwrack asked.

'Yes-yes!'

Bolgwrack growled in anticipation and started to move.

'No!' said Steamclaw, interrupted by a most brilliant thought. 'Wait-wait!' The Master Moulder snarled impatiently, but settled back down. 'We take the tree-thing alive. We torture her, tell the big tree that we will kill-kill if it does not tell us where to find the Grey Lord's realmgate.'

Bolgwrack licked his lips. It was quite clear that *kill-kill* was the only part of that he had heard.

'And if the Treelord fights back?' said Deathskweel.

Steamclaw sniggered. 'You heard. He is caught-stuck. Now, let me think...' He trailed off as he performed a series of rough mental calculations in his head, estimating the Sylvaneth's height and weight, performing some guesswork as to the electrical conductivity of wood relative to flesh, and concluded that a mid-power blast from his warp lightning cannon should be more than enough to stun her. He dialled the power setting from the maximum thirteen claw-scratch mark down to three. *More than enough.*

Deathskweel gave him a warning hiss.

'I am being as quiet as I can be.'

'A skilled assassin can kill-slay from afar. The master kill-stabs in close.'

'You worry too much, Deathskweel. The tree-thing will never hear–'

Unfortunately, Steamclaw's harness chose that moment to belch up green smoke. Sparklers of energy drizzled from the warp-stone reactor built into his back and showered over Croor, who screeched in surprise, as the various alarm systems went off.

'What is that?' Deathskweel squeaked, his paws clamped over his ears.

Steamclaw banged randomly on his war-frame, trying to silence the caterwauling alarms.

'*Warlock?*' came Thanquol's tragically ill-timed voice. '*Why do you not answer?*'

'It is the farsqueaker!'

'Make it stop,' said Deathskweel.

'I cannot!'

'*That is enough fearful cowering. You may now answer the summons of your most magniloquent of masters.*'

The Sylvaneth turned towards them. Steamclaw fought to keep from squirting the musk of fear as the twinkling song of the false forest turned to one of rage.

'Who intrudes upon the grove of Ancient Hruth'gael, Treelord of the Cueth'nhair?'

'She sees us,' Steamclaw squealed.

'I see she sees us,' said Deathskweel.

Bolgwrack looked pleased.

'Defilers,' the tree-thing sang as it strode towards them, unhurried but so appallingly fast with those long legs. Steamclaw fired off a three-claw-mark blast from his warp lightning cannon, but was so unnerved by its turn of speed that he missed.

He looked around for help. Filth Croor, in spite of the lethargic demeanour he liked to put across, had reacted with startling haste in scurrying behind Steamclaw's armoured frame. Deathskweel, meanwhile, had simply vanished altogether. Steamclaw snarled as he swung his ratling gun around. He had given no consideration to how he would go about running away in his war-frame. He had built it to be so powerful and terrifying that everyone *else* could run away from *him* for a change.

Squealing in terror, he closed his grip over the trigger mechanism in the palm of his gauntlet, squeezing off a flurry of rounds that made crashing fountains of broken glass from the crystal trees either side of the charging Sylvaneth – even putting a shot or two in the tree-thing itself, he was sure! – before Bolgwrack pawed him to one side. The rest of his magazine unloaded into the ground as he stumbled, directing all of his genius into not going snout over tail right under the Sylvaneth's feet.

'I in charge,' he heard the Master Moulder growl. '*I* kill this.'

'My boots are wetter than the High King of Ulthuan,' Gotrek complained as he squelched miserably down the corridor, a variation on the theme he had settled upon since he, Maleneth and Jordaius had tumbled through the portal from the flooded chamber. At least he was consistent.

'Stop complaining, Gotrek,' said Maleneth. She had not yet got all of her breath back, and nor had her heart quite forgiven her for the near escape. It was a cold and frighteningly fragile pain under her wet skin.

Gotrek wrung his beard, splattering his hobnailed boots with water. 'I'll be wringing salt water out of my beard for a month.'

'Does being alive enough to complain not bring you any joy?'

'And no doubt we'll still be stuck in this blasted tower too.'

Maleneth sighed. 'How did you know which passage would take us to the portal?'

This was to Jordaius, who shook his head, as though embarrassed at having his contribution noted. 'I did not. I simply took the one that none of the Deepkin seemed to be using at the time. The passage was barely wide enough for me, I did not want to have to push past an aelf as well.' He looked away. 'And I had faith.'

'Luck is what you had,' said Gotrek.

'As long as it is working for us, I will not complain.'

'Maybe,' Gotrek conceded with a grunt. 'But we could be anywhere now.' He shook his wet hair, like a dog who had just climbed out of a river. 'I hate the sea. It's like bathing, only colder, and saltier. And apparently liable to have elves in it. Mind you, if I had to put an elf somewhere then the bottom of the ocean would be as good a place as any. Provided the pointy-eared little beggars would bloody well stay there.'

Maleneth raised a hand for quiet. She cocked an ear towards the passage ahead of them.

'Do you hear what I hear, Darkling?' said Jordaius.

'What do either of you hear? I'm not used to being surrounded by people with sharper ears than mine. I'm not sure I approve of it much, either.'

Gotrek did not approve of anything very much, but Maleneth decided that was obvious enough to leave unspoken. 'Fighting,' she said.

'Fighting, you say?' The Slayer's expression suddenly became serious. 'All I hear are tinkles and chimes. It looks almost like a forest, if you don't look at it too closely, but it sounds like the parlour of a back-alley hedge witch trying too hard to be taken seriously.'

'That…' Maleneth listened for a moment. 'It sounds almost like…'

'Would someone tell me just what it bloody sounds like!'

'It is Druanthael,' said Jordaius.

Maleneth broke into a sprint.

If the Kurnoth Huntress was ahead of them, then that could

only mean one of two things. Either they had both found their way to Xer'ger'ael and it was here, ahead of them, or they were both equally lost. Either way, it sounded as though they could still use one another's help.

'Not like her,' Gotrek muttered to Jordaius, easily loud enough for Maleneth to hear. 'Leaving me behind to run *towards* a fight.'

Khaine help her.

If she was running towards a fight with a Gaunt Summoner then she would take even the Slayer's help without complaint.

FORTY-ONE

Maleneth skidded to a halt on the smooth flagstones. Glass leaves splintered under her wet shoes, crystalline needles tinkling as they rolled away across the floor. The corridor had come out into a forest, but one unlike any she had ever seen before. Light prismed through the crystal bowers, decorating the floor with random displays. The air swirled through the leaves as though it was being brushed across a glass drum. Maleneth could have stood like that for hours, days, just listening, but there was no opportunity. She forced herself to focus. The skaven that Xer'ger'ael had unveiled to them as their rivals were already there.

Maleneth would have panicked at being beaten to the prize had Druanthael not been there too. The Sylvaneth was locked in an embrace with a giant, mutated skaven. Whether he was a small rat ogor of unusual intelligence or a *very* large skaven, the mutant was almost as tall as the Kurnoth Huntress and probably outmassed her in sheer brawn. A tail as thick as a skyship's cable was wound around Druanthael's wrist while Bolgwrack exploited her limited mobility and one-hand disadvantage to pummel her bark in a frenzy.

'The tree-witch!' Gotrek roared, one step behind as usual. 'And the skaven too.'

'It is as Witromm said before the Gaunt Summoner took him,' said Jordaius. 'The maze exists to be conquered.'

'Orange-fur!'

The small piebald skaven carrying the large arsenal pointed to the three of them. The apparatus bolted to the upper back of his fighting harness squealed and shuddered, looking just then like nothing so much as a warpstone bomb strapped to the fool's back as its surplus energies went arcing through the metal frame he wore. Wince-inducing alarms menaced the upper reaches of Maleneth's audial range. The flash of the accompanying beacons, though exceptionally garish on account of poor skaven eyesight, was at least muted slightly by the smoke coughing up from the machine.

'Answer my summons, Galg Steamclaw,' it announced, in a voice like a nail being dragged across a metal sheet. 'Or suffer unimaginable wrath!'

'Deathskweel! Croor!' The one apparently called Steamclaw gestured everywhere and anywhere as he flapped his arms through the smoke. 'Get them!'

A skaven dressed like a monk, in a habit that looked as though it had been dyed using faeces and vomit, turned its snout towards them. A chapped, runny nose poked out from its vile hood. A limp tail lay dead along the ground. He did not appear to be armed at all, which gave Maleneth more cause for concern than Steamclaw's entire armoury.

'Gotrek and I will handle the Plague Monk. Jordaius, you – Gotrek?'

Maleneth swore as Gotrek crashed off into the crystal grove in entirely the wrong direction for the fight. This was a fine time for the Slayer to decide to learn the noble art of discretion.

'I will take the engineer,' Jordaius finished for her. 'Sigmar be with you.' His wings flared with the brilliance of Azyr, driving away all shadows as the Stormcast Eternal took to the air.

Exposed by the unexpected flash, the black-cloaked skaven hidden in the branches above Maleneth's head bared its teeth at her, as though at pains to make it known that it had intended to reveal itself in this manner all along.

Two against one.

Thank you, Sigmar.

'Die-die, aelf-thing!'

Maleneth rolled clear. Its claws sank soundlessly into the flag-stones. She retaliated immediately with a low kick to sweep out the skaven's legs before it could get its balance, but it was faster. It hurdled the arcing foot, turned it into a somersault and stabbed the ground with a weeping knife in each paw. Maleneth gritted her teeth against the pain as a dagger stabbed through her hair. She kicked him in the chest. He stumbled back, half a step, but enough for her to vault back onto her feet. She stabbed her left-hand knife towards the skaven's heart. He blocked with the outside of his wrist and hissed, threw a slice across her belly that she intercepted with a sharply raised knee.

'Fast-quick,' Deathskweel chittered.

'That is why I still have my skin.'

The skaven was fast too but, in a rare turn of events, she found herself with the advantage in strength. Throwing her shoulder into the skaven's snout, Maleneth forced him to give her another handful of paces. She mirrored his retreat, doubling it, sinking into a more favourable fighting crouch and bringing her knives back into position.

'You are trained,' Deathskweel observed.

'As are you.'

'By the Deathmasters of Umbrasan.'

Maleneth grimaced. It looked like they were doing this. 'The Temple of Khailebron, in Azyrheim.'

'Good-good.' Deathskweel saluted her with a tilt of his knife. 'This will be a challenge.'

The assassin leapt, getting more spring out of that standing start than Maleneth could have achieved with the run-up of her dreams. When he descended it was a dervish whirl of knives, teeth and clawed feet that Maleneth strained every sinew of ingrained instinct and muscle memory to match. Counter-attacking became a distant dream.

'It is a rare trick to master,' Deathskweel hissed. 'To wield two knives with the skill of one.' A third blade lashed out from under the assassin's trailing cloak, the hilt firmly gripped in his prehensile tail. Maleneth dropped to one knee, avoiding a gash to her bare thigh in favour of the purple leather of her high boots. Her studies at the temple had taught her all about the Eshin clans' arts of dealing death. The slightest graze would almost certainly prove fatal.

Deathskweel disengaged with a backflip, landing in a mirror of Maleneth's earlier crouch with a long knife held out at each side and the addition of a third, dripping poison like a scorpion's tail. He bared his teeth at her.

'Did you never learn the art of fighting with three?'

Maleneth looked around, hunting for help or any kind of advantage that she could exploit, but found neither. The giant skaven and Druanthael were beating one another to pulp and splinters, respectively, while Gotrek was nowhere to be seen. The Plague Monk, Croor, seemed to have vanished too, which was at least something. As she searched, Jordaius swooped in low. A flurry of glass-shattering green shot and stabbing beams of warp lightning pursued the Stormcast everywhere he turned. Jordaius banked towards Maleneth and Deathskweel, forcing the pair of them to hit the floor to avoid being mown down as an afterthought. The Stormcast swept on, dragging Steamclaw's fusillade along behind him like iron shavings towards a constantly moving magnet.

Deathskweel sprang back onto his footpaws.

Maleneth stayed down a moment longer. She had seen something that the skaven had not.

'I told that metal-brained imbecile to spare his bullets.' He peered down his snout at Maleneth. 'Playing dead, aelf-thing? Clever. Except I see your eyes are–'

The Treelord that had suddenly appeared behind him swiped the assassin from his footpaws. The skaven squealed as he went crashing through the forest's crystal foliage, but the Treelord gave him no further mind. It slumped wearily back onto its roots, as though bedding in for another aeons-long slumber right there.

Maleneth pushed herself up off the ground.

She was, conveniently, already abased in gratitude.

'You must be Ancient Hruth'gael?'

The Treelord grumbled and swayed as if in pain. 'The warlock's bullets are warpstone and his aim is poor. I feel them where they have broken bark and penetrated my heartwood, polluting my sap. I am not long for the place.'

'Not yet, you don't,' said Gotrek, appearing finally, a little flushed in the face and with a scrap of diseased-looking fur caught in his beard. Maleneth felt that she had solved the mystery of the disappearing Plague Monk. 'Not after I came all this way.'

After *we* came all this way, Maleneth wanted to add, but held her tongue.

'For the sake of my lamentiri, I must,' Hruth'gael groaned. 'Lest my soulpod too be corrupted beyond hope of replanting.'

'Move aside, elfling. You're distressing the tree.'

Maleneth stared at Gotrek – renowned lover of all trees – in disbelief until a whipcrack report pulled her gaze away. The smoking wreck of Jordaius Lionheart came crashing out of the sky, accompanied by a shriek of laughter that presumably belonged to Galg Steamclaw. There was a terrific crash as the Stormcast hit the ground, but no blast of lightning towards the crystal canopy. Either Jordaius was still alive or…

Maleneth shook her head. The alternative, that even the soul of a fallen Stormcast Eternal could not escape the Silver Tower without their captor's consent, was too horrible to countenance.

'Get your answers quickly, Gotrek. Before Druanthael goes the same way as Jordaius and we find ourselves outnumbered.'

'Tell me what I want to know, tree, or by Grimnir the fires of this axe will aid you in your passing. Tell me where I might find my axes.'

The Treelord emitted a deep, thoughtful groan. Under circumstances less fraught than these, it might have amused Maleneth how much it reminded her of a senile old duardin. 'Axes. Grimnir. *Yes*. There is a memory, bedded deep in my heartwood. I know you, Doomseeker, older even than I. I do not have your axes, but I know where they may be found.'

'Must I shake it out of you?' Gotrek scowled.

'The realmgate.'

'Realmgate?' said Maleneth. 'Which realmgate?'

'It is the prized possession of the Tyrant of Eyes, for there is no other like it in all existence. A gateway to the World-that-Was.'

Gotrek flapped his lips soundlessly for a long time. 'A realmgate to the Old World? To the Empire, the Border Princes, the Karaz Ankor?' He shook his head, as though a part of him still wished to defy the possibility, however hard he must have wished for it since his arrival in the Mortal Realms. 'I thought the Everqueen showed me the path to my lost axes, but all this time she has been guiding me…' His voice cracked. 'Home.'

'A home doomed to break under the heel of Archaon,' Maleneth felt compelled to remind him. If she did not want Jordaius leading Gotrek on some merry quest across the Mortal Realms then she *most certainly* did not want to have to chase him all the way to the World-that-Was in the days before its destruction.

There was a shimmer in Gotrek's one good eye as he turned to her. 'Aye, elfling.'

Maleneth turned back to the Treelord, but the ancient spirit was still.

When a Treelord died, it died silently.

'Go to the welcome of your ancestors, ancient one. Tell them that Gotrek Gurnisson bids them well.'

An incongruous round of applause startled Maleneth from the moment of passing. The Gaunt Summoner stood before her. In person. The daemon sorcerer was as angular and frail as a skeleton, but nothing in its shape suggested origins as innocent as a human corpse. Its arms, of which it had too many, were sheathed in iridescent carapace and were segmented like those of an insect. Its skull was bifurcated like a blunt fork. The two prongs accounted for half of its gaunt frame, sharing an uneven distribution of smug, cat-like eyes.

Congratulations, Gotrek, son of Gurni. You have bested my maze, found my sanctum, and discovered my greatest treasure. Claim your reward. Whatever you desire, I have the power to grant you.

Gotrek rounded on the Gaunt Summoner with a snarl.

Xer'ger'ael blinked with several dozen eyes. It raised a finger boredly, as though calling the Slayer's attention to something barely worth mentioning, and seized Gotrek where he was. The Slayer grunted, but found himself unable to move, the fire that wreathed him finding new colours and fiercer intensities for every new way he found to struggle.

'Is that... supposed... to hurt?'

Ok utar? the rune echoed in its own golden ancestor tongue.

The Gaunt Summoner smiled. Its many eyes appeared pleased. *I was wondering when he would make his appearance but, as I told you already, there is only one god inside this tower. He has no power here.*

The daemon dismissed the rune's power as casually as one would pinch out a candle. The voice in Maleneth's head cried out briefly before its fire was expunged, pushed deep into the metal of its making. Gotrek sagged, weakened by the sudden absence of the power he had so often sought to refuse.

On the battlefield you would be a most testing opponent, even for me. But not here. Not in any but one of fate's infinite strands.

The Summoner drifted towards Gotrek. There were no legs that Maleneth could make out. It could easily have been nothing more than a floating torso, borne aloft by the fluttering blue gown that draped its lower portions.

Speak your wish, Slayer, and it shall be granted.

'Remember Witromm's warning, Gotrek!' said Maleneth, feeling the desperate need to shout even though all the fighting had stopped and no one else around her was raising their voice. 'Think before you speak.'

Gotrek tilted his jaw belligerently towards the daemon. 'Show me your realmgate to the World-that-Was!'

As you wish.

The Gaunt Summoner cast no spells, and yet suddenly there behind it was a square dolmen of stone. Xer'ger'ael was a god within its tower, and gods created at will. The portal's marble uprights were carved into the stylised semblance of duardin gods. One was male – Grungni the Smith, presumably, as he bore tools rather than weapons – while the other was a robed goddess that Maleneth had never seen depicted before. The argent surface was semi-translucent, a film rather than a barrier, and the landscapes and figures that passed within it were in a state of constant flux. Maleneth could make out nothing from them, but Gotrek stared as if the Cosmos Arcane had just bared its heart to him and him alone.

'It is… No. It can't be. It is the first realmgate I ever passed through, elfling, though I didn't yet know it as such, after I had bested the daemon prince Be'lakor and left that world behind me. It is the gate that conveyed me from Kazad Drengazi to the Realm of Chaos. It is there still?'

With all of her senses captivated by the shimmering wonder before her, the reappearance of Jordaius at her side passed entirely without notice.

'You possess a realmgate to lands undreamt of by all save the gods themselves,' he said. 'Why do you make no use of it?'

The Gaunt Summoner chuckled. *Hammerhal is in anarchy and the Rotbringers returned to the Nevergreen Woods. The Star Titan is cast down. The Oathforged are no more. I would contend that I have made great use of it, Stormcast.* With a flick of the hand, it dismissed the realmgate. As suddenly as it had appeared, it was gone.

'Return my portal to me, summoner!' Gotrek roared.

What you saw was but an illusion, Slayer. A conjuration. Only one of ancient blood can truly command the World-that-Was gate. Only one of that rarest of lines.

'Of which I am one.'

The daemon's eyes smiled in unwholesome unison. *Yes, you are.*

'Careful, Gotrek,' Maleneth warned, but Gotrek had been shown the one thing he desired more than a pointless death or his Shattered God's missing axes and was well past heeding.

'If you can't bring it to me, then send me to it!'

The Gaunt Summoner spread its many arms and bowed.

It would be my great pleasure. But first…

It snapped its fingers.

Where the realmgate had been there now stood a shocked-looking skaven who appeared to have been snatched mid-harangue. His robes were long and patched and dirty grey, but woven with enough painfully obtuse sigils to make clear that the skaven himself was most pleased with them. His white fur had been combed, the curling horns erupting from the sides of his head sheathed in fine plates of gold. Maleneth knew that white fur amongst the skaven tended to signify leadership. Could this even be the near-mythical Grey Lord who had menaced Gotrek's footsteps since the Great Ash Road? The staff in his paw was certainly that of a sorcerer. It glowed an unearthly green, turned towards some no-longer-extant servant who was most likely shocked, but hugely relieved by their reprieve.

'Crank the handle, you lazy-meat...' The Grey Lord lifted his snout, confused. 'What? Where am I? How did I get...?'

He noticed Gotrek and the Gaunt Summoner and bristled in fear, and in anger at being seen to be afraid.

'No!' He slammed his staff on the ground in pique. 'No, no, no, no. *No!* I set the Eye That's Seen to burn Hammerhal, the Three-Fingered to blight the forests, collapsed the so-called Maw of Sotek myself. There is *no way* you could have followed me here unless...' His diatribe descended into a snarl. 'Long-clever is your scheme, Summoner. Rightly do you fear to face the sorcerous might of Thanquol alone. How else to explain this one's untimely reappearance after so many centuries!' The Grey Lord took a generous sniff from the silver box he procured from his pocket, and then let out an ecstatic little shiver of a sigh. Glowing flecks of warpstone green appeared in his eyes and his fur stood on end. 'See how I kill-smite your pawn!'

The skaven sorcerer thrust out with his staff, shrieking as he sprayed about a thousand times the power as had been used to fell Jordaius towards the Slayer.

Maleneth was uncertain about what happened next. The green flash blinded her. Warped thunder rolled and rolled against her ears until she was not wholly deaf but wished for it. By the time her senses did return, Gotrek was standing like someone who had been braced for an avalanche and now looked as though an unexpected breeze might knock him over. Thanquol simply stared, agog. The Gaunt Summoner stood between them with its own staff raised, the Grey Lord's warp lightning orbiting furiously around and around the wide, staring eyeball mounted at its top.

Thank you for the power, Old Blood.

The Gaunt Summoner raised the staff and drew it slowly in a circle. Where it went, it left the shape of a portal behind. Within that shape of the portal, suddenly there *was* a portal, hellish blue faces and grasping hands causing the surface to ripple.

Behold Tzeentch's domain. Dare either of you enter in search of your prize?

'There is naught in that realm for me to fear,' said Gotrek. 'And no horror left to it that I have not bested thrice over. I accept your challenge.' And before Maleneth could so much as scream in horror, Gotrek was striding towards the Ruinous portal.

'What are you waiting for, mouse-brained lazy-meats? After him! After him!'

The Grey Lord hoisted up his robes and scurried after the Slayer in pursuit, and suddenly it was as though the Gaunt Summoner had enacted another of its spells, an enchantment involving neither gestures nor words but which nevertheless caused fighting to break out in the Grey Lord's wake. The skaven scurried past Steamclaw, who swung his ratling gun towards Gotrek only to shriek as a stormcall javelin cast by Jordaius impaled him from behind. Ignoring his dying minion, the Grey Lord fled past the giant skaven and Druanthael. The latter struggled to get up, but the monster had her pinned under his mass. He throttled her with his tail, punching and punching and punching until her head came apart under the blows and spilled pulp over the stones. A final piercing scream shook the leaves of the false forest as the Grey Lord ran past her and leapt into the realmgate.

Maleneth watched in horror. If there was one destination in all creation less appealing to her than a one-way journey to the World-that-Was, it was the plane to which this realmgate would take her.

The Crystal Labyrinth of Tzeentch.

The Realm of Chaos itself.

Knowing what lay on the other side of it only made it worse. Maleneth wanted to surrender to the insanity that it induced, to shut her eyes and run screaming in whatever direction would take her *away*, but deep down she understood that was no longer an option. She had made her choice already. She had made it the moment she stopped trying to kill Gotrek Gurnisson and instead followed him into the Silver Tower. For the life of her, she could not put her finger on exactly when that had been. There had been so many opportunities for her to wipe her hands of him and take her chances, but now it was too late. They were trapped. They would either escape the Realm of Chaos together, or provide the Dark Gods with amusement to the last days of eternity by trying.

And who better to take her chances with than the stubborn fool who had escaped them once already? *By accident.*

With eyes wide open and a curse on her lips, Maleneth leapt into the realmgate. Ready for whatever horror Gotrek's destiny had in store for them next.

PART EIGHT

The Last Gate

FORTY-TWO

The prayer candles flickered, arranged across the huge black altar in a twelve-pointed star. Lightning charms crackled in their sconces. Beyond the thick walls of the Stormkeep's austere chapel, a battle raged. Jordaius Lionheart ignored it. Or tried to. Something about all of this was *wrong*. He knelt before the altar in his heavy armour, eyes watering as he stared unblinking into the image of the High Star painted there in candlelight, and prayed.

'All my mortal life, such as I recall, I dreamed of being a hero in your armies. I wish only to serve you now.'

He heard whispering from the corners of the room. The words meant nothing. It was gibberish, and yet Jordaius felt his skin crawl under the scrutiny of scornful eyes. They saw him, whoever they were, and deemed him to be worthy only of mockery. He closed his eyes, the twelve-pointed star of Sigendil glowing against the backs of his eyelids, and struggled to shut the voices from his mind.

'God-King. Please. If I have failed you in some way then I beg you, tell me. Show me how I might make amends.'

Elsewhere, something giggled.

'What is this voice that speaks to me when you do not? What tongue of the Mortal Realms does it speak? Answer me, Sigmar!'

The door behind him opened. A thrill of dread ran through Jordaius as armoured boots clanked down the chapel's nave, dragging a heavy cloak over the stone flags like a body.

'Would you–'

The voice broke into muffled sniggering. It was the voice of Lord-Relictor Sekrus, only slightly too high of pitch, and Jordaius had never once heard the warrior laugh. For a moment, Jordaius heard what sounded like two identical voices arguing with one another, egging each other on, and then the Lord-Relictor spoke again in the same voice.

'Would you address Lord-Castellant Ansiris Oathforged thus, Prosecutor Jordaius?'

Jordaius looked up, but did not turn around.

He stared into the candles on the altar. They seemed to have shifted into a new *nine-fold* arrangement that made his eyes weep. But he could not tear them away.

'Lord-Relictor Sekrus. Forgive me. I did not mean–'

He turned then, seeking the reassurance of a human face, only to be confronted by the brooding skull mask and jagged golden halo of... *something*. The eyes staring out through the pinhole slits were mismatched: one was a giggling pink, the other a spiteful blue. Jordaius looked from one eye to the other, the mirth in the one growing even as its counterpart hardened with irritation. Words reached his mouth and faltered there.

He did not know where to look.

But then the Lords-Relictor were given to the Stormhosts to provide strength. Not comfort.

'What is it, Jordaius?' said the two voices of Sekrus at the same time. 'Do I disturb you? Is my visage so terrible to behold, or are the doubts you harbour so grave that you fear the view a Lord-Relictor of the Oathforged will take on them?'

'It is not that, Lord-Relictor. I am a Prosecutor of Sigmar's Storm-host. I have a keen sense for that which is false or impure and there is something about all this… something about… you.'

Jordaius started to rise. The thing that was Sekrus planted a gauntleted hand on his pauldron. Weird energies, the colour of confused rainbows, spewed from the meeting of the two plates. Jordaius shuddered at the foulness of the touch. All will to rise suddenly left him.

'Sigmar has it in his power to forgive your doubts,' said the Sekruses. 'But you and I, Jordaius' – another muffled snigger – 'we are merely servants. What would Sigmar suggest as penance were he here, I wonder?' The Lord-Relictor tapped his chin in exaggerated thought. 'Of course! You will recite "I shall not forsake the Everlasting Oath" a trillion trillion times.'

'Lord-Relictor?'

'You can remain in this cell until you are finished. If you hurry then you might yet venture outside in time to see Dracothion's last fires go out. Am I not benevolent?'

Jordaius brushed off the Sekrus-thing's gauntlet and rose. There was no resistance. It regarded him gleefully-grumpily as he turned to face it.

'You are not Sekrus.'

'And by what right does Jordaius Lionheart of the *Oathforged* presume on the wisdom of Sigmar Heldenhammer, God-King of Azyr?' At this point, the thing or things that were masquerading as Sekrus could hold on to the stern façade no longer and broke into fits of giggles. 'Foremost of the gods!' they howled with laughter, gesturing with their relic hammer for Jordaius to get back on the ground. Jordaius struggled against the arcane compulsion, but soon enough found himself back on his knees.

'You have no destiny that is not bound eternally to the Changer of the Ways.'

'I serve Sigmar!' Jordaius protested.

'You are young, Jordaius. And stupid. Oh yes, so very stupid. Fear is natural. But you have been chosen. Remember that. Hold it to that place where a living heart once beat. You have been chosen to glimmer in this cell for my amusement until you fade to nothing. So rejoice!'

Jordaius' armour creaked, lightning spitting between the joints, as he struggled to stand. 'Where... are my... weapons?'

The Lord-Relictor sniggered. 'Have you tried praying for them?'

'There is a voice that speaks to me when I pray.' Jordaius clenched his fist and held it to his heart, felt it vibrate with the power of the storm. 'It speaks in no human tongue I know of, but it is not yours, or that of your infernal master. I see a duardin. A Fyreslayer. His hair is red and struck with gold. His axe burns. He calls to me from beyond the Cosmic Storm. His name is...' He closed his eyes, focusing with all of his might even as Sekrus' insane giggles distracted him. 'His name–'

There was a whoosh of flame as an axe crunched into the back of Sekrus' helmet from behind. Jordaius looked up, feeling a confusion of disgust, relief and horror as the front of the Lord-Relictor's Mortis helm melted away. The flesh underneath bubbled and ran before Jordaius could get a look at the warrior's face. Pink smoke billowed off it in obscene quantities, filling Jordaius' head with giddy thoughts of fratricide.

Two smaller, fouler-tempered copies of Lord-Relictor Sekrus shrugged off the broken armour of the original.

Foresworn your oath, forsaken your brothers, and now a party to murder most unholy, they screamed over one another in identical voices. *There can be no absolution for you, Jordaius Lionheart! Oathbreaker! Oathbreaker! Oathbreaker!*

They continued screaming 'Oathbreaker' until that fiery axe returned to hack the first of them down.

Jordaius blinked, astonished at first to see a flame-haired Fyreslayer wrenching his axe out of a diminutive Lord-Relictor Sekrus while the fallen warrior's identical twin thumbed his nose at his killer and muttered curses. But then whatever force of coercion the daemon had held over him was broken and he remembered everything. The Silver Tower. Their encounter with the Gaunt Summoner. The last battle with the minions of the Grey Lord and then... this. He had followed Gotrek and Maleneth through the portal into the Realm of Chaos, or the Crystal Labyrinth of the Changer of the Ways, to be more precise. That would explain why even Jordaius' powers of perception could not pierce their falsehoods completely.

'It's two of those nasty blue ones,' Gotrek was saying, his voice dripping with disgust. 'Even if they have gussied themselves up a bit.'

Sigmar sentences you to eternal damnation, oathbreaker! said the second of the pair as Gotrek hacked and stamped on the two brimstone Horrors spawned by the death of its twin.

Jordaius summoned a stormcall javelin. It arrived in his hand with a reassuring *snap*, shaking his entire arm with the power of Azyr.

Oathbreaker! the tiny Sekrus shrieked, as Jordaius rammed the weapon through its chest.

The daemon stared at him resentfully as the flames of Change ripped through it. It had never been his Lord-Relictor, but Jordaius could not escape its final judgement, and nor did he deserve to. Lesser daemons, he knew, were mindless wraiths, driven by instinct and caprice. They had little by way of invention or guile, but neither did they need them, for the ambition, grievance and guilt of a man's heart could damn him faster than all the wiles of the Great Four combined. He *was* an oathbreaker. A kinslayer. Perhaps this was no less than the punishment his crimes deserved.

'How… did we get here?'

'There's no *here*, Stormcast,' said Gotrek. 'Not in the Realm of Chaos. There's no part of it sane or permanent enough for that. It is like that old saying. How does it go? About stepping in the same river twice.'

'The last thing I recall was stepping through the Gaunt Summoner's realmgate. It was supposed to take us to the World-that-Was gate. Not…' He trawled his mind for an alternative to *here*, and settled for, 'This place.'

'Daemon trickery, I'd wager. To split us up and turn us about. But the realmgate is here. I can smell it.'

Gotrek turned away from the four brimstone burns on the granite floor. He started down the chapel's nave towards the strong sigmarite doors.

'Wait,' said Jordaius, shrugging off the nagging compulsion to commence the sentence that Lord-Relictor Sekrus had handed down – *I shall not forsake the Everlasting Oath. I shall not forsake the Everlasting Oath* – and struggling to his feet. 'What about Maleneth?'

The Slayer looked back and shrugged. 'What about her?'

Jordaius remembered seeing the Darkling enter the realmgate ahead of him. 'She does not have your experience of the Realm of Chaos, Gotrek. Nor my Sigmar-given sight.' With a terrific effort of will, Jordaius made himself get up and follow the Slayer.

If Maleneth was lost somewhere in this maze of lies, then he dreaded to think what it would have conjured from *her* innermost fears.

'Out of my way, deceiver!' Maleneth screamed, exchanging a flurry of blows with a sneering witch aelf in scythe-edged black armour.

The Darkling quarter of Azyrheim burned. It shrieked for the revels of Death Night. Witch aelves wearing daemonic masks, or perhaps daemons in witch aelf masks, kicked in doors and broke windows, dragged people screaming from their homes to be offered up to Khaine on the altar of the street. A dream. It had to be. It was all exactly as she remembered it, but with the horrible unfamiliarity of a nightmare. That same gnawing uncertainty as to what would come next. That dread.

'Where is the Order of Azyr now, traitor?' The witch aelf cackled as her knives and Maleneth's spun their dance, coming together, breaking apart, switching partners without warning and *clanging* like castanets over their audience's screams. 'Where are your shining protectors?'

Maleneth bent backwards under her opponent's knife, then twisted her body sharply to allow the second to pass beneath her. It was almost too easy. A true Daughter of Khaine would never have been so slow.

'You are no more a witch aelf of the Khailebron than this is Executioner's Row. Do you think me blind, *daemon?*' Bent over and coiled like a spring, she released.

The witch aelf screamed as the knife in Maleneth's right hand pierced her leather bodice. It became a gurgle, Maleneth's explosive uncoiling ending with her left-hand blade sawing into the side of her opponent's neck and her bare arm sleeved in blood. Gurgles became giggles, became grumbles, and then split to become two.

'Where is the rune you promised your new masters?' the first witch aelf asked sourly.

'Perhaps they fear you have betrayed them?' her identical twin offered.

'Returned with the Unbaki weapon to the Khailebron Temple?' The two half-sized witch aelves shrugged, like appalling mirror images of one another being puppeted on strings. Both of their necks were torn, their chests identically slashed with blood.

'It is what I would have ensured the Master of the Order believed,' said the first, 'were I the Hag of Azyr.'

Maleneth backed away from the pair.

They were quite obviously not the witch aelves they appeared to be, but nor were they wrong. She had bided her time in the Mortal Realms too long already, and look where it had brought her. To the very edge of reality, where even the gods went mad.

I need to find the Slayer.

The thought was the truest thing she had encountered since leaving the Silver Tower. She needed to find the Slayer, get the rune out of him, and return with it to Azyr. But first, she had to find the Slayer. The cackling of the two witch aelves receded behind her as she sprinted off between the torched homes.

You will search for an eternity and never cross his path. Stop running. Surrender your heart to Khaine now.

This taunt, however, was far from true. Now that she was starting to think more clearly, she knew it. Whilst hunting Gotrek across the Amethyst Fjords of Shyish, she had placed a Death Mark on his soul. She could have followed him to the bottom of the Well of Eternity, and found her way back out again.

She closed her eyes, trusting to her Shadowblade instincts to hurdle the heaped corpses and debris strewn across her path, focusing instead on the unsubtle pull of Gotrek's aggressive soul on hers. She bared her teeth in a grin. He was nearby. She wondered if he was searching the Crystal Labyrinth for her even as she looked for him, and disgusted herself with the notion. It was far more likely that he had simply found a bottomless pit full of monsters to kill and had jumped into it with both feet. More nonsense for Maleneth to talk him out of if they were going to get out of here alive.

Eyes open, she veered off the main street.

The witch aelves were pursuing now, somehow gaining on her in spite of her longer stride and head start. It was like something from a nightmare, one in which she followed a Death Mark that was forever just around the next bend, scrambling over walls, hacking at washing lines that must have been made of sigmarite while her gleeful pursuers closed, and closed, and closed…

It is Death Night, Maleneth. Do you not recognise it? The one night in the celestial year when the Dark Moon waxes full. When the streets of the Darkling quarters run red and the Cauldrons of Blood run full.

Why does the God-King allow it?

Is his lust for the Oracle of Khaine so great?

Maleneth found a roof that was not on fire and pulled herself up to it by the gutter. Floating cinders crowded out the deep star fields of Azyr. She ran along the narrow ridge, one foot in front of the other, arms out for balance, the hot wind blustering through her cloak as if to drag her back by the neck and throw her down the slope.

The two witch aelves scrambled up behind her.

Sigmar is not the golden paragon that the supine of the Mortal Realms cling to in their millions. He is unkind and unfaithful, doting on young flesh and beating hearts.

You are young, Maleneth. So wonderfully, deliciously young.

Maleneth ran flat out to stay ahead.

'I serve Sigmar's Order because I must,' she screamed over her shoulder, as if Chaos could be reasoned with, damnation delayed. 'But I still live at the pleasure of Khaine. For his glory, and the glory of Morathi.'

Then why do you run? Why do you not rejoice that when your throat is opened it will be for her?

'Who said I was running?'

Maleneth made it to the end of the roof and flung herself from the edge. She flailed her arms and legs with the appearance of panic, but the billowing of her cloak served to slow her descent just enough that she did not shatter her ankles when she landed on the cobbled street below.

'Doomseeker, watch out!'

A blow from nowhere cracked her in the chest. Her heels left the ground again and she struck the side of the building she had just left. She slid down it, crumpled and winded, looking up from the ground with blood in her eyes as a familiarly hateful visage peered down at her.

'Damn it, elfling. You almost stuck that knife of yours right in my neck.'

'She is not at fault, Gotrek. It is this place.' Jordaius stood over the Slayer's shoulder like a shadow that had been absurdly magnified from its source by the distorting magic of the Realm of Chaos. The golden edgework of his black armour had an oily shimmer, as though something in the metal was alive. Alive and resisting the influence of Chaos even as it suffered. 'It is us, Maleneth. Gotrek and Jordaius. We have been searching for you.'

Gotrek scoffed. 'One of us has.'

'Whatever you are seeing here, it is nothing but an illusion.'

'Don't bother trying to explain it, Stormcast. It is as you said it would be. An elf wouldn't know truth for lie if you stuck a beard on it.'

There was a shriek from the rooftop, and Maleneth looked up. Her pursuers flung themselves off.

Gotrek bellowed, hacking his axe clean through one of the witch aelves even as she fell. The two screeching halves splattered the ground like gobbets of burning oil, each splat then picking itself up and running about the alley like decapitated hens that had been set on fire.

'More miserable bloody Horrors,' Gotrek said, scowling. 'Kill yours already, Stormcast, and let's be out of this elvish fantasy.'

Jordaius impaled the second witch aelf on his javelin. Her gasps of pain became the blistering outrage of two smaller aelves, no higher than his knee, which the Stormcast disgustedly crushed underfoot.

Maleneth coughed and got back up. She felt ridiculously glad to see them both.

'The magic of Tzeentch must have separated us,' said Jordaius. 'It is playing tricks on your mind, taunting you with your deepest fears.'

'Aye,' Gotrek added, unwilling to let a thing go. 'You almost stabbed me in the neck.'

It occurred to her that the pair of them thought her completely ignorant of what was going on. She would have laughed at them both if she had not still been desperately wheezing to refill her lungs.

Gotrek, meanwhile, was looking around. 'It's a frightful imagination you've got, elfling.'

'Ignore it,' said Jordaius. 'Have faith instead in Sigmar.'

'Come on then, the both of you,' said Gotrek. 'We've a realmgate to find, and the vastness of Tzeentch's domain in which to search for it.' Without waiting for leave, he turned and walked off.

Maleneth stared balefully after him.

'Do not forget your knife, Darkling,' said Jordaius.

She picked up the blade that she had dropped when Gotrek had struck her.

'Don't worry,' she said. 'I won't.'

Thanquol nudged the slumbering Bolgwrack with the end of his staff, ready to leap back at a whisker's notice should the Master Moulder awake in a less than agreeable temper.

They had emerged from the Gaunt Summoner's portal in dense jungle. The copse Thanquol had chosen to cower in while he collected his bearings and waited for the large, growling things to stomp past was festooned with saw-edged fronds and spiky yellow fruits. A shiver passed down the length of his spine, all the way to the tip of his tail.

To the idle sniffer, like Bolgwrack, their surroundings might have been mistaken for the jungles of Ohlor, which they had not long ago departed for the Silver Tower. But to Thanquol it brought back older memories, deeper memories, of jungles thankfully long gone, of desperate flights through golden temples, pursued by vicious scaly-meat cold-bloods. They called themselves *Seraphon* now, but when he woke from his nightmares of that misadventure it was the older name he screamed.

He resisted the urge for a calming dose of snuff. He needed to think clearly now. The Crystal Labyrinth was superficially much alike to the Realm of Ruin, where the teeming multitudes of skavendom maintained their festering capital, but inferior to it in many ways. Thanquol could endure it, so long as he kept his wits about him, but its effect on skaven of less potent will would inevitably be most deleterious.

'Rouse yourself, lazy-meat,' he said again. 'My patience is short. My time is too precious a commodity while we battle the beard-things for the realmgate.' He kicked Bolgwrack firmly in the ribs.

The Master Moulder stirred with a growl, and Thanquol was prescient enough to scurry clear just as the larger skaven made a grab for his ankle.

'Argh! Deathmaster!'

Deathskweel descended in a flutter of silks, arriving only a little later than an operative of his supposed skill should have been capable of. A knife darkened with the most lethal of Eshinclan poisons appeared against Bolgwrack's throat.

The Master Moulder gave an angry snarl and held up his paws in surrender.

'Better,' said Thanquol.

Thanquol thwacked Bolgwrack across the snout while he remained safely on the other side of Deathskweel's knife, just to reinforce where they all scurried in the hierarchy after the unfortunate business with the Gaunt Summoner. Bolgwrack glared up at him, but did not look as though he would risk a gizzarding in order to act on his displeasure.

Thanquol nodded in satisfaction, setting the butt of his staff back to the ground. 'You may release the Master Moulder now, Deathskweel.'

This time, it was the turn of the Deathmaster to glare. 'Why should I continue as you squeak-say? Kill him now, and then you perhaps. Take my chances. This goes far beyond the payment given to me and my clan.'

Thanquol pinched his eyes, reaching into the pocket of his robes for the reassuring presence of his snuff box. What was it about small minds that they needed to challenge him constantly? Could they not see how fortunate they had been to be stranded in the Crystal Labyrinth of Tzeentch with a skaven of his soaring intellect and powers of leadership?

'Calm your spleen, Eshinclan. I am going to take care of it.'

'As you took care of the Gaunt Summoner?'

'What was that?'

Deathskweel opened his mouth to answer, then licked his teeth, evidently thinking better of it, and shut it again. He lifted his muzzle, just slightly, baring his throat to Thanquol's teeth in the gesture of deference.

'Nothing, Grey Lord. It will be as you squeak-say.' The assassin released Bolgwrack and scurried hastily back in the undergrowth.

The Master Moulder rubbed his neck, casting the occasional

hateful look over his shoulder. So long as at least half of the brute's hate was going in that direction, then Thanquol was as satisfied as he could be.

'You have a tiny mind, Deathskweel, filled with tiny wheels. It cannot comprehend the brilliance that a mind like mine must entertain. *Of course* I could not flex the true magnitude of my terrible power to destroy the Gaunt Summoner. It was the daemon, after all, that brought us here, precisely where I want-wish for us to be. Do you truly believe that I, doyen of the Masterclan, favoured pursuivant of the Great Horned Rat and mightiest of all skaven sorcerers, did not know that the Gaunt Summoner would be able to catch the magic I threw at him?'

'That… does make sense.'

Thanquol nodded sagely. 'That is because I lower myself to the task of explaining it for your weasel-brain.' He waved for the Deathmaster to be silent while he opened up his snuff box. 'But enough, now. You tire me with your flea-like pestering.' He raised the open box to his snout, closed one nostril and took a deep inhale. Sparks flew from his mind. Unstoppable power made his fur stand on end. A long, drawn-out squeak of ecstasy fled from his lips.

Better. That was better.

He toyed briefly with the idea of flaying the ungrateful cretins to their bones right here, but with a sagacity that even he felt humbled to be a party to, he rejected it out of paw. Yes, it would be satisfying to hear their squeals for mercy as their tiny brains finally realised the miniscule and wholly dispensable part they played in his schemes. But the idea that he could have no need of underlings, even underlings as worthless as these, to throw between himself and the difficulties that undoubtedly lay ahead, clearly belonged to the warpstone. Thanquol was not some whelp who had grown his horns only yesterday. He had been using snuff since before the Mortal Realms had congealed out of their birthing aether. He knew that the power it granted, though stupendous, would be gone before he knew it, often leaving him with cause to regret the lackeys he had obliterated while in its throes.

'What of the beard-thing?' Deathskweel asked incautiously.

'Orange-fur?' Thanquol took another quick sniff, just to steady the nerves, before re-pocketing the box. He tapped the lump in his pocket, just to reassure himself that it was in easy reach. 'You worry too much, Deathskweel. Like blind scared-meat. The beard-thing lacks the intellect needed to navigate a maze as fiendish in its complexity as this. He would be dead already if the Clans Skryre had simply killed him as he was told.'

'I think-think he ran out of bullets. I warned him.'

Lucky.

Thanquol stamped his footpaw in annoyance. The Slayer had always been lucky, albeit facilitated by the jealousy, cupidity and uselessness of those beneath him. Somehow, he had survived the destruction of the World-that-Was just to spite Thanquol. Well, not this time. They were deep in the Realm of Chaos. Even his so-called rivals in Blight City could not hope to undermine him here.

A snort of triumphant giggles clouded the air in front of his nose with fizzing green motes.

Bolgwrack, meanwhile, had sat his mountainous bulk upright and was sniffing at his surroundings. 'I remember chase-running after aelf-thing. Through the Chaos-gate. And then… And then…' His eyes narrowed, turning inwards. 'Then I run-run in a giant wheel. Packmasters with warp-prods. And…' He gave a slobbering growl.

'An illusion of your puny mind,' Thanquol assured him. 'Much as the one I spared Deathskweel from, before you.'

'You sound different, Bolgwrack,' said Deathskweel. 'Back to yourself, I think. The influence of the Silver Tower recedes from you. Yes.'

Bolgwrack took another long sniff of the air. 'Looks like jungle,' he said. 'But smells like lies and magic.'

Deathskweel swatted at a particularly annoying leaf. 'If it squeaks like a rat, runs like a rat, and twitches like a rat, then do not be surprised if it bites like a rat.'

'Do not starve your muscles of strength by burdening your mouse brains with unnecessary thoughts. You are accustomed to rodents of lesser potency than Grey Lord Thanquol. Have faith that I will see us through this maze to our ultimate prize.'

'The World-that-Was gate,' said Bolgwrack. 'I remember. How will we find-smell through this jungle? It is an illusion to keep us from finding it, to be sure.'

Perceptive, for a simple brute. Thanquol would have to keep an eye on him.

'The work of a moment for a sorcerer with my knowledge of the Chaos Realms.'

Thanquol picked a spot that he judged to be a reasonably safe distance away and pointed his staff towards it. He gnashed his teeth together and *strained* and a rat the approximate size of a small dog popped into being. Bolgwrack gave a small squeak of surprise. Deathskweel, more adept at controlling his lesser instincts, merely blinked and watched. The rat raised its snout to sniff at the frond wagging over it and, though barely five heartbeats old, immediately urinated on the ground.

'A giant rat?' Deathskweel whispered, as though wary of disturbing it.

'A realmburrow rat,' Bolgwrack corrected him.

'Yes-yes!' said Thanquol. 'You are cleverer than your oafish mien implies, Bolgwrack. With the aether-scent I give, it will hurry-scurry to the World-that-Was gate, and leave behind it a scent that none but skaven noses can follow. Yes-yes.' He preened in appreciation of his own incredible cleverness. 'The Chaos-place holds no terrors for one of my superior cunning.'

The realmburrow rat's inquisitive squeaks became increasingly plaintive, as though it had already managed to devour something that its unnatural digestion disagreed with. Thanquol wondered if it was just his imagination at work or whether the rat really had just trebled in size over the last few moments. He peered anxiously through the undergrowth. No, it was definitely larger than it was supposed to be, and continuing to swell in size, now flattening the leafy frond it had been sniffing at under its hindquarters while it squeaked in pain. Thanquol gnashed his fangs in vexation.

'It should not still be growing. Which of you is doing this?'

'It is the Chaos-place,' said Bolgwrack. 'There is too much magic here for spellcasting.'

'And what would you know of it?'

'I am a master mutator of the Moulderclan, fool-fool.'

Thanquol stared as though the Master Moulder had just tweaked his whiskers. '*I* am fool-fool?' The cheek of him. The gall. The nerve. He was still looking at Bolgwrack as the realmburrow rat gave a last plaintive squeal and then exploded, splattering the leaf fronds that Thanquol had so cleverly bidden them all to shelter under with gore.

They were all thoughtfully silent a moment.

'It is... dead-dead,' Deathskweel observed.

'Obviously, my powers are too great to use to their fullest effect while in this realm,' said Thanquol.

'Ye-e-e-es.'

'What now then?' said Bolgwrack, before adding after a particularly petulant pause, 'Most cunning one.'

'Fear not. While the two of you were squirting fear musk, I was paying close heed.'

Thanquol pointed his staff into what he thought to be the direction that the realmburrow rat had been interested in before its expedited demise. If he was honest, it was barely more than a guess, but he did not want doubts over his leadership to sneak into Deathskweel and Bolgwrack. Such unworthy thoughts would only upset them and make failure as good as certain. And besides, a flash of subconscious insight from a mage of his extraordinary experience and sagacity was surely equivalent to hours of plodding rumination from the likes of those two.

'This way,' he declared, hoisting up his robes, and striding imperiously into the jungle.

FORTY-THREE

Jordaius' footsteps echoed off the faded stones. The corridor ran on without end, branching endlessly like the capillaries in an old, grey hand. It was a maze, another maze, every route through it a memory home to a whispering shade or a group of daemons that sniggered at Jordaius and the others as they passed.

'Stop.' He raised a hand and slowed, Gotrek and Maleneth coming to a halt behind him. He tested the reality of every possible step before him, the eyes of one of Sigmar's blessed Angelos Conclave gazing as far into an infinitely branching future as they could see. 'This way.' He pivoted on the spot, changing direction, and walked on, leading them onto a new path.

'Are you as confident of leading us through this maze as you were in Azyrheim?' Maleneth asked. She was nervous, and was probably right to be.

'It was never Azyrheim, elfling.'

'I know that, Gotrek, but I have to call it something or I will go mad.'

'I see the true path, but… it is becoming more difficult. It is as though the lies become more real, the deeper into the labyrinth we go. But the World-that-Was gate is before us. This much I know.'

'What is this place?' said Maleneth, her voice echoing off into the vastness. 'It is nothing from my memory.'

'Nor mine.'

Gotrek gave a great sigh and spoke. 'These are the great entrance halls of Karaz-a-Karak, what men once called the Everpeak, jewel of the Karaz Ankor. Or at least that is what they are supposed to be. Nor were these the greatest of halls, for this is naught but the Upper Deep, where humans and halflings and hill dwarfs would come seeking entry to the Everpeak, hoping to trade their meagre goods for the gold of the wealthiest kingdom in the World-that-Was. Below this lay the King's Hall, and the Guild Halls of the Lower Deepings.' He shook his head, his spell-ravaged face unreadable as always. 'Ahhh, but those were sights to bewitch the most embittered eye, and to stir even the soul that thought itself numbed to the lure of gold.'

'Was it truly so vast?' Jordaius asked. 'I see no end to these corridors.'

'I could lie to you and say aye, but in truth the grandeur of my world pales in comparison to that of yours. The wealthiest kingdom in the World-that-Was, did I say? Pah! The most dazzling wonder I can recall would be commonplace to your world. Why, Hammerhal Ghyra alone would swallow the High Karak ten times over. The fall of that indomitable city would have been but a footnote in your Realmgate Wars. No. It is the warping influence of Chaos that makes it appear endless, to sap the spirit, to bedevil hope, to gnaw at courage and expose the red meat of fear to whet the appetites of the daemons that lurk in our shadows. It appears that we must walk forever, that we have no destination, but while the former is true enough the latter is naught but another falsehood.'

'I take it then that this has been drawn from your mind,' said Maleneth.

'A fair assumption. Unless one of you two paid a visit to the Everlasting Realm before the end of days.'

'Why are its inhabitants so…?'

'Faded,' Jordaius finished.

Gotrek frowned in thought. 'Perhaps because the memories from which they spring are so.'

Oathbreaker, the wraith-like duardin moaned as they stepped out of faded tapestries and from behind shattered furniture. They reached out for Jordaius' armour as if for his blessing, only to gnash their teeth and fall back as lightning sparked in reprisal at their touch. His armour had been thrice-blessed by the Six Smiths of Sigmaron, and was anathema to daemonkind. *Oathbreaker,* they wept as they faded away. *Oathbreaker.*

'Why do they denounce me?' said Jordaius.

'It's not you,' said Gotrek.

Jordaius almost felt a beat in his reforged heart as he turned towards the Doomseeker. Those terse words had sounded almost like an absolution. But then Gotrek scowled, walking on before either of them could say more. Nevertheless, Jordaius' wings felt lighter as he followed.

'Every figure here is a daemon, wreathed in the garb of a duardin of old,' he said. 'My eyes see through them. They are like children, hiding under blankets and sniggering at the cleverness of their hiding places.'

'Aye.'

'Why do they not simply attack us now? They would overwhelm us easily.'

'Don't tempt fate, Jordaius,' said Maleneth.

'It is because they fear me,' said Gotrek. 'And maybe because they fear you. What you are.' The Doomseeker chuckled grimly. 'And rightly so. Besides, daemons are immortal and quick to boredom. They have seen death a thousandfold and in all its different ways. It brings them little pleasure now, in and of itself. More amusing for them by far to toy with us, to needle us with our own darkest terrors.' He banged against the wall with the flat of his axe. It echoed dully, swallowed by the dark. 'Such things are the blocks and mortar of these walls. It is the air you breathe while in this realm and what these creatures bleed when you cut them. And yet their god and master hungers always for more.'

'It is strange to hear you speak so knowledgeably,' said Jordaius.

Gotrek chuckled.

At another fork in the path, Jordaius raised a hand and came to a stop. The others duly waited while Jordaius looked one way and then the other. Eventually, Gotrek cleared his throat.

'What is it, Stormcast? With every turn you take longer to decide.'

'It is becoming more difficult. I don't know why. I blink and my certainty fades, and each time it does it takes longer for it to return.'

'Then don't blink.'

Jordaius nodded. If that was what it took. Whether it was Sigmar's doing or the work of his ally, Zectoka, or even some mark that Gotrek himself had left on his soul, his destiny was bound to that of the Doomseeker.

'I fear that we venture into a place where the light that guides me cannot–'

'Elfling!' Gotrek barked. 'No wandering off!'

Jordaius turned to find Maleneth having walked halfway down one of the passages that he was still deciding between. She smiled an apology that Jordaius did not need the eyes of the Angelos to see through as she turned back.

'Don't mind me, Gotrek. I just... I thought I saw another way.'

'Do not be lured by their deceptions,' said Jordaius.

The aelf looked irritated at being spoken down to, but no sooner had Jordaius marked that too than she had smoothed it away. 'I bow to your deeper insight, of course,' she said, and did so.

'The maze may be infinite, but there is only one true way to its end.'

'Spoken like a true champion of Sigmar.'

With one more furtive look over her shoulder, Maleneth walked back to them.

'I can find the way,' said Jordaius, more to himself than to the Darkling.

Perhaps it was true that Sigmar could not pierce this maze from Azyr, but he was still here. Jordaius had brought his light in with him.

'You're sure?' said Gotrek. 'Because I've spent a good stretch of eternity in the Realm of Chaos and I'm of no mind to do so again.'

Jordaius smiled. It was the first time he had heard Gotrek recall his damnation with anything other than rose-tinted fondness.

'Quickly, before I lose the true path again.'

He set off once more, almost running this time with Gotrek and Maleneth struggling to keep up.

'The daemons are getting more numerous,' Maleneth panted.

'He's concentrating, elfling. Don't distract him now.'

Jordaius changed course, and then again, making his decisions quickly now and almost without thought. They were close. So close.

'He is leading us into a nest of Tzeentchian horrors,' said Maleneth.

'Good.'

'Jordaius?'

'I see it!' he said. 'The gaze of a Prosecutor pierces all illusion and distance. I see a bridge spanning a great chasm. And beyond it... beyond it lies the World-that-Was Realmgate.'

No further, Oathbreaker.

A duardin stood before them. It was broad enough to block the corridor, but was almost transparent, turning the passage beyond it a smoky grey. It raised a hand to its bearded mouth and sniggered to itself, spoiling the feigned solemnity of its guise.

These are our halls.

'You're no dwarf,' Gotrek snarled, barging past Jordaius and marching towards it. 'You're not even the honest shade of one.'

You've already failed one world to its doom. Why not stay? Fail another.

Gotrek swung at the spectre without breaking stride, his firestorm greataxe *whooshing* down as though he was chopping ironoak. The duardin struck the blow aside on its daemonic axe, giggling as Gotrek's fury forced it to withdraw. Jordaius watched the Doomseeker batter his way down the corridor, even as more duardin began to arrive. They emerged through the walls on either side, banging axes against shields and poking one another in the ribs at the fun they were having as they drew up into sniggering lines.

Their pretence at discipline lasted all of a second, giving way to glee as they rushed at Jordaius. They swung at him with axes like evil children playing a game. His javelin became a blur, a sheet of lightning tracing a thin shield around him, but there was only so much he could fend off without peeling his eyes from the path. This he feared to do, more than he feared a daemon's axe. If he so much as blinked, he knew, he might lose his way forever.

His senses wavered even then. The light brought with him from Azyr grew dim.

One of the duardin landed a ringing blow on Jordaius' armour. There was a flash, a scream, the scent of sweetmeats burned by lightning.

The duardin, unmasked as a gibbering blue-skinned Horror

with long, rubbery arms and crazily rolling eyes, reeled back from him with smoke curling from its fingertips.

Jordaius let it go. He staggered on after the Doomseeker, his eyes fixed on the path to the exclusion of any personal advantage or danger. It was only then that it occurred to him that he had not spared so much as a thought for Maleneth since the attack had begun.

Even his eyes could only hold so much.

'We have to go, Doomseeker! And if we mean to go at all then it must be now.'

From way up ahead, Jordaius saw the Slayer scowl. 'It galls me to leave these capering insults un-slain, but if you insist, Stormcast.' He hacked his firestorm greataxe through his foe, and looked back. 'Be ready to run as fast as your thin little legs can carry you, elfl–' His eyes bulged with shock or fury, both looking much the same on Gotrek's face and having similar consequences. 'Elfling!'

Jordaius grimaced, unable to look, but perfectly able to imagine the sight of a confused Darkling disappearing down one of the innumerable false exits they had passed.

'This place must have driven her mad,' said Gotrek. 'Wait here, Stormcast. I'll go get her.'

'No!' Jordaius snapped. His eyes were burning, his vision starting to waver. He did not know how much longer he could go without blinking and losing the path forever. 'There is no time.' Pushing his way through the press of duardin Horrors, he started to run.

It pained him to forsake another of Sigmar's own to an eternity of tormented wanderings in the Crystal Labyrinth of Tzeentch. But that would be the fate waiting for them both.

If he failed to see Gotrek to its centre while his vision held.

Lost! a long-tailed parakeet with daemonically glowing eyes chirped from the branches.

Doomed!

Flee!

The entire flock squawked and flapped their giddifeathered wings, shaking the branches and setting off an unholy discord that every lizard-thing in the jungle could not fail to hear.

Flee!

Deathskweel hunched into his black cloak, endeavouring to make himself look small and, with Bolgwrack looming beside him, almost succeeding. 'Why do they say that?'

'Ignore them, Deathskweel,' said Thanquol, simultaneously ignoring the clenching of his own glands. 'Show the Chaos-things the selflessness and courage for which all skaven are rightly famed.'

Bolgwrack growled, the simple-minded brute's patience evidently wearing thin. 'Are we nearly there yet?'

'I am a most munificent master, as all who labour contentedly under my charge are aware, but do not think I will tolerate this insolence forever. Do not listen to the chittering of Chaos-things that would deceive you into thinking I have somehow led you astray.'

'Somehow?'

'You think you could sniff-find a path through the impenetrable labyrinth of Tzeentch?' Thanquol gestured wildly about, swatting the drooping fronds with his staff. 'Or you, Deathskweel? Or these Chaos-things that chitter-squeak in your ear?'

Lost!

Thanquol ground his fangs together.

'Die-die, Chaos-thing!'

A bolt of warp lightning leapt from the end of his staff. The offending parakeet exploded into a cloud of white, yellow and green feathers that snowed gently over the three skaven's heads. Thanquol puffed up his chest and straightened.

He felt not insignificantly better.

'But you do not *want* to get out,' said Bolgwrack. 'You want the World-that-Was gate.'

'What does any rat want with a scurry-hole to nowhere anyway?' asked Deathskweel. 'What good is a gate to a dead realm to us?'

Thanquol sighed. 'You cannot bleed an entire man-thing into a thimble. Explaining my plans to the two of you would be no less wasteful or pointless.'

Bolgwrack abruptly stopped walking. His huge shoulders bulged as his fists clenched at his side. He swung around, quickly enough to startle Thanquol into scurrying back out of reach.

He raised his staff warningly.

'What are you doing, Bolgwrack?'

'What I wish-want I had done when you first scurried to my clan-burrow.'

'If your intent is to grovel then that is *quite* close enough!'

Bolgwrack growled. A rope of drool swung from his chin as he stomped closer.

'Deathskweel!' Thanquol squeaked. 'Kill-kill this traitor-meat. He has most clearly fallen under the influence of Chaos-things.' He turned to where he had last seen the assassin, staring up at the daemon birds. 'D-Deathskweel?'

The receding sounds of the Deathmaster of Umbrasan fleeing into the jungle mocked him from afar.

Flee! Flee! Flee! the birds laughed.

'Do not run, fool-fool! Only I can save your measly hide from this place!'

With a terrific, splintering *wrench* and a cacophony of uprooted birds, Bolgwrack wrapped his big arms around a tree and tore it up out of the earth.

'I will kill-smash with this tree, Grey Lord. And I will like-like.'

Thanquol gave vent to a terrified squeal as the tree came down, scampering out of its way in a manner most ill-fitting to the dignity of a Grey Seer. He darted off between the trees, taking a long, deep sniff from his snuff box as Bolgwrack bellowed like a maddened ape and smashed after him. Thanquol shivered as raw power and warpstone-fuelled overconfidence surged through his body and brain like an unholy rapture.

With his loping stride and primitive strength, Bolgwrack was able to quickly catch up, barging through obstacles that Thanquol had to scurry around, but Thanquol did not care. Let him come! Let him scurry straight to his doom! He turned with a furious squeal, flinging out a paw even as Bolgwrack shouldered his way through the last of the jungle and swung his tree.

There was a roar of noise and a blinding flash as Bolgwrack struck an inviolable barrier. The tree exploded in his paw.

The Master Moulder roared in agony. His right arm was now prematurely truncated above the wrist, a few strips of bloody flesh wagging like baby fingers as it spurted over the jungle floor. More amusing still, to Thanquol's view, were the splinters riddling his snout. One of particularly impressive heft had lanced straight through the cretin's eye.

Thanquol tittered at the sight of his erstwhile underling maimed and half-blind. Was he not the greatest of sorcerers, ancient and powerful, devious and wise, subordinate only, and even then just barely, to the god of the arcane who had devised this infernal realm? He barely even needed the warpstone. He could stop any time he wanted.

He took another deep snort from the box and coughed.

'You are the tick on this god's fur, fool-meat. See how I flick you.'

A blast of warp lightning cast the stricken Bolgwrack back into the trees.

'I do not need you anyway. Or Deathskweel. Or Steamclaw. Or Croor. Clearly I have spent too long in the company of inferior minds. I am *Thanquol!* I shall find the World-that-Was gate myself. And I shall keep-keep the rewards for myself!'

To Thanquol's great astonishment and grudging respect, Bolg-wrack heaved himself out of the smouldering trees. He raised his bloody snout and sniffed.

'What is that smell?'

Thanquol laughed, the warpstone buzzing through him making the joke hilarious and his laughter shrill. 'You must think me whelped just yesterday, to fall for the "Do you scent-smell that behind you?" trick.'

Bolgwrack gave him a newly toothless snarl. 'Your nose is dead from too much snuff.' He lifted his snout away and sniffed again. 'Starlight and scaly… scly… slllll…' The Master Moulder's bottom lip went soft, his eyelids drooping. He looked down, and only then did Thanquol notice the dart sticking out of Bolgwrack's chest. 'Mmmrrr,' Bolgwrack said as he pitched slowly forward, hitting the jungle floor with a crash.

'B-Bolgwrack?'

Heavy snores rose from the supine Master Moulder.

The jungle clicked and chirped.

Thanquol froze, listening. What had become of the daemonic aviary that had been pestering him with taunts until now? Where had they gone? Was it only his superior skaven imagination that peopled the jungle around him with burly lizard warriors in golden armour, closing on him even now, licking their cold lips, leading in carnivorous mounts with a particular craving for skaven flesh? He chittered nervously. What a perfectly imperfect time this was to be abandoned by one's own minions! He sniffed at the scent on the air. But Bolgwrack had been right. He had known it, but the cretinous Moulder would not have it! The scent was not that of Chaos-meat.

It was…

The fronds rustled. Thanquol turned to it as though his foot-paws were on a turntable.

'Deathskweel?' he piped hopefully. But the labyrinth was nothing but an illusion constructed by his mind.

Wasn't it?

He was not really *there*.

Was he?

Thanquol shrieked in terror as something *very* large and *definitely* scaly drew back the fronds and bared its teeth. He sprayed it with warp lightning, it and everything else within a dozen tail-lengths, still shrieking as he whirled around and fled into the jungle.

FORTY-FOUR

'You know what I fail to recall ever seeing in the great halls of my ancestors?' Gotrek asked, stomping up to the point where the stone hall they had been traversing precipitously ended. He stopped and peered carelessly over the edge.

Jordaius joined him, his reforged skin sweating in the rising heat. 'A vast chasm filled with infernal flame?' he offered.

'That exactly,' Gotrek said, nodding. 'Got it at the first try. I'll admit, Stormcast, you surprise me. Are such horrors not commonplace in the Mortal Realms?'

'In lands where Chaos has yet to relinquish its grip, perhaps, but I would never call such perversions of nature commonplace.'

'This bridge isn't dwarf-made either.'

The Doomseeker stepped out onto the slender granite arch with the sore look that he reserved for poor masonry. To Jordaius' eye which, though ignorant of the principles of engineering saw nearer to the nature of it, the bridge was not something that had been built at all. Rather, the slender stone span had the look of what had been left behind after the surrounding stonework had been sent tumbling into the abyss. Jordaius winced as Gotrek bashed his heel against it, as though injury might somehow make it stronger.

'Shoddy. Very shoddy.'

'The realmgate is just beyond this bridge,' said Jordaius.

'I feel it, Stormcast, stronger now than ever. It is a sense I have felt on me only when walking to meet certain doom.' Shrugging off some dark memory before it took him, the Doomseeker started forwards.

Jordaius followed.

Or rather, did not.

'What's keeping you, Stormcast? Don't tell me you tire already. Or does your courage waver at the last?'

'No, and never.' This was the path, he knew. He felt it as keenly as the Doomseeker. His body simply refused to take the step. It was as though his upper body was under the command of one will while his legs answered to another. 'There is a... a voice in me that insists I go no further.'

'Well, tell it to sod off and get over here.'

Making the decision to withdraw from the edge, Jordaius suddenly found all of his limbs to be once again under his control. He studied the bridge. His faith in the Doomseeker had cost him too dearly to surrender now. He could not believe that Sigmar would have him follow this far, only to remain in the Crystal Labyrinth while Gotrek went on without him. If he could not traverse the bridge on foot, then he was not without other means of crossing the chasm. He shrugged the black sigmarite and gold wing-frame from his shoulders and waited to take flight.

And waited...

'Well?' said Gotrek.

'It is my wings.' It was the exact same effect he had felt whilst trying to step onto the bridge. The will was there, but the outcome was lacking. 'I cannot make them light.'

'Your power comes from Azyr, is that right?'

Jordaius nodded.

'That'll be it then,' said Gotrek, as though pronouncing on some faulty plumbing rather than the light of the God-King. 'Your furnace has been without a fresh shovel-full of Sigmar's coal since we entered the Realm of Chaos. If I were to guess, I'd say you used up the last of it guiding the Darkling and I through the labyrinth.'

'No.'

Jordaius shook his head. He refused to accept that his purpose amounted to no more than serving as Gotrek's guide and ended here. He opened up his gauntlet and stared down into the palm. Motes sparked from the glossy black sigmarite as he concentrated all of his attention on it and singularly failed to conjure his weapon. He let the hand fall back to his side.

It was true. He had followed the Doomseeker as far as he could.

'An actual blade of real metal doesn't seem so far-fetched now, does it, Stormcast?'

'I wish I could say I find my remaining here forever as amusing as you do,' Jordaius returned bitterly.

'Stow your defeatism, Stormcast. This must be the first chance you've had since dying to show that god of yours what you're really made of.'

Jordaius straightened. 'Where faith remains, you will find my courage unbroken. It is not defeatism. I simply cannot cross.'

'We'll see about that.' Gotrek rolled out his thick neck and turned back. 'Because one of us is getting carried and this time it's not going to be me.' He started back across the bridge, but before he had taken one step the daemon-fire blazing at the chasm's bottom roared upwards. Gotrek bellowed in surprise and turned his head to shield his one good eye as the surging wall of flame singed the ends of his beard and caused the rune in his chest to mutter.

Jordaius gasped in wonder as the inferno soared higher, rising from the abyss but reaching towards the heavens, the variegated colours of Chaos transforming before his eyes into the pure, radiant white of starlight.

But what, or who, had the power to purify the flames of Tzeentch from within the Changer's own realm?

'I do.'

A slender-bodied skink, about as tall and as broad as Jordaius' leg, stepped out of the starfire as though called forth by Jordaius' thoughts. Sparks leapt between the frills of his headdress as he craned his long neck back, eyes that were bright but also cold regarding Jordaius with an appraisal so inhuman he could not begin to contemplate the thoughts that moved it.

'Lord Temekzuqi,' Jordaius murmured, yielding to the instinct to lower his knee to the ground and bow. 'I believed that Maleneth had slain you.'

The skink chirped. If Jordaius had to guess, he would say that he was amused.

'I am the memory of a dream of a time long past. I can no more be killed than a thought.'

On the other side of the barrier, quietened by the silence that exists between stars, albeit with fury writ loud across his features, Gotrek beat his axe uselessly against the starfire. His impotence struck Jordaius as strangely beautiful. Like raindrops pummelling a lake.

'*Keep me from the Stormcast as you did from the Realmserpent and I'll give killing you a good try!*' Jordaius read from his lips. '*You'll find me more thorough than the elfling was.*'

'Why are you here?' Jordaius asked.

'In aeons past, the slann foresaw the end of the World-that-Was. They saw the birth of the realmspheres, the coming of Sigmar, and the golden age that would follow. They foresaw also the fall of the God-King's Pantheon and the resurgence of the Great Enemy. And they saw his return, stronger, wiser, tempered by failure. But the path to the future is a delicate one, Jordaius, easily lost, easily broken.' Temekzuqi tapped on the bridge with his staff. 'Like this bridge. It must be trodden with care lest it crumble. Many thousands of years ago, Zectoka perceived the possibility of the World-that-Was gate, the peril it might pose to the Great Plan. With the combined strength of the slann, he sought to wrest the realmgate from Tzeentch, but it was not enough. Foreseeing defeat, he was able to leave this outpost of Azyr, me, hidden, against the time that the Old Blood would return for the gate.' The starlight of the barrier shimmered across the skink's eyes as he appeared to contemplate Jordaius. 'That was why Starmaster Zectoka devised the Everlasting Oath, and bound the Oathforged to its keeping. He had foreseen *you*, Jordaius Lionheart.'

'I followed the Doomseeker because *Sigmar* willed it.'

'I am sure you believe that.'

'He would not have reforged me with the memories I possess if it was not so. Nor would he have returned me so near to the Doomseeker's side, not with seven vast realms still to be freed from Chaos.'

'Sigmar is noble, and he has recently become wise, but he is a child in the ways of fate.'

'You're more convincing than most of the daemons I've killed, I'll give you that!' shouted Gotrek's lips.

'I am no daemon,' Temekzuqi answered, apparently hearing the muted Doomseeker perfectly well despite having his back to him.

'That's what all the daemons say!'

The skink regarded Jordaius, not unkindly, and offered him his hand. It was so small, and so far beneath easy reach, that it would have seemed ludicrous if not for the power he held inside it.

'As the light of Azyr has guided you in, let it now guide you out. Your purpose here is at an end.'

Gotrek battered at the barrier between them as though mining for sparks. *'Sod that, you scrawny bloody lizard!'*

Temekzuqi blinked then, transparent membranes flickering across his bright yellow eyes, and turned to Gotrek. His long, feathered cloak drew across the stone floor like a silver brush over the skin of a drum.

'And you, Old Blood. All the years you spent looking for the foe who could give you peace, and yet you would abandon this world to die needlessly with yours?'

Gotrek's mouth worked, though not this time with any words that Jordaius could make out.

'The Mortal Realms are all you ever wished for,' Temekzuqi went on, speaking over the Doomseeker's obvious shock. 'Their greatest battles still lie ahead, and you could be a part of them, if you would but have them. You have a part to play in the Great Plan.'

'A destiny, you mean?' Gotrek mouthed. *'The sound of that word grows old on this dwarf's ears.'*

'And yet you go on. You could have died a hundred times over, had you truly wished to.'

'It would've been dishonourable.'

'None would have known.'

'I'd have known.'

'Then why seek certain death now? Your world is doomed and you cannot save it. Grimnir knew as much, though prophecy is not that one's gift. That is why he came here. As you did.'

'How do you even...?' Gotrek snarled, and then shook his head of the question. *'I don't fear death.'*

'But where is the honour?'

Gotrek looked shaken. *'The manling–'*

'Made his choice. As did you.'

The Doomseeker lowered his axe as though it had inexplicably doubled in weight. *'It could just as easily have been Makaisson, you know. He was there. It could've been him that went into the temple at Kazad Drengazi, faced Grimnir, and spent a few days shy of forever battling in the Realms of Chaos.'*

'Could it? Would you have had it any other way? You did not have to step through the realmgate that Grimnir showed you. You wanted it. You knew what it meant.'

'I… wanted to be remembered.'

'Then be remembered.'

'I have oaths still unkept,' said Gotrek, though with the look of one fully aware that he was arguing a losing case.

'And new ones to be honoured here.'

Gotrek glanced at Jordaius.

There was something so close to unmasked affection in that one eye that Jordaius felt the spark in his heart rekindled. The sigmarite scaffold hanging inert from his back twitched as that small morsel of light returned to its frame.

'I saw how you tried to save the Darkling, Old Blood, how you would turn your back on the World-that-Was for this one even now.' Temekzuqi turned back to Jordaius. 'Yes. You have played your part well.'

'So, I never was more than a guide?'

The skink cocked his head in thought. 'Consider yourself more a… compass, pointing the Old Blood to what he already knows is true.'

Jordaius saw then. That was why Sigmar had taken him: a young warrior, untested in battle. It was why he had been reforged in such haste, ensuring he would remember what he did, and been placed with the Oathforged where his path and the Doomseeker's would align again.

Gotrek had a destiny.

Jordaius knew it. Sigmar knew it. *Gotrek* knew it, though he would deny it to its very face if he could. Jordaius' destiny had been to make Gotrek's possible, and now it was done.

'It is time for you to return to the Forge Eternal,' said Temekzuqi.

'And what then?'

The skink chirped. A spoken shrug. 'That is not for even me to know.'

Jordaius nodded. The end of his path was here, and he was surprised to find the certainty and the peace that he had always lacked before reaching it.

'Go, Gotrek,' he said. 'Go find your destiny.'

The Doomseeker scowled. It was a fine last impression on which to return to the Anvil of Apotheosis. *'I'll send no one to a death I'd not gladly join.'*

Jordaius ignored him. He felt only contentment, as he took Temekzuqi's tiny hand in his.

And left the cares of destiny behind.

FORTY-FIVE

The World-that-Was gate was an island. The pinnacle of a sinking iceberg. That was how Thanquol's overheated intellect saw fit to interpret the madness being forced down his five senses' collective throats. The isle of fracturing rock and semi-molten magic hung adrift in the cosmic aether, the last stepping stone to a world where even the daemons no longer cared to go. The realmgate itself continued to thrum with the unknowable magicks that governed the function of such portals. Its argent surface rippled to the vibrations of a voice that was quite clearly coming from the *other* side. It sounded tooth-gnashingly familiar, but in his justifiable and well-earned excitement he had not been able to place it just yet.

The gate was his!

He had overcome the ever-troublesome Gotrek Gurnisson and his aelf-thing pet, the Gaunt Summoner of the Silver Tower, and even his own hapless underlings to beat everyone to the prize. Deathskweel, a paragon of myopia if ever Thanquol had encountered a thousand, had asked what anyone could want with a realmgate to a doomed world. Such foolishness! No wonder the skaven race had not yet risen to its rightful place as overlords of the eight Mortal Realms with such halfwits in charge. Which was why skavendom *needed* for Thanquol to have the realmgate.

He knew that the World-that-Was was doomed to a fiery end. He knew because through sheer tenacity, brilliance, and the affections of the Great Horned Rat, he had survived. He would survive it again. And what knowledge he could whisper to himself! What powerful secrets to be used against his rivals and smooth his ascent to absolute power. Why, even the Verminlords of the Shadow Council – who, in spite of their long memories and apparent wisdom, had reserved an inexplicable antipathy towards Thanquol and his schemes – would have to bow before the threats, blackmail and strategic foresight that he would soon impart upon himself.

This was why he had assumed the title of *Grey Lord* when dealing with the lesser races. Because where smaller minds forgot what true, divinely ordained power looked like, Thanquol remembered.

He squirmed with anticipation.

And if he could zap a few irksome foes during his brief foray into the World-that-Was, one Gotrek Gurnisson, for instance, to pluck a single name from the aether at random, then that would make his possession of the realmgate all the more worthwhile.

He threw a quick look over his shoulder, making sure that no lizard-thing had managed to follow him this far. But of course, they had been thoroughly outwitted by the speed and ingenuity of his escape. He was alone. Chittering in satisfaction, he turned towards the realmgate.

And froze.

His tail went rigid with shock. Not fright, of course. Never that. Not ever. It was an emotion that he was quite beyond. What he felt then was consternation and, dare he say it, outrage at a universe that had been doing precious little to deserve Thanquol as its denizen of late.

The Slayer was down there, plodding through the ruins in typically mulish fashion. A flight of stone steps with the blockish look of duardin-made things led up to the World-that-Was gate. That was where Gotrek was heading. An anxious fright went through him then. By the gnashing teeth and lashing tail of the Great Horned Rat!

The Slayer was going to beat him to it!

'No-no!' Thanquol demanded, in the imperious squeak that all members of the lesser races instinctively recognised as belonging to their natural betters, scurrying from hiding far quicker than he had actually intended. 'Not so fast-quick, orange-fur. The World-that-Was gate is mine!'

With one foot on the bottom step, Gotrek turned.

For one gland-tightening moment, the duardin simply glared at him, and Thanquol rued his warpstone-fuelled confidence. A blast of warp lightning to the back might, in hindsight, have been the more astute course.

'Thanquol?' the Slayer growled, as though the magisterial presence before him had not brought with it the immediate terror of recognition. 'A frail thing you've become, rat, wrinkled and bald. You look each and every day of the thousands of years you've clung on past the end of our world.'

'And you!' Thanquol jabbed a claw at the Slayer while he thought of a suitably withering riposte. 'You have been abandoned by your lackeys.'

'As you've been by yours. Tire of your voice, did they?'

Thanquol snarled. 'I do not need-want such lesser vermin.'

'Just you and me then. As it should be.' Gotrek rolled out his shoulder and hefted his gigantic axe, lifting it one-handed in order to beckon with the other for Thanquol to join him on the stair. 'Come on then, you old rat. A thousand years and then some you've had this coming. Grimnir's blood, but that little skink was right. There are oaths here to be tallied yet. For Felix. And for Gustav Jaeger, his father, slain by your hand.'

Thanquol had only a moment to wonder at who in the realms the duardin was bleating about before the furious Slayer was hurtling towards him. He squealed, looking away in terror at the last moment and striking the fiery axe-blow aside on his sword. It was not a well-loved weapon, nor one he had often felt moved to practise with. The wise skaven, it was said, had only friends in a sword's reach, and made sure he came at those from behind. But, when all else betrayed him and death trod on his tail, it had not failed to save his fur yet.

'You call me weak? You call me frail-meat? But I am neither!'

Magical arcs and streamers of fire strangled the air between the two blades as they rang apart. With so much energy flying it was no effort at all to grasp a pawful of it to him and throw it back into Gotrek's chest.

Karinaz, galdur Karin.

The voice rang off the Slayer like a sonorous note from a bell. A golden shield flickered around him, diverting the elements of Thanquol's spell into the shimmering outline of a rune: a rune that perfectly matched the one glaring balefully from the duardin's chest.

The Master Rune of the Unbak beard-things...

No! he thought. Impossible! It was supposed to have been lost in Hammerhal Aqsha with the Eye Not Seen.

The Slayer snarled and shrugged off the attack, his voice doubled over and over by the ripples of his shield.

'You're not half as strong as you pretend to be.'

'I am *ten* times as strong as I pretend to be, and the Realm of Chaos only magnifies my power.' Thanquol scratched enough magic from the immediate aether for a powerful warp lightning bolt that leapt from his staff and spasmed furiously across Gotrek's rune-shield.

'Mine too, apparently.'

'How many times must you thwart me, orange-fur? How many? Which spiteful god set you upon this sphere to gnaw and torment me yet again? Was one lifetime of unmerited failure not enough?'

'I know not, nor why. When I heard your name spoken in the Silver Tower, I thought perhaps... Well, what does it matter now? Here is where I am.' The Slayer chuckled grimly. The golden rune-light flittering about him lent his muscles an appalling definition as he tightened the choke-hold around his axe's neck. 'The thought of ending your accursed life here lends more strength to these old muscles than all the gold and glory in the Realm of Fire. More even than the hope of returning home ever did.'

Thanquol swept up his staff. 'My magic–'

'Can't hurt me.'

'Or so orange-fur stupid-meats believe!'

With a furious shriek that would have tortured dogs and shattered glass, Thanquol struck his staff against the ground between his foot-paws. The already weakened rock split under the blow, the fissure spearing with a satisfyingly eager haste towards Gotrek and belching noxious gases as it went.

'Yes-yes,' he laughed. 'Run-scurry. Run from the cracks-call!'

The Slayer shouldered his axe and ran, jumping to avoid a fall into the bowels of the Cosmos Arcane while Thanquol gleefully fired off bolts of warp lightning.

Except...

This was odd. The duardin had run right around the widening fissure and was now charging back *towards* Thanquol. He quickly raised his staff, feeling his musk glands clenching as the flame-wreathed Slayer bore down.

'Skitter*leap!*'

There was a puff of green smoke and the abominable Slayer disappeared from view.

Thanquol coughed, wafting vigorously to clear the smoke from his eyes. The skitterleap spell had teleported him onto the stairs a short distance away, but not nearly as far as he would have preferred. He had not even managed to appear *behind* the duardin, who was even then glaring at him with that one stupid eye.

'All of that running away looks like hard work.'

'You will suffer, beard-thing! But only long enough to curse your foolishness for gnawing at the schemings of Thanquol when the gods gave you an underserved second chance at life.'

He took a deep breath, coughed it up almost immediately at the poisonous prickling it brought to the back of his throat, but held it in for a heartbeat longer before sending a pestilential spume washing over the Slayer. Gotrek stumbled through it, teary-eyed and hacking, his axe smothered by a pall of noxious smoke.

'Give me one chance and I'll wring your scrawny neck with your own tail!'

'My tail will always be another length from your grasp.'

The Slayer made a stumbling lunge towards the Grey Lord, his axe coughing up yet more sickly fumes as Thanquol skipped back onto the next step up.

'Yes-yes. Come to me. Tire your muscles. Wear your footpaws to the bone as you *drown beneath the Vermintide!*'

There was a disembodied squeak, then several, the skitter of claws hurrying over stone, the chitter of furry bodies growing louder, louder, until from nowhere there was a swarm of rats tumbling down the steps like a river. Thanquol shrieked with laughter as they flooded towards the Slayer. Biting, nibbling, gnawing, scratching. They scampered around and clambered over him, slowing the Slayer to a crawl as he was forced to wade through them.

'How many of the Horned Rat's children can you kill? How many tiny bites can you suffer before your strength gives in and fails you?'

The duardin shook his head, exposing a dozen large rats clinging onto his beard by their claws.

'As many as it takes.'

'Then I shall summon more! And more! If there is one creature that thrives in all the Mortal Realms, and even here in the hell-spaces beyond them, then it is the lesser harbingers of the great skaven race.'

With another shrill incantation, he brought furry tributaries gushing from newly opened gnawholes. The Slayer flailed, smothered in rats up to the bottom of his crest of hair, but still somehow managed to advance, if slowly. Thanquol took another cautious step back. He had not realised how close he was, but the realmgate was right behind him. That naggingly familiar human voice was still speaking to itself from the other side, accompanied, incongruous as it was, by what sounded like the scratch of a quill pen on paper. Thanquol quivered at the thought of being so close he could literally touch it with his tail. If only the stubborn duardin could die!

'You will never defeat me. Never! Not in this world. In this world *I* am the one who gets to win!'

Rork or gromrhun.

The harsh metallic tones rang from under the seething morass of rats.

Krutkhas dumrhun, ek orf or thaggoraki drung.

Golden bars of light gleamed between the chittering bodies.

Ek kostnakul.

'What is this?' Thanquol demanded. He would have retreated further, but there was nowhere left to go. 'Who is this speaking?'

Rink annar nuzkul a or.

'Just give me the bloody power already, while you've still got an avatar to boss about.'

The Slayer roared, the *other thing* roared, Thanquol squealed, and where there had been a duardin-sized mound of vermin there was now a duardin-sized bonfire of fur and bones. The Vermin-tide broke, rats flinging themselves off the stairs as quickly as they could be summoned, or scrabbling back through the gnawholes into their hellish sub-realms rather than face a duardin wearing the halo of a god. Thanquol trembled as the Slayer crunched over the litter of incinerated rats, recovering his wits at the last moment to scurry around the realmgate and hide behind it.

'I'll have you, you bloody coward! If I have to turn over every stone in the Mortal Realms and outlive them all as I did my own, then I will.'

Blowing with exertion and stinking of cooked rat, Gotrek approached the World-that-Was gate. Close enough, perhaps, for his gnarly duardin ears to pick up on the voice from the other side, because something gave him pause from his purpose of robbing skavendom of Grey Seer Thanquol. He lowered his axe. The burning aura of the *other* grew weak as he laid a hand to the portal stone, not a claw's breadth from where Thanquol clung in hiding.

'Manling?'

Of course!

After so many years it was small wonder that Thanquol had forgotten that insignificant detail. The voice was that of the Slayer's blond-furred human companion, who had thwarted him so often from the duardin's side. Before Thanquol could decide how best to use this discovery to his advantage, the Slayer had inexplicably taken the huge stone ring in a bear hug. Thanquol could actually hear the bunching of obscenely large muscles as golden light once again flickered around the sides of the realmgate.

'Forgive me, manling. They were right, damn their beards. Witromm. Jordaius. That skink whose name I can't get my mouth around. Even the bloody storysmith. I've lived that old life, and so have you. It brought us to where we are, and grander adventures await the both of us, I'm sure.'

Thanquol squeaked in alarm as the realmgate split from the plinth on which it stood, uprooted by the Slayer's ungodly strength, and began to tip.

To tip *towards him*.

For centuries uncounted by rats, it had stood. It had endured the victory of Chaos, the destruction of a world, the cold journey through empty stars and the white heat of cosmic rebirth.

But not until now had it met the stubbornness of a duardin.

'No! No!' Thanquol screamed as he saw all of his ambitions tilting precariously over his head with fifty tons of stone. 'What are you doing?'

'As long as this portal is here and the likes of you and I exist to claim it, then his future is endangered by it. It has to be destroyed.'

With a final roar, Gotrek pushed the realmgate over.

Thanquol watched it come. He wanted to kick and rage and vent and curse and scream, but there was no time. The mad fool of a Slayer had stolen even that from him, again.

He raised his staff as if to brace it against the falling realmgate.

Until next time, he thought, and squeaked the one word that could not wait until then.

'Skitter*leap!*'

FORTY-SIX

Not for the first time in her association with Gotrek Gurnisson, Maleneth found herself picking daintily through corpses and rubble towards the silent ruin of a realmgate. The winds of Chaos whispered across the desolate site. It had been the battleground of gods; now it was just another slowly dying mountain of rock, destined to drift into the outer dark of the Cosmos Arcane and disappear from history. As perhaps it should.

The only recognisable structure still intact was a staircase, rising with a rugged, very *duardin* defiance through the spine of the ruin. Maleneth took it.

The charcoaled remains of what could only have been rats crunched underfoot. Her wince deepened with every step until she made it to the top. There, she crouched, clearing away some of the rubble. She may not have been able to guide the Slayer to the World-that-Was gate as Jordaius had, but wherever he went, she had known that she would be able to find *him*. He had been Death-Marked.

She paused as her efforts unearthed something: a scrap of orange hair, turned belatedly grey with powdered rubble. She sat back, uncertain what she felt, not entirely happy that she *felt* anything at all. She could not deny that her time with the Slayer had been occasionally enjoyable, or even worthy, but every moment that he had lived had been an executioner's draich falling ever nearer to her neck.

Slowly, she drew her knife. It was the one she had been saving, until a Plaguebearer of Nurgle had intervened. Late, perhaps, but all would be forgiven once she told the Order of Azyr everything she had seen this rune do.

A hand broke free of the rubble just as she was about to cut. It grabbed her by the wrist and used her to pull itself up. There was a small avalanche of rubble as Gotrek Gurnisson sat. He blinked until he located her at the end of his hand.

Maleneth gawped.

'You're covered in blood, elfling,' he said, breathing out a cloud of white dust that made Maleneth cough. 'Is it mine?'

'Not *yet.*'

'Then your butchery will have to wait another day. This dwarf breathes yet.'

Maleneth fought to wriggle free of the Slayer's grip, but soon gave it up as pointless. 'I take it the Grey Lord destroyed the realmgate?'

'No, that was me.'

'You?'

'What I needed, if not what I thought I wanted.' The Slayer looked uncharacteristically contemplative. 'That was what the Everqueen promised me, back in the Nevergreen Woods. And she was right too.' He took in the rubble around him, nodding in satisfaction as though he had just built a castle for a Storm-host and it was good. 'I did what I've been needing to do since you found me in Karag Unbak.'

'So, I gather we are stuck with each other then?'

'Don't sound so pleased about it, elfling.'

'Where do you intend to drag me now? Assuming we can find our way out of the Crystal Labyrinth at all, of course.'

The Slayer shrugged. Escaping the Realm of Chaos was, apparently, yesterday's ordeal.

'Now, elfling, we live. And after that, we're going to teach the Mortal Realms my name.'

ABOUT THE AUTHOR

David Guymer's work for Black Library includes the Warhammer Age of Sigmar novels *Kragnos: Avatar of Destruction*, *Hamilcar: Champion of the Gods* and *The Court of the Blind King*, the novella *Bonereapers*, and several audio dramas including *Realmslayer* and *Realmslayer: Blood of the Old World*. He is also the author of the Gotrek & Felix novels *Slayer*, *Kinslayer* and *City of the Damned*. For The Horus Heresy he has written the novella *Dreadwing*, and the Primarchs novels *Ferrus Manus: Gorgon of Medusa* and *Lion El'Jonson: Lord of the First*. For Warhammer 40,000 he has written *Angron: The Red Angel*, *The Eye of Medusa*, *The Voice of Mars* and the two Beast Arises novels *Echoes of the Long War* and *The Last Son of Dorn*. He is a freelance writer and occasional scientist based in the East Riding, and was a finalist in the 2014 David Gemmell Awards for his novel *Headtaker*.

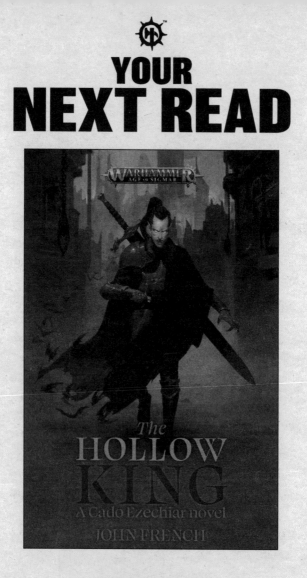